THE TWIN SISTERS

Vivian: Sultry, vivacious, heart-stoppingly beautiful, she married the man her sister loved in an attempt to save the old plantation. But if she saved their precious home, would she lose the one person she adored?

Heather: The intelligent twin, everyone called her—but was she wise enough to understand the dictates of her heart, and choose the only man who could bring her peace and happiness?

AND THEIR DEADLY ADVERSARY

Mrs. DesChamps: A silver-haired beauty and the town philanthropist, she had harbored a bitter hatred for fifteen years, and had plotted and planned to take over the twins' inheritance to avenge an old wrong. But how could the sisters prove that she was behind all the disasters taking place? No one would believe that this generous woman had hired thugs and killers and arsonists in her campaign of evil. For the twins, the struggle with Mrs. DesChamps was a desperate time of terror—and the surprising twists of fate and fortune that befell them will hold readers breathless and spellbound!

Are there paperbound books you want but cannot find in your retail stores?

Nightfall

by
Dorothy Daniels

PUBLISHED BY POCKET BOOKS NEW YORK

NIGHTFALL

POCKET BOOK edition published January, 1977

This original POCKET BOOK edition is printed from brand-new
plates made from newly set, clear, easy-to-read type.
POCKET BOOK editions are published by
POCKET BOOKS,
a division of Simon & Schuster, Inc.,
A GULF+WESTERN COMPANY
630 Fifth Avenue,
New York, N.Y. 10020.
Trademarks registered in the United States
and other countries.

ISBN: 0-671-80831-1.
Cover illustration by James Avati.

Printed in the U.S.A.

Nightfall

One

IT WAS A HUMID VIRGINIA SUMMER NIGHT, FAR WARMER
in the crowded ballroom, so I asked to be excused from
the next dance on my card and escaped, by way of the
dining room and the steaming hot kitchen, to the rear of
the estate. I flipped open my fan, which hung from my
wrist, and used it vigorously as I strolled idly down one
of the wide, cinder garden paths. It wasn't that I disliked
formal dinners and balls. Not at all. I enjoyed them im-
mensely, but it was good to get out of that heat for a little while.

Fireflies were lighting up the night, and beyond the
strings of Japanese lanterns, where the dark was more intense, they seemed to be exceptionally bright. I made a
grab for one of them, missed as I always did, and kept
on walking.

I hadn't seen my twin sister, Vivian, for the last half-
hour and I wondered if she'd also escaped the dance. If
that was true, she was likely with some swain intent
upon vying for her favor. Vivian's charm was as beguiling
as her beauty and that seemed to grow with each social
season. I was her twin, true, but not a mirror twin, nor
was I endowed with her rare form of pulchritude. Not
that I minded. I was proud that I had such a lovely sister.

I was heading in the direction of the barn, well to the
rear of the house, and it was the sharp, acrid smell of
burned wood that made me realize I was wandering too
far. The barn had been afire a little more than a week
ago. It hadn't burned to the ground because the fire had
been discovered in time to douse on enough water to save
the structure, though it had been severely damaged. It
was a mysterious fire because there'd been nothing inside which could possibly have been flammable.

In turning away from that direction, I heard Vivian's voice. It was not the mellow, sultry voice she used when handsome men were around her, and I followed it, my curiosity aroused. I found her standing beside a concrete bench on which a young man was seated. At first I didn't recognize him. He wasn't a guest, for his attire was casual. He was neatly dressed, but not expensively. It was Alex Hale, son of Jacob Hale who managed the plantation.

Even in the darkness, I could see Vivian regarding him haughtily, standing before him so closely, he couldn't have risen even if he'd been of a mind to. The rudeness of her words matched her tone.

"You really don't belong here, Alex. I realize your father is, to a large extent, responsible for the success of this plantation. Papa has said so many times. But that doesn't give you special privileges."

Despite what she'd said, Alex looked amused. "You're beautiful, Vivian, even when you're being spiteful. And forgive me for smiling, but since we grew up and played together, I can't help but find it ludicrous for you to address me in such a condescending manner."

"I thought I could put my point over much better by doing so."

"You mean, of course," he said, "I'm out of place here."

"Definitely that is what I mean and definitely that is what you are," she retorted.

Alex caught sight of me approaching. "Hello, Heather." His manner was still serene as he greeted me.

Vivian stepped back, enabling Alex to stand. Her features were a mixture of surprise and annoyance at my appearance.

"Hello, Alex," I replied warmly, then turned my attention to Vivian. "Alex deserves an apology for your rudeness."

"I was merely telling him he has no business here."

"He has as much business here as any gentleman inside."

"I don't recall our sending him an invitation," she said haughtily.

"If I'd made out the list, he'd have received one," I said.

"I'd have appreciated it," he said good-naturedly, still seeming to enjoy the irritation he'd aroused in Vivian. "And I'd not have embarrassed either of you."

"We know that," I said. "And I apologize for your not being invited. Come in anyway, Alex. You've always been like a brother to Vivian and me. She knows that and is merely being disagreeable to you because you've never fallen victim to her charms."

Vivian now directed her venom at me. "Are you jealous of me, Sister?"

"Why should I be?" I asked, growing tired of the scene she was making. The evening was an occasion for gaiety and I didn't want to lose the mood.

"Because I'm the beautiful twin." She paused, her smile vicious, then lowered her voice to add, "While you're the brainy one."

"Is that what everybody says?" I asked, stung slightly by her cruelty.

"Everybody," she replied, emphasizing each syllable of the word.

"One will never deny Heather's intelligence," Alex said kindly. "Nor will anyone deny your exquisite beauty, Vivian. But remember, goddess, there's also such a thing as character, warmth and compassion. Qualities you've never taken the trouble to develop. It's still not too late."

"Not too late for what?" Vivian's tone was as cold as steel.

"To develop those qualities," Alex went on easily. "They might come in handy once your beauty fades—as it surely will."

"I should slap your face," she retorted. "But all I'll say is, I'd not soil my glove on you. However—and I will use manners—*please* get away from this area of the house. The guests come out here to stroll. You don't fit into the picture."

"You're right, of course," he said, his manner still affable. "And my only reason for being here was to listen to the music. Nothing like music to relax and uplift a person. Especially when one has a love for it, as I have."

"Which interests me not the slightest," she said.

Alex shrugged and again a smile touched his lips. It was an appealing smile, but it seemed to further enrage Vivian.

3

He said, "The only subject which has ever interested you is yourself."

She stiffened and her right hand, holding her folded fan, raised in a threatening gesture. I wouldn't have put it past her to slash Alex across the face with it.

"Don't you dare, Vivian!" I exclaimed. "Go in the house before you forget you're a product of the most expensive finishing school in the country, where you were taught the social graces."

Her hand lowered reluctantly and she turned her venom on me. "You're the worst sister anyone could ever have. And the most disloyal one. You never take my side."

"Not when it's the wrong one." I kept my voice low, hoping none of the guests was within hearing distance.

"I'm always wrong, so far as you're concerned. Papa excuses you when I complain to him, saying you're strong minded. I say you're just plain mean and jealous."

"Please go in the house, Vivian," I urged. "One of us should be there."

"I'll be glad to. There's certainly nothing or no one out here to interest me." She made no attempt to veil the contempt she felt for Alex.

His manner didn't change, but he made no reply and his eyes regarded her scorn-filled ones with pity. Nor did I speak, and so, knowing the argument was ended, she turned sharply and headed back to the house, her heels crunching the cinder path angrily.

I managed a smile, which Alex returned.

"I apologize for Vivian," I said. "I fear everyone has spoiled her, including papa."

"Well, you haven't," he said with a chuckle. "I've never seen two sisters in such constant argument. But she doesn't give you much choice. However, I find her tantrums amusing. I suppose because she looks even more beautiful when angry. She's like a spirited steed that needs taming. One day someone will come along and do just that."

"I hope so. Otherwise, whoever she marries will live in constant misery."

Suddenly the moon came out from behind the clouds, lighting up the area where we both stood. It seemed to brighten Alex's dark red hair. He wasn't handsome and

4

only of medium height, but his face reflected his inner kindness. His eyes were a deep blue, his features craggy. Though college educated, he often worked with the field hands and around the stable, the type of labor that developed a strong body. Alex's frame certainly gave evidence of physical strength.

"Don't you think you should rejoin the party?" he asked.

"Not for a while," I said. "It's nicer out here with you. Peaceful, sort of."

"Don't pity me, Heather." For the first time, sternness crept into his voice. I felt myself resenting it, for if he should have chided anyone, it was Vivian.

"I don't think you need pity." My tone matched his.

"I don't, especially not from you. I go my own way, just as you do. I know my mind, just as you do. And, as Vivian said, I really don't belong here."

"You do, Alex." I forgot my pique in the remembrance of my sister's rudeness. "As for Vivian and me, we've always quarreled, but we're deeply loyal to each other. You know that."

"Better than anyone else," he agreed. "But, then, you're bound to be, since you're twins."

I nodded. "Please come inside and dance with me."

"No, thanks. I'm not dressed properly."

"That's not important." I paused, then laughed uncertainly. "Strange, I don't even know if you dance."

"It's of no consequence."

His manner was brusque, evidence he'd been hurt. I pretended not to notice.

"*Do* you dance?" I persisted.

"A little."

"Then I insist you come in."

"Not tonight."

I reached for his hand and attempted to pull him toward the house, but he didn't budge. Yes, indeed, he was possessed of enormous strength. I desisted in my efforts, lest I pull my arm out of its socket.

"I'll dance with you out here," he said.

He took a light grip on my arm and led me to a tiled terrace, some distance from the house, but close enough so that the music drifted out to us through the open French doors. His arm had just enclosed my waist when the last notes of "Lover's Dreamland" were played.

I shrugged disdainfully. "That was too slow anyway. Let's hope they play a two-step next."

The orchestra began the noisy, fast, exuberant "Hornpipe Polka." We swung into the first steps of the lively dance and before long, we were using the entire area as a dancing platform. Besides the steps which constituted the dance, we improvised a few of our own. We were thoroughly enjoying ourselves, even laughing with delight and pleasure at our foolishness. The dance was almost ended, when Alex grasped both my hands and pulled me closely to him. As quickly, he released my hands and his arms enclosed my waist. Before I knew his intent, his lips were against mine in a tender, warm kiss that shook me to my heels. I couldn't even speak when he freed me, only regard him in open wonder.

"You liked it." His voice quavered slightly with the emotion which had overtaken both of us.

"I didn't," I retorted indignantly. "Vivian was right. You overestimate yourself."

"She didn't say that," he replied, his voice still uneven, though knowing the rapture of the moment was gone.

"Then I'm saying it, and don't ever be so presumptuous again."

"I'd apologize except that I liked it too much and I felt you did also."

"You're quite in error, Mr. Hale." Now I was imitating Vivian and too angry to care. "You caught me by surprise. But I won't be priggish about it."

"Then stop calling me Mr. Hale."

I relented. "Very well, Alex. I'm not going to quarrel with you. I'll express it simply so there will be no further misunderstanding on your part. I think of you as a true and loyal friend. Nothing else. Nor will I ever. What you just did could have spoiled that relationship. I don't want anything ever to spoil it."

He nodded. "I did overestimate myself. I thought you held me in a little higher regard. Which was conceit on my part. Our stations in life are much too different. I know it well and if I didn't before, Vivian made it very plain tonight. But I didn't think you were the type who cared."

"I wouldn't care if I loved you. But I don't. And I never will." I softened my words with a smile.

"You couldn't have expressed it more plainly."

"It's the only honest way."

A smile touched his mouth, but it was a sad one. "Strange, but at the moment I feel you're more cruel than Vivian ever could be."

"That's about the most unkind statement you could make." I couldn't have been more hurt if he'd struck me.

"Now it's my turn to apologize. I do, Heather. Forgive me. I wasn't being fresh. You mean a great deal to me, though I won't waste words on that. Let's say my kiss was one of gratitude. For a few moments, you made me feel important, despite the difference in our stations in life. And, God knows, everything's different. For one thing, our clothes. This suit I'm wearing. The latest style for this year of 1890 came, mail order, from Montgomery Ward and it cost me sixteen dollars, one of the best they offer. Now, let's have a look at you. I don't know too much about women's clothes, but I believe that gown is made of silk and it has some fancy—and expensive—lace covering the material. The choker is real gold and gems. So is the bracelet. All told, you're turned out to the tune of at least a couple of hundred dollars. So no matter how you look at it, the difference is there."

He paused and raised his head, his nose sniffing the air. "Do you smell smoke, Heather?"

"Yes—or burned wood. I noticed it when I came out here. But that's from the barn that caught fire last week."

"No," he contradicted. "This is fresh smoke and I think I hear the crackle of flames." He was already moving away from me. "I'll check the barn. Give the alarm anyway. Hurry! If I'm right, we'll need every man in there."

He rushed away while I stood transfixed for a few seconds, frozen in the fear of fire, no matter where it was located. Then I saw the first of the crimson flames. That brought me to my senses and sent me inside, crying out for attention.

In moments the ballroom had emptied and the men were hurrying down to where Alex had gathered all the pails available. There were quite a few of them because they'd been used in the first fire, then abandoned. Thank goodness they had.

7

Alex gave orders in a voice that compelled obedience. In moments he had a bucket brigade formed. Water from the well and from the kitchen filled pails that were passed from hand to hand. Alex threw most of the water onto the flames. He succeeded in dousing some of the fire, but it was too late to save the barn.

"Get back!" Alex warned. "Everybody, back. The walls are going. . . . The roof is going. . . ."

Five minutes later there was no longer a barn, only a mass of flames that climbed higher and higher until there was nothing more to consume. I stood well back so I'd not be in the way and watched it dwindle. I saw papa disengage himself from the bucket brigade, toss his bucket aside and look around. The embers were still bright enough to make everyone visible and when he caught sight of me, he came my way. He didn't speak, just stood beside me and we both regarded the destruction.

Next, Alex joined us. He was coatless and his shirt was soaked with perspiration, his face stained with soot and ash.

He said, "I'm sorry to have to tell you this, Mr. Gates, but that fire was set deliberately. It raises my suspicions that the first one might have been set also."

"What makes you think that?" papa asked. He spoke without taking his eyes from the ruins, yet I had the feeling his thoughts weren't so much on the destruction as on who had caused it, for he didn't seem overly surprised by Alex's statement.

Alex said, "When I reached the barn, where nothing in the barn was visible, I was able to see an overturned pail with a lot of straw around it. The flames hadn't reached it yet. The straw trailed over to the empty stalls and to the walls. I ran in, but was driven back, though not before I saw the stub of a candle, melting fast, but still attached to the pail."

"And you believe that started the fire," papa said.

"I'm certain of it, sir."

Papa's broad shoulders dropped and his features looked haggard. "I never thought it would come to this."

"What do you mean, Papa?" I asked.

He made no reply. I doubt he even heard, for he turned and went back to the young men who were now sorting out the coats they had discarded and thrown in a pile before fighting the fire. I saw papa talking briefly with each one, no doubt thanking them for their efforts. That completed, he turned and headed for the house.

Only then did Alex speak, for he'd kept his eyes on papa also. "Do you know what he meant by that?"

"I wish I did. Are you sure about the candle on the overturned pail?"

"Positive. I ran in and saw it clearly, but then the straw seemed to explode, as if kerosene had been poured on it, and I was driven back. Also, I saw clear evidence of paths of straw leading to the rotten wood. The way that burned, it was probably soaked with oil also, though it wouldn't need it."

"I'm sure no one who attended the ball would do such a thing."

"Do you suppose they're all accounted for?"

I nodded. "Both Vivian and I greeted them in the reception hall. And no one's been here long enough to carry out such a plan."

"It would take time," Alex admitted. "And the culprit knew it was a good night to do it. Everyone would be occupied and enjoying himself. But why the barn? It was abandoned."

"For which we should be grateful."

Alex agreed, then asked a question that made sense. "If it was an act of vengeance or hate, why not burn the house down? Or the drying sheds? The old barn was of no value. Since it was never used, it should have been torn down."

"Perhaps that's why it was chosen. It was meant to be a warning. Since nobody would be hurt, that seems logical."

Alex looked perplexed. "A warning for what?"

"I have no idea. Neither fire makes sense. I'm going in now. Thanks for all you did."

"Since I couldn't save the barn, I did little."

"If you hadn't been alert and smelled the fire, it could well have spread over the whole plantation. Papa, Vivian and I are grateful and indebted to you."

"No one's indebted to me. I work for my father, who works for you. I'd have been sadly derelict if I hadn't smelled the fire. In fact, if I'd stayed near our house where I belong, I might have caught a glimpse of whoever was guilty of setting the fire."

"You deserve the credit for keeping the fire from spreading. Nothing else matters. Good night, Alex, and thanks again."

He rubbed a dirty sleeve across his soot-smeared brow. I couldn't help but laugh because the gesture only smeared his face more, making it seem as if he were wearing a mask.

I said, "You'd better go home and get cleaned up. Also, a good night's rest."

His returning laughter came easily. "I'll get cleaned up. But before I rest, I'll make certain no one's on the plantation who has no business being here. Though I doubt that there will be. Whoever did it, accomplished his mission. Good night, Heather. At least it wasn't a dull evening."

We exchanged glances. I knew what he meant. First, Vivian's petty behavior when she discovered Alex listening to the music and, in her judgment, too close to the house. Next, our dance, followed by the kiss which I resented. And, finally, our heated words, interrupted by the fire which destroyed the barn.

No, I thought, it hadn't been dull. Nor had the kiss. But I knew Alex too well. We'd grown up together. I could think of him only as a friend, possibly even as a brother. Never as a lover. I walked slowly back to the house, stepped up on the terrace and entered the ballroom through one of the French doors. Almost everyone was still watching the dying embers of the barn. Inside, two members of the orchestra were still playing, the piano player and a violinist, both too old to help form the bucket brigade. In the middle of the dance floor, Vivian and Freddie Faber were dancing in almost sleepwalking steps to a waltz. They stopped and so did the music as I approached them. The musicians used it as an excuse to go out to see at least part of the fire.

"Is anything left?" Vivian asked calmly.

"There'll be nothing but ashes in a few more minutes. Weren't you interested enough to go and look?"

"What for? What good would I have been? What could I have done? And, frankly, what did you do? I don't see any burns, any ash, any water soaking your gown. It's very lovely, incidentally, even if it isn't new."

I said, "Freddie, by the way you're craning your neck, I know you want to go down and look at the fire. Vivian and I are going to have a little talk."

"I'll be back," Freddie said as he loped off to the French doors and vanished through one of them. I ignored Vivian's anger and took her arm, leading her to the chairs lining the long wall of the ballroom. I motioned her to one and I sat alongside her.

"What's the matter?" she asked. "What's all the fuss about? A silly old barn—"

"Somebody set it on fire," I said.

She forgot her anger in the shock of what I just told her. "Burned it down deliberately?"

"Yes. The first time we got the fire out. But not this time."

"How do you know it was deliberately set?"

"Alex was the first to get there and he saw that a lighted candle had been placed on an overturned pail. The candle burned down to where a lot of straw was heaped around it. He was positive he saw that."

"Why?" Vivian asked, finally capable of sober reflection over this news.

"I don't know. But surely we have to find out. Before the dependency house is next, or the summer house, the ice house . . . the stables . . . even the house we're in now. Plus all the drying sheds."

"You don't make sense. Why would anyone want to burn us out?"

"I don't know. But someone wishes us ill. Have you heard any gossip that something like this might happen?"

"No. Have you?" she demanded.

"Not a word. But I wonder if papa knows something."

"What makes you say that?"

"He didn't seem surprised when Alex told him the fire was set deliberately."

"Perhaps Alex set it." Vivian's smile was malicious.

"What a dreadful thing to say."

"I wouldn't put it past him. He did it to spoil the ball. And it did."

"Vivian Gates, you disgust me."

11

"And you disgust me. Dancing with the hired hand outside, with everybody inside watching."

"If they did, they saw a good show. We danced well together. And don't call Alex a hired hand."

I wondered if everyone saw what followed the dance. Vivian's next statement gave me hope they did not.

"They didn't watch long," she went on loftily. "It was more fun in here. I made everyone line up and watch Freddie and me dance. He's excellent, but, then, his mama was a professional dancer."

"You seem impressed," I said, my tone as lofty as hers.

"I am."

"So am I," I said, smiling. "But you're so socially conscious, I'm surprised you would find him acceptable with his mama's stage background."

"His papa's very wealthy."

"That's good. Whoever marries Freddie will need something to take her mind off her boredom. She can spend money."

"You're being very petty, Heather."

"I must have caught it from you."

The return of the guests distracted her and she cried out in dismay. "Oh, look at the men. They're a mess."

"Why didn't Freddie go down and help with the water buckets?" I took no pains to keep annoyance out of my voice.

"Because he preferred being with me."

"I doubt he could lift a bucket—one filled with water."

Vivian's eyes brimmed with tears. I was suddenly contrite and slipped an arm around her shoulder.

"Forgive me. I know I'm being nasty. I'm tired and worried and frightened and I don't know of whom or why I should be. It's almost as if I have a premonition of something horrible about to happen."

"I suppose the party's over." Vivian hadn't heard a word I'd said. She was never interested in anything but her own pleasure. But I had been nasty and I'd bicker no more.

"I'm sorry, Vivian. Yes, the party's over. Come help me bid our guests good night."

"I'll do that. You take care of the kitchen help."

I was glad of the opportunity to leave the chatter and excitement that the fire had caused among the guests. They acted as if it had been part of the entertainment, not even minding their ruined evening clothes. Even the girls joined in, relating to each other and Vivian the way they cheered the men on in their vain efforts to quell the blaze. I paid the help for their evening's work, watched them get in the wagon that would take them to the village, then turned back to compliment Maggie for her evening's work.

Maggie was our cook, who oversaw the servants brought in to clean and for special occasions like to-night.

She said, "It's too bad it had to end the way it did."

"Yes. But we can be grateful it was only the barn."

Maggie was short, rotund, a bundle of black energy and keen intelligence. "I heard them say the fire was set."

"Mr. Alex says it was."

She shook her head. "I wonder who'd want to hurt your papa, doin' somethin' mean like that."

"So do I."

"You think he knows?"

"I wish I knew the answer to that. But I doubt it. Good night, Maggie."

Finding sleep became very difficult. Vivian's room was next to mine. Quite likely she'd fallen asleep in a moment's time, but I was too worried to rest well. The fires frightened me. If someone was going to burn us out, there certainly wasn't much we could do to stop him. I didn't know of any way short of meeting him face to face as he lit the match.

I was concerned about papa's attitude as well. He'd seemed to withdraw into himself lately. During the evening he'd danced his fill, been a gracious host, but the old spirit didn't seem to be in him. I'd noted that for some time now. I'd spoken to Vivian about it but she had derided the whole idea as nonsense. Vivian hated unpleasantness of any kind.

Two

USUALLY, MY SLEEP WAS UNTROUBLED, BUT AFTER LAST night's fire, I tossed and turned restlessly. I welcomed dawn and arose to bathe and dress hastily, though letting my hair fall on my shoulders. I made my way silently out of the house, not even pausing to have breakfast. That could wait. Only a walk in the fresh air of early morn would relax me. The quiet and beauty of the grounds would calm me and help me think.

Papa had begun to instruct me in the running of the tobacco plantation beginning with my twelfth year. I was now nineteen and knew practically everything there was to know about the growing of tobacco. I knew also that we were wealthy and tobacco was responsible for it.

It was one of the largest plantations in the state of Virginia and papa had named it Nightfall. Once, when I commented on the strangeness of the name, he agreed, but added that, to him, it was the most beautiful time of day. A time of tranquillity. He added that, for him, the hour between dusk and daylight had always been a lucky time. He'd met mama at that hour at a soiree. He'd signed the papers to purchase the plantation at that hour. Both Vivian and I had been born as day faded and the softness of night approached. Jacob, recently widowed, and his little son, Alex, had come here at nightfall, seeking work. Papa said he'd been in need of a good overseer and Jacob Hale had been the answer. And so "Nightfall" was spelled out in the arched entrance above the iron-gated fence. I was used to the name now and liked it. So did everyone, once they'd become accustomed to the unusualness of it.

I walked straight along the drive which led to the main road. It was downhill much of the way, for the mansion had been erected on a knoll which overlooked the surrounding area. When I was far enough away, and just inside the gated brick wall surrounding the estate, I turned and looked back at the mansion where I'd been born.

It was a showplace, and rightfully so. The iron gate was set in the red-brick wall and the gateposts were decorated with the heads of ferocious-looking lions. I recalled how I'd feared those two stone animals when I was a child. Vivian had been equally afraid of them, but I'd overcome my apprehension once I'd climbed upon the gateposts at Alex's urging and sat astride one of them, taunting Vivian because she was afraid to climb up onto the other gatepost.

The mansion was three stories in height and the top floor secured daylight through seven dormer windows. There were massive end chimneys. The formal entrance was decorated with four round pillars ascending from a red-brick terrace floor. There were four fan steps of white marble leading to a heavy double door studded with brass. I'd always been fascinated by the sheer beauty of the place. The lawns were well cropped and there was box everywhere. All of this was surmounted by a huge ginkgo tree.

I walked back toward the mansion and around the left of it to the rear. I ambled through random gardens, which were in bloom most of the year. In back were the stables, fortunately not very close to where the barn had been, so none of our horses had been threatened by either fire. There was a neat, two-room cabin where Maggie lived. Close by that was the ice house, a plain, round, gray-painted structure. Our children's playhouse was at the limits of the estate and now sadly neglected, for it had been a long time since Vivian and I played there and fought our childish battles.

Of these buildings, I liked the summer house most. It was large, round, with latticed walls to make it give shade, and also allow the breeze to filter through. It was built on a platform with three steps leading to the entrance. Inside was wicker furniture, painted white and comfortably cushioned, as was the bench that ran around the entire wall. Papa used to say he could have presented band concerts from the gazebo.

Once off the estate proper, I walked between a row of

age-old willows with their lacy-fingered leaves and drooping branches. At the end of this row of trees was what I always said was the cause of their weeping, for it led to the family cemetery. It contained a single grave marked by a large headstone bearing the name of my mother and the dates of her birth and death. I had no clear remembrance of her, for she'd died when I was four. There were a few hazy recollections of a woman with golden hair—exactly like Vivian's—who would sweep me into her arms. I dimly recall mama, Vivian and me dancing in the summer house to a tune she hummed. But it was so vague as to seem more dream-like than real.

I left that area and moved on to the plantation itself, stretching out for what seemed to be miles. The tobacco crop was about half-grown, its broad leaves shimmering in the early sunlight from the dew which covered them.

Further along were the low curing sheds, eight of them, looking for all the world like city factories from this distance. While I stood there, I became aware that papa was approaching from behind me. He invariably carried a gold-headed cane and with it he was in the habit of swishing off the heads of whatever weeds he encountered anywhere on the estate. I didn't even have to turn around to identify him, for the swish of the cane did that for me.

"You're up early, Heather," he said, even managing a smile.

I kissed his cheek and he held me briefly.

"I didn't sleep well last night, Papa. I was glad when morning came."

"I couldn't sleep either. I suppose the fire has you worried."

"Yes, since Alex said it was deliberately set."

"I agree with him—that it was a case of arson. How did Vivian take it?"

"In her usual way. Annoyed because it ended the festivities."

"I thought as much. Well, at least I have you to comfort me."

"You're partly to blame for Vivian's behavior," I scolded him gently. "You spoiled her."

"Yes," he admitted soberly.

"You couldn't help it. Everyone does. She's so beautiful."

"Just as your mama was."

"You never talked much of her, other than to say Vivian is the image of her."

He made no answer and I wondered if he heard.

"Papa, stop worrying about the fire. It seems to have aged you overnight. I'm sorry I chided you about Vivian."

"I deserved it, because I'm guilty. But I didn't do it for the reason you stated."

"Why then?" I asked the question more to let him talk than that I assumed it meant anything.

"I did it out of a sense of guilt. I've carried the burden with me for years and I'll carry it to my deathbed."

"Papa, you sound funereal."

He nodded. "Daughter, it's time for me to talk plainly with you."

"I thought you always did."

"No. I've been quite the opposite. Dishonest would be an appropriate word."

"I'm puzzled, Papa."

"It's the fire. It's once again overwhelmed me with guilt. It's also made me realize how indebted I am to the people in these parts, every acquaintance of yours and Vivian's and mine."

"Whatever are you talking about?" I couldn't keep irritation from edging my voice. It was almost as if he had become disoriented. As if he thought he had set the barn afire.

"Something I've kept from both you and Vivian all through your growing years. The fire made me realize how wrong I was. Especially once I learned it had been deliberately set."

"Go on, Papa." I could think of nothing else to say.

"It's an ugly story, but a true one. I'm ashamed to have to admit it, but I can no longer keep the fact from you and Vivian that I killed a man. I want you to hear it from me first, because now the story will come out."

I eyed him with shock and disbelief and my head moved negatively. What he said didn't make sense.

"Remember, every word I speak is the truth. I learned your mama was in love with another man. He was married and had a son. I found a letter in the summer house. The envelope bore your mother's name—Jessica. She'd apparently dropped it. I don't know what prompted me to take the letter out. Perhaps because the envelope wasn't sealed and I felt I wasn't doing anything wrong. Or perhaps I was beginning to suspect something was wrong. In any case, I read the letter. The contents struck me with the force of a blow."

"What was in it?" At the moment I wasn't concerned with papa's wrongdoing in reading the letter addressed to mama.

"It was from Lemuel DesChamps, the husband of Yvonne."

"You mean Mrs. DesChamps who lives down the road with her son, Joel?"

He nodded. "I went to Lemuel and begged him to stay away from Jessica for the sake of our daughters. Also, I reminded him he had an obligation to his wife and son. The letter named a time and place for him and Jessica to meet."

"Are you saying they were going to run away?"

"Yes. He replied that his wife and son would be well taken care of. And he warned me to remain quiet. That angered me. I told him I'd never allow Jessica to go with him. That even if she no longer loved me, she had an obligation to her two little daughters. He laughed at that. It was too much for me. I slapped him, then sent my seconds to call on him to name a time, place and select the weapon. That was done—in secret, of course. Two days later, I killed him in a duel. With rapiers."

The story was horrifying, but I wasn't so shocked I couldn't make a comment. "So that's why Mrs. DesChamps and her son, Joel, have nothing to do with us."

Papa nodded. I led him over to a marble bench in a secluded garden spot. He seemed grateful to sit down. I was frightened by the gray pallor his face had assumed.

"Strange," I said, "how neither Vivian nor I ever heard a rumor of it. It's a tribute to you, Papa. The people knew you were wronged."

"I deserve no sympathy, Daughter. I made a widow out of Yvonne DesChamps. I deprived her son of his father."

"They'd have lost Lemuel DesChamps anyway," I

said. "Though I know that doesn't lessen your sense of guilt."

"Nor will it ever," he said.

"How did mama react?"

"Outwardly, she forgave me. Inwardly, I fear she scorned me. She moved her possessions to the bedroom Vivian now uses."

"Did mama take her life because Lemuel no longer lived?"

"No. But she never left the house after that day. Many days she never left her room. She became a recluse, except when friends stopped by. They did occasionally, once the scandal died down. Though she became too ill even to see them."

"So that's why we spent all our growing years in private schools in the Midwest."

"Yes. I wanted you away from here as much as possible. I'm grateful that when you returned, no one ever let you know what happened."

"But mama?" I persisted.

"She died a few months later. She'd lost her desire to live. At least, with me. I guess she really died the moment life left the body of Lemuel DesChamps."

"I'm surprised Mrs. DesChamps even speaks to us."

"So am I," papa admitted, "since she swore she'd have her revenge. There were no witnesses to it. She blamed Jessica for Lemuel's infidelity. She shouldn't have. I was the guilty one."

"No, Papa."

But he was insistent. "I have no excuse. I lived solely for Nightfall."

"There was nothing wrong with that," I said loyally.

"My motive was wrong. I wanted to be the richest, most successful plantation grower in the state of Virginia."

"You've practically attained your goal, haven't you?"

"I thought so. But at a terrible price. Now I wonder if my efforts were in vain."

"You're thinking of the fire."

"I'm thinking of a lot of things. Mostly, though, of my selfishness. And cowardice."

"You've never been selfish with us."

"I was with your mother. That's what brought on the

tragedy. I forgot I had a wife and two daughters. I was obsessed with the growing of tobacco. My every waking moment was concerned only with soil conditions, weather, the going price, the highest bidder, ways to make the crops more productive and better in quality. Poor Jessica must have thought she was married to a ghost. She rarely saw me. And DesChamps had a reputation for being a rascal where the gentler sex was concerned. But that still doesn't excuse me. Because of what has happened, I've had to tell you the story, one I'd hoped you'd never have to hear. I don't want to believe that Yvonne DesChamps would carry out her threat in such a way. In fact, at the time I thought it was her overwhelming grief that caused her to speak as she did. I still won't believe her guilty of such an act."

"What of her son?"

"He'd do it only if she taught him to hate me. I can't believe she'd be so set on revenge as to do such a thing."

"Nonetheless, you are going to report the fire, aren't you?"

"I'll have to, since Alex revealed what he saw."

His statement shocked me. "Wouldn't you otherwise?"

"I told you I was a coward."

"You're not afraid of Mrs. DesChamps, are you?"

"For myself, no. I only hope that if she is keeping her word by seeking revenge, she will stop with the destruction of the barn."

"Do you think she'd resort to murder? Yours?"

"I murdered Lemuel."

"That was a duel. I don't condone it, Father. I can't. I hate violence of any kind. But if it had been considered murder, you'd have been arrested."

"I might have anyway, except that Lemuel's reputation in regard to the opposite sex was well known in these parts."

"You weren't arrested, were you?"

"No. It seems everyone knew about your mother's trysts except me."

"Which means they weren't so secret," I mused.

He nodded. "But as I said, if I'd given her the attention she deserved, she'd not have looked elsewhere for love. And perhaps Lemuel really loved her. At least, he was going to run away with her. That's what the letter said, anyway. I can't believe he was leading her on."

"If he was a scoundrel, perhaps he did."

"I never questioned the contents of the letter. Now I'll never know."

"Will you tell Vivian or will I?"

"You, please. She might become emotional, and I'm still too shaken by what happened last night. Also, I must make a trip into the village and report the fire to Deputy Sheriff Tim Oliver."

"Will you mention Yvonne DesChamps or her son?"

"Absolutely not. We've not a shred of proof. Besides, she's highly regarded in these parts."

"I know. She gives generously to the church and does a lot for the poor."

Papa nodded. "Perhaps the fire was started by someone in these parts who is mentally deranged."

"Perhaps," I replied. "Certainly we can't point the finger of guilt at anyone without proof."

"Right," papa said. "And remember this. If anything should happen to me, you have Alex and his father, Jacob, to help you. And you know almost as much about the running of the plantation as they or even I. Your biggest headache will be Vivian. I spoiled her, but my reason was that I'd ignored your mother. I tried to make it up to the two of you. I fear you came off second best, Heather. Not because I don't love you as much, but you're levelheaded. I'd feel better about it if Vivian were married and had a man to look after her."

"Papa," I exclaimed, "you sound as if you expect something horrible to happen to you."

"No," he replied. "But guilt grows harder and harder to live with."

"You wouldn't do anything rash," I exclaimed in horror.

He gave me a direct look. "I may be a coward, but not so much of a one that I'd take my own life."

"Thank God for that." The tension that filled me ebbed and we got up and started for the house.

As if to get his mind off what had happened, he said, "Do you think Vivian will ever fall in love? She's so flirtatious and flighty and—yes—selfish."

I wanted to ask if mama had been like that, but it would only remind him of the past.

I said, "One day a gentleman will come along who won't even give her a second glance. When he does, I doubt she'll ever have eyes for anyone but him."

Papa laughed. "And you?"

"I have Nightfall to help you look after."

"Don't let it consume you as it did me," he warned. "I saw you dancing with Alex last night. Is it serious?"

"No. I know him too well."

Papa said, "It wouldn't be the fact that he works for us, would it?"

"Never, Papa. You know me better than that."

He laughed. "I'm sorry, Daughter. But I'd sort of hoped it would be you and Alex. I suppose it's Rolf Fielding."

"It's not Rolf either. Or if it is, I'm not yet aware of it."

"Well, you've a mind of your own. When the right man comes along, you'll know it. In the meantime, let's get back to the house for breakfast before Maggie sends the bloodhounds after us."

Papa ate hastily and left to inform Deputy Sheriff Oliver of the suspicious fire. I regarded Vivian pouring honey over her hotcakes and wondered how she'd take the news I was about to impart. Not very well, I feared. To her, scandal of any kind was repugnant. Nonetheless, she'd have to accept it, just as I had. However, she kept the conversation light, relating the latest gossip she'd heard at the ball. The burning barn was already forgotten, or perhaps she'd shut it out of her mind so completely that it seemed as if it had never happened. I was about to slap my hand on the table in order to gain her attention and take her mind off the frivolities of the night before when she touched a hand to her brow, complained of a headache and asked to be excused.

I sighed inwardly and reached for the honey. Better to let her rest, so she'd be able to accept the scandal we'd have to live with the rest of our lives. I doubted it was a headache. Merely fatigue. It didn't matter. This was not the time.

So it was late afternoon when I tapped on Vivian's door and awaited her call to enter. She was awake, looking as beautiful as ever. Her room was as feminine as she. There were ruffled pillows in pastel shades, though she favored pink. She kept a tester above her bed, even though Virginia weather, for the most part, was against anything that lent itself to more heat. The bedspread was a series of woven figurines that looked like dolls dressed in the costumes of foreign nations. The furniture was French, dainty and painted in white and gold, upholstered in pink. Twin, full-length mirrors facing each other allowed her to survey herself from head to foot with ease and—yes—open admiration.

She was propped against several enormous, lace-covered pillows and she moved a hand languidly in welcome. I gathered she'd just come awake, for her eyes were heavy lidded.

I sat down. "Papa and I had a long talk this morning," I began.

"You and papa always have long talks." She stifled a yawn daintily, then smiled apologetically. "I'm sorry, Sister, but if your talk was about Nightfall, I don't want to hear about it. I don't have a mind for business and I'll not apologize for it."

"Not business. About papa. And the reason for the barn being burned down."

She shrugged petulantly. "It wasn't worth anything anyway."

"Please listen, Vivian," I said patiently. "I have something very serious and very shocking to tell you."

Her eyes widened in anticipation. "Don't tell me you're in love with Alex."

"It doesn't concern Alex."

"Who then?"

"Papa and Joel DesChamps' father."

"I don't even remember his father."

"No more than you remember mama."

"True. So of what interest could anything about Joel's father be to me?"

"Papa killed him in a duel."

I wasn't sure whether I'd succeeded in arousing her interest or in shocking her.

"I don't believe it." She finally found her voice.

"You must, because it's true."

"Why would he engage in a duel with Joel's father?"

"They dueled over mama."

"In heaven's name, why?" She actually raised herself from her pillows and sat up, still as a statue.

"Mama was going to run away with Joel's father."

"Oh, no!"

I nodded. "Papa blames himself. He challenged Lemuel DesChamps to a duel. Papa won. If you can call such a dreadful thing winning."

"Why weren't we told?"

"Papa didn't want us hurt by the scandal during our growing years and that's why we were sent so far away for our education. We wouldn't even know now except that the barn was deliberately burned down. The first fire was probably deliberate also."

"But what does that have to do with the duel?"

"Mrs. DesChamps swore she would have her revenge. She told papa that one day she would get even."

"Then she should be arrested." Vivian made it sound simple.

"There were no witnesses to the statement she made."

Vivian's head moved slowly in bewilderment. "We don't know Mrs. DesChamps. She barely speaks to us when we attend church services. Neither does Joel, though he's very reserved."

"Their reserve is understandable now. As papa said, he deprived Mrs. DesChamps of her husband, and Joel of a father."

"All because of mama?" Vivian asked, still unable to grasp or accept the dreadful news.

I nodded.

"Didn't mama love us?"

"I imagine she did, but she must have loved Mr. DesChamps more. And as I told you, papa says it was all his fault. He lived for the plantation."

"He still does." A tinge of bitterness touched her voice. "What did mama do when she learned Mr. DesChamps was dead? Kill herself?"

"No. She died shortly after of a natural illness."

"But what about the time before she died?"

I told Vivian of her behavior, just as papa had related it to me. All except the fact that she had moved into this room. I didn't think Vivian could accept that.

24

Her smooth brow furrowed. "Does papa think Mrs. DesChamps burned down the barn?"

"He doesn't know, but he felt that since it was deliberately set, it was time for us to learn about the scandal."

"Do you suppose it will hurt our standing in the community?"

"Is that all that worries you?" I couldn't hide the irritation I felt.

"Why shouldn't it worry me? It could hurt us socially."

"I doubt that, since everyone around here knows about it. No one was ever unkind enough even to allude to it. So I believe our social standing is where it was before the fire and before I informed you of papa's duel with Mr. DesChamps."

"Thank goodness for that." She settled back on her pillows, then sat up straight again. "You don't think Mrs. DesChamps will set fire to the house next, do you?"

"We can't accuse her of setting fire to the barn without proof," I said remindfully. "Neither her nor her son. I doubt papa would even have gone into town to inform Deputy Sheriff Oliver of it except that Alex saw the lighted candle which was still stuck to the bottom of the over turned pail and the straw all around it."

"Why wouldn't papa report it?"

"Probably because even if someone saw Mrs. DesChamps or her son do such a thing, he'd not want to make trouble for her, figuring he'd done enough to her."

Vivian mused over that. "I think we should get married and get off this plantation. Then if Mrs. DesChamps burns the house down, we won't be in it."

"I wish you'd stop pointing the finger of guilt at her."

"Who else would do such a thing?"

"Someone mentally deranged." I repeated papa's statement.

"Hate will do that."

Her sensible statement startled me. "You do think once in a while, don't you?"

"I'm not altogether stupid."

"Just altogether selfish."

"In what way?" she demanded.

"What if the house was set afire and papa and Maggie were burned to death?"

"I never thought of that." Once again she settled back on her pillows. "But I still think it's time we got married."

"You haven't settled down enough," I said flatly. "All you do is flirt."

"You should try it. It's fun."

"It has no appeal for me."

"Nothing but that awful tobacco has appeal for you. Or Rolf Fielding."

"I haven't given him a thought," I said honestly.

"You should. I think he's smitten with you."

"No," I contradicted. "We just enjoy talking about agriculture and business methods as they concern farming. Especially the growing of tobacco. Did you know his plantation is as large as ours?"

"He's terribly handsome. And so tall," she said wistfully. "I wish he'd fallen in love with me."

"Maybe he will."

She'd already forgotten about papa's duel. "I doubt it. We've known him for years and I tried my best to catch his attention."

"Maybe you tried too hard. You might have caught his attention better if you'd ignored him."

"I tried that too. Nothing helped. He just seemed to want to be with you. Even when we were small."

"Maybe he's afraid of a beautiful young lady."

She beamed. "I wish that were so, but I'm afraid he prefers brains to beauty."

"Thank you." I managed a smile, believing she'd not meant to be deliberately cruel.

"Well, you *are* brainy, Heather. But you're not popular the way I am. My dance card had more names on it than there were dances. I made the gentlemen share dances with me."

I stood up, already bored with the direction the conversation was taking. "Just remember, my sweet, you won't be nineteen forever. And while a man enjoys a beautiful playmate, for a mate he wants a woman who will be devoted, loving and have eyes only for him."

"Oh, piff." She fell back on her pillows and made a face at me. "There's no fun in you, Heather. You're getting more and more like a fussy, crotchety old maid every day."

"And you, my sister, seem to grow more childish with the years. I guess it's as well one of us has grown up. Go back to sleep. I'm sorry I had to relate such distressing news to you."

"So long as we won't be hurt by it, I won't worry about Mrs. DesChamps or her son Joel. Or someone mentally deranged."

"Vivian Gates, you are the most selfish, petty individual I've ever known. Why don't you ask papa if you can go on a voyage to Europe? You might meet a prince, fall in love with him and he with you and you can marry and live happily ever after. Just like in the fairy tales."

She picked up a pillow, aimed it and flung it at me. But I expected it and had reached the door as I finished speaking. The pillow smacked the door just as I closed it. I shook my head sorrowfully. Vivian would never change, any more than I. I just wished we could learn to get along. The fault was mine as much as hers. I suppose I favored papa, while she favored mama. That was probably why our parents hadn't gotten along. They were too different. Neither would give in. It was the same with Vivian and me.

Three

THOUGH ALEX OFTEN HARNESSED THE CARRIAGE FOR us when we wished to go to the village, this morning he was nowhere in sight. I had an idea he had accompanied papa so both could relate what they knew about the burned-out barn to Deputy Sheriff Oliver. If so, I appreciated his thoughtfulness. Alex was certainly a credible witness, and should the culprit be caught, any testimony Alex gave would be considered carefully.

And so this morning it was the hostler who had the carriage waiting for us when we came out of the house. He assisted us up to the seat, handed me the reins and

I started the animals in motion. Vivian never wanted the responsibility of handling two animals, fearful something might frighten them and make them bolt. Also, she made a stunning picture in her jade-green dress, with frothy lace edging the collar, which extended to the waist in a fichu. My dress was tailored and without frills of any kind. I suppose it reflected my personality. In any case, I felt it more appropriate, since I was driving the carriage and our journey was merely to do some shopping in Rutford.

The village center had a large, tree-shaded green, with colorful geraniums lining the paths that meandered the length and width of it. Freshly painted green benches were spaced at intervals for the convenience of the folk who wished to rest or relax. In the center of the green was a clock, quite tall, whose four sides were constructed of marble. It was the gift of Mrs. DesChamps and a tribute to her generosity. A bed of roses surrounded it. They were enormous in size and cared for by her private gardener.

I'd always admired it, but now, each time I saw it, I would remember papa telling me of the secret he and the townsfolk had kept from Vivian and me all these years. The fact that we'd not received even a hint nor ever had a snide remark directed our way was proof of how highly papa was regarded in the community. But it had done little to relieve his feeling of guilt at having taken the life of another, even though the duel was considered a matter of honor. His victory had been an empty one. I wondered if it would have been better if he'd let mama abscond with her lover. Knowing him, I felt that what he'd done was done with his daughters in mind, for certainly he'd been a loving father.

Our first stop was at the millinery shop run by Mrs. Loser. She was a hearty, buxom woman, whose skill at copying French originals was known throughout these parts. But Vivian wouldn't purchase a copy. Hers had to be from Paris. Mrs. Loser gladly obliged, and papa paid well for the extravagance.

Mrs. Loser greeted us warmly and led us over to a small table backed by a mirror, with two on either side. They were hinged so that they could be moved to give the viewer a three-angled view of how the hat looked on her.

Though she knew she was going to purchase both, she had to take just so much time trying them on. I sat patiently, watching her preen and pose. Mrs. Loser stood back a way, as silent as I, knowing Vivian and her ways.

But finally, to my relief, Mrs. Loser spoke. "Which one will you wear, Miss Vivian? I'll put the other in a large box."

"Why not the one with feathers?" I suggested, knowing her perverseness. I also realized that was the one she wanted to wear, but I felt it too gaudy for a morning stroll along Main Street.

Her hand had been on it, but she reached for the more tailored one, with the stiff, wide brim. The base of the crown was banded with green ribbon. A rose of matching color was the only other ornament on the straw hat which seemed to be the same color as Vivian's hair. The effect was startling and most appealing.

"Beautiful," Mrs. Loser commented approvingly. "You chose the two loveliest from the catalogue."

Vivian smiled at Mrs. Loser's reflection and the compliment she'd been paid. I excused myself, since Maggie and I had prepared a list before I left, and I headed for the general store.

It took a while to make the purchases, after which the handyman carried them out to the carriage and stowed them on the floor and beneath the seats. I gave him a small gratuity for his efforts, unhitched the animals and waited for Vivian. She came along shortly, a hatbox in each hand. The smaller one contained the hat she'd worn when she left the house. She held her head high, her manner regal. She knew she caught everyone's eye. Those of the male sex regarded her in open approval. Some of her own sex viewed her with admiration; others with envy. I just wished Vivian had a touch of humility. In my opinion, it would have given her beauty far wider appeal.

She placed the boxes on the seat, then climbed in beside me. She spoke without looking at me.

"You don't need to regard me with such disapproval. I know you envy me because I'm prettier than you. I've even heard it said people can't believe we're twins."

"You're not just pretty, Vivian. You're beautiful. And far from envying you, I'm proud of you."

"I wish I could believe you, Heather. But you're for-

29

ever scolding me or correcting me or arguing with me. Nothing I do is right."

"We do argue," I admitted. "And I do scold you, because I think at times you're very rude to people."

"You mean Alex, of course."

"Alex will do as an example. He's as good as we are. Far better educated."

"Because he went to school and studied about plantations?"

"Partly that. And also because no matter what you say to him, he's too much the gentleman to come back at you."

"That's not so. He was rude to me last night. The idea of telling me my beauty will fade. I'll stay young forever if I have to. I'll find a way."

"Now you're being childish." It was useless trying to make her see reason. "And there's no more time for feuding."

"I see what you mean," she said, already forgetting our fussing. "Or, rather, whom you mean. Joel DesChamps."

"Yes," I said softly.

He'd just come out of the bank, and he stood, his features reflective, as if wondering which way to go. He was tall and slender and rather handsome. He had dark brown eyes, bronzed skin and perfect features. His gray cheviot suit fitted him to perfection. His straw hat sat perfectly straight on his head. He was clean shaven and looked every inch the gentleman. Since I'd never conversed with him, I didn't know if appearances were deceiving. Our sole contact had been when we attended church services. The DesChamps pew was close to the front, directly across from ours. Strange, now that I thought about it, I didn't even know if she and papa ever exchanged greetings. She had nodded politely to Vivian and me when our eyes met, but Joel had never seemed aware of us. Shyness, perhaps? Or had he been ordered to ignore us?

His head turned suddenly in our direction, as if he knew my thoughts were of him. For the first time, he seemed to have an awareness of our identity. Not only that, but his hand raised and he lifted his hat to bow to us.

Vivian's surprise equaled mine, for she whispered under her breath, "What do you make of that?"

"I don't know." I spoke without moving my lips. I knew the clatter of the horses' hooves, the squeaking of the moving carriages and wagons and casual greetings called by the townspeople to one another made our words indistinguishable.

He walked the few steps to our carriage, holding his hat before him. "You are the Misses Vivian and Heather Gates."

"And you are Mr. Joel DesChamps," Vivian replied haughtily.

"Forgive my boldness." He spoke with an earnestness that seemed genuine. "But I wish to express my sympathy for the fire on your plantation last night. Particularly since I know it was a special occasion for you."

"How did you know about the fire?" I asked. My manner, though formal, was polite.

"It was quite visible from where we live. In fact, I think it lit up the sky for miles around. I inquired about it in the bank. Freddie Faber was there and I knew he'd attended the soiree. He said it was just a barn and quite valueless. I was glad to hear it."

"Were you really, Mr. DesChamps?" Vivian asked haughtily.

"Yes, Miss Vivian," he replied, quite at ease. So much so, in fact, that I wondered if papa might be wrong in having a suspicion Mrs. DesChamps was the culprit who had had it set.

"How did you know my name?" she asked, her manner quite unchanged. I could see she felt the DesChamps were guilty.

A smile touched his mouth. "Everyone knows your name. No one else on earth could be so beautiful."

Vivian gasped audibly at the compliment.

Mr. DesChamps switched his attention to me. "Meaning no offense to you, Miss Heather, for you're also quite comely."

"Compliments slip off your tongue quite easily, Mr. DesChamps," I said coolly. "I'm usually told I'm brainy. I've learned to content myself with that compliment."

"I doubt any compliment could sway you," he said. "It wasn't my intention to flatter either of you. I

31

was merely stating not only my opinion, but that of the villagers. Convey my sympathy to your father also."

"Thank you, Mr. DesChamps," I said. "And now, if you'll excuse us, please."

"Thank you for your expression of sympathy about the fire, Mr. DesChamps." Vivian bestowed her lovely smile on him. His compliment had quite turned her head.

"I'm only sorry I wasn't among those present to help extinguish it," he replied.

"It was impossible to extinguish it, Mr. DesChamps." I said. "But the bucket brigade prevented it from spreading. As for being present, would you have come, had you received an invitation?"

He smiled. "The fact remains, I did not receive an invitation, Miss Heather."

I returned the smile. "Then you may blame my sister. It was she who issued the invitations."

"Ah." He chided Vivian with his eyes. She colored prettily.

I was finding it difficult to hide my disgust with her behavior, and I was tired of his verbal sparring. I had the feeling he was laughing at us.

"Mr. DesChamps," I said soberly, "after the fire, my father informed me of the duel with your father and the reason for it. I'm sorry for what happened, but since it did, I think your mother did the proper thing in discouraging you from cultivating us."

"What makes you think she did?" I felt he was a consummate actor.

"Papa told us everything. I don't think I need to say more. Or perhaps just one more thing. You exude charm, but I doubt your sincerity."

He had the grace to color. "You have a way with words, Miss Heather, and they cut deeply."

"I'm sorry if I've offended you, but I say what is on my mind. What papa did was wrong. Just as wrong as an act of arson. The fire which burned down the barn had been deliberately set."

"You have proof?" he asked.

"Alex Hale reached the barn in time to see how the fire had been set."

"Then when the culprit is caught, there'll be no difficulty in convicting him. Your father has enough problems without having to worry about someone setting fires on his property."

I made him no answer, lest I lose my temper. I was annoyed with Vivian as it was and I feared I might say too much. A slanderous remark would make me open to a civil suit. I didn't want to cause papa further heartache.

I urged the horses into motion and they trotted briskly off. We left Joel DesChamps staring after us.

Vivian said, "You were very rude, Heather."

"You were very stupid to be taken in by his flattery," I retorted.

"He seemed quite sincere to me."

"Probably he was. I may have made a fool of myself, but you didn't see the agony on papa's face as he told me what he'd done. As a result of it, he's not known a moment's peace."

"I forgot about it," she said. "I mean, what mama did to him."

"He doesn't blame her, only himself," I said. "But he deserves our loyalty."

"Yes," she agreed. "I should have accused Joel of setting the barn afire."

"No, you shouldn't have," I said firmly. "We've no proof he did it."

"His mother, then."

"Her either. We must be careful."

"I wish you'd make up your mind. I don't know which way to go."

"Just don't cultivate Joel DesChamps. I'm afraid to trust him."

"I think I'd trust him," Vivian said ruminatively. "But I'm not sure about his mother."

"We don't even know her." Disgust edged my voice and I urged the horses on to greater speed. I was anxious to get the ride over with.

"Not so fast, Heather," Vivian cried out. She grasped the side of the seat with one hand and held on to her hat with the other.

I ignored her plea, enjoying the wind in my face and the carriage wheels churning the dirt as they rolled along, making it rise and billow around the carriage. Vivian protested again, but I pretended not to hear her. I suppose, in my way, I was as childish as she. I knew she

33

hated fast rides. It was my way of getting even for her allowing Joel DesChamps to sway her with his false compliments. I didn't know if it was he or his mother who set the fire, but I had sense enough to know neither of them cared about us. And with good reason.

Alex met us at the front of the house. Vivian didn't return his greeting, though she accepted his assistance. Once on the ground, she reached in, grabbed her two hatboxes and ran up the front stairs to the door. It was never locked and she was inside in a matter of seconds. It was then she vented her anger on me. A solid slamming of the door made even Alex jump. The horses reared slightly at the sound of the crash, but he got them under immediate control.

"What brought on that fit of temper?" he asked.

"We met Joel DesChamps in town."

He eyed me speculatively. "What about it?"

"This morning papa told me about the duel. It's the first Vivian and I heard of it."

"I'm sorry you had to know," he said.

"We'd have learned of it sooner or later," I reasoned. "Better to hear it from papa than an outsider."

"Much better," Alex agreed.

"Did you know Mrs. DesChamps told papa she'd have her revenge because of what he did to her husband?"

"No," Alex said. "Your papa never speaks of the past."

"It's never been out of his mind, though. Now I believe he fears Mrs. DesChamps."

"If so, he's thinking of you and Vivian, not himself."

"Is something wrong, Alex?"

"What do you mean?"

I knew Alex well enough to realize he was being evasive.

"Is papa in trouble of some kind?"

"Are you asking that because of the fire?"

"No. I think there's something worrying him deeply. I've had that feeling about him lately."

"Why don't you ask him, Heather?"

"I'm asking you. We're friends, Alex. You wouldn't be disloyal to papa by telling me. Perhaps I could help him in some way."

Alex looked around, then said, "Not here. We'll take a ride."

Maggie came out the door at that moment. "You and your sister been fightin' again. She slams that door once more, I quit. You forget the groceries?"

"No, Maggie."

"I'll bring them in." Alex was already shifting them from the carriage to the steps.

Maggie pointed a finger at the stairs. "Leave 'em there. I'll bring 'em in."

"Thanks, Maggie." Alex and I spoke in unison.

He emptied the carriage, then lifted me onto the seat.

"Where you off to now?" Maggie called from the steps.

"China," I called back as Alex got the horses into motion. She shook her head and gave me a look of disgust. I forgot my anger and laughed aloud.

Alex joined me, then paused to say, "I like your laughter, Heather. And when your face lights up with mischief, it's as if a rainbow circled the sky."

"Stop flirting with me," I chided.

"I'm not flirting, but if I were, I'd wish you'd flirt back."

"I won't," I assured him.

"I know," he said. "Besides, you wanted to talk about your father."

"I want your trust and confidence. I love papa and I want to help him, to be at his side when he needs me. I think he does."

Alex drove the horses only a short distance from the estate, for I'd ridden them hard on the way back. He pulled off the road beneath a tall maple, dropped the reins and shifted his position so that he faced me.

"I feel disloyal talking this way—and I wouldn't, except I know how intensely loyal to him you are—but he is in financial difficulty."

"Has he said so?"

"No. But I know about the running of this plantation as well as he."

A sudden thought occurred to me. "Does papa gamble?"

"Once in a while, probably."

"The truth, Alex."

He was reluctant to speak, but he knew how insistent I was. "Oh, there are rumors of two or three games your father sat in on where the stakes were high, but if he placed the plantation at stake, I wouldn't know about it. I can't tell you what I don't know."

"You've told me very little."

"I'm sorry. He can't be in too bad financial condition, going by the ball which you held last night."

"That was Vivian's doing. And papa would make any sacrifice for her."

Alex nodded agreement. "Just remember, Heather, every farmer has good crops and bad crops. Last year's was scanty and not up to its usual quality, but this year— barring storms or other misfortunes—we'll have a bumper crop of the best leaf ever grown on this plantation."

"That's wonderful news." I smiled with relief.

"Now I have a little more news for you," he said.

"What kind of news?"

"I'm going away."

"Leaving the plantation?" I couldn't believe it.

"I've a degree and an education I ought to put to some useful purpose. There's nothing for me on this plantation. My father takes care of everything. Better than I could, too. So I'm going west, where they're beginning to develop big farms."

"I understand, but I'm sorry to hear it. I'll be losing the best friend I ever had. Nothing will be the same without you. I wish you all the good fortune you deserve. And that's an awful lot."

"Thanks, Heather."

"When did you make this decision?"

"Last night. When I found out we could just be friends." He picked up the reins. "I love you, Heather. I've known that ever since I recognized the difference between a–boy and a girl. I always wanted to do something to make you proud of me. I hoped for too much."

"I'm proud I can call you my friend. I wish I were in love with you. You're the finest man I've ever known."

"I have to investigate several offers I've received. I don't want to make any mistakes."

"You won't," I said. "Papa always said you were levelheaded. You're not leaving immediately, are you?"

"I intended to, but after the fire, I'm going to delay

my departure in the hope the culprit will be found and I can give testimony against him. I went into the village and told what I saw to Deputy Sheriff Oliver."

"Have there been any strangers around the village? I mean, unsavory-looking characters?"

"He's not seen any."

"Did papa mention the DesChamps?"

"No." Alex's voice was firm. "Why would he?"

"He told me Mrs. DesChamps swore vengeance. I think papa suspects her, though he doesn't want to."

"I didn't know about Mrs. DesChamps' threat."

"No one ever did until papa told me. She made it only to papa. There were no witnesses."

"She waited a long time to carry out her threat—if it was she. If so, more likely she hired someone to do it."

"Or Joel did it, though he doesn't seem the type."

"No, he doesn't. But we can't suspect the DesChamps without a shred of proof."

"I agree and so does papa."

"Does Vivian know about the threat?"

"Of course. She's my sister."

"And not always discreet."

"Papa felt she should know and I agreed. I'm grateful to everyone for not telling us of the duel before we were grown. I'm repelled by it, though."

"Your father's honor was at stake."

"So was Mr. DesChamps' life. He forfeited it."

"It could have been your father."

"Thanks for your loyalty, Alex. And thanks for confiding in me."

"I wasn't able to tell you much."

"I wish you weren't going away."

"I can't stay here, Heather. I'll never think of you as a friend. I'll never stop loving you."

"You'll meet someone else who'll make you far happier than I ever could."

"I hope so. But I doubt it. Now I'll take you back."

"I'll not betray the confidence you placed in me by telling me about papa."

"I'm beholden to you for that. He'll not worry you unless it's necessary, and if it is, you'll be the first to know. He knows he has a treasure in you."

I colored at Alex's words, but made no reply. He

helped me out of the carriage in front of the house, then brought the horses and carriage to the stable. I went to my room, washed the dust from my face, then sat down and thought about the events of the day. Alex was right. If papa was in trouble, I'd hear about it soon enough.

I shut all worrisome thoughts out of my mind and thought of Rolf Fielding. I hadn't written him in some time and he'd been very faithful in his correspondence. I could tell him about the fire and also imform him I knew of the duel. Certainly he knew of it, since everyone else did.

I went to my desk, inserted a fresh pen point into the holder and dipped it into the inkwell to begin a letter to Rolf, one long overdue.

When I was halfway through it, Vivian came in, wearing the second of her new hats. She posed for me as if I'd never seen it on her before.

"Isn't it beautiful? During the rare times you're nice to me, I may let you wear it. Whom are you writing to?"

"Rolf. I thought it about time."

"You ought to encourage him."

"I'm not encouraging anybody."

"He's so handsome and so rich."

"His looks would have little to do with my falling in love with him, and as for money, we have enough of that."

"There's never enough. Not for my tastes. I saw you ride off with Alex. Why do you persist in being with him?"

"Because he's my friend and I wanted to ask him a few questions."

"What about?"

"The plantation." She expressed no interest in that, so I said, "Alex is going away."

"Leaving Nightfall? Is he out of his mind?"

"He's looking for work on some western farm. He'll have little trouble finding a place. With his education, he'll do very well indeed."

"I thought that someday he'd take his father's place here."

"I predict that one day Alex will be one of the most successful planters or farmers in the country."

Once again Vivian's interest waned.

She eyed my pen, poised just above the paper. "I've got a splendid idea. While you're writing to Rolf, invite him to our next ball. We'll have it in his honor."

"He'll graduate in two weeks," I reminded her. "And we just held a ball."

"The next one will be held as soon as Rolf graduates and gets here." She spoke with quiet determination.

"Vivian, you'll bankrupt papa yet. Have you no idea what these affairs cost?"

"The more they cost, the better they are. This one will be the best ever. I'm going to start planning it now. We'll have two orchestras, so there will always be music, always dancing. And I'm going to insist that Maggie find some new ways to prepare different kinds of food. We'll have twice as many Japanese lanterns. Maybe I'll even have tables set up on the lawn somewhere. I've a hundred ideas, and this is going to be the most lavish ball yet. I'll let you know when I've decided how I want things done. You must invite Rolf. If you don't, I'll never forgive you. Papa isn't going to like the idea of another ball so soon, and I need an excuse. Rolf's graduating is reason enough. Write him now, the next sentence. You hear?"

"I'll finish the letter after supper. We'll talk to papa about it. I can't issue an invitation without papa consenting to the affair, and it wouldn't surprise me if he refused."

"Papa refuse me?" she asked with a little laugh. "He enjoys our formal dinners and balls more than anyone. He won't object. He never has. And he's never refused me anything."

But he did. Not vehemently, though, and he finally gave in to Vivian's blandishments, but it was the first time I felt that his hesitation was due to some very serious concern.

"You girls," he admonished, "must consider the fact that we didn't have a good crop last year. Not that we're headed for the poor farm, but it does mean we have to be more careful in the way we spend money."

"It's Rolf's graduation," Vivian argued. "You know he's in love with Heather and—"

"Nobody knows he's in love with me, including me,"

I said tartly. "Nor has he ever hinted of it. I haven't even seen him in—how long?—five months?"

"Rolf is an excellent young man," papa said. "He would be most welcome into my family, but, as Heather says, Rolf hasn't committed himself. However, we'll have the ball. Give me three weeks or so. Meanwhile, go ahead and plan it."

"That's what Vivian does best," I said with a sigh, because I realized this burden of expense was going to bother papa and I didn't like the idea.

There was no stopping Vivian. If she recognized or suspected that papa's hesitation might be due to something serious, she either forgot it promptly, or refused to consider it. She began planning then and there. Once, I saw papa wince when she suggested some greater-than-usual extravagance.

I would have liked to administer a piece of my mind at that moment, but I didn't. I knew why papa gave in to her.

Yet, for the first time in my life, I was beginning to worry. It was a strange and uncomfortable sensation, and one quite alien. But I was beginning to wonder if papa was as impractical as Vivian.

Four

A WEEK WENT BY PLEASANTLY ENOUGH. SOME FIELD hands removed the debris from the fire and the cleared land was planted in grass. Vivian spent most of her time writing invitations, not yet dated. She changed her mind about the plans twice a day. I was growing more and more concerned about papa. I'd never seen him like this before. I sensed it was more than the fire that had him worried. Which meant it had to be the plantation.

Alex had not yet reached any conclusion as to where he'd go, but he'd already received two offers: one in the

Midwest; a second in California. He worked closely with his father on the plantation, and I knew he kept a watchful eye on it. I'd miss him. He was a friend I could go and talk to, knowing he'd never betray a confidence.

I took to walking the land with him, learning more and more about the growing of tobacco and the way field hands should be managed. Alex instructed me on how to offer cured tobacco for bids, how to improve the crop and fight off infestations of insects. Some of it I already knew; much of it I did not. But I learned and stored the knowledge in my mind to be used later, if need be. Neither Alex nor I ever discussed the financial matters relating to the plantation again.

One evening, papa had Maggie summon me to the upstairs library. Though only the lamp on his desk was lit, leaving the room more in shadow than light, I could see the haggard lines on his face. He was poring over a ledger when I entered, then transferring figures onto a pad to do more figuring. I suspected he was trying to figure out how to make ends meet. There were two leather chairs angled to face the fireplace. The one I chose also faced the desk. I sat, quietly waiting for him to finish, but when he continued on, I glanced at the clock. I'd been sitting there for almost fifteen minutes.

"Papa?" He'd probably forgotten about sending for me, for he jumped at the sound of my voice.

He set down his pencil, rotated his shoulders to get the stiffness out of them, then stretched his long frame and turned the swivel chair so that he faced me.

He rested his head against the high back and gave me an apologetic smile. "Have you been here long?"

"Long enough to know something is weighing heavily on your mind."

He crossed his legs at the ankles and rested his arms on those of the chair, letting his hands dangle from the edge. He was tired and worried though he managed a smile as he spoke.

"I was just figuring out the expenses of the ball I told Vivian she could give."

"And wondering how you could pay for them."

"Oh—there's enough for that."

"Is there enough to pay the hired hands? And Jacob Hale? And his son, Alex?"

41

He sobered. "Yes. But I may as well tell you, our finances are in worse shape than I thought. However, I'm sure the crop will be good and things will be running smoothly once again."

"How did we get into this situation?" I asked. "Or was it due solely to last year's scanty crop?"

"No, Daughter. It happened because I lost quite a sum gambling. I could make the excuse that not having a wife, I had to look for recreation elsewhere, and not being a philanderer where women are concerned, I looked for other means of relaxation. But that's no excuse for letting myself get into such a situation. I have two daughters who depend on me for a livelihood. I should have thought of you, but I'd overimbibed in alcoholic spirits and the company was congenial."

"You mean they were friends?"

"No. I met them in the hotel when I went to sell our crops. I was invited to join them in a game. I've always considered myself a good player, but they were better than I. The drinking made me reckless. I paid my gambling debts, but I had to borrow money on the plantation to do so."

"I've never seen you intoxicated."

"I've taken good care you didn't, but I'm not the strong character you think I am. I'm only human, with the weaknesses of humans. I don't mind paying for my wrongdoing, but I feel very guilty that you and Vivian may have to. That's why I gave in to her and let her send out invitations to the ball she's spending every moment planning."

"Papa, you should never have allowed her such an extravagance."

"My motive isn't the best."

"What do you mean?"

"I'd like to see you both make a good marriage. I thought for a while you and Alex might marry."

I smiled. "He'd scarcely bring money into the family."

"I wasn't thinking of that where you're concerned, because I know you wouldn't. But he's a man of strong character. You'd be in good hands."

"I realize that, Papa, but I don't love him."

He nodded. "Rolf Fielding, then. I didn't know if you and he might have a secret understanding and that's why

42

you denied it in front of Vivian. She's so flighty she'd blab it all over the village."

"If Rolf is interested in me romantically, he's given no indication of it. At least, none that I've noticed. And I've not thought of him in that way."

"Then there's no man you care about."

I smiled at his seriousness. "At present, just one. You."

"I'm very lucky, but I'm your father. And, unfortunately, I won't live to take care of you."

"Then let me live to take care of you, Papa."

"You deserve better than that—especially after what I've done to you. And your sister."

"We'll survive it—all three of us. I can understand your wishing that Vivian would marry and settle down. I do too. But right now, she thinks she'll be nineteen forever. Since she does, let her enjoy the feeling of being beautiful and having the admiration of every swain in these parts."

He laughed softly, but it was rather sad laughter. "Thank God she has you for a sister."

"How do you mean that?"

"I don't mean it in the sense that you're the brainy one. Yes, I've heard that too. Probably as often as you. But you have a quiet beauty that will not only survive the years, but grow with them. I know Vivian glitters like a diamond. Your beauty has the softness of a pearl." He gave a quick shake of his head. "I didn't know I could be poetic."

"Nor did I, Papa," I said softly. "But it's the most beautiful compliment that's ever been paid me."

"It's not a compliment, but a fact. Strange how her skin is so fair and yours has an olive cast. Her eyes are blue; yours a soft gray. Her face is oval; yours heart shaped. And she's golden blonde, while your tresses are jet black."

"There's no picture of mama around. I've been told Vivian resembles her."

Papa nodded. "The image of her. You remind me of my mother. Not only in appearance, but you have the strong character she had. I wish I'd inherited it."

"Don't belittle yourself, Papa," I chided him gently.

"I know me, Daughter. My strengths and my weaknesses. Unfortunately, the latter outweigh the former. I had to let you know things aren't good for us at present. But I don't mean we're in danger of losing everything."

"I'm glad to hear it." I kept my tone light, though I was as concerned as I knew he was. "And thanks for taking me into your confidence. By doing so, I feel you believe me completely grown up."

"You are," he said, "except in one respect."

I sobered. "What's that?"

"The constant bickering between you and Vivian. When will that stop?"

"Probably never." I was relieved that was his only concern. "It's just an outlet. Once whatever we're being spiteful about is over with, we're friends again. You must admit we're loyal to one another."

He looked relieved. "I felt you were. I'm glad to hear you say it. She needs you, Heather. Far more than you'll ever need her. Don't let her down. Whenever I look at her, I see your mama. I guess Vivian's beauty has helped to keep alive my feeling of guilt. Mind you, I'm not soliciting your pity. I killed a man. I should have paid for my crime with my life, but I've paid. I've lived with it every moment. And I will continue to so long as there is breath in my body."

I said, "I can understand your gambling. It helped to take your mind off what happened in the past."

"Thank you for being so understanding, Heather. I hope Vivian will be."

"After all you've done for us, I'm certain of it," I said.

Papa gave a quick glance at the clock. "Eleven. I had no idea it was so late. Run along and get your beauty sleep."

"I don't need too much. Where are you going?"

He was already on his feet. "Oh, Alex, Jacob and I take turns keeping an eye out to make certain there are no prowlers. I don't think we really need to worry. I'm beginning to suspect the fire was set by a disgruntled employee. We've had them from time to time. Transients passing through who want a few weeks work, only they really don't want to work. Once we find that out, we give them short shrift."

"I hope you're right, Papa." I remembered our encounter with Joel DesChamps and told him about it.

"He's a quiet lad. Devoted to his mother. Takes her everywhere."

"He expressed his sympathy about the fire."

"When did you meet him?"

"The morning following the fire. In the village."

"How did he know about it so soon?"

"He had just come out of the bank. He said Freddie Faber was in there and told him about it." I paused, then added speculatively, "Vivian liked him. I had reservations, but I really think he wishes he were a part of the social life here. He hinted as much. At least, that's the impression I got."

"I wish to God I could believe it," papa said. "But I can still see Yvonne's face when I went to offer my regrets. And I still hear her vowing vengeance. Not that I blamed her. My sin was unforgivable."

"So was his," I replied, though not vindictively. "I informed Joel that you had told us about the duel."

"Go to bed." Papa bent down and kissed my brow. I stood on tiptoe and touched my cheek to his and told him that no matter what had happened in the past or would in the future, I'd always love him.

I awoke early the next morning and just as I reached the bottom step on my way to breakfast, there was a sharp rap on the front door. It was Jacob Hale, Alex's father. He seemed shaken and asked for papa.

Maggie had come from the kitchen to answer the door and spoke from behind me. "He's not up yet, Mr. Jacob. But he's awake. I brought him up his breakfast. I been doin' that for the past week to make certain he eats. Once he comes down those steps, he heads straight for the door. Not been himself for some time."

"I know that, Maggie," Jacob said. "And what I have to tell him won't make him feel any better."

"What's wrong, Jacob?" I asked.

"Somebody shot two of our best horses."

Though I could tell from his face he wasn't the purveyor of good news, I didn't expect that, and for a moment I was too stunned to move.

"I'll go tell him," Maggie said.

"No, I will," I told her. "Then I'll waken Vivian."

"I'll get breakfast on the table for the two of you." Maggie spoke as she retreated to the kitchen.

Jacob said, "Please tell your papa I'll be around number four curing shed. I have to oversee some repair work there. One of the hands is standing guard over the dead horses. Alex is on his way there."

Papa was already dressed and opened the door at my knock. When I told him aabout the tragedy, he immediately headed for the stairs. I ran after him.

"Papa, how could such a thing have happened when you, Alex and Jacob have been patrolling the plantation?"

He paused only long enough to answer. "It's so big that we couldn't patrol all of it, and I imagine the horses are at the far end. Alex patrolled after me. I met him on my way back to the house at two this morning and insisted he come in for coffee. We talked awhile. The horses could have been lured away then and not shot till after dawn. We figure it's safe once daylight comes and quit the watch. I'll find out whether I was right or wrong."

I suspected he was wrong. I glanced into his room and saw the tray Maggie had brought up. I decided to bring it down and save her a few steps. I was pleased to note there wasn't a trace of food visible on his plate and the napkin which had covered fresh hot rolls lay open with only crumbs visible. At least, he'd breakfasted.

I set the tray on the table in the hall and went to waken Vivian. To my surprise, she was already up and dressed. Then I remembered. She was still engrossed in making plans for the ball. I asked her to come downstairs immediately, that I had something to tell her. Again, to my amazement, she obeyed. I went back for the tray and followed her down. Maggie took it from me in the dining room and brought it to the kitchen.

I joined Vivian at the table. She'd put her fruit aside in favor of hot rolls and was dipping into the honey jar.

I said, "More bad news, I'm sorry to say."

She looked crestfallen. "I hope the ball isn't going to be called off."

"I wish it were as simple as that. No, sister dear, the ball, as of now, is going on according to the million and a half plans you've made for it."

"I hope so. It's taken every moment since papa gave his permission."

"Two of papa's best horses were shot last night—or this morning."

"What a horrible thing to do!" she exclaimed.

"Yes. Who could be so brutal as to kill two defenseless animals?"

"I can't imagine."

"I can, but I rather hope I'm wrong."

Vivian eyed me across the table. "The DesChamps?"

"I hope not. I wonder if Joel will come to express his sympathy."

"You do believe they had something to do with it, don't you?"

"Only because of Yvonne DesChamps' threat of vengeance."

"But that was so long ago," Vivian mused.

"Hatred can build through the years."

"Why would she wait so long?"

"If she knows papa, she knows he's never had a moment's peace since that dreadful duel which ended in Lemuel DesChamps' death. So she let him suffer through the years. Also, we're grown now and we can be hurt by this."

"How can we be hurt by two horses being killed?"

"You're right. It doesn't make sense," I said, frowning. "I don't know, Vivian. I'm trying to figure out the answer, but it's difficult when I don't even know Mrs. DesChamps."

"I don't either. And her son never spoke to us until that day in the village."

"The morning after the barn burned down."

Vivian chewed thoughtfully on a honey-smeared roll. She wasn't even aware that some of the honey was rolling down the side of her mouth. Despite the gravity of the situation, the sight of it made me smile, for she was a most meticulous eater.

"Why don't we pay her a visit?" she asked.

"Are you serious?" I couldn't believe she was.

"Completely. I'd like to see what her house looks like. I don't even know what she looks like, because at church she always wears black and has a fancy veil covering her face. It's so heavily embroidered you can't see beneath it."

"Yes." We were agreeing for once. "But she's French and they're very fashionable dressers."

47

"What's so fashionable about veils that hide your face?"

"Don't ask me." My interest didn't concern Mrs. DesChamps' veils, but it did concern her. "When will we leave to pay our respects?"

"What excuse do we have for going?"

"We'll need one, since it's still too early in the morning to make a social call."

"I know." Vivian's voice was tinged with excitement. "We'll ask her if she would be offended if we invited Joel to the ball."

"Surely you're not serious." The very thought made me ill.

"Can you think of another reason for going there?" she asked haughtily.

"No," I admitted. "But I hope he won't accept. Somehow, I had the feeling he was laughing at us the day we met."

"I didn't have that feeling at all," she said. She turned her attention to the crisp bacon and fried eggs.

"Once he told you how beautiful you were, you were putty in his hands." Disgust edged my voice.

"If you're going to fight, I won't go." She said peevishly. "I have more important things to think about."

I didn't pursue that topic, knowing she meant the ball.

"I apologize," I said.

"Then I'll go." She added, "I'll wear my hat with the feathers."

I shuddered at the thought, but gave her no argument. At the moment, the hat was of no importance. Meeting Mrs. DesChamps was. I had to know what kind of woman she was, she of the heavily embroidered veil that hid her face. Why, I wondered. Had she a definite reason, or was it an affectation? I'd soon know.

I wore a simple cotton dress and Vivian a pink satin dotted with white polka dots. And, yes, the feathered hat. Scarcely in good taste, but Vivian was so beautiful, she'd be forgiven for overdressing.

Only a hired hand was at the stable. He was in the act of hitching up the buggy, but graciously consented to hitch up the carriage. He told us he had to go to the village and summon Deputy Sheriff Oliver to come and look at the dead horses.

We let the hired hand leave the stable first, knowing

the importance of his mission. He did too, for he sent the horse off at a gallop. We followed more decorously.

"Remember," I cautioned Vivian just before we reached the DesChamps plantation, "we must behave like ladies."

"Don't we always?" she replied peevishly.

"No. We bicker and you lose your temper too easily."

"That's only because you say things to make me."

"My concern is with Mrs. DesChamps."

"And to find out if she and her son are guilty of killing papa's horses and setting the barn on fire."

"We didn't come to make an accusation," I cautioned.

"I'll remember." Vivian spoke like an obedient child, though I knew she was mocking me.

I made no further comment and pulled the reins to guide the horses beneath the wooden archway and onto the drive leading to the DesChamps mansion. It wasn't as large as ours, but it was much more impressive. I knew Mrs. DesChamps was wealthy, for she gave considerable sums to charities and to the church. She had just donated new pews, which were cushioned with dark maroon velvet. The kneeling rails were also cushioned.

We were halfway up the drive when several carriages containing ladies came toward us. Obviously, they'd just left Mrs. DesChamps, and though there was subdued conversation as they approached, it seemed to cease when they saw us. Their amazement was understandable. They had known through the years about the duel, while we had only recently learned about it.

We exchanged greetings with the ladies, most of whom we knew, for their sons and daughters attended our soirees, as we did theirs.

Joel was standing at the foot of the stairs when we drew up before the house. He was dumbfounded at the sight of us.

"We came to pay our respects to your mother, Joel," I said.

"That is, if she will see us," Vivian said, charming him with her smile.

"I'm sure she will." He'd overcome his surprise and helped us alight. A hostler came from around the house and led our horses away from the entrance. I got the idea Mrs. DesChamps was a stickler for perfection.

Joel led us up the steps and into the house. The walls of the hall were mirrored, making it seem enormous and also puzzling, for one didn't know which direction to take. It reflected rooms on either side of the house, their double doors flung open.

Joel said, "I'll bring you into the drawing room and summon mama."

The furniture was French and upholstered in light blue. The draperies were a medium shade of blue and the rug a deep blue. Here, also, mirrors hung from the walls, reflecting furniture and bric-a-brac and, I supposed, when there were guests, making it seem as if there were many more than were present. Vivian and I exchanged glances and nods of approval.

Muted voices announced the return of Joel and his mama. I found my heart beating rapidly, half in fear and half in expectation. What we'd done was most unorthodox. Yet I had no regrets. I had to meet this woman to see if she appeared venomous on the surface.

But I was ill prepared for the petite, doll-like lady who stood in the doorway, pausing to survey us. Or was it for effect? Her arm rested on her son's and they both eyed us with interest. Whether real or feigned, I'd yet to determine.

A smile touched his lips, but it was meant for Vivian. I don't know if she returned it because I was captivated by the beauty of Mrs. DesChamps and wondered why she wore veils which concealed it.

Her face was round, her eyes a deep brown and enormous, her mouth beautifully shaped. Just now her lips were parted slightly, giving her a tremulous, almost helpless look. Her gown was black, high necked and long sleeved. Her silver hair was piled high on her head to make her appear taller, for she was scarcely five feet. But she carried herself so regally, just as Vivian did, that one had no awareness of her shortness of stature.

"Miss Heather and Miss Vivian." She moved forward, an arm extended toward each of us.

We stood up, both of us in awe of her. One of her hands touched Vivian's cheek lightly in a gesture of warmth and welcome. Her other touched mine.

"Please sit down, girls. It was good of you to come. I'm ashamed we've not met before. My son informed me you are aware of the duel, so you know it would have been quite impossible. Also, I am a widow and your papa a widower."

She gave a dainty shrug, as if she'd explained everything, motioned us back into our chairs and took one opposite us. "Joel, why not bring tea and cakes for the ladies?"

"Glad to, Mama."

"No, thank you, we've just eaten," I said. "We came to ask—"

"Regardless of the reason for your coming, you'll not leave until you've had a little nourishment. It would be inhospitable of me."

Joel had already gone, so I made no further objection. I got the feeling Mrs. DesChamps was used to having her own way.

She settled back in her chair. "Now, tell me what you came to ask."

Vivian spoke for me. "We wondered if you would allow Joel to accept an invitation for a ball Heather and I are giving."

"Another? So soon?"

Vivian nodded. "We're giving it in honor of Rolf Fielding, who is graduating from college."

"Ah, yes. Rolf Fielding, whose plantation is some distance from ours. He's grown into a most handsome gentleman. As a boy, he was occasionally our guest." She glanced at Vivian. "Your beau?"

"Heather's," Vivian said without a moment's hesitation.

I didn't bother to contradict her. I wanted no argument in front of Mrs. DesChamps, who turned her attention to me.

"Do you feel well, Miss Heather?"

"Perfectly," I answered quietly. "Why do you ask?"

She was taken aback by my question, but only momentarily. "You look a little peaked. Are you worried about something?"

"We both are," Vivian said. "Two of papa's best horses were shot last night or this morning. Which was it, Heather?"

I stifled my irritation and answered the question. "I would say this morning."

"That is very bad news." Mrs. DesChamps looked properly sympathetic. "I regret hearing it. But why would you say it happened in the morning?"

I said, "Papa, Jacob and his son, Alex, have been taking turns patrolling. Once dawn breaks, they stop, figuring no one will come to burn anything down. Of course, they didn't count on the brutality of killing helpless animals."

"Of course not," she agreed. "It's frightening. Do you have a suspect?"

Neither Vivian nor I answered. Mrs. DesChamps' eyes flashed from one of us to the other.

"Do you?" she asked again. Before we could answer, Joel appeared with a large tray, bearing everything necessary.

I had no desire for tea or cakes, no matter how good, but Vivian's face lighted up at the sight of them and, I must say, we both did justice to what we were served. While we ate, Mrs. DesChamps complimented Vivian on her costume and the two of them discussed the latest in fashion.

Just as with Joel, I felt Mrs. DesChamps was playing a cat-and-mouse game with us. I took advantage of a momentary lull in the idle chitchat to make a statement.

"You never did answer our question regarding your son accepting an invitation to the ball, Mrs. DesChamps," I said.

"Nor did you answer mine," she countered.

"Then I will. I don't believe papa has any enemies in the village," I said. "He did state only last night that the person who set the stable afire could have been an employee who had been dismissed."

"Very possible," Mrs. DesChamps said with a nod. "And I suppose I have entered your mind as a suspect. I imagine that's why you came. You don't really want my son in your home. Nor do I want him there. Not after what your papa did to my husband. Your mama. . . ." She glanced at Vivian. "It's almost as if she is sitting in this room. You are her image, Miss Vivian."

"So I've been told," Vivian said soberly, sensing the change in Mrs. DesChamps' mood.

"Since you are, you have her beauty." Again, Mrs. DesChamps shrugged.

"You too are beautiful, Mrs. DesChamps," I said. I didn't mean it for flattery. My tone was cool.

"Not beautiful enough to hold my husband, apparently. Oh, I'd have held him. He loved me. He worshiped me, really. Though he was comfortably situated, I brought wealth with me. But he trifled with the affections of other women. He would never have run away with your mother. Not permanently. She was a fool to believe him. He was a seducer. Once he'd accomplished that, he lost interest. Your papa was too impetuous. He should have waited. Even if Jessica had left him, she'd have returned. And he'd have taken her back."

"Yes, Mrs. DesChamps, he would have," I said. "But why have you told us this?"

"You're grown-up young ladies and should know the truth," she replied quietly. "At the time of the tragedy, I asked the rector of the church to state from the pulpit that I bore no hatred toward Bryant Gates or any member of his family and I hoped his daughters would be spared the knowledge of what their father had done. I asked Reverend Barton—since deceased—to assure the congregation they'd never learn it from me and I hoped would not from the villagers." She paused and added a simple statement. "Nor did you."

"But you hate us as much as you hate papa," I said quietly. I had seen through her hypocrisy.

"Hate is an ugly word," she replied. She picked up the teapot and held it toward our cups.

We both refused politely and set our cups and saucers down.

"You're right, Mrs. DesChamps," I said. "We came because I wanted to see what you looked like. And what you are like. You're beautiful, intelligent and filled with hatred for the Gates family. Whether you'd commit a crime to avenge your husband's death, I have no idea. I hope not. And you're right. Joel wouldn't wish to accept an invitation for anything from us. It would be embarrassing for all concerned."

"Very," she replied, her smile serene.

"You will excuse us now." Vivian and I stood up as I spoke.

"You never did answer my question," Mrs. Des-

Champs said. "Do you have a suspect, either as to who burned down the barn or who shot the horses?"

"Perhaps you could answer it far better than we," I said.

Her smile faded, but not her poise.

"Just remember." She spoke as we left the room, but I caught a glimpse of her reflected in one of the mirrors. She was standing, her smile venomous. "Just remember," she repeated. "I am highly regarded in the village. I am known for my generosity and graciousness. I have never done anything wrong. No one would believe you if you said I did. Any more than anyone would believe your papa. See them out, Joel."

"Yes, Mama."

I didn't ask him not to, because when we entered the hall, I was utterly confused as to which direction to take. The mirrors made everything seem different than it was. So we were grateful to Joel for leading us to the door.

To my surprise, the carriage awaited us. Apparently, when Joel had gone to get the refreshments, he'd given word to have it brought to the front. Knowing his mother, he was aware the visit would be of short duration. And it was. Yet she'd gone to the trouble of serving us tea and cakes. Of course. That would further attest to her graciousness. I wondered why the ladies who were leaving the DesChamps residence as we arrived had visited there. I voiced the thought to Vivian, who had been sitting quietly with her own thoughts about the visit.

"We could find out easily enough," she replied. "Mrs. Hanes was there and both Cynthia and her brother Bernard attend all our affairs, and we're invited to theirs."

"I'd hate to have them know we were prying," I said.

Vivian laughed. "I'll bet every one of those ladies is dying to know why we were going there."

"I'm sure they were." I didn't join Vivian in laughter, because no aspect of the visit seemed mirthful. I felt we had good reason to fear Mrs. DesChamps.

Vivian, as mercurial as ever, sobered to ask, "Did she frighten you, Heather?"

"A little. And you?"

"Yes," Vivian admitted. "Despite her compliments, I

don't think she likes us. At first, I thought she was pleased we had come. I wish she had been."

"So do I," I said. "But I think she's schemed all these years to make papa suffer as she has suffered."

"No one will believe that," Vivian reasoned. "Especially after what she told us she had Reverend Barton do so we wouldn't be ostracized socially."

"I'm afraid that was part of her scheming."

"But why would anyone want to cover their face as she does? Especially when she's so beautiful."

"And wearing black all the time, as I suppose she does," I added. "I'd say it's to convey the idea she is still mourning her husband."

"Probably she is," Vivian replied.

"Probably," I said, though doubtful that one who hated to the degree that she did would be capable of an all-consuming love for her mate. "Anyway, we met her and know she doesn't like us."

"Are you going to tell papa about our visit?"

"After what happened to the horses, don't you think we should?"

"Do you suppose she killed those horses?"

"I don't know if she did it. I don't even know if she hired someone to do it. But I do know she hates papa. I think she's now carrying out her vow. But we have no proof of her guilt."

"Do you think Joel would do it? For the sake of his mother?"

"He's devoted to her and is proud of her beauty. That was apparent when he ushered her in. But with their money, I doubt either would find it necessary to carry out their evil deeds—if they're guilty of firing the barn and shooting the horses. They could hire a criminal to do it for them."

"We should tell Deputy Sheriff Oliver the things she said to us today."

"There was no one present to back our statement," I reminded her.

"Then we may as well forget it." She kicked at the leather dashboard. "I'd like to forget the whole thing, especially with the ball coming up. I'll concentrate on that to lift my spirits. I was thinking we'd fill the house with wild flowers. Do you suppose papa would let some of the field hands gather them the day of the ball? It wouldn't take them long if he let me have enough of them."

"Do what you want, Vivian. But you ask papa. I have more important things on my mind."

"Like what?"

"Our safety. I wonder if the house might be set afire some night."

"Why worry about it when papa, Jacob and Alex are patrolling the plantation?"

"Three men couldn't possibly cover all the grounds. Papa's going to have to use some of the hired hands. At least Mrs. DesChamps now knows the grounds are being patrolled."

"That might give her pause for thought."

"I hope so."

When we reached the house, a hostler appeared to take the carriage from us. Maggie met us inside and handed me a letter. It was from Rolf. That brought a cry of glee from Vivian. I brought it into the drawing room, slitting open the envelope as I did so. I sat down to read it, with Vivian leaning against the back of the chair and reading along with me. I didn't mind. I was sure there'd be nothing of too personal a nature in it.

"Well," Vivian said, when I replaced the letter in the envelope, "he's accepting the invitation, but there wasn't even a hint of romance in it."

"I didn't expect there to be. Now perhaps you'll believe me when I say neither Rolf nor I have ever had a romantic moment."

"You'd better start thinking of having some," she said spitefully. "Of you'll end up an old maid."

"Only time will tell about that," I said. "As for romance, you make up for my lack of it."

We didn't see papa until supper, at which time he told us Deputy Sheriff Oliver had come, but no one had found any clues to a trespasser.

"When do you suppose the horses were shot, Papa?" I asked.

"They'd not been dead too long," he said. "Probably just after dawn."

"That's what I figured. You'll have to put some hired hands on horseback to patrol the grounds."

"Jacob, Alex and I already discussed that. We'll do it tonight. We can't handle it and take proper care of all that needs to be done in daylight, watching over the crop."

Vivian and I then told papa about our visit to Mrs. DesChamps. He listened quietly, but I could see he was troubled by what we'd done.

"I wish you hadn't gone," he said when we'd finished our story.

"I'm glad we did," I said. "At least we know she meant what she said when she swore to get her revenge for losing her husband. Did you tell the deputy about her?"

"Of course not," he exclaimed indignantly. "He'd never believe me. There isn't a soul in town who would. You just told me how she had Reverend Barton inform the congregation she held no bitterness toward us. Also that she hoped the villagers would never reveal to you what had been done. That's true. I remember it."

"But she was being deceitful," I said.

"Only the three of us know that," he said. "Were I to point the finger of guilt at her, I'd be reviled by all who knew me. I couldn't accuse a helpless widow or her son, whom I made fatherless."

"She said as much," I replied.

Vivian said, "If she's guilty of what happened here, she waited long enough to get her revenge."

"She was probably waiting until you were grown, so you would suffer too," papa said.

"I wonder what she'll do next," I said.

"Maybe she won't do anything," Vivian said. "Maybe she feels she's done enough."

"She has," I said. "But I have a feeling it's only the beginning."

Papa said, "Jacob insisted I let whoever patrols the estate be armed. I was against it at first, but then I saw the logic to it. An intruder would surely be armed. I couldn't send field hands out to be at their mercy. But enough of that. Let's pick a pleasant subject."

"The ball," Vivian exclaimed. "Heather received a letter from Rolf today. He's accepted."

"I should hope so," papa said, "since I believe he's the reason you're giving it."

"Thank you for letting me have it, Papa." Vivian was

bubbling with excitement, already forgetful of the strain we were under because of what had happened and the fear of more of the same.

"Make the most of it, Daughter," papa said, managing a smile.

He said no more, but I could have finished the sentence, since I knew what was on his mind. "In view of what may happen in the future."

Anything could, I thought. I was thinking not only of Mrs. DesChamps and her obsession with the three of us. I was thinking of the plantation and wondering about the extent of papa's indebtedness.

Five

VIVIAN BEGAN ACTIVELY PLANNING THE AFFAIR THE next morning, but I resisted her efforts to have me join in. I had more on my mind than a ball. Papa went into the village early and was gone an exceptionally long time. When he returned, toward evening, he was tired, and while he put on a bright face, I could sense the degree of his discouragement. He was a man filled with fear and anxiety.

I asked him no questions. I would wait until he was ready to talk to me, but I was worried enough to bring up the subject when I met Alex near the stables. We walked through the twilight toward the summer house. As it was a warm evening, we entered the round structure and sat down.

"Have you heard anything about the financial trouble papa is in?" I asked him.

"No, but I think my own father is worried about the situation. He refused to discuss it with me on the theory that it's none of my business unless your father wishes to discuss it."

"Do you have any idea what it's about, Alex?"

"Yes. He took a loss on last year's crops and he wasn't too sound financially then. This year he can make it all up because the crop is high in quality and quantity. I don't even think storms could affect it now. In two weeks or so they'll have the leaves in the curing sheds, and once that's accomplished, he's safe."

"He is upset, but he assured me it was no cause for worry. I wish Vivian would stop having expensive social affairs. She's giving one in honor of Rolf Fielding's graduation."

"So I heard. You like Rolf, don't you?"

"In the same proportion that I like you."

"Are you in love with him? I know that's a very personal question, but I've seen open admiration in his eyes when he looks at you."

"I'm not in love with him, though Vivian thinks I am."

"I thought so too."

"I'm too worried about papa to think of being in love with anyone."

"I'm aware of your concern and I can understand. Just remember, you've a friend in me. I'll do all I can to help."

"Thanks, Alex. Will you walk me down to mama's grave?"

"Of course."

He took my hand as we left the summer house and proceeded down the path to where the fenced-in area held that single grave. I stood at the foot of it and bent my head in prayer. Alex waited for me by the gate.

"I'm glad to see that it has made no difference in the way you remember your mother, after you learned what happened," he said when I rejoined him.

"Papa blamed himself for what happened. I have only vague memories of mama. But what she did is of no consequence now. Not so far as my feelings toward her memory are concerned."

"I asked my father about her, but he wouldn't talk about it. I doubt he'd have spoken against your father no matter what happened, but I don't believe he'd have spoken against your mother either."

We walked slowly back toward the mansion. I spoke my mind to Alex because I knew he would understand,

and talking to him relieved some of the tension which was building up in me.

"I've always had a feeling there was something wrong about the death of my mother. "Oh," I added hastily, "not anything criminal. No such idea ever entered my mind. But papa was always so reluctant to speak of her. And whenever I asked questions, he was evasive. Of course, now I know why, and yet I feel as if the mystery isn't completely solved. As if everybody who knows what happened is holding back. Have you made any plans about going away?"

"I'm not going," he said promptly.

"Alex, you can't remain because of what happened here. You have your future to look after."

"I changed my mind about going at all," he said. I knew he was lying.

"You planned to leave and I want you to. If you stayed and we lost the plantation, I'd never forgive myself."

"I'll do as I see fit and there will be no blame attached to anyone, no matter what happens. Look at it this way. I was born on this plantation and it's all I've ever known. My father's livelihood comes from the land and the crop —and your father's. How can I abandon all this? If I did, I'd not be worthy of everything the plantation has given me."

"I have a feeling you're doing this for me, and it's not right. I can take care of myself. Anyway, we don't really know that papa and the plantation are in a serious situation. There's little sense in anticipating trouble."

"I can wait," he said. "Once I know things are going well, I'll go."

"Promise, Alex?"

"You have my word. All I was doing, I guess, was looking for an excuse to stay here. Though I'd rather the reasons were other than the barn and two horses which were shot. How is Vivian taking this?"

I allowed myself a burst of brief, sardonic laughter. "She isn't even aware there may be trouble hanging over us. All she can think about is the ball. To her, a major decision consists of trying to figure out if tablecloths should be linen or lace. I should be annoyed with her, but I can't."

"There are times," Alex said, "when I wonder if Vivian isn't somewhat smarter than we give her credit for. She's surprised me more than once."

"She exasperates me to the point of anger at times. But she can also apply herself diligently to a cause that interests her."

"Like the ball she's concentrating on now?" he asked with a smile.

I laughed. "She loves laughter and gaiety."

"You should let yourself be more a part of it."

"Oh, I like it too, Alex. But I'm a more somber type. And now, when I sense all is not well with papa, it affects me very much."

"I can see that."

"You were right about his losing money in a gambling game. Or games. He told me about it. He worries me, really. He seems to want to make a clean breast of everything. As if he senses time is running out for him. Have you gotten that impression?"

"No." Alex's reply came immediately, but he did look concerned by my statement. "Have you a reason for saying that?"

I hesitated only a moment. Alex deserved my confidence, and so I told him about the visit Vivian and I made to Mrs. DesChamps and her son. I omitted no part.

Alex seemed bewildered.

"Don't you believe me?" I asked.

"I do. But I always thought she was the soul of integrity, a lonely lady and one devoted to good deeds."

"That's the way she planned it. And as I've told you, she reminded us of how highly thought of she was in the village. I think we have reason to fear her."

"What of Joel?"

"As you and everyone else know, he's devoted to her. Since he's her son, I doubt she'd risk his getting into trouble to carry out any nefarious plan she had in mind. But she's wealthy and could hire a criminal to burn down the barn and shoot our horses and whatever other devilment her mind could conjure up. I believe she's as dangerous as she is vindictive."

"Have you told this to anyone else?"

"No. And papa as much as forbade us to. He also knows of her good deeds and of the statement she made through Reverend Barton after her husband was killed in the duel with papa. He said he'd be reviled by everyone in town if he said anything against her."

"He would be," Alex replied. "I had no idea she was that type of woman."

"No one has. Not even Vivian and I had until we visited her this morning."

"Do you think Vivian will tell what transpired during your visit?"

"Vivian dislikes unpleasantness. She can shut it out easily. I know she was shocked by Mrs. DesChamps' words, for when we entered, the woman was the epitome of charm. But I was wary from the beginning. I felt she was playing a cat-and-mouse game. As the minutes wore on, I was proved right. Only, there's no one who will believe Vivian or me."

"They'd be more apt to believe you than Vivian. Not that she isn't honest, but she's rarely serious. But of course you can't make an accusation against Mrs. Des-Champs without proof."

"I know. And proof we lack. But I feel she's behind what's happened here."

"If so, things won't be so easy for her hired thugs from now on. We'll be on guard."

"She knows that too. Not that the hired hands will be armed, but that you, papa and your father are patrolling the grounds."

"I'll see to it that she gets word through her hired hands that there will be more than the three of us patrolling."

"Papa says the three of you need your sleep for your work in the daytime. I hope you'll let the hired hands take over the guarding."

"I will," he promised. "But I'll do some checking of my own. Not only of the hands to see if they're guarding and not sleeping, but just to assure myself there's no one around who shouldn't be."

"What you're saying is you'll watch the house and other buildings for any sign of fire."

"That's what I'm saying, Heather. So sleep easy."

"I will, especially knowing you're staying. Now, will you walk me back to the house, please?"

He left me at the door and I went inside reluctantly. Even talking with Alex hadn't lessened my worry. I only wished papa had taken me further into his confidence. That problem was promptly solved when his voice called to me from the downstairs library. I hurried there and found him behind his desk. Though I tried not to show it, my spirits dropped further when I noticed his somber mien.

"Close the door, Heather."

I obeyed, walked to a chair facing the desk and sat down. It was up to papa now. I wouldn't ask any questions. Whatever he told me must be of his own volition, and since he had sent for me, I gathered he was ready to talk.

"We are in a sorry financial state," he confessed. "It's not going to cause us to lose the plantation or this house. Nothing like that, but it is a setback. I have to go to Richmond to raise some cash."

"Has the local bank refused you credit?" I asked.

"No, not in that sense. They simply don't have the capital to meet the loan I require. We'll soon be out of this mess. I've every confidence of this. However, just in case things don't turn out as I expect or hope, I wanted you to know. Don't tell Vivian. She's in exuberant spirits just now, getting ready for the ball."

"I won't, Papa."

"Thanks, Daughter. You're my mainstay, the center post that holds up the tent. I can rely on you, and your judgments are as good as mine. Sometimes better."

"Thank you, Papa," I said.

"We've lived well. Perhaps too well, and Vivian is now planning an expensive soiree. That's all right. I've the money to pay for it laid aside. I'll show you where it is later. But all of a sudden things are happening that I can't seem to control. As I said, we've been living in luxury. I'd be less than honest if I said I didn't enjoy it. And I wanted it for you and Vivian. But things have a habit of not enduring forever. It may be over for us."

His words frightened me, but I tried not to show it. "If there is anything I can do to help. Anything, Papa, just tell me."

"You can take charge here while I'm gone. I won't be but a day or two. And I won't leave until day after tomorrow. I need the time to put the plantation records in shape so it can easily be seen that any loan made to us is a secure one. Don't concern yourself about money matters. Leave that to me."

"Whatever you say, Papa."

"I'm going to tell you a trade secret. It's not known to many people and it may be some time—perhaps a few years—before it will come to pass. Inventors are now working on a machine that will roll tobacco into cigarettes and turn them out by the millions. A prepared smoke. This will increase the demand for fine leaf ten times at least. If this was generally known, there'd be a rush to acquire plantations such as ours and harm this business of raising tobacco. However, when the time comes and the machines are ready, we'll be ready. Keep this quiet, please. I wanted you to know so as to further assure you our prospects are excellent."

"Thank you for telling me," I said.

"One more thing. Don't provoke the DesChamps. Don't even go near them. I wish you hadn't talked to that woman, but I can readily see why you did. In a way, perhaps it was a good thing. You now know what sort of person she is and you'll be on guard."

"She's a troublemaker," I said, "but at least I'm forewarned. Also, she knows we'll be on guard."

"It would be wise. Remember, don't concern yourself about our situation and don't worry Vivian by painting a dark picture. Just remain calm. It could well be that in a week's time we'll be out of this, and in three or four more months the crop will be cured and things will go on as before. Good night, Heather."

I went to my room, passing Vivian's door, which was ajar. I didn't want to see her at this moment. I needed time and a quiet place to think. Vivian would see that I had neither. I'd only hear more prattling about the ball.

I sat down close by the window overlooking the front of the estate. It was one of those moonless nights when it's impossible to see a dozen yards away. Looking out of the window was like staring at a black curtain, which suited me fine. There was nothing to distract me from the thoughts which filled my mind.

Papa was in trouble. And it was more serious than he would admit. If this was no more than a routine need for money to carry us until the crop was ready, the local bank would have obliged. To try and convince me they didn't have that much money was a fabrication on his part. Papa was trying to keep the real truth from me.

I didn't like the way he'd talked. He sounded like a man who had given up, which I knew wasn't true, but he was in a very depressed mood. I tried to think of a way to help, but all I could come up with was the cancellation of the ball, which would break Vivian's heart, and it wouldn't help much anyway. Vivian would have her way, and it was right that she should.

I knew now why papa favored her so much. He hadn't granted this attention and devotion to mama and he'd lost her. Vivian was so like mama, and papa was determined to grant her every whim. I doubted that Vivian was benefiting from this devotion on papa's part, and if she had to face the reality of our losing the plantation, the change wasn't going to be easy to bear. However, until something drastic happened, papa and I would cater to her and let her live this carefree life to which she was so accustomed.

I knew I'd be unable to sleep until fatigue made it impossible to think, so I made no attempt to go to bed. Instead I tried to find a way out of our troubles, but there seemed to be none. Vivian's dinner-dance would be a great success, as they always were, but papa and I were not going to enjoy it. To me it seemed so wasteful to spend badly needed money on such frivolity, but papa wished it.

There were times when I resented Vivian's giddy ways, the money she spent so recklessly and her only ambition in life, the pursuit of good times and exciting people. I wondered if she'd ever heard of the word maturity.

Finally, I could no longer keep my eyes open and my troubles seemed to dissolve in my strong desire for sleep. I got into bed and forced all worrisome thoughts from my mind. I slept until almost noon.

When I arose, I washed and dressed as quickly as possible. I was annoyed with myself for having lost most of the morning. I walked past Vivian's open door. She had on a gown and was regarding herself in the twin mirrors, no doubt debating whether or not to wear it to the ball. She wouldn't. So far, she'd never worn the same one twice.

"Well, you're a sleepyhead, Heather," she called to me.

"I know, but I didn't retire last night until very late."

"Why not? And if you couldn't sleep, why didn't you come in to see me and help plan the ball?"

"Because I have more important things to do than spend my time on such frippery. Has it ever occurred to you that the day may come when we might not be able to afford to live in the luxury we've always known?"

"What are you talking about?" she asked, clearly puzzled by my statement.

I could have bitten off the end of my tongue. I'd promised papa not to upset her in any way and I'd just blurted out a matter which could affect her considerably. That is, if she ever stopped to think about what I said and derive some meaning from it.

"You know very well the tobacco crop last year was mighty poor and the market even worse. We have to watch our pennies until the next crop is ready, and that won't be for some weeks. . . ."

She faced one of the full-length mirrors and fussed with the skirt of the gown. "I wore this two years ago. Honestly, it hardly seems possible. Have you noticed that it still fits me perfectly? Two years ago! Imagine that!"

"I can't," I said with a great measure of relief because Vivian hadn't responded to the grim news. It was as if she hadn't heard a word of it. It was just as well.

"No," she declared vehemently. "I'm going to buy a new gown. It's not fair that I should wear the same one. There's time. Heather, will you drive me to the village this afternoon so I can get the dressmaker started? She has some lovely pale-blue silk. I know exactly what I want. Will I look good in pale blue, do you think?"

"You look beautiful in anything. But do you really want to know what I think?"

"Why, yes. I asked you, didn't I?"

"I think you're a selfish girl without a thought of anyone but yourself. All you think of is how to amuse yourself, without regard to what it's costing papa."

"Papa doesn't feel that way. He knows I love him. He knows I have a right to a new gown."

"I've worn the same gown to the last three soirees and nobody ever noticed."

"I noticed. It looked very tacky."

"I'm sorry if I embarrassed you." I switched the subject, already tired of the bickering. "Where's papa? And I'm an idiot if I expect you to know."

"He went riding. So you see, I do know."

"What time did he leave?"

"Oh, I guess about four hours ago."

"Four hours? Where would he ride for four hours? Perhaps he's down at the curing sheds or talking to Jacob. Did he say when he'd be back?"

"Not to me, but he must have something important to do because he didn't wait for breakfast. I met Maggie in the hall carrying down his tray. She was fussing because he hadn't touched it."

I left Vivian, sorely puzzled about papa. To skip breakfast and then be gone for four hours? I went downstairs and ate in the kitchen, but without appetite.

Maggie was hard at work polishing the stove. "Maggie, did papa say when he'd be back?"

"Not as I heard. He's been gone a long time. Didn't even eat breakfast. Guess he wanted to take a ride for half an hour or so, but he was off mighty early and I ain't heard from him since."

"I'm going to look for him," I said. "I'm worried."

"I'm getting to be," Maggie admitted. "He should've been back for something to eat. He's got a good appetite when he takes time to eat, which he ain't been doin' too much of lately."

I hurried upstairs and changed to a riding costume. I walked past Vivian's door without stopping, but I did notice the look of amazement on her face during the fleeting glimpse I had of her. I don't think it ever occurred to her that papa was gone too long and might have had an accident. I kept going. By the time I reached the stables, I was running.

Alex came out to greet me. "If you're looking for your father, I am too. He rode out of here on the chestnut mare and he hasn't come back. He never stays away this long."

"Please saddle up my horse," I said. "I'm going to look for him. I'm worried, Alex."

"I'll saddle up myself and we'll go together. Maybe he's down at the fields or the sheds."

"We'll go there first," I said. "Please hurry!"

We rode through the fields first, but none of the hands

had seen papa all morning. It was now after noontime and my apprehension grew by the minute.

Jacob shook his head when we asked him the same question. "I been wondering about him myself. He was to help me judge some of that new broadleaf that's coming up so well, but he never came."

We rode out along the trail papa usually followed. We galloped side by side, but we were able to carry on a shouted conversation.

"He's hurt," I said. "He must be or he'd not have stayed away this long."

"How far does he usually ride?"

"Depends on how much time he has. Never anything like this."

"I mean, are there any hurdles or jumps he might try? That's where most accidents happen."

I recalled the stone fence. Not too high a hurdle, and any of our horses could take it well. Yet, there was always a chance the horse might not quite clear the fence, or some wild animal might have suddenly scurried in front of the horse and caused it to finish the jump clumsily and spill its rider.

If there was an accident, chances were it occurred at the fence. I sent my horse racing in that direction at top speed, with Alex close behind me.

The first thing I saw when we came into sight of the stone fence was papa, and he seemed to be on his feet, but leaning in the direction of the fence. I shouted to Alex and he shouted back that he also saw him.

It wasn't until I had dismounted and began running toward the fence that I realized papa was dead. Standing up, bent over, but dead. I called to him anyway, but he didn't answer me and he didn't move. I reached his side simultaneously with Alex. I seized papa's shoulder in a frantic effort to move him so I might see what had happened.

Alex took my shoulders in a firm grasp, turned me toward him and walked me some distance away from the fence. "Stay here," he said. "Don't look back."

"But it's my father—"

"I'll come back and tell you about it. Stay here. Do as I say, please."

"Hurry. Maybe he's alive. . . ."

Alex returned to the fence. Some minutes passed before I heard Alex's cry of anguish and dismay. Then I heard him struggling with something heavy.

He came back and touched my arm. "He's dead, Heather. I'm terribly sorry. Nothing can be done. He's been dead for some time."

"May I turn around now?" I asked. "Is it that horrible?"

"I'll tell you what happened and you can judge for yourself. From the way everything looks, your father's horse didn't make the fence. He fell and it seems he broke his neck. I say I think so because the horse was shot through the heart with the pistol your father has been carrying lately."

"But papa! What happened to him?"

"I don't know exactly what happened to your father. There's a bruise on his forehead. Apparently he got that when the horse threw him. Dirt and grass are inbedded in the wound. The fall didn't kill him. Did you know he carried a sword cane? Wherever he went, that cane went with him, even when he went riding."

"Yes, I know about it."

"The crook of the cane, the handle, is lodged between large stones forming the fence. Your father," he paused, then added softly, "was impaled on the sword."

"That's how papa killed Mr. DesChamps." I made it a statement.

Alex nodded.

I felt my knees begin to weaken. Alex quickly drew an arm around my waist to steady me. I pressed my face against his shoulder and I wept. It was some time before Alex spoke to me again.

"You've got to ride back and send help. Tell my father and have him send one or two of the hands to the village. My father will know what to do."

"I want to go to papa first."

"No!" Alex said sternly. "I don't want you to remember this."

He was right. I could withstand the blow of seeing him dead, no matter what the conditions were, but I wanted to remember papa alive. And it was what Alex wanted me to do. I drew away from him, dried my tears and started toward my horse, Alex by my side.

"How in the world could papa have become impaled on his own rapier, which is stuck in the fence?"

"I don't know."

"Does it look as if he killed himself?"

"Yes."

I closed my eyes and covered my face with my hands. A meaningless gesture, for I had a vivid picture of it in my mind.

"I can't believe it, Alex. I won't believe it."

"I don't either. That's why I want to stay here and look about before too many people show up and trample everything into the ground."

"Thanks."

"Please go. And break the news to Vivian. That won't be easy. She'll need your inner strength to help her absorb the shock."

I mounted my horse and rode back in a state of shock and disbelief that it had even happened. Papa was no quitter. Never in his life had he given an inch, no matter how serious the problem. True, he was in serious financial trouble, but the prospects of getting out of it were good. If the present crop were failing, or the market were way down, I might have understood a severe depression on his part, but he hadn't been that discouraged. He was going to Richmond to get money. No doubt he had obtained it there before. There was no reason why he couldn't have done so again. He was an honorable man who met his obligations and had never been suspected of dishonest business dealings.

I found Jacob and broke the news to him. He was shocked, but displayed the same courage as Alex in facing up to this awful situation. I knew he would handle everything capably. Then I turned the horse over to the hostler and headed for the mansion. Perhaps the hardest part of all would be breaking the news to Vivian.

I would need strength for both of us now. She'd be completely ineffectual in handling the details which would follow swiftly.

It was something that had to be done. I walked into the house and encountered Maggie. She took a long look at me and then enveloped me in her arms. Without asking a question, she wept and moaned in her agony of losing someone she cared for with all her heart.

I comforted her as best I could, and in that act I regained some of my courage and composure. I was able to walk up the steps firmly, but at Vivian's door, I hesitated. I could hear her moving about inside, perhaps still posturing before the mirror.

My heart went out to her. I only hoped she'd be able to withstand the shock of the tragedy. I took a deep breath, steeling myself for the ordeal ahead of me, and opened the door.

Six

VIVIAN REMAINED IN A STATE OF COLLAPSE UNTIL THE funeral, which was to take place the following day. Maggie and I alternated through the day and part of the night, sitting at her bedside and placing cold wet cloths on her head. She'd refused to accept the news of papa's death at first. When it finally penetrated her consciousness, she went into violent hysterics. She screamed and cried and raged till I feared her mind would snap.

When she'd exhausted herself and lay across the bed, her body racked now by dry sobs, for her tears had spent themselves, Maggie brought in a sleeping draught. I held Vivian up, supporting myself against the head of the bed, and put the glass to her lips.

"Drink this, please, Vivian. Your throat needs moistening."

She obeyed, but I caught a glimpse of her reflection in the mirror. Her eyes were blank, her features expressionless. I knew my task wouldn't be easy, but I hadn't expected the tragedy to shatter her the way it did.

Maggie took the empty glass from me and I continued to hold my sister until her eyelids drooped, then closed. Once that happened, she became a dead weight. I eased myself out from behind her and Maggie and I lowered her to a reclining position. We undressed her and covered her. I picked up the gown she'd had on when I entered the room to inform her of what had happened to papa. It had been torn almost to shreds.

I handed it to Maggie and whispered for her to throw it out, explaining I didn't want it around when Vivian awakened. It would only serve to bring memory back with a rush. Not that what had happened could be forgotten or shut out of our minds, but I didn't want her to see anything that would set her off on another hysterical outburst. It would do her no good and certainly couldn't bring papa back.

Maggie agreed with a nod of her head, and with the dress in one hand, she moved about the room to lower the shades, then motioned for me to leave the room with her.

"She'll sleep until about eleven in the mornin'," Maggie said. "Services ain't till noon. I don't think she'll carry on like she did. She won't get over that spell for a couple of days. She wore herself out and she'll still be in shock. It's best that way, Miss Heather. Your sister was protected too much by your papa. But he couldn't do it no other way."

"You know about mama?"

"I know, child. I know 'bout all there is to know. Now, go get some sleep. You'll be needin' it. You'll get little enough for the next few days."

Vivian behaved as Maggie had predicted. She wouldn't go into the room where papa was laid out, but she sat in the hall. I thought it was a good place for her, for if anyone came to offer their condolences and pay their respects, it would help to occupy her mind.

But I wasn't prepared for the cry that escaped her, following the stopping of a carriage outside and footsteps that crossed the porch and entered the house. It was someone who knew us, for there was no knock on the door. I left the catafalque, where I'd been sitting beside Maggie, Alex and Jacob, and entered the hall.

It was Rolf Fielding. He held Vivian in his arms and was speaking softly to her. I heard her quiet thank-you, and knew he'd stated his condolences. When he saw me, he released her and came to me. He embraced me also, then held my face between his hands.

72

"I left school the moment I received Alex's telegram stated your father's death was sudden and tragic."

"There isn't time to tell you about it now, Rolf. The services are to begin in half an hour."

"Time enough for me to shave, freshen up and change. I rode all night, hoping I'd make it before the services."

Alex came from the room and the two men shook hands and spoke in an undertone. I went to the drawing-room door and motioned to Maggie.

She came out, saw Rolf and knew why I'd summoned her. His dirt-smeared face was evidence of his travels. A hired hand brought in his suitcase and set it at the foot of the staircase. Rolf picked it up and followed Maggie up the stairs.

Vivian watched his ascent. His sudden, unexpected appearance had seemed to give her a lift. I was grateful to anyone who could do that and especially pleased at Rolf for coming in answer to Alex's summons.

Alex came to my side. "There was only time to tell Rolf that your father's death could have been murder. We'll go into detail after the services."

"Thank you for sending him a telegram," I said.

"Before he went to college, he was really a part of your family," Alex said. "Your father looked after him very closely, after the death of his parents."

I nodded, remembering. "I'd like to walk to the graveside with you, Alex. Vivian can walk with Rolf." I turned to her. "Is that satisfactory, Sister?"

"What?" she turned quickly, her face crimsoning. She'd still been staring up the stairway, even though Rolf was nowhere in sight.

I repeated what I'd said to Alex.

She said, "If that's what you want, Heather, I'll be pleased to have him escort me."

She turned then and went into the room where papa lay to pay her respects. It was the first time and I felt relieved she was finally able to do it. Rolf, by his mere presence, had accomplished what I couldn't. I was glad I suggested he be her escort for the services. It was natural she would feel pleased to see him. As Alex said, papa had looked after Rolf since his parents had been killed in a train accident. He often spent the night here and sometimes he was here for weeks on end, especially during the summer. His attorney looked after the estate he had inherited and he'd also hired a governess for the boy. But once Rolf went to college, he dispensed with her services.

Alex said, "Are you sure you wouldn't prefer to walk with Rolf?"

"Quite sure."

I spoke without hesitancy, but inwardly I knew that Rolf's appearance had lifted my spirits as much as Vivian's. Perhaps we thought of him as a big brother. He was four years older than we; two years younger than Alex. I felt lucky to have two men on whom we could depend. Though I'd not let myself think of it, I feared the plantation was in dire financial straits. Papa had told me we were in trouble, though he insisted it was only temporary. But I had a feeling he hadn't been completely honest with me. I knew the reason. He didn't want me to worry. He felt the situation was his responsibility and the result of his weakness. But now I would have to know the extent of our indebtedness. I'd know soon enough, but I made a silent vow I'd have the same confidence as papa that with the help of Alex and his father, we'd be able to save the plantation.

There was a sudden stir of activity outside which attracted our attention, and Alex and I stepped onto the veranda. I think the entire village had turned out, for the drive was jammed with vehicles of every description. The townsfolk were now in the act of making an orderly line before coming to the door to pay their respects.

I greeted them and accepted the expressions of sympathy each offered as they paused briefly, then moved on into the house. Alex led the way, guiding them into the room where papa's earthly remains lay.

I was touched by the fact that they'd left their work and daily chores to be a part of the ceremony which would take place before papa was laid to rest. I was also relieved that the DesChamps hadn't put in an appearance. It would have been an act of hypocrisy and would have served only to further my dislike for them. I dreaded thinking what their appearance would have done to Vivian.

Once everyone was inside, I went upstairs for my hat and veil. I was already clothed in black, so it took only a moment to put it on and adjust the veil. Vivian was already wearing hers and had only to drop the veil once the services began. I emerged from my room and reached the stairway just as Rolf did. On our way downstairs, I informed him he was to escort Vivian.

Reverend Lumet had arrived while I was upstairs. He was a kindly man in his early forties. He expressed his sympathy in a quiet voice and spoke highly of papa. Then he led me to Vivian, Alex, Rolf and Maggie, who stood to one side of papa's casket. The villagers were lined up on the opposite side, the complete length of the long room.

Reverend Lumet spoke of papa's good deeds, his service to the village and his kindness to his hired hands. He expressed shock for the horrible accident which had taken his life. Then he asked us to bow our heads while he recited the Twenty-third Psalm.

Afterward, he led the procession to the graveside. When the house was empty, the casket was closed and the field hands carried it outside. Alex and I walked directly behind, with Vivian and Rolf following. Maggie followed them and then came the villagers.

The flowers and wreaths which had filled the hall and framed the coffin would be placed on the grave, once it was filled. And so, no one was prepared for the beautiful, oversized pillow of white and pink roses which lay at the head of the grave. I wondered if Rolf had done it—or Alex and his father. I was touched by the gesture and knew it had been a costly one.

The services at the cemetery were mercifully brief. Even so, Vivian sobbed openly. Rolf had an arm around her shoulders and cradled her face against his chest with his other hand. I restrained my tears. There was much to be done afterward and I'd need full possession of my senses. I also had a feeling of foreboding, one not brought on by the sad ritual being performed, but rather a feeling that disaster was building rapidly for Vivian and me.

When the ceremony ended and Reverend Lumet once again offered his condolences to Vivian and me, Alex spoke softly to all who had come and told them that refreshments would be served on the grounds behind the house. I had told Maggie to hire extra help, and between what she had managed to cook and what had been sent by kind neighbors, there was more than enough for all.

Rolf and Vivian went directly to the house. Alex and I lingered with the people, along with Jacob. It was he who suggested to Alex that he bring me inside, stating he would carry on until everyone had left. I was grateful and thanked him.

Inside, I asked Alex about the pillow of roses that lay at the head of the grave.

He looked his surprise. "I thought you had it done. The wreath my father and I ordered is still in the house. Unless the hired hands have taken it to the grave. Oh— my father and I gave orders that we wished to fill in the grave. So all the hired hands will do is bring the flowers there."

"You and your father dug the grave, didn't you?"

"Yes. We wanted to."

"Thank you. Do you know if Rolf sent the flowers?"

"I know he didn't. I heard Vivian ask him. He gave her the same answer I gave you. I also told Vivian I knew nothing about them."

"I don't know who sent them, but here's the envelope that was tied to it."

It was Maggie who made the statement. I hadn't even been aware of her presence, but she'd overheard our discussion and came from the drawing room where she was overseeing the hired hands and making certain they handled the wreaths carefully.

There was no handwriting on the small, unsealed envelope. I drew out the card. On it was engraved the name of Yvonne DesChamps. A brief note stated her sympathy and that of her son for the awful tragedy.

It wasn't easy to restrain my anger, but I did so and handed the note to Alex.

I said, "She is taking great care that no suspicion can be directed at her or her son."

He nodded as he read it. "No one except you, Vivian and I will believe it an act of hyprocrisy."

"Don't you think Rolf will accept our story of what she is really like?"

"I'm sure of it. I haven't told my father what you told me. I felt I should have your permission first. Now I'm asking for it."

"Tell him, please. Only heaven knows what that woman will think up next. We must be on guard."

"Constantly," Alex agreed. "I think Rolf should be informed of the events which preceded your father's death. I'll tell my father about it later."

"I told Rolf to bring Vivian to the upstairs library. It was one papa favored and I believe his ledgers and business papers are all there."

I was relieved to see Vivian sipping a glass of sherry. It would relax her. Her eyes were still dull from the tragedy. She wasn't at all like the gay, vivacious sister I knew.

I addressed my first statement to her. "Alex and I want Rolf to know the story of what's happened on the plantation recently, culminating with papa's death."

"You mean murder," she said tonelessly.

"Yes," I agreed. "But we have no proof. It could be termed an accident."

"The two horses which were deliberately shot was no accident," she retorted, her voice quavering.

"Perhaps you should lie down," I said, keeping my voice low, fearful she was verging on another attack of hysteria.

"I'll stay," she retorted. "I'm not a child."

"We know that. But we don't want you upset again. Another outburst like yesterday's and you could make yourself ill."

"I want to be a part of this discussion," she insisted.

"Good," I said and turned to Alex. "I'll let you tell the story, except for the visit Vivian and I made to Mrs. DesChamps. I'll relate that."

Rolf said, "I was surprised not to see her here. I know she is rather a recluse, though she performs many charitable acts and gives generously to the church."

"We know about the duel, Rolf," I said.

He looked his surprise. "Then there's no need for pretense."

"None at all," I replied. I nodded to Alex to begin.

He told of the two fires in the barn, the second of which burned it to the ground.

Rolf nodded. "Heather wrote me about that, though she didn't make too much of it, beyond saying it was believed to be arson."

"I'm sure of it," Alex said. He told then of the two horses which had been deliberately shot and the unsuccessful search for a clue.

"Didn't anyone see a prowler about?"

"No," I replied. "In the meantime, papa had talked with me. He was concerned once he learned the barn had been deliberately set afire. He told me of the duel and of how Mrs. DesChamps came to him and swore vengeance for papa's having killed her husband. We know it was because of mama. Papa told me to tell Vivian, so she's also aware of what happened. After the horses were killed, Vivian and I paid Mrs. DesChamps a visit to see what she was like."

I continued my story, and by the time I'd finished, Rolf's features were so perplexed that I'd have laughed if the situation hadn't been so grim.

"That lovely lady." His voice further revealed his astonishment. "She was so kind to me. From time to time she would invite me over to play with Joel. They even took me on a visit to New Orleans, where she has relatives. It was great fun. Of course, I wasn't grown up then, but I remember every joyful moment. Forgive me, girls, but this is difficult to accept. I believe every word you said, but what you've told me makes the woman out to be a hypocrite."

"Yes," I said quietly. "The pillow of roses which lay at the head of papa's grave was sent by her and her son. It was clever of her to have it put there. Had it been sent to the house, I'd not have accepted it."

"The nerve of her," Vivian said indignantly.

"Don't get angry, Sister," I said. "We need our wits about us."

"We'll not leave it there," she said, her tone still belligerent.

"Alex and his father can toss it into the forest beyond the gravesite when they go to close up the grave," I said.

Vivian turned to Alex. "You will, won't you?"

"I give you my word," he said. He reached forward, took the empty glass from her and set it on the table. "Will you have a glass of sherry, Heather?"

"No, thanks. Please continue the story, Alex. I'll begin it by saying that papa took a ride before breakfast. Sometimes he did that, but usually he ate first. However, he was worried and he probably wanted to do some thinking. He certainly had enough on his mind. He was leaving for Richmond the next day to raise money. That's what he told me the night before he was killed. You tell the rest, Alex."

Alex said, "Bryant rode out about a mile beyond the estate, up to a fairly high stone fence."

Rolf nodded. "I know the one. I jumped it often enough."

"Then I'll go on. Apparently something happened and the horse either didn't make it over or he lost his footing when he came down. The animal fell and broke its neck. When I arrived on the scene, the horse was dead, shot through the head with Bryant's own pistol. The gun was lying on the ground beside the horse. We can only surmise what happened after that, but the way it looks, he unsheathed the cane rapier he always carried. He mounted the handle in the rocks that formed the fence and . . . he impaled himself upon the rapier."

Rolf uttered an exclamation of horror. Vivian lowered her eyes, but she didn't faint. She was, however, incapable of speech. I kept my emotions in check, knowing Alex hadn't finished.

"That's what appeared to have happened. But—there's another angle we should explore. Someone spotted Bryant riding. Perhaps someone who had gone out each morning, hopeful of finding him alone in the fields. This unknown person hid behind the stone fence. When the horse jumped it, this person stood up, probably waving his arms and screaming at the top of his voice. You know how a horse reacts to the prospect of sudden danger. At least the animal thinks its danger. Bryant was thrown, the horse broke its neck. Bryant was likely stunned. I saw where he fell, and he gouged out a good part of the grass when his head scraped along the ground. Then this person used Bryant's gun and shot the horse, which was probably already dead. Next, he got the cane, exposed the rapier and set it firmly into the stone fence. He then moved Bryant to a point where he could hold him up and . . . push him against the rapier so he'd be run through."

"If you can prove this," Rolf said, "there's going to be a hanging around here."

"I can't prove anything. I saw where Bryant fell. I saw footprints in the grass and on bare portions of earth. They were not made by Bryant's boots. I saw where he had been dragged, hauled over the fence, pushed against the rapier. I saw all these things, but I didn't see who committed this awful deed."

"Joel DesChamps," Vivian said. "He did it. He killed papa because he and his mama hated papa."

"We have no evidence of that," I said remindfully. "And without it we can't make an accusation. However, there is an inconsistency that may help if the murderer is ever identified. What man would impale himself on his own rapier when, if he wished to take his life, he had a pistol?"

"That could be a weakness in the murderer's plans," Alex admitted, "but it still doesn't help us provide the evidence."

Rolf said, "Under the circumstances, about all we can do is wait and see what happens."

"I think I know," I said bitterly. "Papa was in serious financial trouble and Yvonne will profit by that if she can find a way."

"How serious?" Rolf asked.

"I don't know. I'll have to talk to the people at the bank, and papa's books need to be gone over. Meanwhile, to be practical about matters, the dinner-dance is canceled. Do you agree, Vivian?"

She nodded.

Alex said, "Rolf, I wish you'd help Heather when she digs into the family financial condition. You're closer to the family than I."

"Perhaps," Rolf said, "but not as knowledgeable about the plantation as you and your father. However, I've learned a great deal from the overseer of my plantation. So I do understand what it's all about. But I'd like it if you'd check what I did, Alex. After all, you took a course in farming and have had practical experience as well."

"If Heather gives her approval that I do so, I'll be glad to comply," Alex replied.

"You have it," I said.

"When do you wish me to begin, Heather?" Rolf asked.

"Immediately. Papa's books are in the desk and the

cabinet drawers. I really know nothing about the books, but if you have questions, I'll answer if I can. If I can't, perhaps Alex can."

"Papa's been buried less than an hour. Can't it wait?" Vivian complained.

I said, "If matters are as serious as I believe them to be, we can't afford to lose a moment in finding out the truth."

"Heather's right," Rolf said. "If there is trouble of a financial nature, we must know its extent, so we can prepare to meet it. I'll begin work at once."

"You were awake all night getting here," Vivian argued. "It's not fair that you lose more sleep."

"I'm all right," Rolf assured her. "Now, I'd appreciate it if I had this library to myself. I'll come down with a report as soon as I can figure it out. I'm only going to look for tentative figures. The complete examination of the books can be done later."

We filed out of the room and I closed the door. Vivian went to her room. Alex and I made our way downstairs in time to say good-bye to many of the villagers. After that, we automatically drifted over to the summer house and, for the first time, we were able to relax.

"I'm not leaving, of course," Alex said. "So don't try to talk me out of it."

"Thank you, Alex. Even with Rolf here, I know I'm going to need you."

"I just hope I can be of help in solving this murder, because I'm sure your father was murdered. I don't know how the authorities from the county seat will view it. If I know their methods, they'll take the easy way out and say your father killed himself in this bizarre way. They'll be certain of it if we find his finances are in dire shape. But he did not kill himself. Somehow I'm going to prove it."

"I believe Yvonne DesChamps started this reign of terror by burning our barn."

"That was a preliminary step to worry your father and let him know the time for vengeance had come."

"Fifteen years," I said. "She waited a long time. Time for us to grow up."

"The books will show that Yvonne DesChamps was slowly but surely destroying your father. Little things even he wouldn't recognize until too late. Obviously, she's inspired by hate. I wouldn't be surprised to find that her mind has been affected by her obsession with revenge."

"If she has been responsible for a secret campaign against papa, we're in serious trouble. And I don't see any possibility of avoiding her revenge."

"It's a clever scheme," Alex admitted. "Look at the way they set it all up. Your father was in financial trouble and depressed. He went riding, the horse threw him and broke its neck. Nevertheless, he shot it to be sure it was not suffering. It's no easy thing to shoot a favorite horse. That act would have depressed him even more, quite reasonably to the extent that he decided to do away with himself. The only weakness, as you pointed out, is the manner of death. With a pistol in his hand, your father would not have gone about the elaborate and agonizing plan for killing himself in the fashion it seems he decided upon. If there is any consolation in this thought, make up your mind that he was murdered and he did not take his own life."

"Alex, when papa took me into his confidence and told me he was in financial difficulty, I asked him if he would ever be so rash as to take his own life. He assured me he would never carry out such a cowardly act. He had full confidence he would get out of the financial bind he found himself in. He also admitted part of it was due to his gambling debts. He said those were paid, but, of course, he paid them by getting notes from the bank."

"Probably now due," Alex reasoned. "But I'm glad he told you that. It should help to dispel the suicide theory that now seems to prevail. Or will when the state of his finances becomes public knowledge. If they aren't already. Things like that have a way of getting out and being gossiped about."

"I know, but everyone came today to show the high regard in which they held papa. I suppose a few came out of curiosity, but I don't think most of them did."

"I agree," Alex said. "I wish I'd thought to look for strange faces."

"What do you mean?"

"Spies for Mrs. DesChamps. Perhaps even someone in the village is in her pay, but I doubt that. She's too smart to risk being found out. No one would believe what transpired between you and your sister and her the day you visited her. Any more than they'd have believed your father if he had repeated her vow of vengeance."

"Strange, how I never even suspected things weren't going well for papa."

"It's a tribute to him that he kept it from you."

"But sad that he carried the burden alone. That is, until he finally confided in me. I think he may have had a premonition that something was going to happen to him, though I'm certain he didn't believe Yvonne DesChamps would resort to murder. *His* murder. And with a rapier, the weapon used to fight the duel which killed her husband."

"If only her true personality were known, that would be good evidence to use against her," Alex said.

Rolf worked almost all night and we faced a bleary-eyed man when he finally called us to the drawing room. He had made a great many notes and he referred to them as he went along. Things were far worse than we could have possibly estimated.

"Your father," Rolf explained, "was a rather poor gambler. With cards to a certain extent, but mainly in his investments. In a good year he would try to double and triple his income by buying shares in the factories that bought his tobacco. He invested heavily in a scheme to make cigarettes by machinery, an idea that failed miserably."

"He had faith in it," I told Rolf. "He said so just before . . . his death."

"Perhaps it will come to pass. Greater inventions than that, which were ridiculed, are now workable things. Even so, his investments are gone because the firms he bought into are also gone. He borrowed a great deal of money. Most of the time he would meet his obligations, but in the past few years he found it impossible to do so, especially with the failure of last year's crop."

"Are we wiped out?" I asked.

"Nearly so, I'm afraid."

"But there was so much," Vivian cried out in anguish.

"There only seemed to be," Rolf said. "Your father signed countless notes, some for card-game losses, others for business loans. I haven't totaled them as yet because

I don't know the terms and I shall have to consult those people who hold the notes. The bank has a multitude."

"They never pressed him that I know of," I said.

"That's true—and strange. I found no letters of demand and that seems odd to me because many of the notes are considerably overdue. Give me a chance to get a little sleep so I can meet with the people at the bank on even terms. Right now I can barely think. I'll get some rest. Maggie brought me up a tray so I'm not hungry. Don't concern yourself too much yet. Not until we have all the facts."

After Rolf left us, I noted Alex's features, pale with exhaustion. He too was in need of rest, having had practically none since the tragedy.

"I admit it," he said after I mentioned it to him. "You didn't get any sleep either. I suggest the four of us meet about noontime, have dinner and then visit the bank."

"Thank you for all you've done, Alex," I said "I couldn't have held up without you."

"We appreciate it," Vivian added. "Come, Heather, I'm so tired I may need help getting up the stairs."

However, she wasn't too tired to follow me to my room and sit on the edge of the bed while she talked.

"If we're broke, what will we do?" she asked.

"I don't know, but I won't even admit we're broke. Not until after we visit the bank."

"I know about banks and notes. I'm not that stupid. If those people wish to, they can tie up everything we own."

"All but one item," I said. "Papa told me he had set aside the money he would need to meet the bills for the ball you had planned. I found the money in a cashbox. It amounts to almost ten thousand dollars and we can live on that for some time. Please don't tell anyone about this. We should use it to pay some of the notes. But we need it."

"Ten thousand! Do you mean to say it cost that much?"

"No, but plenty. Food, servants, decorations, musicians—there's so much in connection with the kind of soirees you planned."

"You're making me feel awful. I hope not deliberately so."

"I'm not and you know it. But you never had to think

84

of expenses before. Of how much this or that cost. Neither did I. You always acted under the belief that we could well afford whatever it cost. We let papa do the worrying."

"Just the same, don't go around saying I'm to blame for our lack of money."

"Nobody ever implied you were. Now, go to bed. This is going to be a long and unpleasant day."

"Just remember, I've got something to say about what happens to us."

"Of course you have. We're in this together. Whatever happens, we'll face it together. One thing I want you to know and remember. Papa did not kill himself. He was not that cowardly and no amount of reverses would have made him so. He was murdered."

"I know that too," she said. "You might not believe it, but I've been doing a lot of thinking. Maybe I don't like a lot of things you do, and I know you think I'm flighty, but we are sisters and we'll stand up to face whatever comes. Is that agreed?"

I embraced her. She'd surprised me. Vivian was capable of the swiftest changes in character of anyone I ever knew.

"Frankly," I said, "we always did stand up for one another when there was trouble. We may have fought about how to handle things, but in the end we handled them together. If we keep remembering that, everything will be much easier and we'll be in a better position to defy our enemies, no matter how many there are."

"Just two," Vivian declared. "Joel DesChamps and his mother."

I nodded agreement, but I still suspected Yvonne had hired thugs to carry out her devious acts, including the murder of papa. She was too clever to involve herself.

Seven

MR. BRADLEY, THE OWNER OF THE VILLAGE BANK, WAS kind, but he made it very plain that papa had been on the edge of bankruptcy.

"Not that your father was dishonest in any way," he told us. "Bryant was inclined to be reckless and his sense of judgment was not always sound. Also, he paid off personal gambling debts with notes. They were acceptable because he had Nightfall for an asset and everybody knew he'd meet his obligations one day."

"There are innumerable promissory notes," Rolf said. "I found records of them. Some are quite old. Why wasn't payment demanded?"

"If the notes were held that long," Alex said, "I'm sure those who hold them will continue to wait until this year's crop is in. Then they can all be paid. The notes due the bank as well."

"I'm afraid there's more to it than that," Mr. Bradley said. "Far more. The personal notes were purchased long ago. Many of the notes held by the bank have also passed into other hands."

"Who would buy unsecured notes?" Rolf asked. "Even with Nightfall as an asset."

"I'm not certain I'm at liberty to tell," Mr. Bradley said hesitantly. "It was done as a favor to your father, Miss Heather. Not even he knew."

I felt a sinking feeling in the pit of my stomach. "Would it be Mrs. DesChamps?"

His astonishment gave him away.

Vivian said coldly, "How kind of her."

Mr. Bradley mistook her statement as genuine. "She said it was merely a compassionate gesture. She knew how lonely he was, for she too was lonely."

"Are those her words, Mr. Bradley?" I asked.

"Her exact words, Heather. And I was sworn to secrecy, but since you guessed, there's no longer need for that. I have great admiration for the lady. By performing such a kind and generous act, she revealed her powers of forgiveness."

"Will she still continue to hold the notes?" Alex asked. "Or will she demand immediate payment?"

"I have no idea," Mr. Bradley replied. "She sent word through her son, Joel, that she will be here today to discuss the matter."

I closed my eyes, knowing the ultimate outcome. Papa was dead and we would be destitute. Once that was accomplished, and it would be done as soon as possible, her revenge would be complete. I felt I could cope with it. My concern was for Vivian, who had lived in the lap of luxury and relished every moment of it.

Mr. Bradley said, "I wish to take this opportunity to extend my condolences to both you girls in regard to your father. I just don't understand why he would do such a thing."

"What are you saying, Mr. Bradley?" I asked.

"His suicide. It wasn't like him. Especially with two young girls who must now fend for themselves. I mean you, Heather, and Vivian, of course."

"Of course," I replied.

"I'm sorry I couldn't get to the services," he went on, "but everyone else at the bank attended."

"It was good of you to let them," I said quietly. I found it hard to keep sarcasm from my tone, but I did, knowing he meant no harm.

I was sure of it when he rewarded me with a benign smile. "Just remember, if there is anything we can do, we will."

I smiled. "I think you've already done it, Mr. Bradley."

He looked puzzled, not certain what I meant. How could he be when he didn't know the true character of Mrs. DesChamps?

The four of us left and stood outside, determining our next step.

Alex decided for us. "I suggest we pay a visit to the deputy sheriff and the medical examiner. Their offices are in the same building, so it won't take long."

Nor did it. It was Deputy Sheriff Oliver's office we entered. He excused himself, then returned to say the medical examiner had stepped out, but he could give us the information we sought. The verdict they had reached was death either by accident or suicide.

"What about murder, Tim?" Alex became the spokesman.

"That wasn't even considered," he said.

"Why not?" Alex argued. "Since Bryant Gates had to shoot his horse—or felt he did, despite its broken neck—it would have been far easier and less painful to shoot himself than impale himself on his rapier."

"It's a good argument," Tim Oliver admitted. "But we believe when Bryant was thrown, his rapier became freed somehow and imbedded in the rocky stone wall. After he shot his horse, he may have gone to retrieve it, slipped and fallen on the rapier. That is, if he didn't kill himself deliberately. It's questionable, as of now."

"We've learned papa was in dire financial straits," I said. "In fact, he told me that. He also swore he would never take his life. He felt certain that when this year's crop was in, we'd be on firm financial ground again."

"I can understand your grief and know that the shock of what happened is still with you. But I can only tell you the conclusions we have reached. Right or wrong, they must stand for now."

"I hope one day to prove you wrong," I said. "I would like to ask you a question, though. Do you believe the suicide theory because papa owed so much money?"

Deputy Sheriff Oliver lowered his eyes, as if he found the question embarrassing.

"Please tell me," I insisted. "Both Vivian and I know about the duel papa fought with Mr. DesChamps and the reason for it. Don't treat us like children."

"What you've just told me makes your question easier to answer," Tim Oliver replied. "Yes, the duel is the reason we believe your father committed suicide. Remorse, which preyed on his mind. Remorse coupled with his desperate financial condition."

"Thank you," I said. "We won't take up more of your time, though I will leave with a final statement. One day I will prove you wrong. You and the medical examiner. You remember the two horses which were shot, don't you?"

"I do, Miss Heather."

"And the fire which burned down the barn. There were two. If the second was incendiary, the first unsuccessful one was also."

"Do you have a suspect in mind, Miss Heather?"

"Yes," Vivian blurted.

"Name him," Tim Oliver said quietly. "I'll arrest him immediately if you can show proof of his guilt."

"*His* guilt," Vivian blurted sarcastically. "It isn't—"

"That's enough, Vivian," I said sternly. "There's nothing more to say at present."

"Why not?" she demanded. "When you and I know—"

"Your sister's right," Rolf said quietly. "Come along." He took her arm and escorted her from the building. Alex and I followed.

Vivian subsided, but against her wishes, and she sulked all the way back to the plantation.

Alex's father, an older version of his son, awaited us before the house. He asked the question uppermost in his mind. "How bad are things?"

"They couldn't be worse," Alex said truthfully.

"All we can do," I added, "is pick up what pieces are left. I'm sorry, Jacob. You put your whole life into this plantation."

"So did your father," Jacob said. "What's more, he gave his life for it. Don't you go believing any of the bad stories that are bound to spread around now. He was a fine man and I'm proud to have worked for him and to have been his friend."

Alex said, "Rolf, you and my father and I should put our heads together and see if there is anything we can salvage. Maybe we can dispose of part of the crop before Yvonne lays her hands on it."

"I doubt we can," Jacob said. "But we might as well look into the situation."

"We'll leave you then," I said. "Come along, Vivian. We've things to do as well."

"Like packing?" she asked when we were inside. I'd never heard her sound as bitter.

"Not quite yet. We'll have time for that. But in taking over this mansion and the plantation, we'll see that Yvonne gets as little as possible. We have to determine where we'll live."

"And on what."

"With that attitude, we'll not have a good time of it," I said. "Papa wouldn't have wanted us to look upon matters quite so bleakly. We're young and in good health. We can manage."

"I'm used to being wealthy. I don't know any other way of life. I don't care what becomes of us now."

"You'll change your mind. You're not papa's daughter for nothing."

"You're papa's daughter. I'm mama's. I'm like her. I've heard that often enough. And no matter what she did, I'm proud of her. I don't even remember her, but I respect her memory, and if she were alive, I'd love her."

"I feel the same as you about her. But we have to make plans. There isn't too much time."

"Will that woman come here, do you think?"

"I doubt she'd pass up the opportunity. Remember, don't go making rash statements. She can sue us if we can't prove what we say."

"Sue us for what? We're all but penniless."

I spoke sternly. "If you open your mouth in some senseless accusation before that woman, I'll have nothing more to do with you. Papa made me swear to take care of you, but I can't protect you if you refuse to listen to reason."

But there was no placating her. "If she comes here, I swear I won't be responsible for what happens. If you don't like that, I'm sorry, but I will not bow down to anyone like Yvonne DesChamps."

"Nobody asks that you bow down. However, she holds those notes and we can't pay them. She can tell us what we must do, as far as the house and the plantation are concerned, and we can do nothing but obey. We'll not weep and wail, neither will we say anything to antagonize her. Briefly, we're at her mercy."

"I give you my word there'll be no wailing, unless it's on her part."

I left her, hopeful she'd behave, though I wouldn't have guaranteed it. I went upstairs and changed into a more comfortable dress. Then I sat by the window again, in my accustomed chair, to think things out. There was, unfortunately, nothing to think out. It was ended. Yvonne would take over. We couldn't stop her. I could see no way out. I began the process of resigning myself to the situation as it now existed.

Nobody had to inform me that Yvonne DesChamps and her son were arriving. I heard the approach of the carriage. She'd certainly wasted no time and I had an idea that Mr. Bradley, at the bank, had informed her of our visit when she saw him. I had no doubts as to the reason for her visit.

I went to Vivian's room and told her our visitors had arrived. She'd changed to a silk gown in pale lavender, which made her look as fragile as a Dresden doll.

"I saw them," she said.

"Please behave, Vivian. We've everything to lose by making a scene. Perhaps she's had her revenge and has come to make peace with us."

But Vivian was adamant. "She murdered papa."

"I believe she had him murdered, which is practically the same thing," I said. "But if she's come to make peace, let her think we're playing into her hands."

"You mean you'll pretend we don't believe she had anything to do with papa's death?"

"Probably. If I think it's the proper thing to do at this time. Don't forget, Sister, time is what we need. Quarreling with Mrs. DesChamps won't bring papa back. And we're completely at her mercy, of which she has little, I'm sure."

"But we know she's guilty," Vivian argued.

"We're reasonably sure, but she's a clever woman. We must match our wits to hers. Only in that way can we hope to outsmart her."

Vivian eyed me with puzzlement. "What are you asking of me?"

"Please let me do the talking."

"Maybe Rolf and Alex should do it."

"If they're downstairs."

"We left them on the porch with Jacob."

But the men weren't in evidence when we descended the steps. Maggie was, though, standing at the landing, waiting for us.

"I let Mrs. DesChamps and her son in," she said. "They're in the drawing room. Want to speak to you."

Maggie looked as worried as I was inwardly. I felt we could expect little clemency from Mrs. DesChamps, but I hoped I'd successfully hid my fear from Vivian. I also hoped she'd hold her temper.

Mrs. DesChamps was dressed in her usual black, but she'd raised her veil to make conversation easier.

The conversation opened with her expressing her sympathy in regard to papa. Joel added his.

Vivian had taken a seat not too close to them and she assumed a demure pose, but, beyond a mere nod, she made no acknowledgment of Mrs. DesChamps' statement. We both realized it was sheer hypocrisy. Nonetheless, I thanked her.

But I'd not pretend I didn't know the reason for her coming, nor would I curry her favor. I said, "I assume you've come here from the bank."

"We have," she replied quietly.

I noticed her gaze stray to the stretch of wall above the fireplace. I allowed myself a brief glimpse of what had attracted her attention. I was astonished to see mama's portrait hanging there. It had to be mama, because she was the image of Vivian. Or vice versa. Maggie must have had one of the hired hands hang it while we were in the village. Or perhaps she'd had Jacob do it. It didn't matter. Mama was very much in evidence. I suppose papa had had it taken down after her death, the sight of it a constant reminder of what he had done. I hoped Vivian wouldn't notice it until after Mrs. DesChamps had left.

I turned my attention back to the business at hand. "Then you know we've been to the bank and learned that you bought up all of papa's outstanding notes."

"I'm glad you know. We won't need to waste any time on preliminaries."

"You're a very vengeful woman, Mrs. DesChamps," I said.

"And you'll pay for it one of these days," Vivian said. "Just as you'll pay for papa's murder."

"Murder!" Mrs. DesChamps looked aghast. "I have been informed your papa's death was the result of either an accident or suicide."

"You know differently," Vivian retorted.

She smiled bitterly. "All I know is that when I heard the news, I felt it was no more than poetic justice."

"Our grief is still too much with us to bicker," I said.

"What we wish is a statement, down to the last penny, of the total amount of the notes you hold."

She opened her handbag and took out a piece of paper, from which she read. "One hundred nineteen thousand seven hundred and twenty-one dollars. The notes are in my possession. Within the next twenty-four hours I shall petition the court to issue a writ of foreclosure effective on the first legally possible day. At that time I shall take possession of the house and everything in it. Except your personal possessions, which I am not allowed, by law, to take. When the writ is issued and the date set, I shall require that you vacate the premises and that you never come back."

Vivian spoke up, surprisingly, in a moderate tone of voice. "Your boundless hatred is going to destroy you, Mrs. DesChamps."

Again the icy smile, as she said, "You and your sister are the ones who have been destroyed. I'm sorry I can't extend the time on these notes any longer, but you're both so young and know nothing about running the plantation. I'm sure you understand that I must protect my investment."

"We understand only too well, Mrs. DesChamps," I said. There was no longer any need for subterfuge. "You set out to ruin papa."

"The family," she said, correcting me. "I've accomplished my mission in life."

"A sorry mission," Vivian said. She glanced at Joel, whose smile mocked her. "I can see you've also taught your son to hate."

"He was deprived of a father. He has a right to hate."

"We grew up without a mother," Vivian went on. I was proud of the way she was conducting herself, but I was anxious to have the DesChamps out of the house.

Mrs. DesChamps regarded the portrait and Vivian, following her gaze, cried aloud at the sight of it.

"Is this the first time you've seen it?" Mrs. DesChamps was indeed clever.

"Yes." Vivian was so astonished at the resemblance that she couldn't have lied if she'd wanted to. "She's beautiful."

"Like you." But the way Mrs. DesChamps said it

made it no compliment. "Just hope you don't turn into what she did."

I stood up. "Please leave this house at once, Mrs. DesChamps."

"The quicker, the better," she replied, though when she arose, her movements were unhurried and she took time to lower her veil. "Come, Joel."

Vivian turned her attention back to our guests. "If you ever make an unkind remark about our mama again, make certain we're not within hearing distance."

"Your mother was a hussy," Mrs. DesChamps said venomously.

Vivian started to run toward her, but I intercepted her, got my arms around her waist and held her tight. "Get out, Mrs. DesChamps," I cried. "My sister has quite a temper. I doubt even your son could protect you."

"Just remember," Mrs. DesChamps called, and her steps quickened in retreat, as did those of her son. "Waste no time getting out of here once you receive notice. If you do, I'll have you forcibly evicted."

"And spoil your reputation as a kind, generous, compassionate woman?" I asked. It was difficult to talk, for Vivian was struggling to free herself and pounce on Mrs. DesChamps.

"I shan't worry too much about that now," she spoke over her shoulder. "My reputation for kindness is too well established for you or your sister to destroy in the wink of an eye. I've taken good care of that. You did receive the pillow of roses, didn't you? I ordered it to be placed at the head of your father's grave."

"And Heather ordered it to be thrown into the forest," Vivian called after her.

The door closed on her words, but I didn't release my sister until I heard the carriage start and the horses trot down the driveway.

They'd no sooner left than Rolf and Alex entered.

Alex said, "Yvonne DesChamps lost no time in coming."

"Nor telling us why she came," I replied.

"Why did you hold me?" Vivian scolded me, while straightening the dress I'd wrinkled as I held her.

"It would have only antagonized her friends if you'd hurt her. We have a clever adversary."

"You mean victor," she said, still angry.

"Yes," I admitted.

Vivian addressed Rolf. "We've lost the plantation."

Alex said, "I'm sorry, Vivian. I wish I could do something."

"How could papa have made such mistakes?" she asked of no one in particular.

"He was lonely," I said. "He needed companionship. Mama was the only woman he could ever love. He sought escape from his worries in gambling. Apparently, he wasn't good at it."

"Or Mrs. DesChamps had a hand in that too," Alex said. "She could have hired professional gamblers to lure him into a game."

"But if papa was good, he could have beat them," Vivian argued. "He just wasn't a good card player."

"No matter how good a card player is, when he's up against charlatans, he can't win," Alex said.

"What do you mean?" she asked.

Alex explained. "Marked cards. Signals given with their feet beneath the table. Or even a gesture with their hands. Or touching an eye with a forefinger. There are many ways."

"That was probably it," I said wearily. "No matter. It's over now."

"Not entirely," Rolf said. "We may think of a way out of this."

"I've tried every way imaginable," Alex said. "But it's beyond me. And my father. A pity, too, because the crop is excellent and if you could only hold on, you could pay that woman off."

"She'd probably murder us too if we did," Vivian mused.

Rolf said, "I doubt it. She'd be stupid to push her hand too far. One can't reach out and pull the brass ring every time."

I said, "I agree."

"So do I," Alex said.

I stifled a yawn. "I also think it's time to retire. It's been a sad and grim day."

Alex said, "I'm going to patrol the grounds at night."

"No need for that," Rolf said. "I've spent many a night here in my growing years. I'm spending a few more. These girls can't remain here unprotected, even though only we believe Bryant was murdered."

"There are two things that can't be disputed," Alex said. "One is the fire deliberately set to burn the barn down. The second concerns the two prize horses shot."

I sighed wearily. "No one attaches any particular importance to that but us. I don't believe it's even associated with papa's death."

"I'd like a little air before I turn in," Vivian said. "Will you come with me, Rolf?"

"Of course."

They went outside and I bade Alex good night, after thanking him for all he'd done.

"Don't embarrass me, Heather," he said seriously. "I can't even save the plantation for you. For that, I'd accept your thanks. I held your father in great esteem. I'll miss him too."

"I know you will, Alex. Those who knew him will miss him. But thanks for telling me."

I touched my cheek to his and his arms raised to enclose me. But I gave a negative shake of my head and his hands dropped to his sides.

Upstairs, I undressed, slipped my negligee over my nightgown and sat before the dressing table to brush my hair. I wished I could love Alex and I wondered why I didn't. His every thought was of me.

Was it Rolf? He was tall like papa and his perfect features could well be termed handsome. Yet that, in itself, wouldn't attract me. He was kind, as Alex was. He was concerned about us, just as Alex was. I gave myself a mental shake as I realized I was making comparisons.

The fact of the matter was that I had too much on my mind to think of love. And I was insufferably weary. I thought of papa and felt tears trickle down my cheek. I took a handkerchief from the drawer and wiped them away. That would be all Vivian would need to set her off on another fit of hysterics. That is, if she came in after her walk. She often did, even after I'd settled down for the night. Nor was tonight any different. A tap on the door announced her arrival. She came in, moved over to my dressing table and picked up my chamois nail buffer. She used it almost absentmindedly, easing herself into a chair facing the bed I'd just gotten into. The only lamp burning was at my bedside. The soft glow added to her beauty.

"There's nothing we can do, is there?" she asked.

"Nothing," I said.

"I wanted to hit her."

"I'm glad you didn't. She could have had us arrested. Her son would be a witness to your assault."

"I don't want her taking over."

"Well, neither do I, but what can we do to stop her?"

"Are you in love with Alex?"

"I told you before, I'm not in love with anyone. At a time like this, that's the furthest thing from my thoughts."

"I'm only asking. Does that mean you're not in love with Rolf either?"

"It means exactly that."

"Rolf is a very wealthy man. Have you forgotten that?"

I got out of bed and walked over to her. "Vivian Gates, do you mean we should ask him to bail us out?"

"Why don't you marry him?"

"Of all the fantastic ideas—"

"What's fantastic about it? He's a fine man. He's very rich. His money could pay off that old harridan. He's in love with you. He'd marry you like a shot."

"Vivian, if I loved him with all my heart, I would not marry him because he could get us out of this difficult situation. That would be taking advantage of him."

"He's going to ask you. He told me so."

"Then I will have to refuse."

"Why? You could do worse."

"He'd be marrying me out of pity and that I will not have. Now, you stop this nonsense about Rolf and me. I don't want to hear another word. I've enough on my mind now."

"I don't think you're being very wise. You always think of me as being the idiot in the family, but you're not being very smart. If it was a sacrifice on your part, if Rolf was Joel DesChamps, for instance, I'd agree you couldn't marry him. But Rolf is someone we've known most of our lives. He's been in love with you for a long, long time."

"If you continue along this line, I'll order you out of this room. I will not marry Rolf under such conditions."

"All right. Just remember, I asked you."

"What are you talking about?"

"Just what I said. I'll inform Rolf not to embarrass you by asking you to marry him. Tell me this. If we leave here and go to Richmond, we'll have to find some way of making a living. What can I do in that respect? I'm not schooled or trained for anything. You'd be supporting me and that's a certainty. I couldn't even keep house for us."

"You will do whatever becomes necessary," I said. "Now, will you please get out of here? I want to go to bed."

She did a surprising thing. She leaned over and kissed my cheek before she arose and made her grand way out of the room. I shook my head over her. She was impossible.

I did think about Rolf, however. Life with him would be pleasant and he could easily pay off all those notes. But I'd be using him for a selfish purpose and I'd never be sure that I'd married him for love alone. Under such a shadow, I would not take that risk. I intended to make my own way, without relying upon anyone else. I'd prove to myself that I could be independent.

Not even Alex could sway me from that decision. I did realize that as soon as the plantation and the house were in Yvonne's hands, our little group would be broken up forever. Alex would go his way, heading west. Rolf would go to his plantation and look after the land his father had left him. His schooling was done and he was ready to settle down. But not with me.

But, then, why not with me? The thought that he'd told Vivian he loved me made my heartbeat quicken. I loved him. The realization was sudden, but it was certain. However, I'd not let him know just yet. I'd marry him one day, but first I had to prove to myself that I could get along in this world and also support my sister. After that, there would be Rolf. I wasn't putting him second. It was just that I wouldn't take advantage of his love by accepting an offer of marriage when we were financially helpless.

Not that he'd offered it, I reminded myself quickly. Only Vivian had told me he'd said he loved me. But he'd said it. She'd not made it up. I had a feeling she had more than a liking for him and if he favored her, she'd lose no time letting him know. But of the two sisters, he'd chosen the brainy one rather than the beautiful one.

Brainy? That I had yet to prove. But I'd do it.

I put myself to sleep, finally, by listing in my mind the things I would attempt to take from the house before Yvonne became its official owner. And I grew heartsick over the many items I would have to leave behind.

Eight

WHEN I WENT DOWN TO BREAKFAST, ALEX WAS IN THE kitchen talking with Maggie. A feeling of calmness surged through me at the sight of him. Since he hadn't eaten, I asked him to join me. I wanted someone to talk with. I'd made my plans and wanted him to hear them. Maggie brought us fruit, rolls, eggs, ham and coffee and cautioned us to eat everything.

"We'll leave in a few days," I told Alex. "I've decided on Richmond. I think I might be able to find employment there."

"What will you do?"

"I don't know, but I'm not afraid. It's a challenge I intend to meet."

"How will Vivian face up to it?"

"Not easily, I know. But she'll have to face up to the fact that the life we knew is over." I smiled. "I imagine she'd be superb at planning banquets or balls, but I doubt anyone would hire her a second time. She'd bankrupt them the first time."

Alex said, "It's a tragedy all around. And caused by a vindictive woman. I wish Rolf and I had been here to witness what she said."

"It would have done no good," I reasoned. "Even if you both attempted to inform the villagers of what she was really like, they'd say it was because of your interest in us and you were lying for us. But Vivian and I both expected you, Rolf and your father to be downstairs."

Alex's tone was apologetic. "Papa suggested we go back to the spot where we found your father to see if we could find a clue of some sort."

"Did you?"

"No, I'm sorry to say."

"Well, thanks anyway. I'm highly indebted to you for all you've done. I just don't know the words to express it, but I don't think I'd be sitting here calmly discussing the past and our future if I'd not had your strength to lean upon."

"I love you, Heather. But even if I didn't, I respected your father and I wanted to do all I could with his daughters in mind. I'm going to miss you."

"Of course, I know you'll carry out your plans to go west now. I wish only the best for you."

"If I thought there was an iota of hope for me—and you know what I mean—I'd stay. I could do as well here as two thousand miles away. But I can't stay, loving you as I do. Besides, it's my opinion that Rolf regards you with the same warmth as I."

"Everyone seems to think that but me," I said.

"Who else said it?" Alex asked.

"Vivian and papa. I think even Maggie entertains that opinion."

"And Rolf?"

"I haven't the faintest idea."

"You mean he hasn't . . . ?" Alex looked his disbelief.

"He hasn't." I made it a firm statement. "I've had too much on my mind, beginning with the burning of the barn, to entertain romantic thoughts about anyone."

"I know you've been under a strain," he said. "I'm just sorry it wasn't my shoulder you wanted to lean on."

I rested my hand over one of his for a moment, squeezing it gently as I said, "Alex, you've given me so much. I feel I've taken advantage of you, but I'll be ever grateful that you were by my side at a time when I needed you."

Rolf's discreet cough announced his presence. I withdrew my hand and Alex stood up.

Rolf said, "Sorry if I intruded."

"You didn't," I assured him.

I picked up the bell and rang it for Maggie. She pushed

open the door, saw Rolf and told him she'd have his breakfast in minutes. He thanked her and sat down. Alex resumed his seat.

I said, "I was just telling Alex about our plans. I'm taking Vivian to Richmond, where I will seek employment"

"There's no need for that," he said seriously. "I can easily help. I'm saying it merely so you know there is money available to you. In any amount."

"No, thank you, Rolf," I said. "I wouldn't accept it from you under any circumstances."

"I was afraid of that," he said. "You know, Heather, there's such a thing as false pride."

"It isn't a matter of pride," I said. "I must prove myself. I'll not lean on anyone."

"Your father set a great deal of store by this plantation," Rolf went on. "I think he'd like to know I was able to return the kindness he bestowed on me when I was a boy. I spent many happy hours here."

"The four of us did." My glance encompassed both men.

"Yes." Rolf's reply was almost a sigh. "You're certain you won't let me help you? It could be strictly a business proposition. I'll tell my attorney to have the bank draw up the proper papers, making it a loan, even with interest, if you insist."

"My refusal is final." I changed the subject. "Did you know that Alex is heading west to seek a career?"

"And a fortune," Alex added, his voice hopeful.

"You'll make it." Rolf spoke with quiet assurance. "Both of you. Where's Vivian?"

I said, "She's a late riser, usually. But if she isn't up shortly, I'm going to send Maggie to waken her. We've much to do and decisions to make regarding what to take and what to leave. Be assured we'll leave as little as possible. By that I mean we'll sell what we can. There are some valuable pieces here. Of course, we'll have to take them with us and that poses a problem. But one I'll solve myself."

Rolf said, "Since I can be of no further service, I'll leave as soon as I pack. I'm going to Richmond for a day. I believe there's a train out of Rutford in the early afternoon."

"There is," Alex said. "My father and I are staying until after the girls leave."

"Good," Rolf said. "At least I won't have that to worry about."

"I don't want you to worry about anything, Rolf," I said.

His mouth opened to speak, then compressed tightly.

"What is it?" I asked.

"Nothing." He stood up. "Tell Maggie I'm not hungry. I want to pack and go to the village. Please excuse me."

He was out of the room before I could protest. Alex was also on his feet. "I have to go also. My father's getting the stables in order. The hands have been let go, of course. Not only to save you money, but to give Yvonne a problem hiring them back. She'll get them, but not at the wages your father paid—and she won't get my father because he wouldn't work for her. I told him the entire story. He had to know, once we found your father dead. He was as stunned as I to learn of Mrs. DesChamps' knavery. If I weren't his son, I doubt he'd believe me."

"But he does, doesn't he?" I asked, still not completely assured.

"Every word," Alex stated firmly. "Just remember, I'm still around if you need me."

"I will, and thanks again, Alex."

I was finishing my coffee when Maggie entered with a tray of food. She looked at the empty chair Rolf had occupied, then at me.

"Where'd he go?" she asked.

"He didn't want breakfast. He went to pack and leave."

"Leave?" Maggie asked. "I thought he'd stay to look after you."

"Don't leave Vivian out of it," I said, chiding her with a glance.

"That girl can take care of herself," Maggie said. "Want me to go up and wake her?"

I rejected the idea. I could work faster myself and I knew what the process of disposing of our things would do to her. I wanted calm and quiet.

I began the sad task by going to the drawing room first. There, I planned what to take and what would fetch a good price even at a forced sale. I knew there was a tablet and pencil in the chest to one side of the fireplace and I provided myself with them.

I paused to regard mama's portrait. Truly, she was a rare beauty. We'd certainly take that with us. I turned my attention back to the furniture. There were Sheraton tables and French Provincial chairs that would bring a good price if I could find a way to transport them to the city. A sewing cabinet of the pre-Revolutionary War period would be ours. The grand piano and harp, placed on a low dais at the end of the room, both of which Vivian played and which were played at the affairs here, would have to remain. A pity, but they were too cumbersome to transport in a wagon of only moderate size. I heard Rolf's footsteps descending the staircase and I set down the tablet and pencil and went to bid him farewell.

But he was out the door before I reached the hall. I opened the door and stepped onto the porch. Not even his baggage was there. Apparently he intended to return to bid me good-bye. I stood there, breathing deeply of the morning air, heavy with the perfume of magnolia blossoms, whose trees dotted the front of the lawn. I heard the carriage wheels and the pounding of horses' hooves come from the side of the house and I stepped down off the porch, believing Rolf would pause when he saw me.

But he didn't, nor did he even glance my way in answer to my call to him. I felt a pain in the region of my heart and my eyes smarted with tears, which I blinked away. I believe for the first time I understood what papa meant when he had warned me not to be too practical.

I'd not given Rolf even a hint that I cared for him. Of course, I hadn't realized it until hours earlier. I made a resolution that when we reached Richmond, I would write to him, once I'd found lodgings for us. He'd want that. If he responded, I would no longer take pains to hide my feelings for him. I went inside, wondering if I'd been indulging in self pity, and only thought I had been doing what I felt to be my duty toward Vivian and myself.

I made my way upstairs. Vivian was awake and dressed. But her eyes were swollen and she looked as if she'd been crying.

"Rolf's gone," I said.

"I know. He said good-bye."

I sat down on the bench before the bureau. "Did you quarrel with him?"

"Quarrel with Rolf? What a crazy thing to say. Of course I didn't. I'm just . . . feeling bad that he's left."

"Farewells are always sad."

"This one's more than sad. We won't see him again."

"Of course we will. When we're settled in Richmond, he'll come to visit."

"Don't be too sure of that," she said grimly.

"What do you mean?"

"You should have married him. Heather, you're a fool. You never gave him a chance to even express himself. You could have married him and he'd have rescued us. Gotten the plantation back. But you're so proud."

"You're probably right," I admitted. "But it would not be an honorable way of resolving the crisis we find ourselves in."

"In a case of this kind only one thing should be considered: how to keep the plantation and go on living as we always have. I don't think papa would have been very proud of you."

"I don't agree, but that's not important. Besides, Rolf made no suggestions that we marry. Do you think I'd be so bold as to offer myself to him, the price being to rescue the plantation?"

"You and your silly pride." Her voice was contemptuous.

"Marrying under those conditions is not a question of self-respect. It's a matter of common sense. If I married Rolf so that he'd save us financially, I'd be doing both of us a disservice. He might wonder if I really did love him, or if the marriage was one of convenience? And he'd have every right to think that way. As for me, I wouldn't have a moment's rest again, because even if I loved him dearly, I'd always wonder whether I'd married him out of love or gratitude. I will have no part of that."

"Which means the plantation is lost," she said dismally.

"Yes. There is no way we can pick up the notes Yvonne holds. She schemed this for years. She deliberately sought out people to whom papa owed money and who held his notes. She bought the notes when they were due, pretending compassion and insisting the sale be kept secret. She dominated the bank because of her heavy deposits and investments there so she could also buy the notes the bank held. When the notes reached an amount which she knew papa would never be able to pay, she set things into motion."

"Papa knew he was completely in her debt and at her mercy."

"I don't know. He was depressed and worried just before he died. He was going to travel to Richmond and try to get a loan there. I'm inclined to believe that he knew it would be impossible, but he was going to try anyway."

"Maybe he did kill himself." Her voice held a note of resentment.

"Papa did not kill himself. He told me he'd never commit such a cowardly act. He was a fighter. He'd never quit. Even if the plantation had been taken from him, he'd have found a way to get it back or he'd have bought another. Don't ever voice such an ugly thought to me again. I'm ashamed of you."

"I was only making a comment," she said. "You don't have to yell at me."

"I wonder," I said gravely, "how we'll ever get along, just the two of us in some small flat. With your irresponsible statements—"

"Talk about being irresponsible." Vivian's voice rose in anger. "The means of retaining the plantation rested on your saying one word to Rolf. Just one word, and you know what it is."

"He didn't ask me to marry him. How many times do I have to tell you this? He never expressed his love for me."

"You never gave him a chance. I suppose you'll marry Alex. He's as poor as we are, but in your eyes that wouldn't make any difference—"

"In one moment I'm going to shake you so hard, something is going to come loose. I don't love Alex and I am not going to marry him. He's going away—probably tomorrow or the next day. It's even likely we may never see him again."

"I thought you'd go with him and leave me."

She looked so pathetic that I went to her and stood behind the chair she occupied. I placed my hands on her shoulders, bending to kiss the top of her golden head.

"There is one thing I can be definite about," I said. "I will never leave you so long as you need me. Just remember that, sister dear. I love you, despite your irritating ways."

She reached up to touch my cheek with her hand. "Thank you, Heather. That's what I wanted to hear. Promise you'll never stay angry with me, no matter what I do."

"I'd forgive you no matter what heartache you caused me."

"That makes me feel better," she said. "I know there's a lot of work to be done, but I'd like to take the buggy and go for a little ride. Would you mind?"

"It will do you some good. It may even take your mind off the circumstances that have us so upset. Just stay away from Yvonne DesChamps. We want no more trouble with her."

"I wouldn't go there if I heard her hollering for help. When do you think she'll return with the court order to throw us out?"

"I estimate it will be about Thursday—day after tomorrow. She won't waste any time."

Vivian gave a woeful sigh, but quickly brightened at my look of concern. "Don't worry about me, Sister. I'll be bright and cheerful when I come back."

"Fine. You may grow up yet. Now I must get back to my work."

I proceeded to papa's office and began the grim task of sorting out his papers and destroying those of no value. It was painstaking because there was an accumulation of years. Minutes later, I heard the door slam, followed shortly by the buggy being driven quite fast. I didn't even get up to verify it was Vivian, though it should have given me cause for concern. She hated driving and to urge the animal on to such speed was quite unlike her. Yet I was cheered by the thought that she had the gumption to go off by herself.

I became so engrossed in the letters concerning the various aspects of papa's business affairs that I had no idea of the passage of time until a knock on the door announced Maggie.

"You must be starved, honey. Come get your supper."

"Supper?" I glanced at the clock. It was almost six o'clock. "You mean to say I've not eaten since breakfast?"

She nodded. "I looked in on you, but you were bent over those books and papers. I figured you wouldn't eat even if I'd brought you something."

"I probably wouldn't have. Thanks for not interrupting me. I'm surprised Vivian didn't stop in, though."

"She couldn't very well, since she ain't here," came Maggie's caustic reply.

I stood up. "She only went for a ride. Surely she's somewhere on the grounds."

"If she is, I ain't caught sight of her. No tellin' where she is or what she's up to."

"Perhaps she drove to the village, met some of her friends and is visiting them. If so, they'll send a servant back with a message for us not to worry."

"Only thing I'm worried 'bout now is your supper gettin' cold."

"I won't take time to change. I'll be down after I freshen up."

"Don't waste no time. Your sister comes back late, she'll get a warmed-over supper. She should've stayed home and helped you."

"I accomplished much more without her."

"I believe it. But one thing you got to remember. You can't go on spoilin' her the way your papa did."

"I know that. But we can't expect her to change overnight."

"Ain't likely."

"Set a place for me in the kitchen, Maggie. I've been alone all day and I need you to talk with."

"Pardon me for sayin' so," she spoke to my retreating back, "but you're mighty hard up when you got no one better than me to keep you company."

Though she was scolding me, I couldn't help but laugh. Even when I'd reached the landing, I could hear her still fussing. It was her way of showing me she cared.

When I came down, I noticed she'd set a second place. "Just in case Miss Vivian comes back."

"It's so late that I'm sure she won't," I reasoned. I paused and looked up at Maggie, who stood on the opposite side of the table. She knew me better than anyone, even papa, and she'd served us faithfully through the years. I couldn't have loved her more if she'd been my mother. I'd miss her, just as she'd miss us. The sadness she felt was evident in the way she was regarding me and the mistiness in her eyes. "Please sit down and eat with me, Maggie. We won't be together much longer."

"Thanks, honey. I'm sure gonna miss you. I'll worry 'bout you too."

"Please don't. I'll keep in touch with you somehow."

"Sure hope so."

I said, "I almost forgot. Papa had an envelope in the back of one drawer with your name on it and five hundred dollars inside. I'll get it before I forget. I'll be right back."

Before she could protest, I hurried upstairs, found an envelope and printed her name on it in block letters. I opened the cashbox containing the money papa had set aside. I took five hundred dollars from it, inserted the money in the envelope and hurried down to the kitchen. I gave Maggie the envelope.

She didn't open it but held it between two fingers. "Now, ain't that somethin'? I didn't think he took his own life."

"What are you talking about?"

"A man don't leave five hundred dollars in an envelope with somebody's name on it 'less he expects to die. If he wanted me to have it, why didn't he give it to me himself before he killed himself?"

"Papa didn't kill himself," I reiterated. "He was murdered. Maggie, perhaps he had a premonition. I don't know what caused him to set aside this cash for you, but he did and now it's yours. It will help a little."

"It will keep me goin' for a long time," she said. "You sure this ain't your money?"

"Isn't that your name on the envelope?"

She nodded, though she still looked dubious.

I glanced at the kitchen clock. "Good heavens, it's almost eight and Vivian's not back yet. And no message."

"Been worryin' some myself," Maggie admitted. "But eat your supper. Then go lookin' for her."

I obeyed, knowing argument would be useless.

"Do you know if Alex is around?"

"Saw him down near the stables 'bout an hour ago."

I arose. "Please, Maggie, hurry down to the stables and make certain Vivian didn't bring the buggy back. If Alex is there, ask if he'll come to see me right away."

"Yes, Miss Heather, fast as I can."

"If he is there, ask him to harness the carriage and bring it to the front of the house." I hesitated. "Or is the hostler still on duty?"

"Last I knew, he was." She was out the door before she finished the sentence.

I rushed upstairs, unbuttoning my dress as I did so. I changed to a warmer one and provided myself with a shawl and gloves for driving. When I reached the front door, Alex had the carriage waiting and was standing beside it.

The moment I appeared, he knelt to light the lantern beneath the carriage, for it had already turned dark. He helped me onto the seat.

He said, "I didn't take time to hear much from Maggie, other than that Vivian hasn't returned."

"That's all there is to it. I'm worried. I know she had no intention of being gone for any length of time."

"Do you think she might be spending the night at a friend's?"

"If that were it, I'm sure a servant would have been sent with a message."

"Did you see her go?"

"No. But I heard the buggy. She was driving the animal hard. Unusual for her."

"I know you believe there's a need for haste, but give me just a few minutes to talk to Maggie."

He went inside. He was back in a matter of minutes. Maggie stood in the doorway, watching us.

"Before we start searching for her, let's try to figure out a couple of things," Alex said. "We know Rolf left earlier. I helped him harness the horses and carriage he rented."

"Before noontime."

"How did he seem?"

"What do you mean?"

"Was his departure friendly?"

"Quite the contrary. I got the impression he was angry."

"With you?"

I nodded. "He went off in what I can only call a huff."

"He mentioned taking the afternoon train," Alex said.

I nodded. "I recall wondering why he was in such a hurry, because the ride would take him only half an hour or so and he'd have to wait at the depot for some time."

Alex got in the carriage and picked up the reins. "We're going to the depot first."

"But Vivian—" I drew a sharp breath as I realized the thought that crossed his mind. "Alex, no! She wouldn't have followed Rolf."

"Your sister is capable of anything. Maggie just told me that Vivian was not only dressed for travel, but that she carried a small valise out of the house. She thought you knew about it since you said she might have decided to spend the night with friends, but when you received no message from her, you became worried, which is understandable. I doubt we'll have to search much further than the depot."

The carriage was moving now, but Alex was so sure of his reasoning that he didn't make the horses travel fast. His manner was grim and we maintained a thoughtful silence for a while. I was overcome with a frustration often brought on by Vivian's behavior and I was completely puzzled by it now.

"Alex, do you think she followed Rolf?"

"Yes." His reply was immediate.

"For what reason?"

"Money!"

"Oh, no!" Embarrassment flooded through me. "I told her I'd not ask Rolf for help. You heard him offer it and you heard my refusal."

"I did," Alex replied. "And I respect you for your independence. But I'm wondering what your father would have done."

"I think he'd have refused. He was going to Richmond to try to raise money. But papa's dead now and the responsibility for our future rests with me. I can't save the plantation. I'm determined to take care of Vivian and me. I know Vivian is frightened by the idea of having to adapt herself to a new and not-very-easy way of life, but she's going to learn to have to. If she caught up with Rolf and persuaded him to give us a loan, I'll refuse it."

"You may have little to say about it, Heather."

I eyed him with apprehension. "What do you mean?"

"Vivian is a rare beauty and completely aware of it. I was of the opinion Rolf favored you, but no man would be immune to her charm and flirtatious ways. It's quite possible he succumbed to her allure. Or it may be he felt it was the only way he could help you."

"What are you saying?" I couldn't keep the impatience I felt out of my voice. So far as I was concerned, he was talking in riddles.

"I'm saying that in her opinion, she wasn't doing anything wrong. I'm also saying she's not above scheming by telling herself what she did was for both of you. In short, I have an idea she wangled a proposal of marriage out of him."

"She'd never stoop to that," I said indignantly.

"She wouldn't believe she was stooping," Alex reasoned. "She's aware of her beauty. She'd feel she'd be the best asset Rolf could have for his investment. That being the saving of the plantation."

"I'll not allow it," I said sternly.

A smile touched Alex's lips as he glanced briefly my way. "What will you do? Have the marriage annulled?"

"She'd never go that far." Unfortunately, I didn't sound too convincing. Knowing my sister, I realized there was no limit to the lengths she would go in order to attain her objective. She'd save the plantation at any cost. How blind I'd been to her casual manner the night before. I was so tired I didn't know enough to take her seriously. Now I realized she was feeling me out, wondering if she would hurt me by marrying Rolf. She'd probably already "wangled a proposal of marriage out of him," to use Alex's words.

"Prepare yourself." Alex's voice was gentle, for he knew I was shocked by his reasoning and the realization that Vivian was capable of entering a marriage with Rolf.

I clasped my hands tightly in my lap, for I was suddenly so shaken, I was trembling. It wasn't entirely because of what Vivian had done, or what Alex had reasoned she'd done. It was because I was in love with Rolf. It had taken me long enough to realize it. Too long. But I couldn't bring myself to let him know by even a glance because of the situation Vivian and I had found ourselves in.

Yet Vivian wasn't above using him. I recalled she'd said she had practically thrown herself at him to no avail. That it was I he loved. If he married her, loving me, he deserved only my contempt, regardless of his reason.

I came as close in that moment to hating my sister as I ever would. I felt she'd played a trick on me. And on Rolf. Or had she? Did she love him? And did he love her? If so, why hadn't he mentioned it to me? I couldn't answer any of the questions. I only knew I was pained by the knowledge of what I believed my sister had done. I was certain of it.

As if aware of my inner agony, Alex covered my clasped hands with one of his, squeezing them gently, then released them.

"I'm sorry, Heather. I have a feeling that whether you realized it or not before, you do now. I'm referring to Rolf. You love him, don't you?"

I lowered my head, closed my eyes and gave a brief nod. "If what we believe is true—that he and Vivian have eloped—you mustn't ever let him know. Promise?"

"I promise," he said. "Just remember, you still have a friend in me. And don't agonize too much. You love the plantation as much as Vivian. If she and Rolf are married, Yvonne DesChamps' chance for revenge has been wiped out. Your life will go on as before."

Never as before, I thought, but I was grateful for Alex's kindness. He wanted to ease my hurt and he was doing it as best he could. Yes, I had a friend in him.

"If my life does go on as before," I said, "it's because you made me see reason. My dear and trusted friend Alex. I wish it was you I loved."

"So do I. But half a loaf is better than none." His voice was husky and I knew he was hurting inside as much as I. Yet I couldn't comfort him.

Nine

THE TICKET AGENT ON DUTY HAD BEEN WORKING SINCE noon and he remembered Vivian very well. It wasn't surprising. Most men did.

"Right good-looking girl, and she sure was happy."

"Can you describe the gentleman she was with?" I asked.

The reply was typically male. "Can't say I noticed him, miss."

"Can you tell us their destination?" Alex asked.

"Guess there's no harm in it. They were going to Richmond and they took a pullman room, even though the length of the trip sure wasn't worth it."

"Thank you," I said.

Alex drove to the nearest public stable, where we found the buggy. I insisted on paying the bill and I drove the vehicle home. Alex followed in the carriage. I was relieved to be alone. Now that my worst fears were realized, I wanted time to mull the matter over in my mind.

I was hurt and angry that Vivian had played such a game of deceit, both with Rolf and me. She didn't love him and I considered her behavior nothing short of brazen. If they had eloped, she'd deliberately used her flirtatious ways to lure him into making a proposal of marriage. She was well practiced in the art of catching and holding a man's attention. Her beautifully shaped lips that parted in a smile revealing white, even teeth. Eyes that danced with laughter. Lovely hands with slender, tapering fingers that she moved gracefully to emphasize a point. She was not only possessed of exquisite beauty, but she knew how to use it to charm a member of the opposite sex.

She also knew how to hurt me. While she was plying me with innocent questions regarding Rolf last night, when my body was consumed with exhaustion, she had already wangled a proposal of marriage out of him. Her deceitful behavior sickened me.

I was fully aware of her reason for doing it. She was frightened at the thought of being poor, terrified at the thought of having to leave the plantation and everything that went with it. But Rolf was as deceitful as she. He could have told me this morning of his intention to marry Vivian. Though it would have been a shock, especially since I was now aware that I loved him, I felt certain I could have concealed my feelings and wished him well. But he'd been as underhanded as Vivian.

His manner this morning had been almost gruff, in contrast to mine, which had been appreciative of his coming in answer to Alex's telegram, plus his offer of a loan to help us resolve the problem of Yvonne and the plantation.

When we reached home, I drove around to the stable and invited Alex in for coffee and cake. A little refreshment would do both of us good, and talking might quiet the state of nerves I'd worked myself into.

I lit the lamps, started a fire in the stove and put on a pot of fresh coffee. By the time Alex came in, I had everything on the table. I'd also made a plate of ham sandwiches, not knowing if he had even taken time for supper. It so happened he hadn't and he downed every one, plus two servings of the three-layer cake which Maggie had left on the table, awaiting our return.

"You look angry, Heather," Alex said. He got up and refilled his cup, then placed the pot on the back of the stove.

"I'm more hurt than angry. At both of them."

"Then you're convinced they eloped."

"If they went away together, I certainly hope that's it," I said sternly.

I noticed the gleam of amusement in his eyes as he regarded me across the table. There was also the hint of a smile at the corners of his mouth, which sobered only when he sipped the steaming coffee.

"I don't think it's a matter to be taken lightly," I said curtly.

"It isn't." He set his cup down and rested his arms on the table. "Love should never be taken lightly."

"Love," I scoffed.

114

"It could well be." He was unaffected by my disdain.

"My sister is too much in love with herself to care for anyone else."

"Now you're being petty and as cruel as Vivian can be sometimes."

"How can you say such a thing?" I exclaimed, cut to the quick by his statement.

"How can *you?*" he asked. "You and Vivian bicker and sometimes quarrel, but it comes and goes like quick-silver. You're hurt because Rolf married her instead of you."

"If he loved her, then it's she he should have married."

"I agree. I also understand why you're hurting. You'd never admit even to yourself you loved him. Now you've lost him to your sister."

"I can't lose someone I've never had," I retorted angrily. I picked up my cup, but it was empty. Before I could move, Alex was on his feet. He brought over the pot and filled my cup.

"True," he replied. "And perhaps I was wrong about thinking Rolf's interest centered on you rather than your sister."

I felt color flood my face. "Perhaps you were. Certainly he never gave me the slightest hint his interest in me was more than friendly. But, then, he didn't Vivian either."

"How do you know?"

"Only last night she asked why I didn't marry him and save the plantation. I told her I felt that would be a despicable thing to do. To me, the only reason for mar-riage is love."

"And you love Rolf."

"We'll waste no more words on that. If I do, I'll get over it."

"Will it be so easy, living in the same house with him?"

"I'm certain they'll live on Rolf's plantation," I said.

"I'm just as certain they won't," he replied.

"Why not?"

"Your sister may be conceited and selfish, but she loves this house and the plantation. If she connived to marry Rolf—and I wouldn't put it past her—it was a des-perate move on her part to save what she values most on this earth. Your father valued it too. And so do you."

"But I have a high sense of ethics."

I know I sounded self-righteous because a smile touched Alex's lips, which he quickly repressed.

"Didn't your father?"

"Of course."

Alex's voice softened. "Heather, if I didn't love you so, and a hopeless love it is, I'd give you the dressing down you deserve."

"What are you saying?"

"Not as much as I'd like. But I'm going to say this: when Vivian returns, greet her with love and understanding and the compassion you're usually so filled with. You're hurt and bleeding inside. I bleed every time I look at you. That's how much I love you, and because it will do me no good, I'm going away. I can't stand being around you. What I mean is, sooner or later I'd lose control. I don't want that to happen. While you'll never love me, I don't want to instill hatred in you for me. However," he paused and his brow furrowed thoughtfully, "I'm staying until Vivian and Rolf come back."

His goodness and decency made me ashamed of my trifling arguments and I felt my anger fade. "I talk of Vivian's selfishness when really I'm just as selfish. I'm also resentful because I believe she got Rolf to propose to her. I thought that when she and I went to Richmond, he would come and call on us. Then, following a suitable interval after papa's death, he would court me and propose marriage to me."

"You can still go to Richmond and make a life for yourself," Alex mused. "But I think Vivian will be hurt if you do. She's not stupid. She knows what she's done and she'll have to live with it. It will be up to you not to make it harder for her."

"You tell me to stay here for a reason similar to the one that is forcing you to go away."

"You're a highly disciplined young woman. You'll not only keep your emotions under control, but no one will ever suspect you love Rolf."

"Loved." I made it the past tense.

"It doesn't go so easily. I know." His smile was bitter. "However, I'm not remaining here to await their return just to assure myself you'll behave. I have faith in you."

"I don't know how I'll react," I retorted, again with a hint of anger.

"Sensibly," he said quietly.

"What is your reason for remaining here, if not to see that I behave?"

"I can't explain it yet, because I'm not sure. There are certain measures to be taken, certain avenues to explore. When I know what I'm talking about, then I'll tell you and not before."

"Does it have to do with the plantation? Or Rolf?"

"It has to do with you and Vivian. Now, please don't ask any further questions. I can't answer them. When the time comes, you'll be told. In fact, you'll have to be."

"I seem to be surrounded with half-truths and vague statements. Regardless, tomorrow I go right on preparing to abandon this house, just as if nothing new has happened. If I delay, and there is no rescue of the plantation, Yvonne will take over with too many valuable and precious articles still in the house. So I must ask you to excuse me, Alex."

He stood up and moved around the table to face me. "Please don't think me unsympathetic. You've had a grim time since the burning down of the barn. It's been catastrophe piled on catastrophe, culminating with the murder of your father."

"At least you believe he was murdered."

"I never doubted it," came his prompt reply.

"Oh, Alex, thank you."

I was so grateful, I placed my hands on his shoulders. I'm sure all my eyes expressed was gratitude, but his were devouring my face hungrily, as if he'd never see it again. Before I could protest, his arms enclosed my waist and his lips came down on mine. Gently at first, then with a demanding firmness. I was shattered by the depth of his passion, so much so that I couldn't even resist when he held me so tightly I could scarcely breathe. It was only with difficulty I managed to slide my hands down to his chest to push myself free.

He was caught unawares, for he'd thought I was responding to his embrace. So when I used all the strength at my command, freeing myself, he was caught off balance and almost fell. But he made a grab for the counter beside him and regained his balance.

"I won't apologize, Heather. I had to know the thrill of holding you close, of my lips pressed against yours and feel the warmth of you. For a few precious moments, you were mine."

"Don't ever do such a thing again," I retorted, my voice quavering as much as his, though with me it was caused by indignation.

"I'll try not to," he replied huskily. "The next time you may not have the will to fight me and that would really make you angry, wouldn't it?"

If he'd dared to smile, I'd have slapped his face. But without even a good night, he turned and left the house so quickly that the door didn't catch. I went to it, opened it wide and slammed it shut. I couldn't believe my ears when I heard his uneven laughter drift back. Never before had I been subjected to his impudence. As for his behavior, it was not only insulting, it was inexcusable.

I rinsed the dishes and put out the lamps, taking one to light my way. But halfway up the stairs I had to pause and hold onto the railing. I was still trembling and felt a weakness I'd never experienced before. It was so strong I feared I might drop the lamp. I didn't move until I had control of my emotions again.

Once in my room, I bathed my face with cold water and immersed my hands above my wrists in it. It served further to calm me. I undressed quickly and went to bed. I shut out all thoughts of what had happened. It would only unnerve me again and I'd felt enough anger for one day.

I'd make certain that for the remainder of time Alex was here, I'd not be alone with him. I wanted no repetition of what had taken place. And with that determination, sleep overcame me.

When I awoke, I felt refreshed and was able to think calmly. The thought of Alex no longer frightened me. I could handle him. After breakfast, I went outside and walked to the cemetery, where I stood between the graves of my father, whom I had loved dearly, and my mother, who had apparently taken her marriage vows lightly. Yet papa placed the entire blame for the tragedy of their lives on himself. At least, now they were together and at peace.

I felt better after that and I went back to the house and

my work in clearing out papa's papers. There wasn't too much left to do, but I busied myself examining a mound of letters in a bottom drawer. They were business types, old and without value. Then I found an envelope that was postmarked more than four years ago. There was no return address in the corner of the envelope, but it had been mailed in New Orleans. The postmark was very clear. It was addressed in a woman's hand. I withdrew a single sheet of paper.

There was no heading on the note, no date, only a few words.

> Bryant:
> *I have no reason to respond to your letter except*
> *to say that I am not interested in you or yours now,*
> *or at any time in the future.*
>
> J.T.

I leaned back in the ample chair to wonder who J.T. could possibly be. Also, what could papa have written to her to have brought this cold and callous reply? Evidently J.T. was someone papa had known. Perhaps he'd asked a favor. But I doubted that, because this woman, whoever she might be, had stressed the fact that she didn't want anything to do with him or his. That meant his offspring. Vivian and me.

I slipped the letter back in its envelope and determined to keep it. Certainly I didn't need another problem to add to those I already had. But it might prove important.

I spent the rest of the day hard at work. I tried to keep my mind busy so that I'd not think about Vivian and Rolf. I was no longer worried about my sister, which was a good indication that I fully believed she was with Rolf and if not already married, about to be. As for Alex, I shut him and his behavior out of my mind.

My work in the library done, I went downstairs to resume my inventory of furniture, china and silver. The work was a waste of time and effort, but it kept me busy. Maggie stayed away from me. It was possible Alex had spoken to her, though I didn't know that for certain. She served me a fine dinner at one o'clock and took my suggestions for supper. I didn't know if I'd have to dine alone, but I knew Maggie would be prepared for any eventuality, even the return of Vivian.

The rest of my day was taken up in more checking of rooms and noting details of every item of furniture in them. By the end of the day, I was feeling lonely. I actually missed Vivian's chatter. Alex didn't come near the house. I even missed Rolf.

Maggie stayed aloof, probably because she sensed I was still on edge because of Vivian's absence. While I'd accomplished a great deal this day, it had been a drab and lonely one. And I'd itemized possessions I'd never be able to take. It was over, however, and tomorrow might spell out for me what my future would be. I was certain of one visit. Yvonne DesChamps would call with her court order to pay up or get out. Perhaps Vivian and Rolf would return. That I wasn't sure of, but if they were going to circumvent Yvonne's years of scheming, I hoped they'd get here in time. Otherwise, Vivian's chicanery would be for naught.

I felt a strange calmness now that the crisis was nearing. I could only wait and see what fate had in store for me. I retired early and I slept well.

Next morning, I ate a solitary breakfast, pleased by my serenity. Maggie bustled about as if nothing out of the ordinary were about to take place. If Yvonne had her way, I would have to clear out within forty-eight hours. Vivian and I—if she was still my unmarried sister—would check into a Richmond hotel and look for a place to live. I had changed none of my plans, though Vivian may have done so for me. I was seated in the drawing room when Maggie entered. She stood before me, her features contemplative.

"You want me to get the big bedroom ready, missy?"

"What big bedroom?"

"The one Miss Vivian and Mr. Rolf is goin' to use."

"Maggie, did they tell you to get the room ready?"

"Nobody told me anything. But I got ears and I can think. It didn't mean nothin' to me when Miss Vivian went off with that little valise at first. But I can put two and two together well as you. Miss Vivian run off to marry Mr. Rolf an' he's goin' to bring money so the plantation won't go to that mean woman an' her son. Leastwise, I hope it turns out that way."

To my surprise, I said, "So do I, Maggie."

She said, "Which room, then? Your papa's? It's the biggest."

"We don't know that Vivian is married. We don't know that she's coming back. If she is married and if she does come back, we don't even know if she and Mr. Rolf will stay here. We don't know that he will pay off Mrs. Des-Champs. So how can we plan anything?" I paused, then shrugged and said, "Oh, go ahead and fix up the room. Get all of papa's things out of there and pretty it up."

"Right away."

"Want me to help?"

"No, thanks. I know how to fix it up."

"Have you seen Alex this morning?"

"Reckon he'd be down at the stables. Hostler's gone. Mr. Alex said he'd take over."

"Thank you, Maggie."

She bustled off and I began to feel the first pangs of uncertainty, of actual fear. How would I act when Vivian and Rolf came back? What if Yvonne arrived first to serve me with the papers that meant the end of this house? How could I handle such a situation? The answer came quickly. Accept defeat in good grace.

I left the house and headed for the stables. Alex was just leading a horse to his stall. I waited until he came out. He stopped short at the sight of me.

"I want to talk with you, Alex, please." I spoke quietly, not certain whether he'd ignore me.

"About what I did?" He didn't move from the spot and his tone was noncommittal.

"Partly."

"I'll not apologize for my behavior," he said firmly. "I love you and when your hands touched me, I lost all control."

"It was my fault, knowing how you regarded me. You mistook my gesture of gratitude for one of love."

"I mistook nothing," he replied firmly. "I wanted to kiss you, to hold you close, and I did. I'll carry the memory with me the rest of my life. There's no more to be said regarding that."

"No more," I agreed. "But I'm very nervous about Vivian and Rolf. That's why I want to talk with you."

"Why? They're married and there's no more to be said about that either."

"We assume they're married," I replied. "And I'd like you to be with me when they return, which I believe will be today. At least, if Vivian hopes to save the plantation, it had better be today, because there's no doubt in my mind but that Yvonne DesChamps will be here with the proper papers, ordering me to vacate the premises."

"It isn't easy to be with you, loving you as I do," Alex said.

"It won't be easy for me to be living in the house with Rolf," I replied. "But you told me that with my discipline and strength of character, I'd manage."

"I also said you're a woman," he replied quietly. "I'm a man and quite aware of it when I'm around you. If you want me to be with you, you'll have to keep that in mind."

"I want you to be with me," I said firmly. "We can sit on the porch."

"Why not have Maggie come with us to chaperone?"

"Don't be sarcastic, Alex. It isn't like you."

"Perhaps because I don't feel like a big brother to you." For the first time, anger tinged his voice. "And I'm not going to be one. Why don't you have Maggie keep you company? I have enough around the stables to take up my time so long as I remain. And as I've already told you, I've a specific reason for staying. When Vivian returns, I'll tell you both about it. But it has to wait until then. After I reveal that, I'll be on my way."

"I don't want Maggie with me," I said irritably. "I want you."

"For God's sake, Heather, what's wrong with you? Haven't you heard one word I've said?"

"Every word, and if you wish, I'll repeat it."

"Don't bother."

"Then stay with me, please."

His eyes feuded with me for a few moments, then he gave a reluctant sigh. "All right, Heather. We will sit on the porch, very prim and proper. I'm beginning to think that's the way you wish to go through life. You'll end up a maiden aunt to Vivian and Rolf's brood."

I turned away and blinked quickly to shut off the flow of tears that threatened to come.

But Alex saw and his voice softened. "Don't cry, Heather. I couldn't stand that."

"I won't," I said. "I deserve everything you said to me. I'll say one thing more. I know I couldn't have gone through with this if you hadn't been here for me to talk to."

"Thanks, dear Heather." His eyes held no hint of mockery. In fact, they regarded me tenderly and revealed he would remain with me. "I'm the one to apologize. I hurt you. Perhaps I did it deliberately because, in my way, I was getting even with you for having repulsed me."

"I was prudish," I admitted. "I wasn't repelled by your embrace, but I was tired and nervous by what Vivian had done. The kiss served to unsettle me further."

He regarded me somberly. "You've been through a lot, and since your father's death, you've not had a moment free of worry and concern regarding your future."

I smiled. "Don't excuse me, Alex. I guess, in a way, I'm glad you just spoke as you did. Papa warned me not to become too engrossed in the plantation. He said I was as deserving of fun as Vivian."

"It will come. Let's go sit on the veranda. It's too hot to stand here and talk."

"When do you think they'll arrive?"

He took out his thick gold watch and snapped open the lid. "Getting on to noontime. Half past eleven. There's a train in from Richmond in about an hour. They'll have to rent a carriage when they find the buggy gone. I'd say they'll be here in an hour and a half—if they come."

"I hope they do," I said. I smiled at Alex's look of surprise and continued to speak as we crossed the lawn. "I know I sound contradictory, but I love this plantation as much as Vivian. It was the realization of all of papa's dreams. I want to preserve it and I know Vivian does too."

"I'm hoping they'll come and that Rolf will pay off Yvonne DesChamps. I'm hoping for it most of all because it will take a load off your shoulders."

"Do you think Rolf is capable of running it? He has a caretaker looking after his."

"That's a question that can't be answered until they come—if they do—and we learn what their plans are."

When we reached the porch, Maggie came out with

tall glasses of ice-cold lemonade, cucumber sandwiches and cake.

"You two better put somethin' in your stomachs," she said. "No tellin' what this day is gonna bring."

As usual, she was right. She set the tray down on the wicker table and we took a chair on either side. We maintained a thoughtful silence while we ate. When we finished, Maggie returned for the tray.

She picked it up and looked down at me. "Relax, honey. It ain't the end of the world, you know."

"I know, Maggie. I'm still finding it hard to accept the fact that Vivian is married."

"Guess she had more gumption than we give her credit for."

Alex laughed and stood up to hold open the door for Maggie. When he resumed his seat, he said, "You know, she may be right at that."

"To me," I said, "Vivian's like a child, really not old enough to be married. And not settled enough."

"I agree, despite the fact that she's only five minutes younger than you. I always thought, when I'd see her in one of her tantrums: five minutes younger and five years less mature. It could be we've both been wrong. Only time will tell."

"I hope I won't behave foolishly when they come."

"I'll see to it that you don't." He spoke with mock sternness. "Just remember, you're the older sister. You're also a lady, and you'll behave like one."

We caught sight of a carriage moving down the road. My hands gripped the chair arms tightly as it reached the plantation. Not until it passed, did I relax. I believe I feared Yvonne's arrival more than that of Vivian and Rolf.

But our wait was finally rewarded when a second carriage came into view. This one turned down the drive. I scarcely dared breathe, fearing once again it might be Yvonne DesChamps and her son, come to gloat.

Not until the carriage neared did my hands loosen their tight grip on the chair arms. There were three persons in it. A driver and a couple seated in the back. When it neared, I recognized Vivian and Rolf. They'd rented a carriage for their return. It drew up before the house and Rolf jumped out to help Vivian alight. Both Alex and I stood the moment the carriage stopped and I sensed his eyes on me. I felt rooted to the spot. Rolf and Vivian hadn't moved either, but their eyes were on me, as if awaiting their cue to come to the porch or get back in the carriage.

Alex spoke under his breath. "Go down and welcome your sister. She's as frightened as you."

I looked at him and felt the tension I'd been so filled with leave me. I even smiled as I said, "Come, Alex, let us welcome Vivian and Rolf."

"Good girl," he said quietly. His eyes bespoke his admiration for me.

I descended the steps, my arms extended as I said, "Welcome home, darling."

Vivian looked radiantly beautiful as she called out my name. The next moment we were in each other's arms, laughing and crying at the same time.

When I stepped back, holding her at arm's length, I said teasingly, "I trust you're married."

"Very much so, Sister!" she exclaimed happily and thrust her left hand before my face. A diamond and wedding ring were on the third finger.

I turned to Rolf, who had just received a handshake and congratulations from Alex. I touched my cheek to Rolf's and added my congratulations to those of Alex.

"Why didn't you tell me?" I scolded him lightly, laughing as I did so.

"We thought you'd not permit it so soon after your father's tragic death," he replied, at ease now that he knew the welcome was genuine. "And when you refused my offer of help yesterday morning, Vivian and I knew there was no other way of saving the plantation."

I sobered. "Surely that wasn't your reason for marrying."

"No." His glance switched to Vivian and warmed at the sight of her. "Your sister is without equal in charm, beauty and warmth."

Vivian came over and slipped her arm around him. "We're very happy, Sister. And happier still that you're not angry with what we did."

Alex was already taking their baggage from the carriage. Rolf went over and paid the driver. He gave a wave of farewell and drove off.

I said, "Alex, please take Rolf into the drawing room and have a brandy. You must toast the bridegroom. Vivian and I will visit Maggie first, then we'll go upstairs."

Vivian said, "Did we get here before Yvonne Des-Champs?"

She looked her relief when I replied affirmatively.

Vivian opened her handbag as we entered the house. "I've a gift for Maggie." She took out a small, colorfully wrapped package. "A pin with lots of glitter. I was with her once when we paused to look in a jewelry-store window. She pointed to one similar to this and said she'd always wanted one just like it."

I was touched by the gesture and felt assured that Vivian had matured greatly during the few hours she'd been gone from the plantation.

"It was very thoughtful of you, and Maggie will be thrilled."

In the kitchen, Maggie hugged Vivian, then took her hand and exclaimed over the beautiful diamond ring. She also observed the wedding ring, to assure herself Vivian was now Mrs. Rolf Fielding.

She accepted the gift with another exclamation of delight and ripped the paper off in her eagerness. When she removed the cover, a cry of "oh, my" escaped her. Her eyes brimmed as she hugged Vivian, then turned and hugged me too.

"I got a feelin' this is goin' to be a real happy day," she said.

"It is already," I said.

Maggie gave a quick nod of her head and wiped her eyes with a corner of her apron. "I also got a feelin' things are gonna turn out jus' fine. Jus' fine."

"They are, Maggie," Vivian said with quiet assurance. "Let's go upstairs, Sister."

In my room, I closed the door and regarded Vivian again. Her dress was new. Part of a trousseau she'd purchased in Richmond, no doubt. It was ready made, but fit her perfectly.

"There is one question I want to ask," I said.

"There's one I want to ask also. Are you angry with me?"

"I was. Angry and hurt that you had indulged in such deception."

"It was the only way," Vivian said. "You refused Rolf's offer of a loan."

"Don't you love him?" I was stunned by her reply.

"Of course I do!" she exclaimed, her face coloring with indignation. "Why should you doubt it?"

"Because only two nights ago you were urging me to marry him," I said. "You did so after you came in from a stroll with him. I assume he proposed to you then."

"He didn't."

My features revealed my disbelief, and I knew my eyes betrayed the contempt I felt.

"It's true. He didn't propose that night. He talked only of offering you a loan to save the plantation, but was reluctant, knowing your fierce pride. Those are his words, not mine."

"Then, after talking with him, you came back and tried to persuade me to marry him to save the plantation."

"I thought you loved him."

My mouth opened to say that I did, but I caught myself. Instead, I said, "No matter how much I loved him, I'd not marry him so we could continue to live here."

"I hope you won't leave," she said.

"So far as I know, I'm going to have to," I replied, though I sensed what was coming.

"You're not going to have to," she replied gaily.

"What does that mean?"

"I have in my bag a bank draft for the entire sum and it will be a delight to present this to Yvonne DesChamps. But not until after she spells out the dire things she intends for us. Will you let me wait until the last moment, so that her defeat will be complete?"

"It's Rolf's money. I have nothing to say about how or when you present the check to her. I'm only human enough to feel a slight sense of satisfaction in knowing, despite what she's done, she'll not achieve the triumph she sought. But I don't feel vengeful. Not only because I'm still spent from what we've been through, but because I have no desire to get even with that woman. I think she has an evil streak in her and is one to be feared."

Vivian shrugged. "Once the debt on Nightfall is paid, we'll have nothing more to fear from her."

"I'd like to believe that," I said quietly. "But I don't

think she'll be happy until she has exterminated the Gates clan."

"You mean murder you and me as she did papa?" Vivian exclaimed in dismay.

"I hope not. But what you're about to do is only going to make her more angry."

Vivian dismissed it with an airy wave of her hand. She was once again the happy bride. "I saved the plantation, thanks to Rolf."

"You didn't marry him just to do that, did you?"

She pouted prettily. "He's the only man who ever ignored me, and now he's mine."

"Vivian, I don't understand you."

"Don't worry about it, sister dear. You never will."

"Well, you understand this. If you married Rolf without loving him, I'll find it very difficult to forgive you."

"What if he married me without loving me?" she countered.

"He'd never do such a thing."

"Not even to save the plantation?" she queried.

"Why should the plantation mean that much to him?" I demanded.

"Probably because you are so noble." Disdain touched her voice.

"You're talking in riddles."

"Perhaps. But just remember this: I saved the plantation. The new crop is excellent. Alex and his papa have sworn to that. Since you're so proud, when it's sold at a very high price, we will pay Rolf off."

"We certainly will." I found it hard to keep anger out of my voice.

"In the meantime, I don't have to think of the horror of a rooming house or flat in Richmond. Or you hunting for a position when you were taught nothing but the social graces."

"I was also taught about the business end of this plantation by papa. I learned how to use my brain, and because of that, I had no fear of the business world. I'd have found work. I may still leave."

To my dismay, she ran to me and held me close. "You wouldn't, Heather. Promise, please. I need you here."

I freed myself from her arms. "You no longer need me. You have a husband to look after you now. Just make certain you love him and charm him as you did your endless other suitors whose affections you toyed with."

Vivian eyed me carefully. "Why, Heather, you actually sound jealous."

"Don't be so childish," I retorted.

"You're the one being childish," she replied, her smile superior. "But you must remember, I gave you your chance to marry Rolf. Once you gave me a firm negative response, I had to make plans on my own. As for Rolf, does he look like an unhappy bridegroom?"

I rubbed my furrowed brow. "Forgive me, Sister. You've only just got home and we're quarreling again. Probably you're right. I am a little jealous of your handsome husband."

"He is handsome, isn't he?" Vivian exclaimed happily.

I'd already succeeded in getting her mind off our bickering. She hadn't changed in that respect. Pleasant things occupied her mind much more readily than unpleasant. And whether I liked her method or not, she had got us out of a dilemma.

"The handsomest man I've ever seen," I admitted. "Just as you're the most beautiful young lady he's ever seen. Or anyone else, for that matter."

She colored prettily. "Thank you, Heather."

"Maggie fixed up papa's room for you and Rolf. It's large and I imagine she dressed it up attractively, knowing what you like."

"If she didn't, I'll attend to it. Goodness knows, we've no money worries now."

"Just one more question. Did Rolf bankrupt himself to help us?"

"I'm sure he did not."

I wished I were as sure, but even if he had, I know he'd not have worried Vivian with the thought.

"Run along and freshen up," I said "I'll see you downstairs."

"I have a very chic Paris tea gown. I must be suitably garbed to present the lovely Yvonne DesChamps with the check that will make her ill. Positively ill."

She left with a light step, but I could still hear her giggling as she ran down the hall. Nor did it stop until she'd entered papa's room and closed the door, shutting out all sound.

I wished I could laugh with her, but I felt the situation was too grave to treat lightly. I was worried about her and Rolf. Though they had appeared radiantly happy when they arrived, I was quite aware that Vivian had parried my questions with evasive answers.

My attention was distracted by the sound of a carriage approaching. It became more evident as I walked to the open window. The curtain hid me from view, but I was able to observe Yvonne and her son, Joel, both sitting erect, he driving and she by his side. They had come with the proper papers to issue their formal demand that we vacate the house. It was apparent they hadn't the vaguest suspicions that their plans would be thwarted. I couldn't blame Vivian for wanting to have her moment of triumph. I wished I could have shared it, but I had a feeling that Mrs. DesChamps was not so easily defeated. And we would pay dearly for the humiliation she was about to suffer in being ordered from the house. I was certain Vivian would settle for no less than that.

I decided to allow Maggie to admit them and bring them into the drawing room to join Rolf and Alex. I knew the gentlemen would give no hint of what was to come until Vivian and I made our appearance.

I went over to the mirror, picked up a brush and used it to catch a few stray hairs and urge them into their proper place. I was surprised at my paleness and pinched my cheeks to bring color into them. I looked better and more at ease, but inside I was trembling. And I knew why.

I feared Yvonne DesChamps. I'd never feared another human being before, but I feared that woman. I felt she was the epitome of evil. She'd plotted well and, up until today, all had gone as she wished. I stopped thinking and left the room, my steps brisk.

Ten

VIVIAN AND I MET AT THE LANDING. SHE LOOKED RAPturous in a light-blue chiffon tea gown. I noticed she kept her left hand in her pocket.

"To hide my rings," she whispered, pushing out the pocket, her hand still inside. "I'm also holding the bank draft."

My smile was a mixture of gratitude and relief. Regardless of the inner pain I felt at what she'd done, she had saved the plantation. And certainly, when she and Rolf had stepped from the carriage and stood motionless, uncertain of their welcome, there had been a softness to their features that bespoke their love and happiness. I told myself that with time, my pain would ease.

As we descended the stairs, I caught her free hand, gave it a light squeeze and our eyes exchanged looks of understanding. Male voices, intermingled with that of Mrs. DesChamps, drifted from the drawing room. Though we couldn't make out the words, I gathered the conversation was informal and neither Rolf nor Alex had given the slightest hint that Mrs. DesChamps would be thwarted in her attempt to take over the plantation. Apparently, the gentlemen had succeeded in completly disarming her with their charm, which, I am sure, matched hers when she chose to use it—whenever she appeared in public. I doubted even her servants were aware of her true nature. She conspired and revealed her true self only to her son.

Maggie stood at the entrance of the room, as she always did. She would wait until I either excused her or asked that she bring beverage and cakes. Though she was as aware as my sister and I that this was not a social occasion, she was as well versed in the social code as we.

She regarded us hopefully as we approached and I gave

a bare nod of encouragement, but it was enough to assure her that all was not as bleak as it seemed. She acknowledged my signal with a hint of a smile and maintained her position.

Mrs. DesChamps' back was to us, as was that of Joel, for they were ensconced on a settee. On either side of it, Alex and Rolf occupied chairs facing them. They stood up as we entered. Joel, sensing our approach, rose also. We had to walk around one end of the settee to face Mrs. DesChamps. Joel couldn't take his eyes from Vivian, nor could I blame him. She'd let her hair down and its curly ends rested on her shoulders in a tousled fashion, giving her a little-girl look.

Even Mrs. DesChamps' eyes widened at the sight of her. But she quickly switched her attention to me. I asked that the gentlemen be seated. Vivian and I occupied the settee facing the one on which Mrs. DesChamps and her son had seated themselves.

I opened the conversation by saying, "I know this isn't a social visit, Mrs. DesChamps, but the day is hot and your journey was long. May we offer you a beverage and cakes? Or at least a beverage to quench your thirst?"

"No, thank you," she said. "We'll not tarry longer than necessary."

I nodded to Maggie, who stood in the doorway. Since she'd heard the conversation, she returned the nod and went to the kitchen.

Mrs. DesChamps regarded both Alex and Rolf. "Since our visit today is of a business nature, I think it would be more fitting were we to excuse both gentlemen."

I softened my refusal with a smile, saying, "I would ask that they leave, but Alex has lived on the plantation with his father for so long that both Vivian and I consider him one of the family. And, as I'm sure you know, papa appointed himself a sort of guardian for Rolf, following the death of his parents. He spent many summers with us, so he, too, is as at home here as Alex. Be assured you may speak freely in front of the gentlemen. They know the dire circumstances we found ourselves in upon papa's untimely death—if such it may be called."

"That's all it could be called," Mrs. DesChamps said. "And both you girls have our deepest sympathy."

"Let us be done with the hypocrisy," I said. "We believe one day we'll prove papa was murdered."

"You're the only two who do," she replied calmly. "I spoke to Deputy Sheriff Oliver about it and he is of the opinion it was either suicide or accidental. He leans toward the accidental version."

"Why?" Vivian asked in sweet innocence.

"He knew your father well and believed him a man of strong character. Oh," she shrugged daintily, "he had a weakness for gambling, and when away from home overimbibed in spirits. Tim Oliver excused that since your papa was a widower and had eyes for no other woman once your mama passed away."

She gave a momentary glace at mama's portrait above the mantel and lowered her eyes quickly. But not so fast that I didn't see the hatred she still bore my dead mama revealed. While pretending to express her sympathies, she was belittling papa for his weaknesses, which had forced him into a situation where he was at her mercy. But she'd not been satisfied with seeing him lose the plantation. She had had him murdered.

"Suppose you get to the reason for your being here," Vivian said quietly. "I dislike subterfuge."

"So do I." To my surprise, it was Rolf who replied and it was Vivian to whom he addressed his remark.

Fortunately, she was so intent on Mrs. DesChamps' reason for being here, and now impatient for the opportunity to spoil the woman's chance for vengeance, that she was unaware Rolf's sarcasm was directed at her. I glanced casually in his direction. His eyes were on his bride and there was a coldness in them that frightened me. He no longer seemed the happy bridegroom. I wondered if he already regretted his generous gesture.

But Mrs. DesChamps felt the remark was directed at her and she colored slightly.

Joel, for the first time, spoke up. "I resent the rudeness you directed toward my mother."

Rolf, with no change of expression, said, "I apologize. It comes as a shock to learn your mother is not the gracious lady I thought her to be."

I relaxed, believing I'd been wrong. He *had* meant Mrs. DesChamps.

She opened her handbag and removed what was obviously a legal document. She held it up as she spoke. "I have here a court order that requires you girls to pay me the sum I have already stated. It must be paid immediately or this house, its entire contents—except for very personal property—and the plantation intact become legally mine. I'm sorry I have been forced to take action against you. If you were older and better versed in the running of a plantation, I could afford to be patient, knowing that, in time, I would get a full return on your papa's indebtedness to me. I bought his notes as a gesture of compassion, knowing his loneliness equaled mine. However, I did insist that my identity not be known to him, lest he refuse and lose everything. The banks felt they could no longer carry him after the poor crop of the previous year."

"There's no need to say more," Vivian interjected.

Mrs. DesChamps' smile was apologetic. "Please forgive my verbosity, but I wanted no misunderstanding either on your part or on the part of your friends, whom you consider members of your family."

"We're completely aware of the situation," Alex said. "And speaking for myself, I believe you are taking great satisfaction in this moment."

"Scarcely a gallant statement," she said.

"I agree," Alex said. "But a true one. At least, in my estimation."

"You're completely wrong." Mrs. DesChamps raised her arms, palms upward, in a gesture of helplessness. "While I may lay claim to anything in this house, I wish the girls to know they may take anything or everything from this house they wish."

"We have no desire to take anything from the house," Vivian said.

"Not even your mama's portrait?" Mrs. DesChamps asked in feigned innocence. "But, then, I suppose since you know the true story of what happened—your mother's infidelity—you may be excused from thinking ill of her. Even though she has been dead these many years."

"We do not think ill of mama," I said. "We revere her memory."

"Then you believe what she did—or attempted to do—is to be condoned." Mrs. DesChamps kept her tone casual.

"No," I admitted. "But neither my sister nor I will hate her because of it."

Vivian stood up and her left hand slipped free of her pocket. She spoke as she extended the bank draft. "Mrs. DesChamps, this is payment in full of every claim you have against our plantation."

Mrs. DesChamps was too stunned to accept it. She still couldn't believe what she'd heard.

"Please, Mrs. DesChamps, take the bank draft," Vivian urged. "A pity your day has been spoiled."

But Mrs. DesChamps was not one to lose her composure for long. She replaced the legal document in her handbag and reached for the piece of paper Vivian held, still extended. As she did so, she noticed the rings on Vivian's hands and a bitter smile touched her mouth.

"So," she said, "you are wed. Quite recent, isn't it? And scarcely in good taste so soon after your papa's tragic demise."

Vivian's face flushed with anger. Joel seemed to be in a state of shock, for his mouth hung open and his eyes were on the bank draft his mother held, then stuffed into her handbag.

I decided to say a few words, now that Vivian had presented the check. "Yes, papa's death was tragic, especially since we believe it to be murder, and one day we will prove it. Just as we will prove the barn was burned down deliberately and two of papa's prize horses were shot with malicious intent. We will also prove, Mrs. DesChamps, that you are not the kind, gracious, charitable lady everyone in the village believes you to be."

"That will take quite a bit of proving," she replied serenely. "I doubt you have that many years left to do so."

"Are you planning on murdering me—and Vivian?" I asked boldly, sickened by the woman's hypocrisy.

She got to her feet with a suddenness that almost threw her off balance. The gentlemen arose also. I was the only one still seated.

"You are a bold one," she said, her voice as cold as steel. "As for murdering you or your sister—or anyone —I wouldn't stoop to such viciousness."

"There would be no need for you to do so," I replied quietly, and though seated, I felt the advantage was mine, for I'd managed to keep my emotions under control. "You can well afford to hire thugs to do your dirty work."

"How impudent you are!" she exclaimed.

Vivian said, "You should have been an actress, Mrs. DesChamps. Anyone who didn't see the real you would certainly be fooled."

"You are looking at the real me." Her eyes, which had conveyed her disgust, were brimming with tears. I only hoped Alex and Rolf weren't being taken in by the act of humility she was putting on.

"No, Mrs. DesChamps," I replied serenely. "You revealed your true self the day Vivian and I visited you. Though you denied any guilt regarding papa or the other tragic events that happened here, you swore you lived to get your revenge. Unfortunately, only Vivian, your son and I were in the room at the time."

"Do you recall the ladies who were leaving in their carriages as you arrived?" she asked.

"Yes," Vivian and I replied simultaneously.

"I am donating an enormous sum of money toward the building of a hospital in the village. It will serve the people, both rich and poor, for miles around. The plans for it are now being drawn up."

"You planned for it to be done at just such a time, didn't you?" I asked.

"Oh, no." Her smile was one of sweet innocence. "It just happened that our plans came to fruition at this time. I am also donating the land and there will be a celebration to which everyone will be invited when the cornerstone is laid. Which will be very soon. The ladies and I are working on that now and it was the reason for their being at my home the day you visited my son and me. There will be music, dancing, refreshments and even a small circus with clowns, a merry-go-round, Ferris wheel and various other forms of amusement to keep the children occupied and happy."

I said, "Congratulations, Mrs. DesChamps. You think of everything. I agree. It will be difficult to reveal your true self to the good people around here."

She eyed me speculatively and I actually saw apprehension in her eyes. "It is my opinion, Miss Heather, that you are the one to be feared. You sound very vindictive. Be assured I will be most wary of you."

"And I suppose you will pass the word around the village that my sister and I were most ungrateful that you allowed us—or, rather, papa—extended credit."

"You misjudge me," she replied. "I really came today to tell you that though I had the papers to do so, I could not, in all good conscience, force you off the land."

It was my turn to smile. "Fortunately, there are two gentlemen who can, when the time comes, testify in court, if need be, to the opposite."

"Wasn't it you who said the gentlemen were members of the family?" she asked.

"Yes."

"Then they might be accused of being biased, wouldn't you say?" She eyed Vivian speculatively. "I assume your sister is the bride of Rolf Fielding."

"I am." There was pride in Vivian's voice.

Mrs. DesChamps was triumphant. "Now I understand the reason for the hasty marriage."

Rolf moved to Vivian's side and placed an arm about her shoulder. "Call it any kind of marriage you will. We were wed in the church and Vivian is my beloved wife."

"Congratulations, Rolf, and to you, Miss Vivian, my wishes for happiness. And I mean that sincerely, regardless of the reason for the marriage."

The words were spoken so sweetly, one wouldn't believe the venom they contained unless one knew the true character of the woman.

"I will now take my leave and I wish you luck in the managing of the plantation. You will run it, won't you?" She directed her question at Rolf. "Particularly since it was your money that saved it for the two sisters."

"I'm hoping Jacob and Alex will remain," Rolf replied quietly. "If they do, I anticipate no problems. I'm sure you'll see to it there are none which will involve you."

Her smile was solicitous. "I have no further interest in it."

Rolf's features were somber. "I appreciate hearing you voice that."

"So do I," Alex added, as serious as Rolf.

Only Mrs. DesChamps and Vivian saw anything to

smile about. The former's was one of face-saving grace. Vivian's, one of triumph.

Joel took a step toward Vivian and Rolf. "I wish to add my best wishes to those of my mother. I'm glad things turned out as they did."

He sounded very sincere and when he bade his farewell, he gave a slight bow in my direction. It was as if he were congratulating me for besting his mother. Though that seemed incredible. I wondered what Joel would be like away from his mother's domination.

Maggie appeared in the hall and opened the door for them. None of us moved or spoke until we heard the carriage wheels and horses' hooves pound the earth.

When Vivian was certain the DesChamps were no longer within hearing distance, she burst into peals of laughter. Laughter which none of the three of us joined in. The air was still too charged with the tension of the ordeal. I felt we'd not heard the last of Yvonne DesChamps.

Vivian half turned, still convulsed with laughter, and looked up at Rolf. For a moment she didn't seem aware of his somber features regarding her almost with distaste. Her arms raised to move about his neck, but he caught hold of her wrists, lowered them to her sides, released them and stepped back.

"I want to talk with you. We'll go upstairs to whatever room we've been assigned." His tone was cold, his eyes contemptuous.

I moved up to them, astonished at the change in him. "What is it, Rolf?"

"A private matter between Vivian and me." He spoke without taking his eyes from her.

But I couldn't refrain from asking the question which came to mind. "Are you sorry about the magnanimous gesture you made?"

He regarded me impatiently. "That has nothing to do with it."

Vivian had sobered and was regarding him with as much puzzlement as I.

"Lead the way," he ordered her. "Now."

She'd never been spoken to in such fashion before and had never been treated with contempt except by Yvonne DesChamps the day we paid her a visit. My sister's eyes actually held a touch of fear, for Rolf's behavior was completely unexpected. But she still didn't move. He reached out, grasped her by the shoulders, spun her half-way around and pushed her toward the door.

She ran the rest of the way and the laughter that had spilled through the room was replaced by hysterical sobs. I wanted to run to her and comfort her and apparently took a few steps in her direction because Alex, standing behind me, reached out and caught my arms in a firm grip. Rolf had followed her and I could see them both ascending the stairs.

Alex didn't release me until the upstairs door slammed shut. I turned to face him.

"What happened?" I demanded rather than asked.

"I don't know," Alex replied, yet the way he avoided my eyes, I knew he was lying.

"You do," I asserted firmly.

"Whatever it is, it doesn't concern us or Rolf would have revealed it here."

"Are you sure he doesn't regret having given that money to us?"

"Positive."

"Did he say so?"

"He did."

"He mentioned you and your father staying. Are you going to?"

"It would be less than gracious not to, under the circumstances."

"Under what circumstances?"

"Rolf does need help with the plantation. Also, there's another matter I mentioned."

"Oh, yes." I remembered. "You wouldn't discuss it until Vivian returned."

Above our conversation, Vivian's hysterics, coupled with her shrieked replies, which were as indistinguishable as Rolf's words raised in anger, rang through the house. Alex moved about the room nervously, visibly upset by the quarrel upstairs.

"Alex, please tell me what Rolf is angry about."

"No." His reply was quiet. "And don't ask me again. I suggest you go to your room."

"In heaven's name, why?"

"I have a feeling Vivian will run to you shortly for

consolation. When she does, tell her I have something to reveal to both of you and to Rolf. This can't wait."

But I didn't obey, saying, "Alex, I'm tired of mysteries. If there is something else wrong, please—"

"Do as I say." His voice was as stern as Rolf's.

My mouth opened to make an angry retort, but his eyes were so filled with irritation, I dared not. I turned and moved briskly to the stairs and on to my room.

Eleven

I HADN'T LONG TO WAIT. I HEARD RUNNING FOOTSTEPS, my doorknob turned and Vivian entered the room. She closed the door behind her and leaned against it, her eyes closed, her chest heaving with her uneven breathing. Her tears hadn't been faked. She was genuinely upset and exhausted from her emotional ordeal. She'd had little time to gloat over her triumph. Perhaps that was what had angered Rolf. She'd been too glib. And as vengeful as Yvonne DesChamps.

Once her normal breathing resumed, she walked with leaden steps over to the chaise longue before the fireplace and dropped onto it. There was no posing or attempt at gracefulness in her manner and it was difficult not to go to her and comfort her. But I maintained my silence and walked over to a chair facing the chaise. I sat down and waited for her to speak.

Her eyes were swollen from crying and there was a slackness to her features that revealed she had met her master in Rolf. Whatever the cause of their quarrel, defeat was registered in every line of her face.

"Rolf is leaving me." Her voice was expressionless, but not her eyes, for at mention of his name, they filled with the agony of her loss.

"Why?" I barely spoke the word, so great was my shock.

"He found out I lied to him."

"About what?"

"You—and Alex."

"What about us?"

"I told him Alex was leaving the plantation."

"It's true."

"I know. But I told him you and he were in love and you would go with him. That you were going to be married at a decent interval after papa's death."

"Why did you tell him that?" Again my voice was scarcely audible. I was shocked by her deceit, though not yet cognizant of the reason.

"Because I wanted to save the plantation." Feeling crept into her voice. "You were doing nothing about it other than planning to go to Richmond and seek employment. What could you do there? What were you trained for?"

" 'Where there's a will, there's a way,' " I quoted.

"Bosh," she derided. "In the meantime, we would be starving. I couldn't see that."

"But you could see luring Rolf into a proposal by using your womanly wiles on him, wiles in which you are well versed."

"I only did it after he told me he wanted to offer you the money to pay off Mrs. DesChamps. He didn't use the word offer. He said 'give' you the money."

"He did make such an offer," I said.

"And you refused it," she retorted.

"I did."

"He said he knew you would. He was aware of your pride. There are times when pride is a stupid virtue. If, indeed, it is a virtue at all."

"I wasn't thinking of virtue. I don't use people to get out of difficult or impossible situations."

"He loved you. He still does." Her voice quavered.

"Please," I entreated. "No more tears."

"I have no more. They're spent." She paused, then asked slowly, as if fearful of my answer. "Do you love him?"

"How I feel about Rolf has no meaning now. He's your husband."

"Do you love him?" she demanded.

"What if I do?"

"Don't take him from me!" She jumped up and knelt before me, burying her head in my lap. "Don't take him from me, Heather. I love him. He despises me for what I did, but I honestly love him."

"Was that your sole reason for marrying him?" I didn't remind her she'd already told me he was leaving her.

"No. I love it here. I couldn't bear the thought of living anywhere else."

"What about Rolf's plantation? As his wife, wouldn't you move there if he wished it?"

"I'd live anywhere with him. But he doesn't love me. He consented to marry me only after you refused the loan he offered yesterday at the breakfast table." She raised her head and looked up at me. "Don't forget the night before I eloped, when I suggested you marry him. I told you he loved you and he never even gave me a glance. But no! You were determined to go to Richmond."

"I may still go," I said quietly. "I'll be ill at ease here now."

"Not now!" she exclaimed and held onto my wrists tightly. "He won't share our nuptial bed. He told me so. He's leaving. I shouldn't have laughed at Yvonne Des-Champs. Now she'll laugh at me. The entire village will laugh. You wouldn't leave me alone here."

"You won't be alone. Maggie will be here. So will Alex and Jacob."

"But you're my sister. You're the one I want with me. The one I need. Especially now. I've lost my husband. He loathes me." She released my wrists and let her hands drop to her sides. "Do you loathe me too?"

I looked down at her swollen eyes and tear-stained face. She was still on her knees and sitting back on her heels, looking up at me.

I said, "I almost wish I could loathe you for what you did."

"I did it for both of us."

"Oh, no, I'll have none of that. You did it for yourself."

"I love Rolf. Despite my flirtatious ways, I've always loved him. Even when he spent summers here. I worshiped him, but it was you he always wanted to be with."

"I was never aware of it."

142

"Sometimes I think you're incapable of love. Probably like mama."

I gave a slow negative movement of my head. "I revere mama's memory, but she was fickle."

"Papa didn't pay any attention to her." Vivian was already excusing mama, just as papa had.

"She should have remembered her marriage vows. No matter how busy he was."

"You sound priggish."

"I suppose I do and I suppose I am. But I could no more be like you than you could be like me." I stood up, reached down and drew her to her feet. "There's no longer time for bickering. No matter what subject we start on, we end up in an argument. Alex wants us downstairs. He says he has something important to tell us."

"Let him tell you. I don't want to see him. He knows."

"Knows what?"

"About Rolf and me. Rolf asked Alex today when you and he were planning to get married. Alex replied he'd marry you within the hour if you'd have him, but you didn't love him and never would. He'd already pleaded his case."

So Alex had lied to me downstairs when he stated he didn't know the reason for Rolf's wrath. I could understand why.

"Did Alex say anything more?" I wondered if he'd told Rolf it was he I loved.

"I don't know," she said. "All Rolf cared about was that I had lied to him. He believes I married him only to save Nightfall. I'll get a divorce. It will be a disgrace, but I'll go away from here and that will leave you free to marry him."

"You'll do no such thing. This family has had enough scandal."

"There'll be scandal anyway. Rolf won't stay."

"Perhaps he will," I said hopefully. "He's angry now. When he calms down, he may change his mind."

"He won't—ever. I have to ask Maggie to bring my baggage back to my room. He may stay here tonight, but he can use papa's room."

"We've no more time for talk. I'm going downstairs. Go bathe your eyes and wash your face, then come downstairs. And please—no more scenes."

"Don't worry. I'm not capable of it." She headed for the bathroom as I went to the door.

At the landing, I spoke Alex's name softly. He came from the drawing room. "Is Rolf with you?" I asked.

Alex's head moved negatively.

I said, "Do you wish him to hear what you have to say?"

"I do," came his quiet reply.

"I'll get him. And Alex," I added, staying his return to the drawing room, "Vivian has told me the reason for her quarrel with Rolf. He told her he's leaving. Do you think what you have to say will cause him to remain?"

Alex looked his consternation. "I certainly hope so."

I had to ask a final question, lowering my voice still further. "Did you tell him anything?"

"You mean," Alex gestured with his head in the direction of papa's room, "your feelings regarding him?"

I nodded.

"I said nothing. He's Vivian's husband."

I smiled my gratitude. "I'm beholden to you. I'll get Rolf."

I moved on to what had been papa's room and tapped lightly on the door. Heavy steps approached and the door opened. Rolf, still stern faced, regarded me almost belligerently.

"Rolf, please come downstairs."

"I have no time. I'm leaving. I'd be grateful for the loan of a horse and buggy. Perhaps Alex would drive me to my plantation."

"It's Alex who wishes us downstairs. You as well as us. He has something important to reveal. I'm as much in the dark as you. But he said it's important that you hear what he has to say."

He debated it in his mind a few moments, then gave a reluctant nod.

"Immediately," I said. "You may leave whenever you wish afterward. Vivian told me you're leaving."

"Did she tell you why?" he demanded.

"Yes. She did lie to you about Alex and me. But she loves you."

"It's the plantation she loves. Well, I saved it for her."

"We're both grateful for that. But she didn't marry you merely to save Nightfall."

"I don't care to discuss it further."

"Nor do I, except to say we will pay you back when the crop is harvested."

"That's not important, the payment."

"It is to me."

"Yes," he said quietly. "It would be to you."

For a moment I thought he was being sarcastic, but he wasn't. He looked very weary, but he did manage a smile, which I returned, though I felt no more like smiling than he did, and I wondered why my heart didn't beat madly at his nearness. Perhaps because I'd been through too much. We all had, thanks to the viciousness of Mrs. DesChamps.

And so the four of us reassembled in the drawing room, Rolf in a chair, Vivian and I on one of the settees and Alex standing.

Alex said, "I'll be as brief as possible, but be prepared for a shock. When your father died," he switched his glance to Vivian and me, "papa and I dug the grave. We wanted to do it out of respect to a man who had both courage and character."

"Thank you, Alex," I said. "It was a beautiful gesture."

"As you know," he went on, "your father's grave is beside that of your mother. However, while digging his grave, the side of your mother's collapsed and a part of the coffin fell into the hole we'd dug. Naturally, we had to take steps to conceal that. I tried to replace the piece of wood that formed a large part of the side. Before I could get it into place, I could see inside the coffin."

Vivian gave a cry of dismay.

"Relax, Vivian," Alex said. "The coffin was empty."

"Empty!" My dismay matched my sister's.

"You heard me right. However, there wasn't time to make a further examination. But that's why papa and I insisted on closing up your father's grave. We didn't want any of the hired hands to throw a shovelful of earth carelessly and have the same thing happen. What I'm saying is that we must open your mother's grave and see if I was correct. I'm sure the coffin was empty. There was no evidence of a body or the skeleton of what was once a body. Nor a sign of a woman's dress or rotted fabric of any kind."

"But surely someone must know if mama was buried

there. Certainly, papa wouldn't say she died if she didn't," I reasoned.

"Unless he murdered her and hid her body." Vivian spoke without viciousness, but was using her brand of logic.

"I'll never believe that!" I exclaimed indignantly.

"Nor I," Alex said.

Rolf addressed Alex. "Didn't you and your father live here at the time?"

"Yes," Alex replied. "But my father said that Bryant sent him to Richmond for some supplies. The shipment hadn't arrived and we stayed over until it did. When we returned, your mother was buried. The headstone hadn't been erected, but it had been ordered."

"What about the undertaker?"

"Your father sent mine into Rutford to pay Seth Lomas, the undertaker, for the coffin. Seth sold his business shortly afterward and went north to live with his daughter. He was elderly then and I imagine is long since dead."

"There's Maggie!" I exclaimed. "Perhaps she knows something."

But when we summoned Maggie, she could offer nothing except that after the duel, mama refused to eat and took to her bed, getting up only when there were visitors. After a while, she wouldn't even get up for them and was so weak, she finally got the lung sickness. She told how papa pleaded with mama to take food to get her strength back, but she refused. Then she forbade Maggie entry into her room, finally insisting she leave the house. Papa paid her fare to Richmond and told her he would send for her when mama said she could return.

I asked Maggie who took care of us. She replied that we had been sent north to papa's sister and we stayed with her until after mama's death.

I said, "That was Aunt Samantha. She died long ago."

"Not long after your mama," Maggie said. "Which meant you didn't have a livin' relative other than your papa. I had to be your mama."

"You were a good one, Maggie." I was touched by the compassion with which she regarded us. I got back to the subject which was uppermost in our minds. "Did papa call you back for the funeral?"

"Not until after the burial. The headstone came along 'bout a month later. That's all I call tell you."

"Thank you, Maggie."

She turned to go, then paused. "Supper will be ready in about an hour. Shall I set the table for four?"

"Yes." It was Rolf who gave the answer. Vivian looked her surprise. I gave him a smile of gratitude, which he didn't return.

Maggie retreated to the kitchen.

Alex said, "I suggest we get to the grave. We've got to dig up your mother's and see if her remains are there. If they aren't, it means she could still be alive."

"Or murdered," Vivian said morosely.

"Stop talking that way." I spoke harshly, thoroughly irritated by her reference to such a thing.

"I'll help you, Alex," Rolf said. "Do you girls wish to come?"

"I'm coming," I said. "I hope Vivian will."

"I don't want to!" she exclaimed.

"None of us wants to," I countered. "But if we see an empty coffin with our own eyes, we'll know mama may not be dead. Or if she is, she wasn't buried on this plantation."

"But why would papa do such a thing?" Vivian asked.

I thought a moment. "Pride. And to lessen the scandal he felt you and I would have to live with."

"What do you mean—scandal?" Vivian asked.

"I don't know," I said wearily. "The first thing to learn is if the coffin is empty. Or if the bottom collapsed and the body or skeleton sank into the earth."

Vivian covered her face with her hands. Rolf followed Alex out, using the kitchen exit, and I hovered, waiting for Vivian to make up her mind. She looked up at me, her features plainly revealing her dislike for what she had to do. After the scene with Rolf, I believed she'd dare not refuse to go to the gravesite.

We moved down the path to the cemetery. Papa's grave was still covered with fading wild flowers. I was pleased to see the enormous pillow of roses was nowhere in sight. Alex and Rolf, in their shirt sleeves, had already dug out a good portion of the earth above where mama's coffin should be.

Vivian grasped my arm tightly when we were a brief distance from where the grave was. I shrugged free of her hold and moved up to the gravesite just as their shovels struck wood, making a hollow sound. Both men pulled themselves upward quickly as the top of the coffin caved in. Then Alex got back in the hole and moved the rotted wood aside, handing some of it up to Rolf so that he could make a complete inspection of the casket. It wasn't difficult to see that it was empty. The bottom was intact and it was lined with puffed satin, now rotted and water stained, but there wasn't a sign of what had once been a body in it.

"No one was ever buried in this casket," Alex said quietly.

"I can see that," I said. I turned around to Vivian. "Mama's skeleton isn't here. The casket is empty."

"Does that mean we'll have to go to the police?" She looked frightened.

"It means no such thing," I said. "We'll keep quiet about it. The only other two who will know are Alex's father and Maggie."

Alex said, "My father would have been here, but I stepped out when you went upstairs and told him the plantation would stay in the family. He immediately set off to rehire the help."

"Tell him what you found," I said. "I'll tell Maggie. She'll not betray our confidence."

"But what does it mean?" Vivian asked.

"It means one of two things," I replied. "Either mama is buried elsewhere or she isn't dead."

"But if she's alive, where is she?" Vivian persisted in her questioning.

"If I knew that," I said patiently, for Vivian was genuinely moved by what we'd learned, "I'd go to her and ask why papa felt compelled to do such a thing."

"Do you suppose she ran away with someone else?"

"No." I kept my reply brief because I felt Vivian was asking questions more for the sake of talking than because she believed such a thing. We'd all been through too much today. The men remained behind to fill in the grave. Vivian and I returned to the house. She continued on through, but I remained in the kitchen and related the grim news to Maggie.

She was visibly disturbed by it and as puzzled as we. "I don't understand it. I sure don't."

"Papa had a reason," I said. "But I don't know what it was."

"I don't either, child. It's as big a shock to me as it is to you. I don't even like to think about it."

"You don't believe papa would have harmed mama, do you?" I had to ask the question, since she knew both of them.

"I sure don't. Not the way he worshiped her."

"That's what I wanted to hear you say, Maggie. Thanks." I embraced her and went into the drawing room to join Vivian. I knew the men would join us as soon as their task was completed and they had washed up.

In the meantime, there was the present to consider. I turned my thoughts back to the plantation. Tomorrow the hands would return to the fields and in a few weeks the crop would be curing in the sheds. On this crop we could borrow whatever was required, for the sale was guaranteed and the price would be high.

I also recalled papa's reference to the advent of the cigarette manufacturing machines. The tobacco we raised was perfectly suited to that purpose, but by changing some acreage to a lighter leaf there'd be a new mildness which cigarettes would require. I made up my mind to see that the next crop consisted of that different strain. And as soon as I found out that these machines were coming to perfection, I'd plant three-fourths of the fields in bright leaf.

I was thinking like papa, in practical terms, at last. We were, I guessed, headed for prosperous times beyond anything we'd ever known. A bright future in bright leaf —clouded by Vivian's hasty marriage and my hopeless love for Rolf.

Twelve

THE GENTLEMEN HAD NO SOONER JOINED US THAN Maggie came striding in with the family Bible. She set it on the table before the settee and stepped back. "I want the four of you to take a good look at this. You'll find your mama's name listed in the deaths. I stood right by your papa when he put her name in."

"Why?" I asked.

" 'Cause he asked me, that's why," she replied with a firm nod of her head. "Your mama's body has got to be in that grave."

"It's not, Maggie," Alex said.

"You have to accept it just as the girls have to," Rolf added.

Maggie's head moved in slow, negative fashion and she pointed to the Bible. "Do like I say, please. Look up the deaths. And while you're lookin' them up, put your papa's name in, Miss Heather."

"I'll do it later, Maggie," I said, more anxious to discuss our newest problem of what had happened to mama.

"You'll do it now." She opened the drawer, took out a crystal inkwell, pen and wiper and set them on the table. Then she eyed me sternly.

I opened the Bible to the page marked "Deaths," lifted the sterling-hinged top of the inkwell, dipped the pen in the ink and wrote papa's name and date of death. She took the pen from me, used the wiper to clean it, then replaced the articles back in the drawer.

"Now read your mama's name up above his out loud."

Not one of the four of us gave her an argument. She'd not seen the empty coffin and apparently she'd had second thoughts about what I'd told her.

I read: "Jessica Gates, died June 16, 1874."

"Well?" she questioned. Her eyes encompassed the four of us.

"That's papa's handwriting," I admitted. "But you must believe us, Maggie. The coffin never contained a body. Do you know if anyone helped him in the burying of mama?"

"I know Reverend Barton came when the headstone was set down and said prayers over the grave. Your papa and I were there."

Alex said, "I remember now. I was there with my father."

"You were," Maggie said. "Also a few hired hands."

"But who dug the grave and buried her?" I was more perplexed than ever.

"Only your papa, far as I know. You can't ask Reverend Barton anythin' 'cause he's dead."

"I know," I said. "Yvonne DesChamps must be greatly relieved at that."

Vivian said bitterly, "Just as papa must have been relieved when Seth Lomas, the undertaker from whom papa purchased the coffin, sold the business and moved away."

"What are you talkin' 'bout?" Maggie demanded.

"If mama wasn't buried there, papa couldn't very well let anyone know when she died—since she obviously *didn't* die. Also, how could he carry a coffin by himself? He was strong, but. . . ." Her voice trailed off, a mixture of anguish and disgust.

"It's a mystery and I'm not certain how to go about solving it," I said.

"Why would papa do such a thing?" Vivian demanded.

"You jus' remember this, young lady," Maggie asserted firmly. "He had a reason—maybe two. Both of them right here, an' I guess you know who I mean." She eyed Vivian and me sternly, then turned on her heel and walked out of the room.

Alex said, "In case you don't know it, you've just been scolded."

"We deserved it," I said.

"I'm not so sure," Vivian argued, "since papa indulged in trickery."

"Just don't say he murdered mama," I cautioned.

"I'm not stupid and I don't want to hurt papa," Vivian replied. "But don't forget, he had us to raise. If he did hurt mama—and you know what I mean—he might have lived with the guilt of that also until we grew up."

"We are grown up," I replied. "And if he lived with it during our growing years, he'd have confessed now."

"Yes," she admitted. "But with the problem of money and the danger of losing Nightfall, he may have decided to wait."

"We're arguing again," I said. "Let's not waste any more time on that. Besides, it's mere supposition. We must get at the facts. There has to be a clue somewhere, something that will point to where mama is."

Vivian motioned to mama's portrait. "We never even saw that until after papa was murdered."

Maggie spoke from the doorway. "I took it down when I came back from Richmond. Couldn't stand seein' your papa walkin' the floor at night. He wouldn't let your aunt bring you home where you belonged. I told him he needed you girls. An' you needed him. One night he drank himself into a stupor here in this room, facin' your mama's portrait. I got Mr. Jacob to bring in a ladder an' take it down. I wrapped it up in cloths an' hid it in the attic behind trunks which were never used. Once your papa died, I felt it only fittin' that it be put back there. After the hired hands finished takin' the flowers to the grave, I had Mr. Jacob come in late that night an' hang it. That satisfy you?"

"Yes." Vivian's voice was barely audible and she had the grace to look embarrassed.

"I just remembered something," I said. "When I was sorting the papers and letters in papa's desk, I came across a very brief note written in a woman's handwriting. It puzzled me and it still does. Not only because of its brevity, but its curtness."

"Was it a recent letter?" Alex asked.

"No. I believe the date on the envelope was about four years ago. It was from New Orleans. The signature bore only the initials of the sender. I don't remember what they were."

"It might be a clue," Alex said.

"I'll get it." I went to the upstairs library. The letter still nestled in a separate corner of the center drawer, for I'd thought it might be of some importance. I hoped it was.

Downstairs, I took the letter from the envelope and handed it to Alex. "Please read it aloud."

He read:

Bryant:
 I have no reason to respond to your letter except to say that I am not interested in you or yours now, or at any time in the future.

J.T.

"What do you make of it?" I asked.

"It's a woman's handwriting. She knew your father well enough to address him by his given name. It seems she rejected a plea by your father for help of some kind. Do the initials J.T. mean anything to you?"

"Your mama's name was Jessica." Maggie again pointed to the Bible. "Look on the marriage page."

I did so and exclaimed aloud. "Jessica Taylor! Taylor was mama's maiden name. I didn't know. Papa never spoke of her. Now we know why. This has to be mama's letter. If she hasn't died since it was written, she's alive."

Vivian said, "We've got to find her."

I agreed, adding, "Even if she isn't interested in us."

"How will we go about it?" Vivian asked. "New Orleans is a big city."

"Big enough to hide in," Alex ventured.

Vivian spoke hesitantly. "Could the four of us go?"

"No," Alex replied abruptly. "We can't leave the plantation unguarded. Nor can the crops go without overseers. If you girls wish to go, you'll have to do it on your own. Unless Rolf cares to accompany you."

"Couldn't you use my help here?" Rolf asked.

"Very definitely," Alex replied.

"Then I'll stay."

Vivian was hurt by his reply, but I felt it would be better if only the two of us went. I wasn't afraid and I was well aware of how important it was that the crop be attended.

Alex said, "Do you have any funds in reserve?"

"Papa had ten thousand dollars set aside. All I took out of it was the expense of papa's funeral and a donation to Reverend Lumet for the service."

"Plus the five hundred dollars you pretended your papa

left for me." Maggie took the envelope I'd given her from her pocket and set it on the table. "Use that for your trip. You can't fool me, honey. I had no intention of keepin' it, but I wouldn't hurt you right then by turnin' it down."

"Thanks, Maggie," I said. "You'll get it back."

"I ain't interested in gettin' it back. Just want to save the plantation."

"You're one of the family, Maggie," I said.

"If I didn't think so," she retorted, "I wouldn't be in here speakin' my mind."

"And since everything's on a very personal basis, I have a question to direct to you, Rolf. Did the check you gave Vivian to present to Yvonne DesChamps leave you in a vulnerable position regarding your finances?"

His face reddened, assuring me it had. But he quickly recovered his composure. "I have my plantation, you know. The overseer told me he expects to harvest an excellent crop."

"But that's about all you have now," I said.

"Yes. Just now, my concern is for you and Vivian. You'll need money for supplies and new equipment. Alex tells me a lot of yours is beyond repair."

"Can we get a loan from the bank, now that we're in the clear?" I asked.

Alex said, "I should think so."

"We're playing into Yvonne DesChamps' hands again," I said. "But it's a risk we must take."

"When will you girls leave?" Maggie asked.

"Tomorrow," I said. "I'll go upstairs immediately and start packing."

"So will I."

"You can pack tonight," Maggie said. "Your supper's 'most ready. Go upstairs an' change. An' don't come down in black. Your papa hated it. I didn't want to tell you before 'cause it wouldn't be fittin' not to wear it at his grave, but don't wear it now."

"Wearing black won't make me more aware of what happened to papa," I said. "So we'll do as you say."

I wore a deep-maroon afternoon dress. It was tailored, with high neck and long, tight-fitting sleeves, but it was respectful of papa without being morose. Vivian was a dream in pale green. She'd tucked a green silk rose in her hair and when the gentlemen met us at the foot of the stairs, I saw her cast a shy glance at Rolf. He couldn't help but reveal his admiration for her beauty, though he gave her no compliment. But he took her arm and guided her to the dining room. Alex and I followed. In an undertone he informed me that Rolf would remain at the house while we were in New Orleans.

I was relieved, for after the incendiary fire at the barn, I felt there was no limit to Yvonne DesChamps' quest for vengeance. Perhaps more now than ever, since she'd been deprived of her moment of triumph—the taking of the plantation.

Rolf and Alex gave us all the information regarding New Orleans they could. We could only absorb so much, but it helped to pass the time. Certainly, there were no love glances exchanged between Vivian and Rolf and I feared that after the crops were harvested, he would take his leave. There would probably be a divorce after all, for he made no pretense of being a happy and devoted bridegroom.

I didn't like such worrisome thoughts, so I turned the conversation back to the purpose of our journey. "Where do you think we should begin?"

"I suggest the city hall," Rolf said. "Check the names under Taylor. If she owns property, her name will be there."

"What if she married again?" Vivian exclaimed in horror.

"She couldn't with papa still alive," I said. "Besides, she used her maiden initials."

"Do you suppose she got a divorce?" Vivian asked, avoiding Rolf's eyes.

"How could she," I queried, "since she was supposed to be dead?"

"Maybe she doesn't know that," Vivian ventured.

Neither Rolf nor Alex could refrain from laughing, nor could I. At first, Vivian didn't see the humor in it, but then she joined in, though not too heartily. I didn't blame her. The occasion wasn't a joyous one. I even wondered why we were going to attempt to locate a woman who was responsible for our being on this earth and who, from the brief note, indicated she hadn't the slightest interest in us.

Thirteen

VIVIAN AND I, IN STREET APPAREL, EMERGED FROM THE St. Charles Hotel and had our first close look at New Orleans. We'd seen, heard and smelled the streets during our brief ride from the railroad depot but now, as part of the everlasting bustle, we were more able to absorb the flavor of this unique city.

The street vendors fascinated Vivian, who said she couldn't have imagined this even in a wild dream. They sold everything from strawberries to hot coffee and pancakes. They called their wares stridently and in good humor. They asked people to buy, but were never insistent.

"Look!" Vivian exclaimed. "It cannot be, but that woman sells coffee from a pot she carries on her head."

"And from what I have heard," I said, "the coffee is excellent. But we have more important things to do."

"I know." Vivian nodded somberly. "I wish we were here on a vacation. I'd like to see everything."

"We will probably be required to move about a great deal in our search for mama," I told her. "That means you will likely see all of this city you care to. We are now going to go to the city hall and ask to see the real-estate records so we may look for mama's name among them."

"A stuffy old place where there are nothing but stuffy old books," Vivian commented. Her eyes were following the weird spectacle of a man on whose back was strapped a deep basket filled with brooms and mops. That alone intrigued her, but this vendor also played four instruments at the same time: small drum, brass cymbals strapped to his knees, a banjo which he plucked with his long fingers, and a harmonica somehow attached to his head.

Vivian clapped her hands in delight and, quite impulsively, she opened her handbag and pressed a half dollar into his hand before she moved away from the somewhat startled man.

I had to urge her, by constant tugs on her elbow, to keep her mind on our mission here and to get on with it. Vivian's brief marriage hadn't turned her into a mature woman. She looked for pleasure wherever she went and had a difficult time being serious. It seemed to me, though I knew it was not true, that she'd forgotten she had a husband who no longer respected her because she'd lied to him and was going to leave her within a short time after we returned.

At city hall we were granted the privilege of looking through their index of names. It was a dusty, somber, large room where we searched, and Vivian was forever brushing dust off her white gloves. I'd removed mine, but she was too much the lady and too concerned with her appearance, for she knew very well that every male eye in the place was on her.

I looked for mama under both her marriage and her maiden names, but it didn't take long to ascertain the names were not on file. I thanked the official in charge and went out into the hot sunlight with Vivian. She promptly opened her mauve-colored parasol and assumed that regal walk which was so much a part of her. I was proud of her appearance and the fact that she caught and held the eye of both sexes.

I seized her arm and brought her to a halt. "Wait! The building we just left also is where the names of people who have died are kept. Vivian, we have to be sure."

"Oh, no!" she exclaimed tremulously. "Let's not think of mama dead."

"I don't want to, but we have to be practical. I'll meet you back at the hotel."

"Heather, you wouldn't leave me alone on the streets of this city!"

"I intend to see if mama died in this city and the place to do it is at city hall. You may accompany me or not, as you see fit."

She sulked, but went with me, and we discovered a death, two years ago, of a woman named Jessica Taylor. Her age corresponded to mama's and I felt my heart begin to sink.

"I won't believe it," Vivian said angrily. "Mama is not dead."

"This Jessica Taylor was mama's age," I reminded her. "She appears to have been buried in the Metairie Cemetery. I don't know where that is, but no doubt a coachman will. We're going there at once."

Surprisingly, Vivian made no further protest. The first carriage we approached took us to the cemetery. The driver knew it well and made comments on the fact that it had once been a racecourse and was now one of the grandest burying grounds in the state. It had, he proclaimed, some of the largest and most elaborate mausoleums and the handsomest ovens to be seen anywhere. He was quite proud of it.

We soon discovered the ovens were merely crypts containing simple niches and, when empty, they did look like ovens. As neither of us had any strong inclination to browse among these macabre structures, we sought out the superintendent of the graveyard and, through him, we located the tomb of Jessica Taylor.

We found it to be a mausoleum on a grand scale and for a few moments I was convinced this was mama's last resting place. We opened the creaky iron gate and stepped inside to discover the engraved slab bearing Jessica Taylor's name.

SACRED TO THE MEMORY OF

JESSICA TAYLOR

born in Morrie Parish
March 12, 1850,
died November 10, 1888

Wife of William Taylor
Mother of Sarah, Anna
and Michael

Vivian bolted out of the cramped space amidst the tombs. I followed in more dignified fashion, certain and relieved that it was not our mother interred here. The engraved legend did not agree, only the name and year of birth.

We returned to our hotel in the carriage which we'd ordered to wait for us. Vivian, still affected by the ordeal of the cemetery visit, lay down to rest. I sat at the window, looking at the bustling streets below, and tried to think of some other way to locate a person missing from our lives for fifteen years.

Vivian declared herself unable to carry on, so I began a tour of the better hotels located not too far from ours. No old registers—where there were any—bore my mother's married or maiden name. I even visited the police station to make inquiries there without any result.

I returned to find Vivian just out of a hot bath, with three gowns laid out on the bed, one of which she would pick after much deliberation. I took my own bath and felt better for it.

"No doubt," Vivian said, "this hotel is famous and quite likely will have the most fashionable dining room in the city. Is it agreed we shall dine here?"

"As you wish. I'm here to find mama. It doesn't matter to me where I eat."

"There's nothing we can do this late in the day anyway."

"There is much, but you'd not be inclined to do it. We could walk the streets and look at faces. I believe I would recognize mama if I saw her."

"Not me. If she still looked like the portrait, maybe I could, but that was painted at least twenty years ago. She will have changed."

"I suppose so. We'll suspend our search for tonight, but tomorrow we'll think of some other way to look for her. Wear the pale green. It looks so well on you."

We dined, though Vivian nearly did not, for she became too lost in the grandeur of the dining room and the open stares of admiration from the men, accompanied by some hostile looks from a few of the women whose escorts eyed Vivian too frequently. It was, in Vivian's eyes, a memorable and lovely evening. I enjoyed the food, but my mind kept reverting to the plantation. Many problems were present there. I thought of Rolf, wondering what he would do when the emergency was over. He had already told Vivian he would not live with her because she had lied to him about Alex and me. Though it was cruel on my part, I was relieved that Rolf would not stay at the plantation as Vivian's husband. It would be an impossible situation living in such close contact.

Then, too, there was the loan to pay back, for I intended to repay Rolf at the earliest opportunity.

Life was going to be no picnic at the plantation, once things were straightened out. We'd be in debt, no doubt until the crop one year hence would mature. That was a long time. Vivian would have none of her famous balls and dinners, which would not make my life easier.

Alex would tarry no longer than necessary. I'd miss him, for I'd have no one with whom I could discuss my problems and ask for advice, advice wisely and freely given. There'd be only Vivian and me to take care of the plantation, with the help of Jacob. It wasn't going to be easy. If Vivian could help, that would be an asset, but she had neither the desire nor capability for it. Her chief asset was charm.

I knew I'd feel better about all of these matters if I could learn what had become of mama. And why papa had maintained an empty grave all these years to further the pretense that mama was dead. And I'd have Yvonne DesChamps to contend with. She'd not be apt to surrender in docile fashion. I had few doubts but that her antagonism toward us would fester and grow to become more deadly than ever. As a neighbor she'd not have a difficult time keeping track of us. I had no doubt she knew now that we were in New Orleans. I didn't believe she knew the reason why, however, since only Alex and his father had discovered papa's well-kept secret. Now, besides Vivian and me, only Maggie and Rolf knew, neither of whom would betray us. If mama was alive and Yvonne DesChamps ever learned of it, I dreaded what would happen. Her hatred for mama would be as unbridled and dangerous as it had been for papa.

Though I arose early, Vivian slept late as usual. I contacted the manager and made inquiries about the services of a good attorney and, in Edmund Latimer, I found one. Elderly and wise, he listened to my candid story, pressed his fingertips together and delivered to me the one method left for discovering someone missing for fifteen years.

"You have exhausted the real-estate records, death notices and police files. Hotel records are poor sources of information, when they are available, and hospital records fall into the same category. However, if your mother came here alone, determined to make her own way, then she would likely have either found a job or have begun a business. We shall assume a business. In New Orleans, a business requires a license, and to obtain a license one must have proof of identity, so your mother could not have used a false name. She might have used her maiden name, which is legal and can be backed up with documentary proof. So I would suggest a long examination of the city license bureau. I wish you all manner of luck, young lady, and I fully sympathize with your desire to find your mother."

He refused a fee, and I went out to find a carriage that would take me back to city hall, where the license bureau was located. Two hours later I entered our hotel room in a high state of excitement, and startled Vivian, who was again in the tub.

"I've found her," I said. "I've found mama."

"You mean you've seen her?" Vivian looked apprehensive.

"No, no. I've only found a record of her, but she's still here. I'm sure of it. She's right here in New Orleans."

"How can you be sure of that?"

"Fifteen years ago Jessica Taylor took out a license to operate the Café Brulot Ballroom."

Vivian reached for a towel and stepped out of the tub. "The what?"

"A ballroom. Vivian, I recall that papa once said she loved dancing and music. You've taken after her. And since she did love dancing, wouldn't it be natural for her to begin a business where people would come and dance?"

Vivian looked dubious. "It sounds like a very strange business for a lady. Are you sure?"

"She had to have a city license, and I found it."

"But after fifteen years . . . would she still be running it?"

"She is required to take out a license every year and she took one out this year. She's here, she's alive and we know where she can be found. All of a sudden I'm confused."

"So am I," Vivian said. "But it's strange to hear you say that."

I tried to explain. "It's just that I thought I'd be so excited, I'd hire a cab and go directly there. But all of a sudden, I realize what we've done is reckless."

"I agree. But go on."

"Well, suppose no one here knows she was once married and bore two children, now young ladies. Suppose she doesn't even want to recognize us as her flesh and blood."

"How can she refuse us recognition? I look just like the way she once did." Vivian toweled herself dry, slipped on a negligee and took the pins from her hair to brush it.

"Yes. And she may resent it."

"In heaven's name, why?" Vivian looked properly indignant.

I shrugged uncertainly. "She isn't young anymore and in you she'll see her lost youth."

Vivian set down the brush, placed her hands on her hips and eyed me speculatively. "I never saw you so uncertain of yourself before."

"I've never been so confused and uncertain of myself. My heart is pounding madly. I'm nervous and jumpy and I feel we've done a very reckless and unwise thing in coming here."

"What perplexes me is that for once in my life I agree with everything you say."

"Then again," I reasoned, "there is the mystery of mama's empty casket."

"You want mama to solve it," Vivian said.

I nodded.

"So do I. I also want to see what she looks like. And the surprise on her face when we identify ourselves."

"I would have to, but after viewing that painting, I doubt you would."

"So what do we do?" Vivian picked up her brush and started running it through her hair.

"We find the Café Brulot Ballroom and see what it looks like. Tonight we'll go there and mingle with the people who attend. Somehow we'll arrange to see her or meet her."

"What will I wear?" Vivian asked.

Her question relieved the tension and I broke into laughter. Despite the uncertainty of our reception, her main worry was her appearance.

But I quickly sobered, wondering how mama would

react to her daughters who came out of a past she surely had wanted to forget. She might resent us to the point where she'd refuse to see us, even send us away with harsh words.

The situation had to be faced. The day became interminably long, despite the fact that we explored many streets before we finally developed the courage to find the Café Brulot Ballroom. We regarded it with considerable dismay, for it was located in an area known as the Vieux Carré, a section of what seemed to be ancient, shabby buildings on an incredibly narrow street. The houses had high balconies decorated with ornamental iron grillwork. The structures actually appeared to share the same walls with their neighbors, so they looked somewhat like a single, long building, the separations evident only by the doors.

The only indication that the ballroom was here consisted of a small, unobtrusive sign stating the Café Brulot Ballroom was upstairs, beyond a gaily painted door.

"It can't be much of a place," Vivian observed. "Mama must be terribly poor."

"That's of no consequence," I said. "But I disagree. Mama began this ballroom fifteen years ago and never changed its location, so it must pay something and it must be well known."

"To those who would frequent a place like this—yes. Can't we make some sort of inquiries about it?" Vivian was regarding the shabby building with distaste.

"Why waste more time? We came to find mama. Don't you want to see her?"

"I—don't think so. Maybe we should just go home."

I spoke sternly. "We came here to find her and we're not going away until we do. If she needs help, she'll certainly get all we can supply. If she dismisses us without showing a trace of affection, then we'll go. But we are going to meet her and talk to her. Tonight, if possible."

To my amazement, Vivian agreed to the logic of my statement. We walked back to our hotel and there we planned our method of reaching mama.

"The only thing we can do," Vivian said, "is to go there and, I suppose, buy a ticket at the door."

"Without escorts?" I asked scornfully.

"From the looks of the place, they're not going to care

if girls have escorts or not. I've heard of these places, where they have girls to dance with unescorted men and men go alone, through preference, to dance with unescorted girls."

"I read of them too, in *Scribner's* Magazine, but I can't say I approve. And, frankly, neither did *Scribner's*."

Again Vivian surprised me. "I do, if mama runs it."

"Very well. But the moment we find the opportunity, we'll face mama."

Vivian looked alarmed. "Do you think she'll turn her back on us?"

"No." I spoke with far more conviction than I felt.

"But she didn't come near us once through our growing years."

"She was supposed to be dead," I said remindfully.

"It's all so puzzling."

"That's why we must have a face-to-face confrontation with her. I hate puzzles."

"Perhaps it had something to do with Yvonne DesChamps," Vivian reasoned.

"Let's not play a guessing game. But since you mentioned that woman's name, I hope she doesn't learn mama's alive."

"How could she?"

I thought a moment. "She's so vindictive, I'm sure she thinks of everything."

"What do you mean?"

"Nothing." I wasn't going to worry Vivian further, but the thought occurred to me that Yvonne DesChamps had probably kept a very close watch on everything that happened on the plantation. And on the owner and his daughters. If so, it could well be she'd had us followed here. I thrust the frightening thought from my mind. If she knew we'd gone on a journey, she'd probably think it was to get away from the shock of papa's death.

Vivian broke into my thoughts. "How do you think we should dress?"

"Not spectacularly. We don't know what sort of place that is."

Vivian agreed it would be wiser to look subdued rather than flamboyant. We had our supper in the hotel, but we were too nervous to more than nibble at our food, and Vivian was oblivious to the admiring looks she merited.

At eight o'clock we found the street door to the ballroom wide open. As we approached, a carriage pulled up and two extremely well dressed young gentlemen got out. They entered the building and proceeded up the stairs.

"If mama attracts that kind of clientele," I said, "it must be a respectable establishment."

"I want to see it." Vivian was suddenly bursting with excitement, imbued with a spirit of adventure.

"Very well. We'll be ladylike, but also insistent. We must not fail."

I led the way up the narrow staircase. At the top we heard the strains of lively music. We also encountered a large, closed door with a slim, middle-aged man in white trousers and a bright, red coat over a ruffled shirt. His skin was a handsome copper tone; his dark eyes regarded us curiously but respectfully.

"Bon soir," he said with a little bow. "You look for someone, *oui?"*

"We wish to dance," I said.

His smile was disarming. "You are no doubt strangers in New Orleans."

"We are," I admitted.

"Mademoiselles," he bowed again, "I am sorry, but ladies are not permitted in this ballroom."

"And why not?" I asked indignantly.

His smile was apologetic. "Here, the girls are . . . well . . . they are previously invited. No strangers allowed."

"I don't understand," I said. But I was not giving up. If we were refused entrance, then we must ask for mama.

"It is simple, mademoiselle. You and the beautiful girl with you cannot enter. In fact, it would not be safe for you to do so. With such beauty in the ballroom, our clientele would go mad over both of you. Please, go away."

He was trying to get rid of us through flattery. I would have none of it.

"Does Jessica Taylor operate this ballroom?" I asked.

His manner changed, just as mine had. *"Oui,* that is so. Why do you ask?"

"Because we came here to see Jessica Taylor, mostly." Vivian used her sultry voice. "It is most important."

"Ah, I see. She knows you, then?" He turned back to me.

"Please tell her that Miss Heather Gates and her sister, Miss Vivian Gates, wish to speak to her."

"Please wait," he said. He disappeared inside, opening the door enough to enable us to see a gaily decorated room with a long bar against the far wall facing the door. A few couples were on the floor; others were gathered in small groups. It seemed sedate enough, and pleasantly so.

"Did you see that big sign inside?" Vivian asked. "They have dancing every night and on Thursday's there's a masquerade."

"I saw it. And I'm more confused than ever. I can't make up my mind what sort of place this is."

I tried the door and found it locked. I had barely moved back when it opened and the man in the red coat stepped outside again, closing it quickly, making sure to bar our way.

"Mademoiselle Taylor says she does not know anyone by the names you gave me and she is much too busy to see you. *Au 'voir*, mademoiselles. I am indeed sorry."

We could do nothing but retreat down the stairs. A cab pulled up as we stepped out of the door. Two more well-dressed young gentlemen alighted and smiled at us.

"How lovely you ladies are," one said. "Why are you leaving so early? It might be beneficial if you remained. Is that not so, Alfred?"

"Oh, *oui*, that is so." His companion was eyeing Vivian in a manner that displayed more than ordinary interest.

"We do not speak to strangers," I said haughtily and I seized Vivian's arm in a tight grip. I propelled her along until we reached the corner. I gave a brief glance back to see the two disappear into the building.

"What in the world kind of establishment is mama running?" Vivian asked in a voice that threatened to break with anxiety.

"I can tell you one thing. We're going to find out. We're going to walk about this area until we find a policeman and ask him."

"Why a policeman?" Vivian asked worriedly.

"Because I'm as confused as you. Mama certainly recognized our names."

"I wonder why she refused to see us."

"She refused," I said, "because she doesn't want to see us."

"Do you mean the place she owns is disreputable?"

"That's what I intend to find out."

Vivian gave a quick, negative shake of her head. "I think we ought to go home."

"You may if you wish. I'm seeing mama if I have to break down doors to do it."

"I'll stay," she said in a small voice. "I'll not let you go back there alone."

We found a policeman not a block away and we stopped him. He was a middle-aged, graying man and he looked trustworthy and intelligent.

"Please," I said, "we would like some information. We're strangers in New Orleans and, of course, we are not familiar with the way some things are done here."

He smiled. "It is said we don't do things that are ordinary, miss. How can I help you?"

"My sister and I sought to enter the Café Brulot Ballroom in the next block and were refused admittance. It seems to me that it is a public place and we should not be barred, even if we are unescorted. The man at the door didn't say there were rules against unescorted women. He merely refused to let us in."

The policeman tried to repress a smile, though not too successfully. "And no wonder."

"What is amusing?" Vivian asked.

"My dear young ladies, that ballroom is reserved for use as a quadroon ballroom. Perhaps the term has little meaning to you, so I will try to explain. This is a modern city with ways perhaps not agreeable to someone from, say, New England. At this ballroom the most beautiful girls of mixed blood come to meet wealthy young white men who are looking for a mistress."

"Good heavens!" I exclaimed.

"Please go on," Vivian urged, suddenly quite curious.

"Well, it's not quite like it sounds. You see, these young men select one of these girls; one he favors the most only after coming here several times, dancing and talking with her. I might add that this is with the express and open permission of the young man's father—who likely did the same thing in his youth—and the pretended ignorance of his mother. The young man will never marry the girl he chooses to live with. He could not marry a quadroon under any circumstances. Once the girl accepts him—and it is all done in the most graceful fashion—he then goes to the girl's mother and arranges payment to the mother. He also signs papers that he will support children born of this union and he will see to it that the girl never regrets what she has done. Mind you, some of the young men who installed a favorite in a beautiful apartment will often marry some other girl of his own color if he was not married beforehand. But he never ceases to visit the girl he has chosen as his mistress. If he does, she's well taken care of. Some relationships last for years, until they are both old. Of course, he has obtained a written agreement from the girl that she would never name him as the father of any children she bears him, and that he would be obligated to them in no way as a legal father. Though, morally, he is. I never knew of a man who did not further the ambitions of these children, in a quiet way, of course. Everyone here understands. While some may not approve, they nevertheless tolerate this situation."

The revelation left Vivian and me speechless.

"Now," the policeman said, "do you understand why you were denied admission to the ballroom?"

We nodded bleakly. I felt sick inside, wondering what kind of woman mama was.

"Is the ballroom run by someone who profits from all this?" I asked.

"Indeed, miss. She's one of our more prominent citizens."

He touched his helmet and bowed before he resumed his beat. Vivian and I strolled in a daze toward the center of the city, where our hotel was located.

"What do you think of mama?" I asked.

"I'm disgusted," Vivian said. "I think we should go home."

"That's the first thought that occurred to me," I said. "But as the policeman said, it's not considered shameful here. It's acceptable."

"Not by me," Vivian said.

"Nor by me," I said. "But I still feel we should have

second thoughts about it. I can't condemn her without talking with her."

"How can we when she won't see us and we've been barred from the ballroom?" Vivian argued.

"I've thought of a way. If you're game."

"Tell me."

"The masquerade. It's held tomorrow night. Perhaps, wearing a costume and mask, we could gain entry."

Vivian pondered that, though not for long. She had a greater sense of adventure than I and I could see from the way her eyes lit up that the idea appealed to her.

"How can we get in?" she asked.

I considered that for a few moments while we strolled along the gaslit street in the direction of our hotel.

"I was thinking about finding the back entrance—sort of a performers' entrance—and staying there until mama came out."

"Think of the fun we'll have buying costumes. What will you choose?"

"I haven't the faintest idea. Just any sort of costume that will get us inside."

But in my heart there were doubts. Strong ones. If mama didn't wish to see us, we were not going to trick her into anything. Yet to return without seeing her would be to admit defeat.

Like Vivian, I began to think of a costume.

Fourteen

CHARACTERISTICALLY, VIVIAN CHOSE TO DRESS AS A LIT-tle girl in a starched dress, white with a blue sash and tiny matching ribbons for her hair, which she fashioned into pigtails. She wore sandals with a single strap and white cotton hose. Some cleverly applied powder and rouge created the look of extreme youth and when she was finished, she appeared ten years younger and very, very fetching.

"With a mask, we'll be certain to get in," she said.

"Perhaps, but don't forget, those girls must enter by some rear door. It's not going to be easy. If they suspect we're not one of them, we'll again be denied entrance."

I stayed in character in selecting my costume too. It was that of Evangeline, a long, gray dress, black-laced shoes and a poke bonnet. All very staid, but the way I felt at this moment. Finding costumes was incredibly easy, for I learned that each year, prior to Lent, the New Orleans citizens dress in costumes and roam the streets after looking at a long and impressive parade with everyone also in costume. We purchased long cloaks and on Thursday evening we were prepared to make our furtive way into the questionable establishment that mama ran.

We hired a carriage and reached the ballroom early. We paid the driver and went to the rear. As we expected, there was a stairway leading up to the back of the ballroom itself. Vivian and I had found a sheltered area where we were not visible, but had a clear view of the girls' entranceway.

It was dark by the time they began to arrive. Vivian and I studied them as they passed under a gaslight, which illuminated them well. I didn't think I'd ever seen so many beautiful girls at one time. Even Vivian was impressed.

"Those are the girls content to live with a gentleman who will eventually marry someone else? They must be mad. With their beauty, they shouldn't cheapen themselves."

"Neither they nor the gentlemen consider it in that vein. It's a question of mixed blood. Sad but true. And I'm sure you observed the fact that they are ladylike in dress, posture and walk. Also, their voices are modulated and pleasing to the ear. They've been taught all the social graces."

"I'm more interested in how we're going to get in."

I was myself, but pretended complete confidence because Vivian was suddenly nervous and unsure of herself.

"It's simple," I said. "When the next group arrives, we'll wait until they've started up the stairs. Then we will don our masks and move quickly to catch up with them, but remain behind them. When they enter, we'll follow."

"But what about once we're in there?"

"We'll just keep our wits about us."

"You're not very reassuring."

"I can do no better. We'll watch the others and act accordingly. Just remember—we must not fail. It's our last chance to see mama."

"I wish she were as eager to see us," Vivian said.

"No matter. We want to know the reason for the empty casket."

"She may not know the answer to that."

"We'll find out shortly."

"You hope."

There was no time for further talk. A group of six young ladies arrived, conversing softly to one another. Their costumes were elegant. Vivian and I moved in behind them. They were masked and chattering amiably, so they paid no attention to us. At the top of the stairs we were admitted, along with the others, and we found ourselves in a long corridor behind the bandstand. As the music had already begun, we followed the girls to the end of the corridor. As we did so, we passed a door marked "Private." I glanced at Vivian significantly and she nodded back that she understood.

There were four steps leading down to the dance floor, already fairly well filled. The men were also costumed elaborately. Someone approached Vivian, called her "little one" in French and took her in his arms to dance. She sailed away happily, I thought. A moment later I was dancing with a gentleman costumed as Satan. But he was well mannered, a fine dancer, a brilliant conversationalist and extremely intelligent.

I couldn't converse easily with him for any length of time without being discovered. There was a certain rapport between these girls and the men who came to curry their favor. Inexperienced as we were and naïve as Vivian was, we had to put our final plan into motion at once.

When the dance ended and serious conversation began, I made my way to where Vivian was talking to a dauphin in silk finery. I excused myself, telling her there was a gentleman who had an important matter to discuss with her. The dauphin bowed graciously and I led Vivian to the steps leading to the corridor behind the ballroom.

We lost no time getting to the door marked "Private." We were both frightened, but determined, and we exchanged glances of encouragement to bolster our courage.

Vivian said, "Shall we remove our masks?"

Before I could make a decision on the wisdom of that, we heard heavy steps ascending the stairway. I gripped the door, turned the knob, hoping that it wasn't locked. It wasn't, and we stepped inside. I closed it behind us. Vivian was holding my hand so tightly, it was painful. I was sure her heart was beating as rapidly as mine. I viewed the room briefly. It was large, fitted as an office, but an impressive one. There was a red-velvet chaise before the fireplace and several chairs cushioned in the same red material. A deep burgundy carpet covered the floor. Gas lamps were on three different tables, and directly ahead of us was a large mahogany desk, also with a lamp. A large bowl of roses stood at each end, the perfume of which reached us. But our attention was centered on the woman seated behind the desk, wearing a blue satin evening gown. She hadn't even raised her head at our entrance. Her attention seemed riveted on a ledger.

I touched a forefinger to my lips in a motion for Vivian to remain silent. I figured it was the best way to get the woman's attention.

It worked, for she finally raised her head. It was difficult to appraise her reaction to our appearance, for her features were noncommittal.

Finally she spoke. "What is it, my dears? What prompted you to come in here when your place is in the ballroom?"

I took a few steps forward. Vivian followed. We were still wearing our masks, so it was only natural for her to assume we were two of the girls from the ballroom.

I said, "Good evening, Mama."

She was too astonished to answer and could only stare at us. When she found her voice, she said, "Take off your masks."

I removed mine first. Vivian was slower. In her nervousness, it caught on her hair and I had to help her free it.

We turned our attention back to mama. She was still slim, her hair the exact color of Vivian's, without a trace of gray. A beautiful woman, despite her years. An older version of Vivian, as she realized, for she gasped aloud when Vivian faced her.

Her glance then switched to me. "You're Heather. You resemble your father."

She regarded Vivian again. "You're the image of me when I was your age. Yet you're both attractive. I guess I can be proud of myself."

"Can you?" I asked.

She rested her head against the back of the tall chair and eyed me speculatively. "So you know about the scandal."

"We do," I said.

"I thought everyone did except the two of you."

"Papa told me about it," I said.

"Why?" Her voice hardened.

"I think he had a premonition of death and he wanted us to learn about what happened from him."

"He was always so noble."

I resented her sarcasm. "He was also a gentleman. He blamed only himself for what happened."

Her smile was bitter, her eyes disbelieving. "I would like some coffee. Will you girls join me?"

"No, thank you," I said. Vivian gave a negative shake of her head.

Mama shrugged and lifted a small bell. Its silvery ring brought a girl in maid's uniform. Mama merely waved her hand and the girl understood. She brought a tray minutes later, making it evident that mama wanted coffee ready at any time she snapped her fingers. But this was a somewhat different coffee. It was served in a tall, delicate china cup. After the intensely black coffee was poured, tiny bits of citrus peel were added and then brandy poured on the top. Mama struck a match, set the brandy flaming and waited for the blue flame to die down. I almost wished I'd accepted for the fragrance of the citrus peel teased my nostrils.

"Café brûlot," she said. "The best coffee in the world. I named the ballroom after it." She took an appraising sip and nodded. "Now—where were we?"

"Talking about papa," I said. "He's dead. He was killed a week ago."

"I read about it in the newspapers. A detailed account. The story stated it was either an accident or suicide."

"It was neither."

"Why didn't you come back?" Vivian spoke for the first time.

"How could I," mama retorted, "since he'd already buried me?"

"Why did he do that?" I asked.

"Why drag up my scandalous past?"

"As your daughters, don't you think we have a right to know the complete story?" I asked.

"So you can hate me thoroughly?" she asked.

"We don't hate," I said. "It only destroys one."

"Didn't you ever think about us?" Vivian asked.

"Never," mama replied. She took a few sips of her coffee. "I learned I had a talent for business. I'm proud of my success."

"You did better than papa," I said. "He almost lost the plantation."

"Through stupidity. He trusted everyone. He played with professional gamblers. I believe he was lured into the games. Of course, he'd been drinking."

"You were responsible for that." I was afraid my tone was as hard as hers. I couldn't sit there and listen to her belittle papa.

"I suppose I was responsible for him almost losing Nightfall," she retorted. "He did write, asking for a loan. He even offered to bring you here. I refused both the request and the offer. The latter would have only reopened the scandal."

"He fought a duel and killed a man because of your indiscretion," I said.

"He needn't have if he'd paid even a little attention to me. But it was always the plantation. He worked twelve to sixteen hours every day. He wanted to be the biggest and most successful plantation owner in the state. And the richest, I suppose."

"He did it for you," I said.

"No. His foolish pride. And for his heirs. Or heiresses, I should say."

I said, "Why did he pretend you had died?"

She gave a brief shake of her head as if she didn't want to discuss the subject further. Then, with a discouraged sigh, she said, "I suppose I'll not be rid of you until you know the entire story. When I've told it, get out. Both of you."

"We will," I said quietly, though I was seething with anger. "But first, the story."

"After the duel, I took to my room. I hated your father because he'd killed a man who had made me feel desirable."

"Papa knew you were desirable," I said "Maggie told me how he walked the floors at night before your portrait after he'd supposedly buried you. One night he drank himself into a stupor. She had Jacob come in and take down your portrait. I guess it was too much for papa to look at. He missed you so. She had Jacob hang it after papa was murdered."

"Are you certain he was murdered?"

"Very."

"Who would do it?"

"It's more a case of who hired a criminal to do it."

From the faraway look in her eyes, her mind was back to the days of her young womanhood. She said quietly, "Yvonne DesChamps."

"Yes," I replied. "She told papa years ago she would one day get her revenge."

"But she had Reverend Barton tell of her forgiveness from the pulpit. She also asked that the townspeople never reveal it to either of you."

"They didn't," I said. "Papa told me. I told Vivian."

Mama said, "I guess I am curious. Tell me all that happened."

"First, the barn burned down. Alex Hale, Jacob's son, saw enough before it was consumed by flames to know it was incendiary. Then, two of papa's best horses were shot. We visited Yvonne DesChamps. She admitted nothing and told us we could never convince anyone she was other than kind and compassionate. She has used the years building that reputation in the village. It was she who bought up the notes which papa had signed and were overdue. The banker was pledged to secrecy, after being told by her that she didn't want to embarrass papa. It was the gesture of one who felt no bitterness because of the past. She also said her husband, Lemuel, might have run away with you, but he'd have come back to her. That he had a weakness for a pretty face and for him, once he'd made a conquest, he lost interest."

Mama's face flamed. "He made no conquest, though I was going to run away with him. He was killed before we could do so. A letter your papa found brought things to their tragic climax."

"We know," Vivian said. "But we still don't know why he pretended to bury you."

"Then I'll tell you. When I took to my room, I refused nourishment. I believed I hated your father at the time. I also believed Lemuel loved me. His wife is right. I learned later he was a scoundrel and no doubt he'd have discarded me once he tired of me."

"Papa would have taken you back," I said. "It was Yvonne who said so."

"I told your father I wished to leave him. He begged me to stay. To forgive him. Perhaps if you two had still been there, I'd have given in, but your aunt was visiting us at the time of the duel and he packed you both off with her and told her to keep you until he sent for you. It was as well. I took to drinking spiritous liquors. I refused food of any kind. I lost weight. I said I'd starve myself to death if he didn't let me go. He had no choice, but he had a great deal of pride. We made a bargain. He would send Maggie and Jacob off and he and I would be alone on the plantation. I was quite emaciated by then and Dr. Dillon told him if I didn't take nourishment, I'd live only a matter of days. Your papa said he would give me a generous sum of money if I would go a considerable distance from Virginia. He would purchase a casket, bury it in the cemetery and announce I had died. Enough people had seen me to know I was in failing health. I agreed to the arrangement. He was most generous and with what he gave me, I started this establishment. I am respected here. And I prefer that Jessica Gates remain dead."

"Amazing that no one from Virginia ever came here and saw you."

Her laughter was soft and reminded me of mine. "I'm sure they have been here, merely out of curiosity, but I kept away from the ballroom. I've lived a quiet and retiring life. I do my business from this office. When I go out, I am heavily veiled. Many women use veils to protect their fair skins. Any invitations I accept, I insist on a guest list first. I always get it. So I've been very careful."

"As careful as Yvonne DesChamps, who almost got possession of the plantation."

Mama sobered. "Tell me about that."

I did, as briefly as possible. "Vivian saved it. She is the bride of Rolf Fielding."

"The orphan," mama said.

"Papa was good to him."

"I suppose it was his way of doing penance."

I resented her statement. "He was a good father to us, loving and generous."

"Making up to you for his lack of attention to me," she said. She regarded Vivian. "I wish you happiness, my dear. But I do have a question. How did you know I wasn't buried in that grave?"

I explained that also.

"Things have a way of coming undone, don't they?" she mused.

"They did in this case."

"And how did you know where to find me?"

"I found a letter in papa's desk, signed J.T. Apparently, papa knew you were successful. You've already told us he asked if you would give him a loan."

"I refused. I knew of his gambling, but I didn't believe he was in danger of losing Nightfall."

"Why did you refuse?" Vivian asked.

Her mouth opened, then closed abruptly. "I've said all I'm going to say. Now, get out. I've given you enough of my time. I'm sure you're shocked by my way of life."

"Why should we be?" I asked.

"I'm not certain how you mean that, but I'm going to enlighten you about this business I have developed. What I do is approved in all circles, small and large, poor and wealthy. I have too many friends to count. I do my business fairly, morally and I am held in the highest regard. I supply a vital need—on both sides. The young men and the girls. From my endeavors are created years of happiness for both parties with no heartbreak for anyone. These are fine girls, besmirched only because of traces of alien blood, a state of affairs that is abominable, but it will not change in my lifetime. These girls could never

177

marry except below the class which they have attained. So I give them a chance at happiness. Whether you like it or not, every word is the truth."

I said, "Mama, we understand. We came here because we wanted to see and talk to the woman who gave us life. There was nothing more to it than that. We grieved over an empty grave. We wanted to know the reason for it."

Vivian said, "I thought papa might have murdered you."

"I wish he had," mama said. "Now, get out. Don't come back. Remember—I'm dead."

I bit my lip in exasperation, seized Vivian's hand and we turned and walked out. We were both in tears before we reached the street to search for a carriage.

We locked the door of our hotel room, removed our masquerade finery and sat down to discuss our visit to a mother who showed us not a trace of affection.

"What can we do now?" Vivian asked.

"Go home, as she directed. Remain away from her. Consider her dead."

Vivian said, "You're right. It wouldn't surprise me that if we tried to see her again, she'd have us escorted out of the place forcibly."

"As far as the plantation is concerned," I said, "we're back in business and we've bested Yvonne. At least, for the time being."

"Forever, I hope."

"So do I."

For a change, Vivian was the first in bed. I sat by the window in darkness. Sounds of revelry drifted up from the street, yet they didn't intrude on my thoughts. They were somber, going back to the burning of the barn, which started a chain of events that led to our being in a hotel room in New Orleans. It had also led us to our mother, who openly resented our presence and ordered us from her business establishment. We were to consider her dead.

"What is it, Heather?" I was startled by Vivian's voice, believing her to be asleep.

"I was just sitting here thinking."

"What about?"

"Alex. Papa. Yvonne DesChamps. Mama."

"And Rolf. You love him, don't you?"

"I wasn't thinking of him."

"You were. You love him. I think he loves you too."

"That's nonsense."

"It isn't. He has great respect for you. He admires women who have learned how to use their brains. He told me."

"What kind of talk is that?"

"Woman talk, I guess. I wish, for Rolf's sake, I could be brainy like you. I wish I could be like you in every way because he admires everything about you. He says you're warm, compassionate and have all the desirable qualities a woman should—"

"Stop it, Vivian," I commanded. I got up and walked over to the bed.

"I have to say it. I have to tell you. I want terribly to grow up. The best way is to be honest. I know that now. I'm frightened, Heather. When I saw mama tonight, saw how hard and unfeeling she was, I realized that's how I was. I schemed to get Rolf. I lied to him. But it wasn't only because of the plantation. It wasn't only because he paid no attention to me. Alex didn't either, but that didn't matter. It hurt that Rolf didn't. And do you know why it hurt?"

"Yes."

"You don't."

"I know, Vivian. You love him."

"It's so hopeless. It's like a great big pain inside. I hurt all over and it's a strange kind of hurt."

How well I knew her agony. But I'd not admit my love for Rolf to her. It would only make her more miserable. I had gripped the brass knob at the foot of the bed, but I let go and went to sit in the chair on her side of the bed.

"I think it's Rolf's pride that's been hurt," I said. "I'll ask a question that's very personal, if I may."

"You may."

"Was he loving after your marriage?"

"Yes." Her voice grew tremulous. "He made me feel like a queen. And I worshiped him. He was so tender and considerate."

"Then be assured you won his heart. You must be patient. Don't plead or beg him to come to you. And don't

179

try to flirt with him. The time will come when once again he'll make you feel like a queen. Just now, we're all under a strain. None of us is thinking straight, but we're trying to. I believe Alex is the most steadying influence we have."

"I was so unkind to him the night of the ball." Vivian actually sounded ashamed.

"Yes, you were. And if it weren't for Alex, you might not have got the reception you did on your return. He told me to behave like a woman."

"Alex said that?"

"Oh, I'm not perfect, Vivian. I resented your trickery. I felt you and Rolf should have told me what you were about to do."

"I was afraid you would forbid me to elope," she replied, "so soon after papa's death."

"I'd probably have tried to reason with you, using that as one of the arguments."

"We'd have quarreled again."

"Yes," I agreed. "I'm tired of quarreling and being lonely and pretending I'm so brave when I'm scared to death. Just as mama's scared."

Vivian sat up in that quick manner she had when I made a statement that caught her unawares. "Mama, scared?" she exclaimed.

"Yes. Remember when you told her you thought papa might have murdered her when we discovered the empty casket?"

"Yes."

"What did she say?"

"That she wished he had."

"Her voice was filled with agony. The agony of loneliness. She's not really happy. She's in business to keep busy, to forget her loneliness. She had a reason for saying she wished he had killed her. I'd like to know what it was."

"So would I. But she'd never tell us."

"Not if we leave tomorrow. But suppose we stay over."

"She won't see us."

"That's something we're going to find out."

And on that note, we retired and slept the entire night. I suppose because of exhaustion, but I'd like to think it was because we'd not admit defeat.

Fifteen

THE NIGHT'S REST HAD DONE VIVIAN A LOT OF GOOD. At least, I thought so, for she was bright and cheerful as we dressed and later when we breakfasted in the downstairs dining room. We had a window table which gave a view of the passersby. The townspeople, in their street finery, occupied our attention as we sipped our coffee.

"Would you like to live here?" Vivian asked.

"It's a fascinating city," I admitted. "But I love the quiet and beauty of the country."

"I wonder if mama likes it," Vivian mused.

"Who knows what she likes?"

"What do you mean?"

"I have a feeling mama wears a perpetual mask."

"I don't know what you mean."

"I'm not sure I do either. But I think she keeps so busy that she has no time to think of how unhappy she is."

Vivian pondered that a moment. "How are you going to contact her?"

Though Vivian didn't know it, I'd wakened at dawn and tried to think of a way of doing so. I hadn't and so decided to tell the truth.

"I haven't been able to figure out a way."

"Then let's go home. Why bother her? She doesn't want us around. Why should we want to see her again?"

"Because we wouldn't be on this earth if it weren't for her and I'm not completely satisfied she has no love for us."

"What you're saying is that she feels it's better for her to remain dead, as far as Rutford is concerned. She'd only be an embarrassment to us."

"Yes. She puzzles me." I paused and smiled as I added, "Just as you often puzzle me."

"Papa spoiled mama just as he spoiled me," Vivian said.

"Perhaps when they were first married," I reasoned. "But then he neglected her in his ambition to become a successful plantation owner. He didn't realize it until too late."

"But why did he spoil me?"

She smiled as I started to protest.

"I know he did, Heather, so don't play a game with me."

"Very well. You're the image of mama. He tried to make it up to you. He told me so when he confessed to the duel with Lemuel DesChamps."

"Let's get back to mama. How are we going to see her?"

"I told you I don't know."

"Do you want to?"

"I don't know that either."

"Then let's go home. I want to be close to Rolf. Oh, I remember what you told me last night. I won't flirt with him or try to lure him into compromising situations. But I'm so unhappy and lonely away from him. Just knowing he's close by will help."

It wouldn't help me, but I could understand her anguish. "Very well. We'll go upstairs and pack."

"First, let us go on a shopping expedition!" she exclaimed, once again the old Vivian now that I'd given in to her.

"We can't afford to!" I exclaimed. "We must be very thrifty."

"Then let's go through the stores as if we were going to make purchases. The windows are so beautiful and exciting."

"Are you sure that will satisfy you?"

"Positive."

I wished I were, but I couldn't resist her appeal. Also, it would take her mind off Rolf for a little while and give us something to chatter about on our journey home.

It was mid-morning when we left the hotel. We visited several shops and, true to her word, Vivian refrained from making any purchases, though she eyed several gowns with longing. And the salesladies viewed her with anticipation, for her fashionable street dress matched her beauty and they expected she would make a large purchase.

It wasn't until we paused before a millinery store that I knew I'd met defeat. There was a soft-brimmed hat trimmed with rows of fine lace that matched Vivian's hair. She cried out in delight at the sight of it, then switched her gaze to me.

When I gave her no encouragement, she said, "At least, let me try it on."

"It probably costs a fortune."

"I'm sure it does," she replied, "but I don't have to buy it."

"Come on."

I led the way inside, knowing if I could possibly do so, I'd purchase it for her. After all, the money was as much hers as mine and it would be something to take her mind off our journey, which had been a complete failure. Well, not complete, I reasoned. We'd found mama. We'd also learned she wanted no part of us. I just wished there was no gnawing doubt in my mind about that.

The clerk and I exclaimed aloud when Vivian put it on, for it seemed made for my beautiful sister.

"What is the price?" I asked the saleslady.

"Forty-five dollars, mademoiselle, but it is a French original and the only one in the whole world."

Vivian appealed to me with her eyes.

I spoke as I opened my handbag. "You must have it, Sister. It was made for you."

She removed it almost reverently and embraced me. I paid for it and asked that it be delivered immediately to the hotel, giving our name.

The clerk bowed us out, assuring us it would be there before we returned. Outside, I paused, wondering which direction to take. I noticed a man leaning against the wall of the building next door. He was a shifty-looking character, branded with a large, badly healed scar that ran from the left corner of his mouth almost all the way to his left ear. For some reason, I thought he was interested in us, not by the attention he paid, but the clumsy lack of it. After we'd passed him by and continued on for two more blocks, I looked back. It was a relief not to see him.

"What's wrong?" Vivian asked.

"Probably nothing. There was an especially ugly man who I thought was watching us."

"Maybe eyeing us is the better word," Vivian said complacently. "I guess we made a mistake carrying our parasols this morning. There isn't much sun. It's a dreary sort of day, if you ask me."

"Even a folded parasol is an asset to a lady's stroll. I see a little shop just ahead that sells trinkets and jewelry. I think we should buy Maggie another sparkling article. Perhaps earrings. Or a bracelet."

We entered the shop and studied the items in the display case, deciding on a pair of hoop earrings with flashing stones in it. It was pretty and modestly priced.

We'd wandered from the center of the business area, and once back on the street, I was confused as to which direction to take.

I questioned Vivian, who said, "I think we should go left."

We did so, but after continuing a few blocks and making a left turn, which Vivian felt might bring us back in the direction from which we came, I was certain we'd made a mistake, for there were no pedestrians and the street was littered with papers and even discarded pieces of broken furniture.

I began to feel uneasy, remembering that man with the ugly scar, the way he'd looked at us, and the fact that he'd disappeared immediately after we passed him by. He could have followed us very easily without our having been aware of it.

It was only the silence of the deserted street that enabled me to hear padded steps behind us. I looked over my shoulder and cried out a warning to Vivian. The man with the scar, accompanied by a bulkier individual, was running toward us and they both held some sort of club. We were going to be attacked. They probably thought we were wealthy and were going to rob us. Or with such weapons, murder would seem more likely.

Though neither Vivian nor I had ever encountered an experience like this before, we reacted instinctively. Our parasols came up. I thrust mine forward in a hard jab aimed at the face of the shorter and the end of the parasol struck him close to his right eye. He emitted a scream of pain and clapped a hand to the injury. He dropped his club and bent over in agony.

Vivian hadn't fared so well. The scarred man had already struck her one blow which glanced off her shoulder. She'd managed to deflect the full force of it with her parasol.

I raised mine now and belabored him with it, striking him across the face. Vivian, her ire aroused, used her parasol like a rapier and she thrust the point of it at the man's throat. This too landed where it did the most damage, and the man turned away, gurgling in pain as he choked from the force of the thrust.

Vivian and I turned in the opposite direction from which we'd been going and began to run. We didn't slow down until we were once again in the crowded area. There we encountered a policeman and told him our story. He took our names and the name of the hotel where we were registered and jotted down a brief résumé of what we told him.

"I'm sorry this happened, but please do not allow it to affect your love for our city," he said. "We have an evil element here, like any other city I'm afraid there's little we can do, though the description of the man with the scarred face may help. If we find him, we shall call upon you at once. Again, mademoiselles, my sincere apologies."

When we reached our room, we unbuttoned our shoes, kicked them off and lay down to catch our breath and rest from our ordeal.

I said, "You'd make a good swordsman. I'm proud of the way you fought back."

"I was terrified," she admitted. "But angry that they'd attack us. I suppose they wanted our money."

"I saw him strike you. Are you hurt?"

"I think I'll have a black-and-blue shoulder. If that club had struck me on the head, I think I'd have been killed. Do you believe they meant to kill us, Heather?"

"I don't know. I'm wondering if their motive was robbery or murder."

"But why? And who would want—" She paused and cried out in dismay, "Mama? Even if she hasn't a spark of feeling for us, do you think she'd hire thugs to kill us?"

"If mama wanted to harm us, she could have seen to it we never got out of that building."

"I think we should leave immediately," Vivian said.

"What about your hat? It hasn't arrived yet."

She sighed. "It probably won't get here until afternoon. I imagine the lady believed we'd be shopping most of the day. I wish I could."

"I'm sure you do. After we've rested, we'll go downstairs, have something to eat, then return and pack our clothes."

"Did you notice the policeman didn't seem at all perturbed by what we told him?" Vivian mused.

"He's probably used to it," I reasoned. "Cities have a great deal of crime."

We recovered after an hour and ate a hearty meal in the large restaurant. So much so that we decided to take a walk to work it off, though we'd be careful not to wander from the busy business sector. We strolled the streets, window-shopping, and I kept a wary eye out for that man with the scar. I was, by now, convinced that we'd been selected by these two men because we entered so many stores. They must have thought we were spending a great deal of money. Perhaps that was the way some robbers worked. Find a victim who was bound to have enough money to make the risk worthwhile. Then the scarred man and his partner had followed up and been fairly clever at it.

They'd not get far if they attacked us again on one of the streets we now chose. There were far too many people about, so we felt safe enough. It was late afternoon before we returned to the hotel. The moment we entered, we saw the man waiting for us. Not the one with the scar, or the other criminal, but the man in the red coat and white trousers who had barred our way to mama's ballroom.

Vivian said curtly, "What's he doing here?"

"Don't make a scene," I warned. "He may only have a message for us."

"I doubt it." Anger edged her voice.

The man, now wearing a nicely cut suit of British origin, unless I was greatly mistaken, bowed slightly and gave us a warm smile.

"Mademoiselles. It is my pleasure to see you again."

"That is difficult to believe," I retorted.

"I only follow orders," he said politely. Then he grew serious. "It has come to the attention of Mademoiselle Taylor that you two lovely ladies were subjected to physical abuse by two robbers this morning. Is that true?"

"How did she learn that?" Vivian asked.

"Mademoiselle Taylor, she knows very much of what goes on in New Orleans. She has asked me to extend her apologies that such a thing would happen to you in our city and she requests that you accompany me that she may speak to you and perhaps discover who is guilty of this most serious crime."

"She asked you to take us to her?" I couldn't believe my ears.

"At once, please. I have a carriage waiting and you will be brought back here at your convenience."

Vivian's surprise matched mine and her curiosity equaled mine, so we left the hotel with this man. A carriage was waiting, and a handsomer one I'd never before seen. The mahogany body was lined in light brown leather with gold stampings. There was a uniformed coachman on the seat and I know Vivian and I felt like royalty as we were driven through the streets in this grand style.

"Just a moment." I expressed immediate concern. "This is not the way to the ballroom."

"But no, mademoiselle. You are to visit at her home. It is in the Vieux Carré, not far from the ballroom."

The attack on us had achieved what I'd been unable to. A visit to mama. The carriage stopped before an iron gate, behind which were so many thick shrubs and trees that it was impossible for the eye to penetrate this maze. I began to develop the idea that perhaps this French Quarter was not quite as shabby as its exterior seemed to indicate.

Our escort opened the gate, closed it after we were through and he went off by himself after indicating with a sweep of his arm that we were to seat ourselves on this patio.

It was very large. So big, in fact, that it had a sidewalk running clear around it. In the midst of this were tables and chairs, and so many colorful flowers and leafy plants that I couldn't count them. Some of these gave off a mild, beguiling aroma. I had never seen a place quite so suited for relaxation.

The house itself was entered through French doors off the patio, and it was through one of these that mama appeared. This time she was dressed in a more simple style. A white gown, high necked and long sleeved, touched with black at the edges. Her hair was modestly and attractively arranged. She wore less powder and rouge, though it seemed to me, on closer inspection, that she required a minimum of either.

"I brought you back because I want to know about the attack made upon you this morning. Was it for the purpose of robbery?"

"Or murder. I thought you sent them," Vivian said sternly.

Mama's eyes widened in shock. "Kill my flesh and blood?"

"We didn't think you cared anything about us," Vivian said.

Mama turned to me. "Did those men want to rob or kill you?"

"We don't know," I said. "They attacked us with clubs."

"Criminals who rob women do not usually use clubs. Their fists are sufficient. It is more likely these men meant to do you serious harm." She looked at Vivian. "I had nothing to do with it. Do you know who would wish you harm?"

I said, "Not in this city. One man followed us for quite a distance before he and his companion set upon us."

Mama clapped her hands once. The man who escorted us here came from somewhere behind the plants and bushes.

"You heard, Marcel?"

"*Oui*. May I ask mademoiselle to describe these men, please."

I said, "One was short and heavyset. I didn't get too good a look at him, but the other man was tall with a wide, lumpy scar from the left corner of his mouth clear up to the left ear."

"Find them," mama said.

"*Oui*, mademoiselle. At once." He hurried away.

188

"I want to know why you were attacked, why singled out," mama said. "I do not like this. There has to be a reason. We shall see. In a few moments my maid will bring you coffee and cakes. You will remain on the patio until Marcel returns."

"We will not have your company even for this short time?" I asked.

"I am busy. You will be comfortable. Ask for anything you wish."

I could have wished for just a little more warmth from this woman who was our mother, but apparently that was not to be. As she swept across the patio and into the house—which I would have dearly loved to see—a maid emerged from another door and served us tiny, delicate cups of coffee, strong and hot. There were little cakes of a quality I had never tasted before.

Vivian looked at me after she'd eaten one. "I don't know if mama made those, but if she did, I wish she'd come home."

I smiled, glad Vivian took mama's indifference so lightly.

"I'm beginning to think," she said, "that mama is wealthy and influential and we are underestimating her."

"Not her disposition or her nature," I argued. "Money and influence, of course. Otherwise, how could she afford a home like this? And how would she have learned of the attack on us so promptly?"

An hour must have passed. Vivian and I relaxed in the beautiful surroundings, limiting our conversation to our observations of the city. The maid replenished our coffee and supplied us with more of those tantalizing small cakes. Mama never came near us. I told myself it didn't matter. I was already inured to it.

I heard loud voices somewhere inside the house and then Marcel appeared holding the scar-faced man by the scruff of the neck. Mama followed and behind her came two more men grasping the arms of the chunky assailant bearing a black eye from contact with my parasol.

Mama said, "Can you identify them?"

"Yes," I said. "The swollen eye of that one was caused by a jab from my parasol. The other is easily recognized by the scar. I have no doubt."

"Nor have I," Vivian said. "How did you find them when the police were unable to?"

"Because the police did not look for them," mama said. "Besides, I have sources of information the police do not. Do you still think they attacked you only to get your money?"

"I can't see any other reason," I said.

"I don't think so." Mama faced the one with the scarred face. "You—it is best that you tell us who hired you to harm these girls."

"Nobody," he grumbled. "We don't hire out."

"Liar." Mama turned to the chunky one. "You—what have you to say?"

"Nothing. I was not even there."

"Marcel, take the one with the scarred face and see if he will not oblige us with the truth. If he does not, take care of the matter. Then return for this fat one—also a liar—and give him the same treatment."

The scarred man was propelled from the patio to somewhere in the house. After a short time we heard him scream and then yell again in terrible agony. The chunky man was growing paler. His hands shook, his mouth was partly open and stark fear was beginning to develop in his eyes.

Mama said, "It will be your turn next. You'd better talk."

"I am innocent. I was passing by and mistaken for the one who attacked these girls. I swear I was there only by accident."

There was one more sharp scream, cut off in its midst. The chunky man tottered over to a chair and collapsed in it. Marcel and the two men returned, grim faced.

Mama said, "He did not speak?"

"No, mademoiselle, nor will he ever speak again."

"Bien," she said coldly. "Take this one out now. If he does not speak, give him the same treatment. And, Marcel, when you're finished with them, be sure they don't float."

"Mademoiselle," the chunky man said. "Please . . . I am innocent—"

His plea fell on deaf ears. Marcel seized him by the collar and hoisted him out of the chair. His two assistants closed in. The chunky man sagged in their grasp.

"I do not know who he was, mademoiselle. I swear I do not know him."

"Who?" mama asked.

"We were paid twenty dollars each to . . . scare these girls."

"Scare them? With clubs? That proves you lie. Take him out of here, Marcel."

"We were to kill them," the man blubbered. "That is the truth. We were to kill them and make it seem we killed only to rob them."

"That's a little better. Did you see this man with his bribes?"

"I saw him. We both did."

"Describe him. And remember this. If what you say is not the absolute truth, you are finished. Do you understand that?"

"*Oui*, I will tell you the truth. He was not old. Maybe twenty-two or three. He was handsome and rich. His hair was dark, maybe dark brown. His eyes were also brown. He met us in a saloon. If we succeeded, we would each get fifty more."

Mama looked at me. "Does the description fit anyone you know?"

I nodded, horrified at what I'd heard. "It could."

Mama gestured. The chunky man was hustled out. Mama sat down.

"Now, tell me who it could have been."

"The description could fit Joel DesChamps," I said, "Yvonne's son."

Mama's features hardened. "First she does in your father, then she brings legal proceedings, which fail. She has nothing left but to resort to violence. I didn't know she was such a vindictive and dangerous woman."

"We did," I said. "And we'll be on guard from this moment."

Vivian seemed badly shaken by the revelation. "She won't stop until she's killed us. She'll never give up."

"No doubt," mama said. "And she is clever enough to insure that you will be unable to supply any proof. If we brought charges against this Joel, we would have only the word of the two ruffians he hired, and their word is worth nothing."

"We shall be very, very careful," I vowed. "With the help of Alex—"

"Who is he?" mama asked sharply.

"Jacob's son."

"Jacob? Oh, yes, I remember him. He did have a son. I'm glad he is alive and still at the plantation. Then there is your husband, Vivian. At least you have some protection." She arose and looked down at us. "Good afternoon. I have done my best to uncover this plot against you by a woman whose hatred has robbed her of sanity. You are now forewarned. You have no further need of me. I suggest that you go home. At once. There you will have the protection of three men."

She turned and entered the house, closing the French door behind her.

Vivian got up. "We'll go home now."

I said, "I want you to do something and don't question it. Leave the patio by the door to the street. It is of metal. Let it clang shut behind you."

"But what—?"

"No questions. Do as I say."

For once, she was too puzzled to do other than obey. The door made a metallic ring as she closed it. I had, by this time, moved up to the French door which mama had closed. I cupped my hands to my face and peered inside.

Mama lay on a large chaise and I could see her shoulders rise and fall as she wept softly. I opened the door soundlessly. The carpeted floor gave no hint of my approach. When I stood beside the chaise, I spoke quietly and unemotionally.

"You can stop crying now, Mama. You're a good actress, but I saw through your charade."

"Oh, no!" she exclaimed through her tears. She stopped crying and looked up at me.

"Oh, yes," I replied quietly.

She sat up, took a handkerchief from her pocket and dried her eyes. "How did you guess?"

"Guess what?" I asked.

"That I love you both."

"It wasn't difficult," I said. "Perhaps you tried too hard to pretend your indifference, though you had just about persuaded me you didn't care about your daughters."

"Where did I fail?" she persisted. "What did I say that gave me away?"

"The other night, when Vivian said she thought papa had killed you, you replied that you wished he had. It wasn't the words that gave me pause for thought, but the way you said them. You were tortured."

"Where is your sister?"

"I'll get her. She helped me play a game that enabled me to uncover the real you."

I went outside and summoned Vivian, who stood at the gate, both fearful and puzzled.

"What's going on?" she asked.

"Come inside. Mama wants to see you."

She made no move to obey, saying, "That's difficult to believe."

I reached for her hand and pulled her onto the patio. The gate clanged behind us. "Mama is waiting for you. Hurry."

Her features were a mixture of doubt and hope, but her steps now matched mine. Once we entered the house and mama's arms extended at the sight of her, she uttered a cry of delight and ran to her.

They embraced, then mama released her and embraced me. Finally, we settled down and began to talk coherently. Mama was in full control of her emotions and she held one of our hands in each of hers.

"Thank you, girls, for forgiving me. I pretended disinterest because I didn't want to embarrass you. Nowhere but in New Orleans would the work I do be accepted by society. But that's today. It was in my yesterday that I left your papa, because I had hardened my heart to him. I suppose if he'd allowed your aunt to bring you back, I'd have softened. I like to think I would have, but I don't know. I felt he'd disgraced me and himself by the duel which cost Lemuel DesChamps his life. Your papa refused to allow you to come back because I had changed so. And he was right. I had. I was drinking. I wanted to forget. I was a fool. I fell for a weakling because of loneliness. I believed the lies he whispered into my ear. But I was not an adulteress and I felt that all of Rutford believed I was because of the duel."

"That's over now, Mama," I said. "We must live in the present."

"I want you to live. But Yvonne DesChamps evidently has other ideas and is using her son to carry them out. I only wish that when your papa wrote asking for financial aid, I had given it. He'd be alive today if I had. I'm as guilty of his death as he was of Lemuel DesChamps'. Now I've endangered your lives."

"Jacob, Alex and Rolf will watch over us," I said. "Won't you come back with us?"

"Never. Your papa buried me. Let me stay buried. Just remember, I love you both. I refused your papa financial aid because he had deprived me of both of you years ago. I wanted to love you and I wanted your love in return."

"You have it, Mama," I assured her.

"Yes, and I don't derserve it. What a terrible thing pride is. It is as destructive as hate."

"May we tell Maggie and the men that you are alive?" I asked. "It will be difficult for us to return unless we do. They know the reason for our journey here."

"You may." She worried a jade ring from her finger and handed it to Vivian. "Give this to Maggie. She was always kind to me and I know she regards you as her own. Jacob will look after you. He held your papa in high esteem, but he's fair minded and will bear me no grudge."

She released her hold on us and stood up. "Just remember that I love you both. Come visit me when you can. Bring your husband, Vivian. I wish to see him as a man. I remember the Fieldings. And their son. A handsome lad. Orphaned so young. Another tragedy.

"And you, Heather," she regarded me with motherly concern. "Have you met no one who has captured your heart? Or are you too serious—like your papa?"

"I'm serious, Mama," I replied. "And with good reason."

"Yes." She understood. "Love will come. Be patient."

I nodded, pleased the ache in my heart didn't reveal itself in my eyes.

Mama sighed, then favored us with a smile. The harshness so evident in her face the previous night had gone and her features were soft with the love she bore us.

"I will embrace each of you once more," she said, "then I will leave the room. Marcel will bring you back to your hotel and he will remain to take you to the train.

With so many people around, you will be safe. Just send a telegram to Nightfall, stating when you will arrive."

She held us close and smiled through her tears, then turned abruptly and left the room. We exited through the French doors. When we reached the street, Marcel awaited us. This time we rode in a landau, of equally expensive trappings. The seats were covered with moiré satin. Marcel sat facing us and the landau made a majestic drive through the streets.

To my amazement, people waved and smiled. Some called out friendly greetings. It was all so spontaneous and genuine that I was astonished.

"Does mademoiselle have so many friends?" I asked.

"*Oui*, very many," he replied.

"But she's not with us. Yet they seem to think she is, or they act that way."

"Mademoiselle, your sister, she is the image of Mademoiselle Jessica. Perhaps they are mistaken. And take your lovely sister for your mama."

"Do they really think I'm mama?" Vivian asked, highly pleased at the compliment.

"It would seem so." Marcel looked as amused as we.

"Bow nicely—mama," I said with mock seriousness.

We made no attempt to stem the hysteria that convulsed us. It was the release we needed. One of the first light moments for me since the burning of the barn.

Sixteen

OUR RETURN JOURNEY WAS SHEER DELIGHT BECAUSE Vivian and I were closer than we'd ever been. Happiness overwhelmed us now that we knew mama had never ceased to love us. I'd been right in believing she'd kept very busy to forget her loneliness. As I said to Vivian, every individual on this earth needed the love of another human being.

She agreed, then made one of her surprising statements. "You miss papa, don't you?"

"Just as much as you," I replied.

She nodded. "I know you love me and Maggie does too, even though I irritate her at times. But papa was especially nice to me."

"After seeing mama, don't you know why?"

"I can see how I reminded him of her. It must have been hard for him."

"I suppose it was, but it's a credit to him you never knew."

"What do you mean?"

"He might have hated you."

"And with good reason, considering what mama did. That awful Lemuel DesChamps making up to her."

"In her innocence she mistook his flattering attentions for love."

"Isn't it sad, Sister, how one person's weakness can make trouble for so many people?"

"Change their entire lives," I said soberly. "And endanger others."

Vivian gave a delicate shudder. "Let's not get morose. Talk about something pleasant."

"Like the compartment mama secured for us?" I ran my hand over the soft, plush seat. "It's elegant. So is the hatbox."

Vivian was seated facing me, the box beside her. She patted it gently. "I love what's inside."

"You should, considering the cost. But it's worth it. Wait till Rolf sees it on you."

She lowered her eyes and regarded her clasped hands. "I'd like to think wearing it would exercise some sort of magic that would lure him back to me."

"*You* will have to do that," I said. "But very discreetly."

"I'm not clever like you, Heather. But I hope one day I will be. We got along very well all the time we were away, didn't we?"

"We had to. We had no one but each other and our mission was an important one." The train whistle hooted twice and we began to slow.

"We'd better put on our gloves," I said. "We're coming into Rutford."

We did so, also pinning on our hats. Vivian carried the hatbox as if it were a delicate piece of china. She loved beautiful things and I hoped she'd never be deprived of them.

I'd sent the telegram as mama had ordered and was pleased to see Alex waiting at the station to greet us. He stowed the baggage beneath the seats, then he helped Vivian into the back seat. I handed her up the hatbox and she set it alongside her, anchoring it firmly with the palm of her hand. I sat in the front seat with Alex.

He cast a smile my way as he started the horses in motion. "You look well and happy."

"We have reason to," I said. "Our mission was a success."

"You found your mother?" he asked.

"We did. But we'll let the telling wait until the four of us are together."

"Rolf insisted on remaining at the plantation to help my father. He said he has so much to learn and he'll learn more there than at his own place."

"That's a tribute to your father," I said.

"Yes," Alex agreed. "But it's also an indication of Rolf's modesty. He feels the overseer on his plantation wouldn't be so apt to tell him when he's doing something wrong. Not so with my father. I know. When I returned from college, where I studied agriculture and farming, he made it quite clear I had much to learn in actual experience. And he was right. Rolf realizes that also."

"I hope there was no more trouble."

"None," Alex replied. "Perhaps Yvonne DesChamps has had her revenge and will let you alone."

"I'm not so sure, but since that's part of the story, it can also wait until Rolf is present."

"And Maggie," Alex added with a smile. "She reminds me of a mother hen who's lost her chicks. She's worried about you every minute since you left."

"It's understandable," I said, laughing. "She raised us and I guess she thinks of us as her own."

"Be assured she does."

Vivian didn't utter a word during the entire ride. I knew her thoughts were on Rolf and she was wondering what kind of reception she would get. It was on my mind also. Maggie must have been watching or listening for the carriage, for she was standing in the drive as Alex drew up. She embraced us both, eyed each of us carefully to see that nothing was amiss, then sent us into the house with an admonishment to freshen up.

We didn't need to be told twice. We were glad to get out of our travel clothes, soak in a warm tub and dress in something soft and dainty. I chose a simple voile. Vivian, a beige organdy, sashed with a large bow, the ends of which almost reached the tops of her shoes.

Maggie had a table set on the side porch which was screened and shaded by magnolias. A pitcher of iced lemonade, plus salads, rested on a serving table and Alex, in a white suit, was filling the tall glasses. Vivian had come down before me and she and Alex were serving the salads and cold cuts.

When I saw my plate heaped with food, I exclaimed in dismay. "You're worse than Maggie," I scolded. "If I eat all that, I'll not get into my clothes."

"If you don't eat it all, you'll hurt Maggie's feelings," Rolf said. "She worked all morning preparing it, making it just the way you both like it."

It was delicious and we did justice to it. I asked Alex to have his father join us, but he replied the hands needed someone to oversee them. Maggie hovered about the table, seeing that when one hot roll disappeared from our bread-and-butter dish, another was placed there. Lemon meringue pie topped our meal, and it was delicious.

While we ate, we told Alex and Rolf of our efforts at finding mama, our success in doing so and her rebuff. They listened attentively, as did Maggie—without seeming to—and evidenced no shock at any phase of my story. That is, not until I related the incident of the two men who attempted to flay us with the thick, heavy sticks they carried.

"How did such a thing happen?" Rolf asked.

"Did you stray from the center of the city?" Alex added his question to Rolf's.

"Yes, though purely by accident, and we thought their motive was robbery, for they were ill-dressed, evil-looking men. But we managed to fight them off, though Vivian's shoulder was bruised. She didn't manage to deflect the full force of the blow with her parasol, but it helped. However, we kept our wits about us and inflicted enough pain on the two so that we were able to flee. We ran at a speed we didn't think ourselves capable of."

I noticed Rolf gave Vivian a look of concern, though he made no comment. I was pleased that her manner remained calm, though I knew his casual manner cut deeply. However, she wasn't being babyish, nor was she doing anything to curry his favor. The fact that she helped him fill our plates while they talked of the fascination of New Orleans pleased me as much as it surprised me. However, it also told me there'd been no affectionate reunion.

I went on with my tale, stating we had believed the men were ruffians who sought to take advantage of two young women they'd observed going in and out of stores and believed they carried a considerable sum of money on them. They had no way of knowing we'd made only one purchase. "However, later that day," I went on, "Mama sent her servant to bring us to her."

"What do you know 'bout that?" Maggie observed. She stood on the opposite side of the table, facing me, drinking in every word I spoke.

"I didn't know what to make of it, but we lost no time accepting. We'd wanted to see her again, but couldn't figure out a way of reaching her, since her dismissal was so final and so cold. In a way, I'm glad those ruffians set upon us. Except for Vivian's injured shoulder, of course."

"It's really not that painful," she said. "Please go on with the story, Heather."

"Anyway, we were pleasantly surprised to see mama's home. It is luxurious and furnished in excellent taste—the one room we saw. But mama was aware of the incident and was greatly concerned about us."

Alex said, "She may have been having you guarded, without your knowledge."

I looked my surprise. "I never thought of that."

"I apologize for the interruption," Alex said. "You were speaking of your mother's concern."

"She questioned us regarding the men and we gave a description. Mama had a man named Marcel listening. She sent him out to get the two, which seemed rather like a fool's errand to me. But in no time he was back with them. I would rather not think what was done to one, but his cries persuaded his companion to talk. He described a man who might well be Joel DesChamps."

Alex said, "How did he come into it?"

"He bribed them each with twenty dollars to attack and kill us. If they were successful, they would each get fifty more."

Alex and Rolf looked their anger.

"Of course," I went on, "we'll never be able to prove it."

"Why not?" Rolf asked.

"As mama said, who would take the word of two ruffians against that of Joel DesChamps?"

"True," Alex agreed. "But it will put us on guard. Obviously, the fact that Rolf put up the money for Nightfall is more than Mrs. DesChamps can tolerate."

"She's determined to destroy us," I said. "I'm sure she's already planning ways and means of getting her hands on the plantation. At the same time, she's thinking up some intrigue for getting rid of Vivian and me."

"She'll not succeed," Rolf said. "I think we should inform Deputy Sheriff Oliver about the incident in New Orleans and what that man revealed."

"It would be a useless gesture," I said. "Perhaps you don't know it, but she has donated money to build a hospital in Rutford, plus the land on which to build it."

Alex's head moved slowly from side to side in wonderment. "She thinks of everything."

"She's schemed for years to get her revenge for what papa did to her husband. I only hope she doesn't know mama's alive."

"So do I." For the first time, alarm tinged Vivian's voice. "Mama should be warned."

I smiled, thinking of Marcel and his aides. "Mama is well protected. But she'll be on guard."

Vivian was still not reassured. "Do you suppose Mrs. DesChamps had us followed while we were in the city? And she knows about mama?"

"Anything is possible with that woman," Alex said. "We can only hope, if she did, that she thought that your going to that ballroom was the mischievous act of two adventurous young ladies."

"It would be a relief to think that," I said.

"Mama wishes to remain dead so far as Rutford is

concerned," Vivian said. "She feels she'd be an embarrassment to us because of the business she has established. It's not acceptable anywhere else."

"I'd like her to come back anyway," I said. "But New Orleans is such a sophisticated city—so gay and fun loving, I doubt she could adjust to the quiet of a plantation again."

"I believe you're right," Vivian said. "She made the proper decision."

Alex said, "Well, at least you're back and safe. I was waiting for you ladies to return so we could discuss a little business. It concerns getting a loan from the bank for sorely needed equipment."

"Of course," I agreed. "I thought you'd already done it."

"We need your signature."

"May I be excused?" Vivian asked. "I'm travel weary and would like to rest. You can handle it, Heather."

"Yes," I admitted. "But first, I would like to see your father, Alex. We're all one family now. We must stick together."

"He's in the kitchen," Maggie said. "He wouldn't come out here 'cause he's in work clothes."

"Then you'll excuse me. And run along, Vivian. Take your nap. You deserve it. I'm still too excited that all went well while we were gone to feel fatigue."

I headed for the kitchen, eager to see Jacob and discuss the plantation with him. He greeted me heartily and we sat at the kitchen table while I repeated everything I'd told Alex, Rolf and Maggie. He was as pleased as the others at how things had turned out.

My thoughts switched to the plantation. "Now—what of the crop?"

"If you're not too tired, Heather, I'd like you to walk with me to the nearest field. You should see for yourself."

And so, presently, I stood looking over the tops of the man-high stalks of tobacco.

"It's been a fine year so far," he said. "No hail, no blight, even the pesty insects weren't too bad. The weather never turned heavy and all the tobacco plants had to do was grow. And grow they did."

He led me between the rows of the green plants, which were now beginning to fade to a ripe yellow. The leaves, when exactly matured, would be cut from the stalks, beginning at the bottom. Then there'd be a wait for the higher leaves to mature, which meant there were five and six harvests from each plant.

Jacob reached down to pull a sucker from the junction of a stalk and a leaf. "We've got a fair crop in two of the curing sheds now and the flues have been going. We can walk down there and look them over, if you like. I've got all the hands I need for the harvest and then some. They were glad to come back. Every one of 'em felt real bad when they thought you were going to lose the place."

"In good years, papa always paid a bonus. If this year turns out as well as we expect, they'll also get one. You can tell them that."

We cleared the first field and turned in the direction of the fourteen large curing sheds. Wisps of smoke came from one of them and we headed there. Jacob opened the door and we stepped back to let the entrance clear of the smoke from the flues. Inside, it was incredibly hot, as it should be. Jacob snatched a leaf from one of the sticks hanging from the rafters. We lost no time getting back to the sunlight and open air. I was already drenched with perspiration from those few seconds inside.

Jacob handed me a piece of the leaf and, as I'd so often seen papa do, I examined it to make certain it was a rich brown. Then I crumpled it between my fingers to find it satisfactorily crisp. When the curing process was finished, the leaves would then be baled, allowed to absorb moisture to their normal content and finally shipped to the auction rooms.

"What do you hear of the cigarette machines?" I asked Jacob.

"Not much. They've been working on them, but so far they haven't turned out anything worthwhile. It's coming, though. Likely next year we'll see the first of them. I can't wait."

"It would be a boon to our plantation," I said. "Thanks for all you're doing, Jacob."

His only reply was, "The day before your papa died, he said we'd have the best crop yet. I'm going to see that we do."

I strolled back to the barn, hoping Alex would be there. I wanted to discuss more in detail about the working of the plantation, but he was nowhere in sight. But I did catch a glimpse of Rolf, once again in work clothes and heading for the field. I called his name. He stopped and waited for me to approach.

"We've not had a moment to talk since you returned after your elopement," I said. "Would you mind taking a little longer from work? Can you give me a little time?"

"As much as you want, Heather," he said graciously.

"Let's go to the summer house. I've been in the curing shed with Jacob and I'm still soaked with perspiration."

He laughed. "I know what you mean."

We directed our steps to the gazebo and I repeated what Jacob had told me about the crop. Rolf agreed, adding, "I've learned so much about the planting of and caring for tobacco in the brief time I've been here. You have experts in Jacob and Alex."

"We're very fortunate," I agreed. "Blessed, I might say."

We'd reached the summer house and we took seats on either side of the center table.

"I suppose you're referring to finding your mother," he said.

"That too," I said. "But I meant it in the sense that papa had the foresight to find someone like Jacob, who stayed with him through the years, and taught Alex all he knows."

"Alex knows almost as much as his father and applies it too."

"We've been blessed in another sense also. You."

His face shadowed, but even so, it did nothing to detract from his handsomeness. Being in the sun had bronzed his fair skin, adding to his masculinity. His blond hair, with a soft wave, had already begun to show signs of bleaching, again from the sun. It was only with difficulty that I brought my mind back to my reason for bringing him here.

"I really feel I've not expressed my appreciation to the extent I should for what you've done for us. Without your financial aid, neither Jacob nor Alex would be here. There'd be no need for them."

"I did only what I wanted to do and I don't want thanks. I'm married to your sister. As a member of the family, it was to my interest to save this land. Your father worked too hard to lose it."

"Of course, he didn't know he was playing into the hands of Mrs. DesChamps. Not until it was too late."

"Did he know she held the notes?"

"I have a feeling he did. Though not until near the end." I spoke slowly, thinking back to the night of the fire. "It wouldn't surprise me but that she had, in some devious way, warned him that the hour of reckoning was at hand."

"Amazing how that woman has hidden her true self through the years. I really thought I knew her."

"She's very clever. We'll have to go some to outwit her."

"The four of us should be able to."

I was pleased he'd included Vivian. "I wish you could have seen the way your wife conducted herself when we were set upon by those hoodlums."

"I wasn't referring to your sister. I was thinking of Jacob."

Though there was no change in his voice, his eyes revealed quiet resentment.

"I think Vivian should be included in our efforts to thwart any further destruction Yvonne DesChamps has in mind."

"Even if she were interested, I doubt she'd be capable," Rolf said.

"I don't agree, but neither do I want to quarrel with you about her. If you feel so bitter toward her, how can you stay here?"

"Not to protect my investment," he said. "So far as I'm concerned, it was not a loan. Vivian is my lawfully wedded wife and I want to see her with a roof over her head."

"Under such circumstances, I will consider your generosity only as a loan. It would be nothing short of immoral to accept such a sum of money. Vivian would no more do so than I."

"That's not true," he said. "She married me to save the plantation."

"I won't dispute that, because she admitted it."

"I don't want to talk about it." He stood up and headed

204

for the steps, but I moved quickly and blocked his path. My hands gripped his arms.

"You must talk about it. Or, at least, you must listen. My sister loves you. She's miserable and you've made her so."

"She lied to me the night before we eloped. She told me you were going to marry Alex. She said you loved him. She added how pleased she was that you would be taken care of. She told me she was going to Richmond and try to find work of some kind. I told her there was no need for that. I would furnish the money for the plantation and she could remain here. I was certain Jacob would look after the crop and her. I was glad to know that at least you would be taken care of. I figured, after a suitable time of mourning, I would court her."

"I appreciated your offer of help that morning," I said. "But I fear I'm cursed with too much pride. Even if love were involved," I took care that I not express my true feelings for him, "I'd not have accepted money from you."

"Your sister wasn't so reticent. That morning, when I went upstairs, she professed her love for me. Believing her, I proposed and suggested we elope. In that way, you couldn't refuse the money."

"I think you're the one who did her a disfavor by marrying her and not loving her."

"But I did love her," he said fiercely. "I've always loved her. But I felt she'd not be content with the love of one man. No man wants a flirtatious woman for a wife."

"And so you'd settle for second best," I said, managing a smile.

"What are you talking about?" He regarded me impatiently.

For a moment, I was too stunned to reply. I realized I'd been consumed by conceit, one as great or greater than Vivian with her regard for her beauty. Rolf didn't love me. He never had. It had always been Vivian.

I shrugged. "I'm not quite sure. I'm as confused as you."

His features softened. "Do you think I'd be such a cad as to propose marriage to you without loving you just so that Vivian would have a roof over her head?"

"You are very gallant, Rolf. Also, noble."

"And still damn mad at my wife for lying to me."

I regarded him thoughtfully, wondering if I dare bare my foolish thoughts. I had no choice. We had enough problems without the friction between Rolf and Vivian adding to them.

"Vivian thought you loved me."

"What?"

I laughed at his bewilderment. "That's exactly what she thought. The reason she gave was that you were always staring at me when I wasn't looking at you, but you never gave her a glance."

"I deliberately ignored her because of the reason I stated."

"And pretended your interest in me was more than friendship?"

"No," he replied. "I have always had tremendous admiration for your intelligence. Most women in our set are determined to catch a husband by any means they can. Either they flirt or they pretend disinterest."

"As you did with Vivian," I interposed.

"Yes," he admitted.

"You know," I went on, giving him an arch look, "even Alex thought you loved me. And so did papa. I suppose they misinterpreted your admiring glances."

"I'm afraid they did," he said. "With me, it was always Vivian. I know she's frivolous and that she dislikes unpleasantness of any kind and loves dressing up. But despite all those things, I love her."

"Even when you act as if you hate her?"

"I despise deceit. Or lies. Vivian dotes on such."

I regarded him with dismay. "If you ever make your peace with her, you may as well know she will always play teasing games with you. Unless," I added, "you assert yourself, so she will know just how far she can go."

"At present, I'm not certain I'll stay once the crop is gathered and sold."

I tried pleading with him. "Think of what pride has done to this family. It's been one tragedy piled on top of another. Are you going to make Vivian suffer as mama and papa suffered?"

"Heather," he smiled down at me to soften what he was about to say, "my marriage with Vivian should not concern you in any way, and I'm sure you know why."

"Suppose you tell me, then there'll be no question in my mind."

"Very well. I will. It's none of your business." He spoke quietly but firmly.

I felt my face flush with color, but I managed a smile. At least, I tried, but I'm sure it was more of a grimace.

He grasped my shoulders lightly. "I didn't mean to hurt you. But I happen to be a very honest person. You know I respect you, far more than I do my wife. But I love her, despite her shortcomings. Regardless of that, as of now, I intend to leave her at the proper time. I've already said when that would be. And if you wish, you may repay the loan, as you refer to it."

He bent and kissed my brow. "I'd better get back to work or Jacob will give me a dressing down. And don't think he wouldn't. Are you angry with me?"

"No," I replied. "You put me in my place and you cleared the air. I only hope you will give Vivian—"

"Stop it, Heather." His voice became stern again.

"Run along," I said. "I want to rest here awhile."

"You're not angry?"

I gave his arm a light pat. "You'll probably not believe it, but your talk has done me a great deal of good."

"I wish I felt differently about it," he said. "But I don't and I doubt I ever will."

At least he used the word "doubt," so I felt there was a glimmer of hope for Vivian. But a glimmer was better than nothing. As for me, I'd had my eyes opened. Rolf had never loved me. The very thought of it was embarrassing. I even felt a sense of shame because my thoughts had strayed to him even after his marriage to my sister. Thank goodness, I'd never been alone with him. I may have made a fool of myself. As it was, Rolf, by his frankness, had prevented that.

I sat down listlessly, propped my elbow on the arm of the chair and covered my face with my hand. Tears stung my eyes, but I managed to control them, knowing they'd be shed in self-pity. I don't know how long I sat there. It was only the sound of footsteps that brought me to my senses. I raised my face and looked at Alex, ascending the steps to the summer house.

Concern etched his features at the sight of me. "Are you ill, Heather?"

"No. Just resting."

"Want me to move along?"

"If you have the time, please stay. I was looking for you awhile ago. Instead, I met Rolf. I had a talk with him here."

Alex made no move to sit down until I motioned to the chair Rolf had occupied.

He eyed me critically. "You look as if you've been dealt a severe shock."

"I can't think of a better way of expressing it," I said.

"I don't like to pry, Heather, but where you're concerned, I can't help myself. Did your conversation with Rolf concern Vivian?"

"Yes," I admitted. "He loves her."

Alex looked his surprise.

I couldn't help but smile. "I flattered myself thinking he cared for me. You can laugh if you wish."

"Why should I?" he demanded.

"You wouldn't," I said. "You're too kind. I'm afraid you've spoiled me the way papa spoiled Vivian."

"If concern for you is spoiling you, then I've spoiled you. But you're too level-headed to be spoiled. And you'll accept what you've just learned. You never let your feelings for him be known anyway."

"Vivian guessed, I'm afraid. Though not even to her did I ever admit it."

"Then your secret is safe." He paused, then added, "Were you really looking for me?"

"Yes. I talked with your father and that lifted my spirits."

"Barring a stroke of ill luck, you and Vivian will have no further worries. You can repay Rolf—though he doesn't expect it—and you'll still have enough left over to relax and enjoy life."

"Without Rolf, I don't think Vivian will enjoy anything. She really loves him. And I'm proud of the way she behaved today."

"I think she's growing up," Alex observed.

"What we learned in New Orleans helped us both. We're getting along beautifully."

"I noticed that too," he said with a smile.

"Perhaps our troubles are behind us."

"Don't forget Yvonne," he warned.

"I said 'perhaps.' I fear her."

"After all we believe she's done, you have reason to. I only hope if she is up to more mischief, she'll give herself away or leave a clue that will point directly at her. There's no other way we can convince the authorities of her guilt."

"Let's talk about the plantation."

"There's enough to talk about and it might help to get that woman off your mind. First of all, I'd like you to accompany me to the bank tomorrow. The payroll is due and you'll have to sign the papers. Then there's farm equipment to order. Much of what we're using is beyond repair."

"You know I found some money, but I'd like to keep it for an emergency. Do you think the bank will grant us a loan?" I asked dubiously.

"They have no reason not to, with the plantation owned by Vivian and you."

"What about Rolf?"

"He wants no part of it. He has his own."

"And that's all he has, isn't it?" I asked.

"Yes. But he's not worried. He's been assured by his overseer of a good crop."

"I hope Mrs. DesChamps doesn't transfer her hatred to him."

Alex smiled. "No matter what we talk about, she somehow gets back into the conversation."

"The woman haunts me. And Joel. He seems manly enough, but apparently he's completely under her influence."

"No doubt about it, after the description those men gave of the individual who paid them off to do their dirty work."

"I only hope that woman doesn't know mama is alive," I said. "Not that I'm ashamed of her. I know her business would be held in low regard here, but she commands respect in New Orleans. Yet I know Yvonne DesChamps would hold her up to ridicule, first, through bringing her back to life."

"Don't bring on fresh worries," Alex cautioned. He stood up and extended a hand. "Come on. I'll walk you back to the house."

I placed my hand in his, smiling as I did so. "It's so

comforting talking with you, Alex. I wish you never needed to leave."

"So do I. And you know why."

When I sobered, he added quickly, "Don't worry. I'm not going to force my attentions on you. I know better. While I'm here, I'll be your devoted friend. When I leave, I'll do my best to thrust you from my mind. It won't be so easy to harden my heart against you. But, then, you know what unrequited love is."

I made no answer. There was no need to. We walked in silence to the house.

Seventeen

I WAS UP EARLY AND DRESSED FOR MY JOURNEY INTO THE village with Alex. Maggie told me that Alex said we would leave as soon as I was ready. I asked that she inform him I'd like to depart immediately after breakfast, particularly since I'd slept late and it was almost ten o'clock.

Vivian entered the dining room just as I took a final sip of coffee. She'd pleaded a headache the night before and asked that a tray be sent to her room. I looked in on her later, but her light was out and when I spoke her name softly, there was no answer. I was pleased to know she was sleeping. At least, it meant she wasn't grieving over Rolf's disregard for her. I hoped he'd have a change of heart, but I could think of nothing to say or do to bring it about. He'd told me it was none of my business and he was right. It wasn't.

To my amazement, Vivian was wearing riding clothes.

"Where are you going?" I asked, astonished at her apparel.

"Well, I'm not going to plant daisies," she retorted, her eyes flashing angrily.

"What's wrong with you?"

"Not a thing. Just don't talk to me."

I ignored her request, for her change of behavior was too much to bear.

"Vivian, after what happened to papa, you can't be serious about going for a ride on the plantation."

"That's exactly what I'm going to do."

"With Rolf?"

"With myself," she retorted. "I'll leave Rolf to you."

"Behave yourself," I said sternly.

"You're a fine one to talk about behaving oneself."

"What do you mean?" I demanded.

"Do you really want to know?" Her eyes as well as her voice mocked me.

"I really do."

Her eyes were contemptuous as she said, "It was a very touching scene in the summer house yesterday."

"I don't know what you're talking about."

"Don't you, sister dear?"

"No, I don't, sister dear." My anger was growing with hers.

"Then I'll tell you. I saw my husband kissing you. Before that, I saw you gripping his arms, pleading with him, I suppose, to give me up."

"That's not so. And if you'll listen, I'll tell you."

"I don't want to hear it. If you've finished breakfast, I'd like you to leave the table. Your presence doesn't help my appetite."

"You're very rude."

"You're very sneaky."

"Vivian, let me explain, please."

"No," she shouted. "Get out of this room. I want my breakfast so I can go riding."

I stood up and set my napkin on the table. "Good luck. And keep a sharp eye out."

"I'll ride as fast as the wind. I'll do anything that will take my mind off the trickery of my sister. I thought we could be friends. I thought our quarreling days were over."

"So did I. I also thought you'd grown up. I was wrong."

"Now, what's goin' on?" Maggie came bustling in from the kitchen. She glanced from Vivian to me and back to Vivian. "You two fightin' again? Thought you'd both come to your senses."

211

"So did I," I said.

"Get out!" Vivian's voice was a scream.

"Run along, Heather. Alex is out in front," Maggie said, then turned to Vivian. "You calm down. You eat as upset as you are, you'll just throw it up soon as you get on the horse."

Alex was waiting outside the door, a rifle under his arm.

"Why are you taking a gun?" I asked.

"It's a payroll mission," he said. "I'm riding shotgun. After all that's happened, I'd be stupid not to have a weapon."

He helped me into the carriage and he drove rapidly to the village. There, we tied up in front of the bank and went inside. Mr. Bradley greeted us cordially. We discussed a loan for new farm equipment and were told there would be no problem. While doing that, the payroll was being made ready for us. I asked Alex to wait for it. I left to make my purchases, first at the general store, then the pharmacy.

At my first stop I had quite a wait, for my order was extensive and took time to be filled. There was the coffee to grind, the butter to be cut out of the tubs, pickles to be taken from the barrel. A wheel of cheese teased my nostrils and I ordered a pound. I wandered about the store buying various other items. Maggie loved hard candy so I purchased several flavors to keep her sweet tooth satisfied.

Once the groceries were boxed and I paid for them, the handyman brought them out to the carriage. Alex had ridden it up to the grocery store. I went the few doors down to the pharmacy and made my other purchases. The carriage was in a location where I could keep an eye on it and watch for Alex's return. Since there was no sign of him, I ordered a cherry phosphate and took it to the door, standing just inside as I sipped it.

I finally caught sight of Alex, moving briskly along the street. His pace was much too fast for midday. Especially when the temperature hovered near ninety. He disappeared briefly, then reappeared, carrying the canvas bag. I set my half-finished soda on the counter, picked up the items I bought and met him at the carriage.

"We have to go back immediately," he said, practically lifting me into the carriage.

"What's wrong?" I asked, confused by his abrupt manner.

He didn't reply until we were beyond Main Street and on a dirt road. Then he urged the animals on to a gallop.

"I'm not certain anything's wrong," he replied, raising his voice above the noise of the creaking wheels and horses' hooves. "But I've been following Joel DesChamps. He's been going from one store to another. He entered the tavern, ordered a glass of beer, then presented it to one of the hangers-on there. In fact, he ordered four more for a group of cronies seated at the end of the bar. He went into a dressmaking shop, apparently on an errand for his mother. He entered the grocery store after you left and came out chewing on a piece of candy from a bag he'd purchased. It's as if he wanted to be seen in as many places as possible."

"I still don't understand," I said.

"I got the feeling he's up to mischief of some kind, though I can't figure out what it is. But I feel the wise thing is for us to get back to the plantation as fast as possible."

I gave him no argument. Even though I knew it was only a hunch, his features gave evidence of his concern. The carriage rocked and swayed and I held on for dear life, bracing my shoes against the dash to further steady myself.

Rolf and Maggie were standing in the drive when we returned.

"What is it?" I asked, all too aware now that their features displayed the same anxiety as Alex's.

"Miss Vivian ain't back from her ridin'," Maggie said. "I just told Mr. Rolf. I think all four of you better go lookin' for her."

"Get in, Rolf," was all Alex said.

The three of us drove to the stable. Rolf saddled his horse and Alex saddled two. I rode sidesaddle, not daring to take the time to change. I couldn't ride as fast that way, so I suggested they go on ahead to the area where we'd found papa. It was where Vivian and I chose to ride also.

213

The men looked grim. Alex had taken his rifle and started off, but Rolf turned back to the house.

"I'm going to get a gun," he said. "I'll catch up."

I followed the path Alex had taken. He was already out of sight, losing no time. My concern grew as I moved along, seeing no evidence of Vivian. Then I caught a glimpse of Alex as he slowed and studied the area on either side of him. Before I could reach him, he was gone again, entering the forest that abounded on the land.

The further we progressed, the stronger became my feeling of foreboding. I thought of Joel and Alex's comments regarding his strange behavior. If he had seen Vivian riding her usual route, he could have informed someone. Perhaps someone living in their house, though keeping under cover, while Joel rode swiftly to the village to establish an alibi, so he could not be accused of harming Vivian. It was a dismal thought, but one I couldn't dismiss. I had the horrible feeling that her life was in peril. She was long overdue at the mansion. She'd always enjoyed riding, but not for any prolonged period.

Alex had stopped again. He looked back and raised his arm in a signal for me to pull up.

"I thought I heard a shot," he said. "It came from our left. Where's Rolf?"

"I haven't seen him. I don't know if he came along this forest trail."

"The shot may have come from his gun. I hope so. Let's veer to the left anyway. That direction is away from Yvonne's place. She wouldn't want any tragedy to happen close to her property. Ride more slowly now and keep a sharp eye out."

Before we were started, we heard another shot. "A pistol," Alex said. "That won't be Rolf. Come on!"

We veered to the left. The shot was followed by a scream and Vivian's voice calling for help. Alex pulled up and dismounted. I went on past him because I couldn't stop in time. Armed with his rifle, he began running toward the direction of the scream, which had ceased abruptly.

When I finally dismounted and caught up with him, he motioned for silence. We crept forward. We couldn't be too hasty, for if she was being threatened, whoever menaced her might panic and shoot again. It was a mild comfort to me to realize Vivian's scream came after the second gunshot.

We reached a small clearing and there we saw the tragedy about to be enacted. Vivian, her riding costume torn, her face so deeply scratched that blood ran down her cheek, was backed against a tree, and slowly advancing on her was a man I'd never seen before. He was in the same category with the two would-be murderers in New Orleans. He held a pistol aimed at Vivian, who was so beside herself with terror that she could no longer cry out. Or perhaps she realized how vain her screams might be.

Alex raised his rifle, but he hesitated. If he fired and missed, the bullet might hit Vivian, for she was directly in line. But the murderer was about to finish his threat now. He was slowly bringing the pistol down for the final aim.

The shot that rang out came from the killer's right. The bullet hit him at the temple and hurled him to one side. The pistol dropped from his hand and he went down hard. Rolf came out of the surrounding forest. He was holding a rifle, but he threw it aside and rushed to where Vivian cowered in her terror, still too paralyzed with fear to believe she was no longer in danger.

Rolf's arms went about her. She clung to him and he held her close, talking softly to her, calming her, letting her know that she was safe. Alex sped to the side of the dead man, knelt and searched him. He discovered one significant thing. The man had two hundred dollars in one wad of tens. It had been tied with a piece of stout cord to keep it intact.

I felt my legs begin to buckle and I staggered over to a tree to sit down with my back against the trunk. Rolf had picked up Vivian and was carrying her toward where he'd left his horse. He was talking softly to her. I couldn't hear him, but his face rested against her head. He had no awareness of Alex and me. His sole concern was for his wife.

I didn't try to get up. I doubted that I could. Alex came over to join me.

"Please hold my hand, Alex. I was never so frightened in my life."

He placed an arm around my shoulder and drew me

close. "Rest your head on my shoulder. You're trembling from the shock of what you witnessed."

"Yvonne," I said.

"Of course," Alex agreed. "The money that goon had on him is proof she's still out for revenge. In a way, it's a pity he's dead. We can't question him."

"Even if we could, Deputy Sheriff Oliver would never believe him."

"Nonetheless, Tim Oliver can't ignore the fact that tragedy has built on near tragedy here."

"If you hadn't noticed Joel's strange behavior in the village, Vivian would be dead." I shuddered at the thought and Alex's arm tightened. It was a comforting gesture. "I don't know the words to express my gratitude."

"I don't want gratitude," Alex replied soberly. "I do want assurance of your safety and that of your sister. It's something we don't have. We have a dangerous adversary in that seemingly helpless widow. She's heartless. And to instill in her son the hatred she bears your family shows her mind has become affected."

"No one will believe that either. She is still able to control her madness."

"I'd like a confrontation with Joel," Alex said. "Perhaps I could bring him to his senses. He knows, as well as his mother, that we're aware of what they're up to."

"He seems so manly, but he can't be when he conspires with his mother. For a mother to destroy her own son by sowing the seeds of hate in his mind . . . I can scarcely accept it."

"Mother is just a word," Alex said kindly. "It's the woman who gives it meaning."

"I hope she doesn't know mama is alive. I don't know what nefarious plot she would conjure up to do away with her."

"Just now, we have Vivian's welfare to think about. And there's a body lying a short distance away. I'll remain with it so it won't disappear."

"You'd better hold on to your gun. There may be other thugs about."

"I'll be on guard. Ask my father to saddle a horse and ride to Rutford. Tell him briefly what happened and ask him to inform Deputy Sheriff Oliver we need him here at once."

He helped me to my feet and lifted me onto my horse. I lost no time getting back to the house, going directly to the stable. Jacob was there and had a fresh horse saddled. He informed me Vivian's horse had returned alone and he was just about to set out and look for her when Rolf brought her back. I repeated to Jacob what Alex had told me. He wasted no time setting out to the village.

I went into the house and met Maggie at the foot of the stairs. She was bringing up a glass of water and had a folded paper in her hands.

"A sleeping draught for Miss Vivian," she said. "She's in one of the guest rooms."

"How seriously is she hurt?" I asked.

"Scratched up, mostly. You can tell me about it after I give this to her."

"Where's Rolf?"

"Where he should be," she replied sternly. "With his wife."

"Because it's his duty?"

Maggie knew why I asked.

"No, child. Because he loves her and he's at her bedside comforting her. No need to worry about them no more."

"Thank God."

Maggie had started up the stairs, but paused and looked back at me. "You really mean that?"

"With all my heart," I said. "I had a talk with Rolf yesterday. He assured me his love for Vivian was genuine. But she'd damaged his pride!"

Maggie gave a knowing nod. "He's forgotten about that now. I had to order him out of the room while I bathed her scratches and examined her to see if she had any broken bones. But she better have a doctor look in on her."

"She will have."

"Not that he can do anything for her. What she needs is rest. She's trembling awful from shock." Maggie held up the folded paper. "A sleeping draught. Rest and sleep is what she needs."

I suddenly remembered Vivian's bitterness of the morning and of the sharp words we'd exchanged. "Do you think she'll see me?"

"I'm sure of it. Rolf told her if you and Alex hadn't

217

come back, he wouldn't have known she was in danger."

"Then I'll go up and speak briefly with her."

Rolf was at her bedside, one hand resting lightly on her brow, his other holding her hand which lay on the coverlet. He looked up at me and said, "Thanks, Heather."

"I did nothing. Alex realized there was peril of some kind lurking here. Joel was showing himself in too many places in the village. Alex figured it was to establish an alibi. We know now it was."

I managed a smile when I looked down at Vivian, but it wasn't easy, for her lovely face was terribly scratched. "I'm sorry about this morning, Heather. Rolf told me about your talk in the gazebo yesterday."

This time I did smile. "Then you know he really loves you."

She nodded and winced. The slightest gesture was painful. "I must tell you what happened."

"No," Rolf said. "I will. You must lie very quiet."

Maggie said, "Mr. Rolf, just move away from the bed long enough so I can give this to your wife. She got to get some sleep. Take away the aches and pain."

Rolf moved to the foot of the bed and explained that when she entered the forest, a man, concealed behind a tree, pulled her from the horse and struck her. She managed to free herself and played a hide-and-seek game with him until she was breathless and he came upon her just before we reached the scene. He'd already shot at her once, but missed. Then he tried again, but missed. However, he cornered her finally, and backed against the tree as she was, she was a perfect target. Fortunately, Rolf had entered the forest on a different path and caught sight of them. He managed to dismount without either Vivian or her would-be murderer hearing him. Still concealed, he took aim and shot him.

"He's dead," I said.

"I'm not sorry," Rolf said. "Yvonne DesChamps, I suppose."

"Who else? Jacob's gone for Deputy Sheriff Oliver."

"I hope this time he'll listen to reason."

"So do I. But Yvonne has conducted such a perfect campaign, I doubt he'll believe in her treachery. We've still no proof."

Vivian swallowed the sleeping potion dutifully. Rolf moved a rocker to her bedside. He said, "If I need you for anything, Maggie, I'll let you know."

"You do that." I knew it was all she could do to repress a smile. It was Rolf's way of telling her he was taking charge.

"And Maggie," he called to her as she reached the door.

She turned and gave him her full attention.

"Will you please move my wife's belongings back to the room you assigned us when we returned?"

"It'll be a real pleasure, Mr. Rolf," Maggie said with a nod.

Vivian murmured, "Darling," and raised a hand for his.

Maggie closed the door and looked up at me. "Does it hurt much, child?"

"Strangely, it doesn't hurt at all."

"Then you're over him." She gave a satisfied nod and headed for Vivian's room. I followed. My sister's wardrobe was so extensive, it would take both of us an hour to move it back to papa's room.

Eighteen

DEPUTY SHERIFF TIM OLIVER WAS A MAN OF MIDDLE years and had been born and raised in Rutford. However, he had spent several years as a member of the police force in Richmond and was familiar with the workings of the law. He was held in high respect by the citizens of Rutford because he was fair, but stern when the occasion demanded. I felt this was a time for sternness on his part and I hoped he'd act when I revealed the true character of Yvonne DesChamps.

Alex, Rolf and I retired to the drawing room after our evening meal, the gentlemen sipping an after-dinner brandy. They poured me a glass of sherry, stating it would relax me and help me sleep. I wasn't in agreement, but maintained a thoughtful silence, my mind concerned with the shock of what Vivian had undergone.

I was by her bedside when she wakened an hour ago. Rolf had gone for Dr. Simms, who returned with him. He examined her carefully, and stated that though she was covered with bruises and suffering from shock caused both by the fall off her horse, then subjected to the terror of believing she was going to be murdered, a few days of rest in bed would help her recover from her ordeal. As for the multitude of scratches on her face, he suggested they be kept clean and exposed to the air, which would do more to heal them than any medication.

We'd just finished our drinks when Deputy Sheriff Tim Oliver arrived. He expressed his regrets over what had happened to Vivian and his delay in arriving, then asked if he might speak to her. Since the doctor hadn't forbidden it, Rolf consented, though he asked that the questioning be kept to a minimum.

I felt the deputy would cooperate, especially since Vivian had actually witnessed the gunman aiming the gun at her with intent to kill. While he and Rolf were upstairs, I told Alex that I intended to inform him of everything Yvonne DesChamps had said to us.

"I think you should," Alex said, "though I fear your revelations will prove fruitless."

"What do you mean?"

"You know as well as I how well that woman planned her strategy. She's built up an image of herself through the years as an angel of mercy. Even I believed it. You have no witnesses of your first meeting with her, other than Vivian, who happens to be your sister. Even her statement, added to yours, won't hold water. Any more than Rolf's and mine will regarding the day Yvonne Des-Champs came to lay claim to Nightfall."

"Nonetheless, he's going to hear the complete story."

"Including the empty grave?" Alex asked.

"Oh, no," I exclaimed. "Mama wants to remain dead. And to reveal her existence would make the memory of papa less than honorable."

"And further weaken your story," he said.

Alex took my empty glass and set it on the tray alongside his. "I think you should reveal what she said to you.

Inform Tim Oliver of her quest for revenge. Even if he doesn't believe it, at least he will know of it, and should something else happen—God forbid—his mind will go back to your story. Also, if Yvonne should tip her hand, what you told could be the turning point."

And so, when Deputy Sheriff Oliver came downstairs, as somber faced as Rolf, he again expressed his regrets at what had happened. Rolf poured a brandy, which the deputy accepted with thanks. He also accepted my offer to be seated and we formed a circle, making conversation easy.

"I think there's one or more goons skulking around these plantations," he said. "The lands have so much acreage that it's almost impossible to track them down. Of course, the one today will never threaten anyone again."

"What about the two hundred dollars that we found on his person?" Alex asked. "Certainly one wouldn't expect someone like him to have that kind of money on him. His suit was cheap and frayed. His shoes had holes clear through the soles. His face hadn't been washed in days, nor had he shaved."

"It added to his ferociousness, I'll admit," Deputy Sheriff Oliver said. "But as for the money, he could have stolen it or won it in a gambling game of some kind."

"Don't you think it's more likely he was paid to kill my sister?" I asked sternly, displeased with his reply.

"There was nothing on his person that would lead me to that conclusion," Deputy Sheriff Oliver said quietly.

"To leave such evidence on his person would be stupidity on his part or the individual who hired him to murder," I replied, though softening my voice and being careful not to lose my temper. It would serve no purpose and I could better serve our interests by remaining calm, difficult though it would be.

"I agree, Miss Heather. And after observing the scratches on your sister's face, I can understand your indignation."

"I hope you will understand it when I tell you who is behind it," I said.

"You can name a suspect?" His keen eyes brightened with interest. "Name him and I'll have him behind bars immediately."

"It's a woman." I refrained from saying "lady." Yvonne DesChamps did not qualify.

His brow furrowed in puzzlement. "Are you saying a woman would hire a thug to kill a young girl? What could possibly be her motive?"

"Revenge," I said.

"Against whom?" he asked.

"My father, first of all. She was successful in having him murdered. Now we're her targets, along with the possession and ownership of Nightfall."

"You're talking in riddles," he said. He studied me carefully, then looked down at the brandy he'd not touched. He set the glass on the table, gripped the arms of his chair and turned his attention back to me. "Are you willing to name her?"

"Yvonne DesChamps." I couldn't help the bitterness which slipped into my voice as I spoke her name.

"Good heavens, girl, do you know what you're saying?"

"I do and I hope you will listen carefully to every word I speak."

"I'll listen, but you'll have to do some mighty hard convincing."

"That's all I ask. An open mind."

"You have that, Miss Heather. I will also want evidence. Concrete evidence to back up what you tell me."

"First, my story," I said, fearful he'd not remain if I admitted I had not a shred of proof. And so I began my tale, starting with the night papa confessed to the duel he had engaged in with Lemuel DesChamps. I spoke of the burning barn, which we knew to be incendiary.

"You know I told you about that, Tim," Alex said.

"Yes, but there again, no proof as to who could have done it."

I moved on to the morning Jacob came to the house to inform papa that two of his best horses had been shot.

"I saw them," Deputy Sheriff Oliver said. "But again, no proof as to the culprit." He glanced at me. "Your papa did say that a disgruntled employee could have been guilty of the act."

"You've forgotten I told you that papa informed me that Yvonne DesChamps swore vengeance for having killed her husband in a duel."

"Were the two of them in the presence of anyone who can vouch for that?" he asked.

"Unfortunately, no. The woman is clever. She's a genius at intrigue."

"That's an unkind statement to make about so charitable a woman," Deputy Sheriff Oliver observed.

"That was part of her scheme, to perform so many good, charitable deeds that no one would suspect her of chicanery. Even now, she is building a hospital and donating the land for it."

"And everyone in the village is grateful," Deputy Sheriff Oliver said. "It's something you must bear in mind."

"I'm coming to realize that more and more," I said. "But I haven't finished. After the horses were shot, Vivian and I decided to pay Mrs. DesChamps a visit. She admitted she was out for vengeance and she would destroy us. I know she's intent on obtaining possession of Nightfall. Later, she told us we would be either ridiculed or scorned were we to voice a word against her. That very morning, as we arrived, many ladies from the village were leaving, after discussing the building of the hospital with her."

"My wife was one of those ladies," Deputy Sheriff Oliver said. "I recall now her mentioning seeing you and your sister riding up the drive. She replied the others in the carriage were surprised that you came. Not that Yvonne wouldn't admit you or ever referred to you in any slighting fashion. I recall years back, when Reverend Barton informed the congregation she had forgiven your father his transgression and she wanted no one in the village to hold him responsible. She even asked that one and all of us refrain from giving either you or your sister a hint of what Bryant Gates had done."

My smile was one of defeat. "I know all that, Deputy Sheriff Oliver. But she was playing a game. That was the beginning. I don't condone what papa did. Nor did he ever forgive himself. He carried the guilt of having taken a life through his every waking moment. He told me. I believe that's why he had periods when he drank spiritous liquors to excess. He was trying to shut it out. It didn't work."

Deputy Sheriff Oliver's eyes widened in surprise when he realized I was aware of papa's indiscretion.

"Oh, yes, papa admitted his weaknesses, his gambling and the losses which forced him to sign notes at the bank. We'd probably have made out if the crop last year hadn't been poor. But that caused him to sign more notes, so that he was very deeply in debt. I suppose you know who held those notes."

"Yes. But neither you nor your sister made any secret of it."

"It would have been difficult to do so since we were going to lose the plantation. That we could have stood. Papa's murder was something else."

"It could have been an accident."

"Never. Nor was it suicide. Papa swore to me he'd never commit such a cowardly act."

"Perhaps he was of unsound mind, brought on by his debts."

"He was worried," I admitted. "The burning barn and the horses which were killed didn't help matters. I believe Mrs. DesChamps let him know, in some way, she was behind it. She wished to instill fear in him. He probably thought she'd be satisfied with taking over Nightfall. But first, she wanted his life. I'm sure she wouldn't be capable of committing his murder. Nor would she allow her son to. But she hired thugs to do it. Thanks to Rolf, the last one met his Waterloo."

Deputy Sheriff Oliver didn't doubt my earnestness and he was disturbed by what I'd said, but I could see he wouldn't accept it.

"Miss Heather, if you had a single shred of evidence against the woman, I would go to her and charge her with the crime of your father's murder—as you call it—and the near murder of your sister. But you've given me no evidence."

Alex broke into the conversation for the first time. "Rolf and I were here when Yvonne came with a writ ordering Vivian and Heather off the plantation."

"I know about that," Deputy Sheriff Oliver said. "Yvonne hated to do it, but because the sisters were so young, she felt they couldn't run it competently and she had to protect her investment. She stated that if your father had lived, she would still have continued to hold the

224

notes. As you know, he never was aware that she was his benefactress."

"She was not a benefactress." Alex spoke with quiet firmness.

"I'll vouch for that, since I was present also," Rolf said.

"You'd hardly be credible witnesses, since one of you is married to Miss Vivian."

"Do you believe us?" I asked boldly.

"I kind of wish I could," he said, speaking slowly. "But I know what Yvonne DesChamps has done not only for the village, but for the poor and the sick. They'd be wards of the county if it hadn't been for her."

A general could have set a course of action no better than that woman, I thought. It had been a complete waste of time, revealing all I had to him. But I had no regrets. At least, he knew.

I said, "You know, of course, it was Rolf who furnished the money to save Nightfall."

"Yvonne said she was pleased she didn't have to carry out her plan to take it over. She told the ladies on the hospital committee that it was a great relief to her that you girls could remain here. My wife told me Yvonne's eyes brimmed as she related her reluctance to lay claim to Nightfall."

"The woman," I said firmly, "is a liar. I'm referring, of course, to Yvonne DesChamps."

"Of course," he replied, though his shock at the boldness of my statement was evident. He reached for his hat, which rested atop a table nearby, and stood up.

"I hope that with the death of the vagrant, there'll be no more trouble here, Miss Heather. I know you and your sister have been through a lot. I can understand your bitterness toward Yvonne once she came to take over the plantation. But you still have it. What happened to your sister today could be coincidence."

I made no reply. There was no need. I'd failed to convince him, just as Alex had predicted. The three gentlemen were standing.

I said, "Thank you for listening to my story. All I'll say now is that every word I spoke is the truth."

"It's still only your word against that of Mrs. Des-Champs," he replied quietly. "I couldn't arrest a woman who is a pillar of the community on such flimsy evidence. Evidence which really isn't any such thing."

I'd heard enough. "Good-bye, Deputy Sheriff Oliver."

"Good-bye, Miss Heather. If anyone here, and that includes the hired hands, sees a strange face on the plantation, let me know. I'll come out immediately and bring other officers to make a search of the entire grounds."

I could have told him he'd be searching the wrong property, but it would have been a waste of time and words. I murmured my thanks and asked the gentlemen to see him out.

I went to the window and watched him get into his buggy and start off. He hadn't paused even a moment to chat with Alex and Rolf. It was as if he were eager to leave. There was no doubt that he'd found his visit quite distasteful.

Rolf and Alex came back in. Rolf excused himself and went upstairs to Vivian.

Alex joined me at the window. We stood there looking out, watching Deputy Sheriff Oliver's buggy until it turned off the drive, onto the road, and disappeared behind tall trees.

"Don't be too discouraged," Alex said. "There has to be a way to outwit that woman. At least, you've given Tim Oliver the story."

"Not one iota of which he believes," I replied wearily.

"He'll have to, one day." Alex was doing his best to brighten my spirits, but his words did little to cheer me.

"I think the four of us will have to be murdered before anyone will believe the evil that woman is capable of," I said. "Oh, Alex, I don't know what to do."

I couldn't hold back the tears and I turned my face away. He gathered me to him gently and told me to cry on his shoulder, slipping his handkerchief into my hands as he did so. I let the tears flow and I was once again comforted by his presence. His hand rested lightly on my head as Rolf's had rested on Vivian's upstairs.

When I was able to speak, I said, "At least, what happened today accomplished one good thing."

Alex stepped back and his hands moved to my shoulders. He grasped them lightly as he looked down into my tear-swollen eyes.

"You mean Rolf and Vivian are together again."

226

"And this time for good."

"Does it hurt?"

"Maggie asked me the exact same thing."

"What did you tell her?"

"Not a bit. And that's the truth. I mistook infatuation for love. Thank God I have you for a friend, though. You've always been close by when I needed you."

"Yes." His reply was barely audible. Then he managed a smile as he asked, "Feel better after your cry?"

"Much. A little foolish too. You must think me a fool."

"You know differently. I think you'd better retire early. This has been a hard day for you."

I wanted to reach up and touch my cheek to his, but feared he might mistake the gesture, so I said, "Will you walk me to the foot of the stairs?"

"It will be my pleasure." He bowed slightly and offered his arm. I rested my hand on it and together we moved slowly into the hall. I didn't pause at the landing, but went directly upstairs. At the top I looked down. He was still standing there, a lonely and forlorn figure. I felt a sudden impulse to go to him. But I resisted it. I was too emotionally unsettled.

Instead, I put my fingers to my lips and blew him a kiss. His only response was the merest hint of a smile that touched the outer corners of his mouth.

I moved on to my room, for the first time aware of my quickening heartbeat. Could it be I was falling in love with Alex? Was I the fickle one? I'd believed that of Vivian, yet with her it had always been Rolf. I'd thought only recently I was in love with Rolf. Now I knew it was mere infatuation, caused probably by his handsomeness.

But Alex. Would I one day say: "Dear Alex," "My beloved Alex?"

I was thinking foolishly. I had too much to concern myself about to allow my emotions to take over. I opened my door and closed it softly behind me.

Nineteen

A WEEK PASSED DURING WHICH ROLF MADE NO SECRET
of his love and devotion to Vivian. Whenever he wasn't
working on the plantation, he tended to Vivian's slightest
wish. Fortunately, her scratched face was healing and
would soon show no sign of the ordeal she'd endured.
However, I was beginning to fear that Rolf was spoiling
Vivian in the manner papa had, but I kept my silence,
since the household was running smoothly.

If it hadn't been for the threat of Yvonne DesChamps'
evil ways hanging over us, I would have said that a new
life had begun for us. But, try as I might, it was difficult
to keep her out of my thoughts. Though I managed an
outward calm when I was around Vivian, Rolf and Alex,
I wondered what devilment she was conjuring up for us.
She had waited years to carry out her threat of revenge
and I imagined she would delay no longer, lest time run
out on her. Nonetheless, I took care that her name didn't
slip into my conversation. I noticed also that Vivian
avoided any mention of her, as did the men.

But there came a day when Rolf's own plantation required some of his time and he began to make frequent
trips there. Though he had asked Vivian to accompany
him, she showed little inclination to do so. I tried to
discuss the matter discreetly with her, stating that her
place was with her husband, and since he wanted her with
him, not only because he loved her, but because he feared
for her safety after her near murder, she should abide by
his wishes. But she was adamant, asserting that despite
what had happened, she felt more secure here.

However, she moved back to the bedroom she had
used before her elopement, stating that it was less lonely
and the room was next to mine. I resigned myself to her

contrary and puzzling ways. I realized that no matter what, Vivian would never change. At least, not completely.

But it was while in her room that she came upon the small, satin, quilted bag in which she'd placed the jade ring mama wanted Maggie to have. She brought it to my room and suggested we both bring it downstairs and present it to Maggie. In the excitement of our return and all we'd had to tell, plus Vivian's near murder, we had forgotten about it.

But there was no need for us to go downstairs, for a familiar tap sounded at the door. I called to Maggie to enter.

Before she could say a word, Vivian told her we'd brought her back a gift from mama, which we'd both forgotten about. Her eyes widened in pleasure as Vivian extended the small bag. Maggie loosened the braided cord which held it shut, looked in and cried out in delight.

"A ring," she exclaimed. She took it out, slipped it onto her little finger and held it up to admire it herself and for us to exclaim over it.

Vivian said, "Mama wanted you to have it. I'm sorry, in all the excitement of our return and what followed, that I forgot."

"I forgot too, Maggie," I said. "It looks beautiful on your finger."

"Real jade too," Maggie said reverently. "Your papa always gave your mama beautiful things. And often sent her out to get somethin' real beautiful too. She liked to pick out things herself."

Her features sobered.

"What is it?" I asked.

"I can't wear this around here," she said, regarding it forlornly.

"Why not?" I asked.

"This is a real unusual ring an' I'll bet there are women who'd remember it."

"Are you thinking of Mrs. DesChamps?"

"Her and others. Though she's the only troublemaker." She slid it off her finger and returned it to the little bag. She drew the cords closed and tied them securely. "I'll wear it in my house when I'm sure no one's skulkin' about."

229

"Why don't you move over here?" I asked. "I worry about you there by yourself."

"Unless you want me here 'cause you're scared, I like to be in my own house. Your papa built it for me an' I'm proud of it. An' I got the land it sets on. Of course, if that awful woman gets this land. . . ." Her voice trailed off and her face took on a worried look.

"That parcel of land would still be yours and so would the house," I said. "You have the deed to it."

"She'd burn me out, child," Maggie said. "Besides, I couldn't live here if she took over. Not jus' that I don't like her, but she'd make my life plain miserable."

Neither Vivian nor I disputed that. Maggie turned and headed for the door, then did an about-face so quickly that she startled us.

"Good gracious," she exclaimed. "You got a special delivery letter. Jacob jus' came back from the village and brought me groceries. He met the postman there an' he gave him this letter."

She reached into her apron pocket and brought out the envelope. She extended it to Vivian, who was closer, but she drew back.

"You take it, Heather," she said. "It might be bad news."

I reached for it, saying, "Good or bad, it has to be opened."

There was no return address in the left-hand corner and the typed heading read "The Misses Gates."

I said, "It's for both of us."

"Where is it from?" Vivian asked fearfully.

I glanced at the cancellation stamp. "New Orleans."

"Mama," she said, her voice barely audible. "Open it and see what it says."

."I will, if you'll stop talking." I'd already reached for a letter opener and was slitting open the envelope.

There was a folded sheet of paper, plus a smaller envelope.

"Read it to yourself first," Vivian urged.

"For goodness sake!" I exclaimed tartly. "Stop being so childish."

"I can't help it. I'm frightened."

Her voice quavered and she was on the verge of tears.

I relented, suddenly remembering what she'd been through. I placed an arm about her waist and led her over to the chaise longue, settling her comfortably against the cushions.

"You better stay, Maggie," I said, noting she was heading for the door, not because she too feared the contents of the letter, but she wasn't one to intrude, though I knew her curiosity was as great as mine. The letter was a surprise, for I'd not expected to hear from mama. I didn't even know yet if the missive was from her, but since we knew no one else in that great city, I assumed it to be. Once I opened the page, I recognized mama's signature.

I sat down facing Vivian and scanned the contents of the letter, which consisted of only one page. The smaller envelope was unsealed and I opened it. It contained a clipping from a newspaper and when I read it, I couldn't help but cry out in dismay.

"What is it?" Vivian asked apprehensively.

Maggie moved over to stand beside the chaise and rested a comforting hand on Vivian's shoulder. "Whatever it is, you gotta know it sooner or later, child. So jus' lay back and let Miss Heather read it to you."

"The letter first," I said, and began to read:

> *My dear daughters,*
>
> *It is with reluctance I write this and send the enclosed. As you know, I said I would never return to Nightfall and preferred to remain dead. But I invited you to visit me whenever you wished. It was my secret hope that your visits would be frequent. That is still my hope, as it was my desire to remain dead and still is.*
>
> *However, I am enclosing a clipping that fills me with alarm. I have the feeling I am about to be resurrected and with vicious intent.*
>
> *The clipping is from a New Orleans paper. This is a city that loves riddles and gossip. So the paper devotes a column headed "Today's Tattletale," and allows the citizens to send in limericks and poems, hinting of an illicit romance, a scandal in the making, an unlawful political alliance. Anything to set the tongues wagging.*

All of it is done in a spirit of jest. And, of course, because of the nature of the column, the sender may remain anonymous. What I have sent you is not only vicious, but also a lie. Not completely, of course, since I am alive. But my love for you is genuine. My concern for your safety, grave. Do be on guard.

I leave it to you to identify the writer of the poem. Having contacts with the paper, I had an emissary make discreet inquiries of the paper as to where it had come from. The envelope bore a local stamp. The words of the poem were cut from a newspaper and glued onto the white sheet of stationery. In that way, there could be no attempt to make comparisons of the handwriting.

It was sent in a large envelope so the banner of the newspaper could be glued to it. I fear for you both and I am at a loss as to what to do . . .

I do not wish to return to Nightfall and, as I told you, I wish to remain buried in the cemetery beside your papa. As of now, that seems remote, but hopefully, the tide of misfortune directed at you will, through some miracle, end. That is what I pray for. Though that may sound strange to you, it is true. I do pray.

I beg of you both to inform Jacob, Alex and Rolf to guard you constantly. Coward that I am, I cannot go back.

I suppose in view of my above statement, it's asking too much of you to believe it when I say I love you both. But it's the truth.

Your loving mother,
Jessica

"What's mama talking about?" Vivian's voice was barely audible.

"Whatever it is," Maggie said sensibly, "it ain't good."

I said, "I'll read the poem. It will tell you as well as I. Or do you wish to read it, Vivian?"

She gave a quick, negative shake of her head and reached up to get a grip on Maggie's hand.

I said, "The column is headed 'Today's Tattletale,'" and proceeded to read aloud:

A coward killed upon his sword
Now lies beside his wife
Or so 'twas thought
But he did give
His wife a second life!

She's widowed now and sinful too,
For the business that she chose.
Her siblings know
Since they did go
To spy in strangers' clothes.

She scorned them both, despite their pleas
And sent them on their way
Then hired two thugs
To kill the twins
Lest they her sin betray.

But when that failed, a messenger
Was sent to bring them to her.
She swore false love
And feigned concern
For the two she'd sought to murder.

They do not know she lied to them
For with guile and trickery
She persuaded both
Ne'er to reveal
Her wretched grave is empty.

"Mrs. Yvonne DesChamps," Maggie said angrily. "Somethin's gotta be done 'bout that woman before she does somethin' to you."

"Why did Yvonne send that to the New Orleans newspaper?" Vivian asked. "Why not to the Rutford newspaper?"

"They wouldn't print an anonymous poem or even a letter," I said. "Besides, that would be risky for her, even using words cut from a newspaper. Also, don't forget, she had it mailed in New Orleans."

"The Rutford paper wouldn't print that sort of thing anyway," Vivian mused, more thoughtful than scared now that she was aware of the contents.

I was filled with trepidation and wondered what we could possibly do to outwit this woman. This was so unexpected, I could think of nothing at the moment, though my thoughts did turn to Alex. I would discuss it with him at the earliest opportunity. I also hoped Rolf would return so he would know of Yvonne's latest bit of satanic evil. She'd give us not a moment's peace.

I said, "I'm going to take a walk. If you want me, Maggie, I'll be in the summer house. I can think calmly there. Would you care to join me, Vivian?"

"No thanks, Sister," she said. "I'm going to my room and lie down. I have a headache."

"Yvonne DesChamps is enough to give anyone a headache," I said. "Besides, after what you've been through, this latest worry isn't going to do you any good."

"Come," I extended a hand to her, "I'll walk you to your room."

Maggie followed and went in to draw the shade. I heard her soft voice, talking to Vivian in a soothing manner. I wondered what we'd ever do without her.

I walked along the gravel path, my hand in my pocket clutched tightly around the envelope containing mama's letter and the cruel poem. I wondered how long it had taken Yvonne DesChamps to compose it. Though it didn't show any particular talent, it revealed the workings of a mind filled with hatred and the imagination to put it into words. Certainly the newspaper had thought it worth printing. I suppose everyone in New Orleans was wondering who the woman was that had borne twins and, though believed deceased, still lived.

No one, other than mama's trusted lieutenants, would think of mama, but it assured me of one thing. We'd been followed. Of course, we knew that once we were set upon and mama had found the would-be murderers. Despite what the poem said, mama hadn't feigned her love or concern. Everything in the poem was a lie except the line about the grave which was empty. That added to my concern, for it was Yvonne DesChamps' way of telling us she knew mama was alive.

Since the time we'd entered the Café Brulot Ballroom and had been trailed there by Yvonne DesChamps' goons, who undoubtedly reported to Joel, he must have checked the ownership of the business establishment.

While the name Jessica Taylor would have meant nothing to him, it would to Yvonne DesChamps. And since Alex and Rolf had dug up mama's grave, the earth would still have been soft enough to push a thin pole down to check as to whether there was a casket there. There was. That we knew. But it had rotted and collapsed. If the woman had the slightest doubt, she undoubtedly had had the grave dug up and discovered what we already knew.

I thought I heard a sound behind me and I turned, but saw no one. I was hoping for a glimpse of Alex. I saw him only during our evening meal and afterward we discussed the plantation, its maintenance and taxes, the equipment he had purchased and its cost. Rolf spent all his time with Vivian and so I appreciated Alex's help. He was teaching me the fine points of keeping the books and meeting the payroll, as well as listing new employees. As for those, Alex took care that he knew their background. He was taking no chances on one of Mrs. DesChamps' spies acquiring employment here for the purpose of bringing back information to her which she would use to do us harm.

Once again, I thought I heard a sound and a shiver of trepidation swept over me. Perhaps it was the letter, coupled with the dismal day. The sky was gray, foretelling the coming of a storm, which we could use, for the weather had been hot and sticky and not even a breeze stirred the leaves into movement. It was almost an unnatural stillness, the quiet before the storm. Or was it a warning of another impending catastrophe? I hoped not. Vivian's nerves were on edge as it was. It wouldn't take much to send her over the brink into a nervous breakdown. I didn't want that to happen. The difference between us was forgotten. In fact, I was grateful she'd married Rolf. I realized I'd never loved him, though not until some time after I'd talked with him.

I hoped I wasn't one of those women incapable of giving love. I wondered if I'd ever be free enough of worry and concern regarding Nightfall to find out. I envied Vivian and Rolf, for I'd seen them in endearing moments and it was beautiful to behold. Their features soft with their love for one another, embracing each other with their eyes across the table, oblivious to the conver-

235

sation Alex and I were holding. Not even aware there were others in the room.

I heard the sound of footsteps. Not leisurely ones and not on the graveled path. These were running and were those of a heavyset person, for they pounded the soft earth. Only the deathly stillness of my surroundings made them audible.

I'd reached the gazebo and debated whether to sit there and contemplate what, if anything, I could do to counter this latest bit of knavery thought up by a vengeful woman, or to return to the house. I decided to remain here. Vivian would be resting. Sleeping, I hoped. I also hoped Rolf would return so he could learn of our latest worry.

"Heather." My name was spoken softly and the voice was that of Alex.

It was as if the sun had come out.

"Alex," I replied, even before I turned to see him moving up the steps. I stood up and extended both hands to him.

He extended his, palms upward, and revealed the earth clinging to them. "Much as I'd like to, I'd better not. I've been grubbing in the earth."

"It's beautiful earth," I replied, taking a firm grip on his hands. "And I just need to know you're with me for a little while."

He studied me carefully. "You're very pale. Are you ill?"

"Just with worry," I replied. I released his hands and took the letter from my skirt pocket.

I extended it to him, but he'd moved to the edge of the summer house and was looking over the heavy shrubbery.

"What is it?" I asked.

He turned. "I thought I saw someone skulking around the shrubbery near here when I was down in the field. That's why I came up. When I saw you, I believed it was you."

"Did you run to get here?" I asked. "I heard someone running."

"No," he said. "I sort of kept to the trees, hoping to surprise whoever it was. Did you see anyone?"

"No. But I had an uneasy feeling while walking along the path. Perhaps I felt I was being followed."

Alex's features grew stern. "It's possible that you were. My father, Rolf and I have been very watchful and have had a few of the most trusted hired help keeping an eye out, though stating we believed there were poachers of some sort roaming about. It sounds logical in view of what almost happened to Vivian and did happen to the two horses. We can't include your father in it, since his death hasn't been considered murder, though we know it was."

"I appreciate all you're doing, but I know the acreage is so vast, it's impossible to cover all of it."

"And, of course, the tobacco fields as well as the heavy shrubbery and trees afford excellent shelter for spies or ruffians."

I'd forgotten the envelope I was still holding until I noticed Alex regarding it.

"Oh, I really was hoping I'd see you. This just came special delivery. It's from mama. I'd like you to read it."

"Suppose you read it for me. My hands are so dirty."

I laughed. "So are mine, after holding yours. So it won't matter if the letter and the poem that accompanies it get dirty."

Alex joined me in laughter and gave me an admiring look. "Heather, I love you. And don't get frightened. I won't get romantic. But you're quite a woman."

I colored with pleasure. "That's the most beautiful tribute you could pay me. Now, sit down and absorb the contents of the envelopes. And don't tell me you're too dirty. You belong here as much as I."

He regarded me soberly. "No, I don't. But thanks for making me feel important."

He sat down and took mama's letter from the envelope, along with the smaller envelope which held the poem. He read the letter, then the poem. He replaced them in the envelope, handed them back to me and sat back, his brow furrowed thoughtfully.

"That woman is a devil," he said. "It's a shocking statement to make, but I believe there is one thing on her mind. The utter destruction of the Gates family, followed by the possession of Nightfall."

"Please don't say that in front of Vivian. She's terribly frightened."

"Are you?" Alex asked.

"I'm trying not to be," I said. "Or at least to maintain a calm exterior. Do you know if Rolf is coming back tonight?"

"He wasn't certain. His overseer is having a problem with some of the help."

"You don't suppose Yvonne DesChamps is behind that?" I said.

"Only God knows," Alex said with a sigh. "I know Rolf will be back if he possibly can. You know how much in love he and Vivian are."

I nodded. "I'd feel she was safer if she was with him."

"She should be and not only for the reason you state," he replied.

"Somehow, she feels this is her sanctuary," I said. "I suppose because papa always protected us."

"Her especially. But he can't now. I believe that in time she'll get over her obsession about Nightfall and make a permanent move to Rolf's place."

"Does he want to be there permanently?"

"Yes. I believe he mentioned it briefly to Vivian, but her reaction was such, he told me he'd not bring it up again until she was over the shock of nearly being murdered. He feels she'd be safer in his home than here."

"I agree," I said quietly. "But you know Vivian. She's stubborn. And this is no time to argue it out with her."

"About that poem," Alex mused. "Do you think Yvonne sent it to the paper with the idea of scaring your mother?"

"Mama doesn't scare easily," I replied. "She's self-reliant and possessed of great poise."

"I know the people who inhabit the city of New Orleans are extremely tolerant of things we aren't here," he said. "I have a feeling they'd believe her to have been very clever at having carried off such a thing for years."

"I'm beginning to see what you mean," I said.

He eyed me speculatively. "I wonder if you do."

I nodded slowly. "I didn't think of it before, but Yvonne's idea was to have it printed in a newspaper, then to spread the word through Rutford and the entire countryside in some devious way. It will make fools of mama and us."

"It will also make your mother less than honorable. Not only because she is alive and well, but because of the business she carries on in New Orleans. The fact that it is accepted there will have no bearing here. She'll be despised."

"And so will we," I said. "I hope Vivian doesn't think of that. She's very social minded."

"How well I know." Alex gave me a knowing smile.

I managed to lighten the moment by leaning forward and, in mock seriousness, saying, "I believe she has finally accepted you into the family."

He laughed. "I can think of an answer to that, but I'll not say it."

"Why not?"

"Because it doesn't pertain to Vivian."

"Alex, last night," I smiled uncertainly, "when I stood at the head of the stairs. . . ." I paused uncertainly and he finished the sentence.

"And you blew me a kiss."

"For a little while, I felt very close to you."

"Don't do it again, please, unless you mean it." He was suddenly serious. "I almost ran up the stairs and took you in my arms again."

"Perhaps that's what I need. Or what I want. But I don't know. I'm under such a strain, I don't know how I feel toward you. I don't want to mistake gratitude for love. I was infatuated with Rolf. Love goes much deeper."

"I'm glad to hear you say that. I'll remain here until this plantation is no longer in danger of being taken over by Yvonne DesChamps. And I'll stay until I'm certain you're no longer in danger. I'll say one thing more. It's the hardest thing I've ever done, because my love for you —hopeless though it is—grows stronger each day."

"You know," I said, "Vivian made a very wise statement. She said everyone needed someone to love. It's true. I have a very empty feeling inside because I have no one."

"So have I." He stood up. "Come. I have to get back to the fields, but first I want to make certain you reach the house safely."

"I'm not afraid," I said.

"I know that," he replied, "but I am—for your safety."

"I was going to sit here and try to think of a way to best that woman."

"There's only one way."

"What do you propose?"

"Your mother has to return to Nightfall."

"She'd never do that!" I exclaimed.

"She has no choice. If she loves you both as she states in her letter, she'll return."

"She also stated in her letter she would never return."

"If she values the lives of her daughters, she'll come back."

I was at a loss for an answer.

Alex said, "If you don't write, telling her that, I will."

"Oh, Alex, no."

"Are you ashamed of her?"

"How can you ask me such a question?"

"I'm asking you." He spoke with quiet determination.

"Of course I'm not," I exclaimed indignantly. "I'd stand beside her proudly, in front of the whole village, and tell them I loved her and was grateful Vivian and I found her alive."

"Then that's what you must do."

"How could I get her here?"

"That's something for you to figure out," he replied. "Once the answer comes, write to her and give her the details of what must be done. It must be done as quickly as possible. I have a feeling Yvonne DesChamps is up to something. There's no limit to the evil that woman can conjure up."

We'd reached the house and stood at the foot of the steps. I said, "I'm going to papa's upstairs study and sit in his chair. Perhaps that will help me think of a way of getting mama here."

"Please do. You know Yvonne had you followed in New Orleans, since you were set upon and nearly killed. You went to the Café Brulot Ballroom and it was as easy for Joel to check the ownership of the place as it was for you. While the name may have meant nothing to him, it did to Yvonne. The rest was easy."

I nodded. "I'll try to have the solution tonight."

He gave a nod of encouragement, bent and kissed me lightly on the cheek. Then he turned and strode briskly away. My hand raised and touched the area and my eyes followed him until he turned off the path to take a short-cut through the fields and was no longer visible.

I entered the house, still under the spell of Alex's kiss. I'd liked it. I'd more than liked it. Whether from loneliness, or gratitude, or what, I didn't know. But it gave me renewed courage and a determination to once again rob this Yvonne DesChamps of another triumph.

Inside, Maggie had just descended the stairs. She said, "Your sister's sleepin'. Let her rest." She gave me a closer look, started to smile, then sobered. All she said was, "Humph," and continued on her way to the kitchen. Nothing escaped Maggie's keen eye.

I sat in papa's chair until it was nearly time to dress for our evening meal. Only then did the answer come. It was simple and I wondered why it had taken me so long to think of it.

I heard Vivian stirring when I passed her door and I tapped lightly, entering when she called out.

I said, "Did it occur to you why Yvonne DesChamps sent that poem to the newspaper?"

She was seated before the mirror, brushing her hair. Without pausing, she said, "To frighten mama."

I nodded at her reflection. "True, but she doesn't know mama won't frighten so easily. Her real reason is to humiliate us."

"We don't know anyone in New Orleans."

"We do in the village and the surrounding country-side and practically everyone knows who we are. They also believe mama died years ago and her remains lie beside papa's."

"And that's the way mama wants it." Vivian resumed brushing her hair.

"But she can't have it that way," I said.

Vivian set down her brush and turned to look up at me. "What are you saying?"

"That mama must come back to life."

"Why?"

"So Yvonne DesChamps can't make a fool of her or of us. Mama loves us. We love her. We've nothing to be ashamed of."

"Mama has," Vivian retorted.

"You mean the business she's engaged in?"

"That's exactly what I mean. It's shocking."

"To us. But not to the people in the city of New Orleans."

"We don't live there."

"Vivian, don't you love mama?"

She shook her head uncertainly. "I love her, but I don't want her back. We've our lives ahead of us. We are invited to the best homes. We're socially important here. We'll be the laughing stock of the community. We'll be scorned."

"What if we are?" I exclaimed. "Mama's paid for what she did to papa. And papa paid. I believe he'd want her back here. At least, he wouldn't mind if she revealed she isn't dead."

"It will make him out to be exactly what that poem said—a coward," she blurted. "Heather, you can't be serious."

"I am serious. And you must be grown up about it."

"What will Rolf think?"

"We'll have to wait until he comes back to find out. But I believe he'll think as I do and as Alex does."

"Alex again," she exclaimed impatiently. "You talked it over with him."

"It was his suggestion she come back."

"He should mind his own business."

"Nightfall *is* his business. I don't know what we'd do without him and his father."

"Nor do I!" she exclaimed sarcastically. "You don't make a move without consulting him."

Her comment made me smile. "You know, you're right. But the thought never occurred to me before. Anyway, this is my plan."

"I don't want to hear it." She swiveled back on the satin stool and picked up her brush. She used it savagely and cried out when the bristles pierced her scalp.

I reached over, took the brush from her and held it beyond her reach. "You listen, Vivian Fielding. You eloped with Rolf Fielding."

"Do we have to go through that again?"

"No. Only that your marriage has never been announced. It's going to be. Because of papa's recent death, we will have a quiet soiree. Ladies and gentlemen will be invited. As your older sister—"

"By five minutes," she said, giving me a look of disdain,

which I ignored and continued as if I'd not been interrupted. "I will announce the marriage. Afterward, I will tell our friends we have a beautiful surprise for them. At that time, you will go and bring mama into the room. With the two of you standing side by side, no one will doubt the relationship. After everyone has recovered from the shock of the revelation, mama will talk."

"About the Café Brulot Ballroom?" Vivian asked sarcastically.

"If she wishes. After all, it's a part of her life. If we are scorned afterward, so be it. But at least the truth will be known and Yvonne DesChamps' attempts to hold mama and us up to ridicule will be thwarted."

Vivian's lips pursed thoughtfully before she spoke. "Suppose mama won't come."

"She has no choice other than to come," I said, though I spoke with far more conviction than I felt.

"It will be the end of our social life here."

"If Yvonne DesChamps isn't stopped, we may not have a life of any kind. Have you forgotten what almost happened to you?"

By the startled look on her face, I knew she had. She nodded slowly, then looked up at me. "You're right, Heather. We are fighting for our lives. Mama must come. Even if we're ostracized socially, I still have Rolf."

"And you still have me, for what it's worth," I said, smiling down at her.

"It's worth a great deal." She stood up, embraced me and stepped back. "I know I'm difficult. But I'm trying."

"It isn't easy for either of us. But I'm grateful you have Rolf."

"So am I. And I'm sorry I spoke slightingly of Alex. I know what he's done for us. And so do you. I wish I could be the woman you are. I never will be, except perhaps sometimes."

"For Rolf, you're perfect. And don't ever forget it." She smiled with pleasure. "I wish he'd come home."

"He is home," I replied quietly. "And he wants you with him."

Her mouth opened to say something, but then compressed. It was as if she feared starting another argument. I didn't want that either, so I switched the subject back to the one we were discussing.

"We'll tell Alex what we've decided to do tonight while dining," I said.

She amended that to, "You mean you'll tell him what you've decided we will do."

I nodded agreement. "I must hurry. I don't even know what I'll wear."

She looked perplexed. "I never heard you say that before, I never thought you felt it terrible important."

"Maybe I didn't before. All of a sudden, it seems to be."

"May I have my brush?" Vivian's laughter filled the room and her eyes teased me.

I tossed it to her and closed the door quickly, lest she see my face flush with color. Her observation had been keen. I was filled with confusion, misgivings and a feeling of having imbibed too much champagne.

Twenty

REGRETTABLY, ROLF HADN'T RETURNED TO JOIN US, so we couldn't reveal our plans to him. I'd already made a list of those to be invited before I dressed. I'd chosen a tangerine dinner gown with gold threads woven into the fabric. It complimented my olive skin and black hair which I wore piled high. Even Vivian gasped when I went to her room and handed her the list of people I'd invited for the soiree. I would spend the evening after our meal writing the invitations, which would state it was to be a quiet evening, out of respect to the recent death of papa. It would only be from the hours of seven to nine, and its purpose would be to formally announce the marriage of my sister, Vivian Gates, to Rolf Fielding. The formal note seemed a little foolish, since just about everyone knew them, but it was a social custom, and in view of the elopement, was necessary.

Vivian complimented me on the note and asked if I

was going to send mama one. I replied that I intended to send her a letter, along with a copy of the invitation, telling her that her presence here would be necessary, and if she really loved us, she'd not refuse. I would send her letter special delivery, as she had sent the one to us. Since the affair was to be held in one week, there'd be no time for correspondence back and forth, in the course of which she might think of a way to wheedle her way out of coming. I could well imagine her anger and indignation when she received the letter, because I'd been on the receiving end of Vivian's often enough and they were carbon copies of one another.

To my delight, Alex could scarcely find his voice when he caught sight of me descending the stairs. He was dressed conservatively in a dark business suit, and except for his deeply tanned face, one would never know he worked in the fields, sometimes supervising and sometimes working alongside the hired hands.

He complimented me and I'm sure once again I felt color flood my face, though I managed to keep my emotions in control. Vivian, whether deliberately or not, remained upstairs a little longer. She said she wanted to check the list again, lest I may have omitted a name or two. But I was feminine enough to want to observe Alex's reaction to my appearance and I was amply rewarded.

At dinner, we discussed the soiree. Vivian and I were in agreement for once that it should be kept simple and brief. Our only concern was whether or not mama would put in an appearance. Alex felt certain she would. Vivian and I did not, knowing that she had no desire to return to Nightfall, and knowing also that she wished to remain dead, though that possibility now seemed remote in view of the fact that Yvonne DesChamps was aware that she lived. I knew better than to go and plead with her, for she'd flaunt her knowledge in my face. I did wish I knew how she intended to inform the villagers she'd learned mama's grave was empty. But I believed that in due time, I'd know.

Alex told me he would take the letter to the village once it was written. I told him tomorrow would do, but he was adamant, stating there was a train that came through Rutford at dawn and Abe Brown, the postmaster, a congenial soul, would see that the letter was in the mail pouch.

"Abe is only twenty-seven and your mother's name would have no meaning to him. Besides," Alex added, "he's not the type who looks at the names on envelopes."

And so I went upstairs directly after dinner, wrote mama a brief letter stating the conclusions Vivian and I had reached, what we intended to do and told her we would expect her on the date which was on the invitation, preferably before, if she could manage it. I informed her it was no longer possible for her to remain dead. Yvonne's poem was proof of that and it was up to us to outwit her. I added I'd have the soiree sooner, but doubted she could get here before then, considering she had business dealings to attend to. But I reminded her she also had two daughters now completely at the mercy of a vicious, scheming woman, who sought vengeance against them and would stop at nothing to achieve her ends unless we finally outsmarted her. I made a final appeal to mama's vanity by stating that certainly, having been in the business world for a number of years and having dealt with women of all types, she should have no difficulty in playing a victorious role in the plan we had thought up.

I addressed the envelope, slipped the folded letter inside, sealed it and added stamps, including extra ones to insure its being sent special delivery. Then I brought it downstairs and presented it to Alex.

He didn't tarry, other than to tell me he had never seen me look so beautiful. I told him it was the gown. He disputed that, saying it was the lady who wore it, for she glowed like a precious jewel. I scoffed at his reply, though softening my rebuff with a smile. Then we both laughed foolishly and I sent him on his way.

For a moment, I didn't think he would go, but he did, and after I closed the door, I stood there, wishing he hadn't. But I knew if our friendship—or what I'd thought was friendship on my part—was to assert itself, the next advance would have to come from me. Inexperienced as I was, I wasn't certain how to go about it. And, of course, a lady wouldn't assert her love without a little encouragement from the gentleman. Or would she? I chided myself for such idle thoughts when I had so much writing to do. Vivian, who always wrote invitations and loved doing it, could not do it this time. It was up to me. Once again, I had no time to think of love or the tender moments that led to it.

I had to keep blinking my eyes when I wrote the final three notes, for I could scarcely keep awake. But finally, the chore was done and the invitations piled in two neat stacks, ready to be mailed tomorrow.

I lost no time undressing and preparing myself for sleep, for my eyes were closing. I debated about whether or not to shut the two open windows, for I thought I heard the distant rumble of thunder. But I compromised and lowered them to about four inches from the sill. The air was so close, I couldn't wait for the storm to hit. Even if I woke up to rain, the floor could be dried with no harm to the wood. The thought of a breeze stirring the curtains would have cheered me had I not been so overcome by exhaustion.

I set the alarm clock, then turned down and blew out the lamps. I wasn't in bed longer than a minute before sleep claimed me. I don't know what pulled me awake, whether the light patter of rain against the windows, the low roll of nearing thunder or the welcoming breeze wafting gently across my face, filled with the sweet scent of rain. I opened my eyes, but my lids fell shut, for I was still sleep filled. Then I felt a strong burst of wind blow through the room.

My first thought was to get up and close the windows, for a downpour was imminent. My hand raised to throw off the light cover, but before I did so, something cautioned me to remain quiet. I sensed the presence of someone in my room. Someone had opened the door and caused the draft crossing my face to waken me. I slitted my eyes to make certain there was no light. The darkness was intense. That was a relief, for if I couldn't see anything, neither could the intruder.

The only other person in the house was Vivian, and she was a sound sleeper. And it wasn't she or she'd have wakened me by speaking my name. My right arm slipped from beneath the cover and my hand carefully reached for the alarm clock on the bedside table. But my relief at locating it was quickly dashed when, in my haste, I scraped it against the tabletop. It gave warning to the intruder that I was awake and since forewarned, perhaps forearmed.

Then a flash of lightning silhouetted a figure in the room. It was that of a man. As he lunged toward the bed, I threw the clock. It must have struck him because he uttered a grunt and stumbled over a piece of furniture, sending it clattering across the room to hit the wall. But the moment I threw the clock, I jumped from the bed. I knew my path to the door was clear and I ran, screaming for help as I reached the corridor. It could only come from Vivian and be of doubtful value at best. But the scream was meant to frighten the intruder into thinking there were others in the house, causing him to panic and run.

He must have lit the lamp on the hall table—or left it there to aid his escape. He came out of my bedroom, a tall, uncouth-looking man with a shock of black hair that looked as if it hadn't been combed in weeks. He had a wide, cruel face with a slash of a mouth that was widened in a sneer or perhaps a smile of victory. In his right hand he held a long-bladed knife. I had not the vaguest doubt but that he intended to kill me and this was his reason for invading our home.

I screamed again, over and over. The only indication that I'd been heard was the sound of a bolt being hastily pushed in place. Vivian was taking no chances. I ran to the head of the stairs, the man following close behind me. I fled down them, grateful I was familiar with them, enabling me to move fast. The intruder had to be more careful. The lamp upstairs was no help. I had one wild hope that he might stumble and fall, but he didn't.

Just as I reached the landing, the front door swung wide. My first thought was that there must be two of them, which meant my exit was now blocked and I had no chance whatsoever.

But it was Jacob who entered. He held a knife in one hand, a lantern in the other. The knife was one used in slashing off the tobacco leaves. It would be razor sharp. Jacob would know how to use such a weapon.

The intruder was within three steps of the reception-hall floor when he realized he was about to be attacked. Unfortunately, the lantern silhouetted Jacob, making him a perfect target.

However, Jacob, unafraid, raised the blade, preparing to set upon the intruder, but he was handicapped by the lantern. Also, the intruder, no doubt more experienced in this sort of thing, raised his knife and threw it. Jacob gasped in pain and staggered to one side. The lantern fell from his hand as did the knife. The intruder skipped the final step and, still moving, flung me aside and raced out into the night.

I reached for the lantern, which had somehow landed upright. I set it to one side, closed the door, took the key from the hook, slipped it in the lock and turned it. Not until later did I realize that it was my carelessness that had allowed the intruder to gain such easy entry. When I'd let Alex out, I'd forgotten to lock the door.

Jacob was on his knees and I went to him. His breathing was heavy, but he ordered me to light some lamps. I did so, hastily and stupidly, for my hands were trembling, making my movements awkward.

Jacob was bent over in pain, the intruder's knife still lodged in his left shoulder. I saw him grasp the knife handle and, with one powerful yank, pull it free. But the pain of this sent him crashing to the floor.

I got a soft pillow from the drawing room and slipped it beneath his head. Then I went to the kitchen for a basin of water, clean towels and peroxide with which to wash and sterilize the wound. There was also a stack of pillowcases. I took some to make bandages. I got scissors from the pantry, moving with certainty now, for the gravity of Jacob's need for help made me forget my fright.

I cut open the shirt around the area of the wound with the scissors. I was surprised at the small amount of blood surrounding the wound.

"Don't move, Jacob. You might start it bleeding. As it is, there's very little blood."

"I'm sure it didn't hit a vital spot. It doesn't hurt much."

"How did you happen to hear me scream above the noise of the storm?"

It was a downpour now, interspersed with heavy thunder and sharp crackles of lightning.

"Alex and I have been taking turns watching the house. We were afraid something like this was going to happen.

You screamed loud enough to wake the dead. A good thing the storm was still approaching."

"You saved my life." The statement was true, but I was talking in an effort to take his mind off the pain he must have been filled with.

"Where's your sister?" he asked.

"She's safe. I heard her throw the bolt on the door of her room."

He made no reply. He couldn't, for when I applied peroxide to the wound, he winced from the sting of the antiseptic.

I tore the pillowcase into strips and bandaged the wound as best I could. It would do until we got the doctor here.

"How did he get in?" Jacob asked.

I motioned with my head toward the door. "I forgot to lock it. Lie there until I come back. Sorry you can't be more comfortable, but you'd better be quiet for a while so the bleeding won't start up."

He gave me no argument. I brought the cloths to the kitchen, dropping the soiled ones in the sink. Maggie would attend to them in the morning.

I returned to check on Jacob, who assured me he was all right. I told him I was going upstairs to close the windows in my room and also to let Vivian know she was no longer in danger. I warned him again not to move until I returned.

I tapped on Vivian's door and called to her that she was safe now and could come out if she wished. Before she could reply, I went on to my room, picking up the lamp in the hall so I'd not step on the alarm clock which lay on the floor somewhere.

It lay in the center of the room. I picked it up, noting the glass covering the face was shattered. There was no ticking sound. The time on the face was four-thirty. I closed the windows and got towels from the bathroom to mop up the rainwater beneath both windows. There was a goodly amount, for the rain was coming down in torrents. I returned to the bathroom and tossed the towels in the tub.

I picked up the lamp and was in the hall when Vivian's door opened. Light flowed from her room, indicating she had every lamp lit.

"What happened?" Her features still showed the terror aroused by my screams.

"Nothing much," I said dryly. "Someone got in the house and came to my room. He tried to stab me with a knife, but I threw my alarm clock at him and got out of there. Jacob heard my screams and came in the front door. He also had a knife, but the lantern he carried made him a perfect target for the intruder—or would-be murderer, I should say. He threw the knife, which struck Jacob in the shoulder. I've cleansed and bandaged the wound and he's lying in the hall downstairs."

"I'll come down with you."

"There's no need. I can handle things. I imagine Alex will be along shortly. Go back to bed."

"Thank you, Heather. Your screams were horrible. I hope you're not angry because I threw the bolt on my door."

Despite the gravity of the situation, I couldn't help but laugh. "It was the smartest thing you ever did. He might have turned on you."

She nodded. "I knew you were in danger, but what could I do?" She was rationalizing her behavior.

I took compassion on her and went over and touched her cheek. "You couldn't have helped me. So what you did was wise. I can't tarry longer. I'm afraid Jacob may decide to get up and go in search of his assailant. He's in no condition to move, much less search for anyone."

Vivian closed her door. Apparently, she wasn't taking any chances, for I heard her slide the bolt again. It was better for her to be there. If the intruder should come back, at least I'd not have her to worry about.

But Jacob, true to his word, still lay prone, his eyes closed. I didn't know if he was sleeping and was about to go for a light blanket to cover him, when there was a heavy banging on the door.

Without opening his eyes, Jacob said, "That's Alex. But better call out and make sure."

I did and was reassured by Alex's voice. I opened the door, but he didn't enter until he took off his raincoat and hat.

"It's all right." I reached for his arm and urged him inside. I took his wet coverings and tossed them on the stair rail. Once he closed the door, he saw his father lying there, his shoulder bandaged.

Before he could ask what happened, I told about the intruder, ending my story with, "I forgot to lock the door last night after you left. That's how he gained entry."

Jacob's eyes were opened now and he smiled reassurance at Alex, who was regarding him with concern. "I asked a dumb question of Heather, when I asked how the goon got in," Jacob said. "I opened the front door just by turning the knob. Never even thought of using the key I had."

Alex said, "I'll saddle up a horse and get Dr. Simms."

Jacob said, "No need trying to get him now. Wait till daylight. I'll be all right."

Alex looked down at his father. "I intend to make sure."

I had squatted down and was carefully examining the area beneath the bandage to see if the bleeding had resumed.

Once reassured, I said, "There's no bleeding, Alex. I believe it's safe to wait until daylight, then send a hired hand. I'd feel more secure with you here. Certainly there are men on the land who have no business being here. I know now I was being watched today or probably even followed when I went to the summer house, the idea being murder. It could have been the same one who came here tonight, but he caught sight of you today and knew you'd seen him. That would explain the running footsteps I heard. I'm glad you saw him."

I looked down at Jacob. "Would you like some nourishment?"

"A little brandy, please," he replied.

"You'll have it." I turned to Alex. "Could we help your father to the leather couch in the library? He'll be more comfortable there."

"A good idea." Alex kneeled on the floor and with one of us on either side, we got his father to his feet and insisted he move very carefully to the library. I carried the lantern to light our way. Once there, Jacob stretched out on the couch and sighed gratefully.

Alex went for brandy and a glass and poured a moderate amount into the glass.

Jacob eyed it and said, "A little more would help. Put me to sleep."

"I agree," I said. "Pour it, Alex."

Alex eyed us both, gave a brief shake of his head and obeyed. I held the glass until he raised his father sufficiently so he could swallow the liquid comfortably. I handed Jacob the glass. He took a few sips and smacked his lips appreciatively. When he finished, I took the glass and Alex lowered him back on the raised head of the couch. Jacob closed his eyes and gave another sigh of contentment. I reached for the throw which lay folded at the foot of the couch and covered him with it.

"Would you like some brandy?" I asked.

Alex gave a negative shake of his head, but took out his pocket watch and snapped open the cover. "It's only five o'clock, but I'd appreciate some breakfast."

"So would I," I said. Alex picked up the lantern and we went to the kitchen. He struck a match and started a fire in the stove, which Maggie kept in readiness. Then he lit two more lamps while I bustled about getting eggs and sliced ham from the icebox and fresh bread from the pantry. I'd already filled the coffeepot and placed it on the stove, and soon the tangy aroma of the beverage filled the kitchen. At the same time I let out a cry of dismay.

Alex, expecting trouble, turned quickly and raised his hands, making fists of them. He expected someone else had gained entry to the house. But it wasn't anything like that. Suddenly, I'd become aware I was wearing nothing over my nightgown. He relaxed and started to smile, but quickly sobered, aware of my embarrassment.

"Run along. I'll look after the cooking until you get your wrapper on."

"Thank you." I was already fleeing up the back stairs to the hall which led to the bedrooms. I wondered if things would ever gain a normalcy here so that we could resume a quiet way of life. But as I slipped into the robe and tied the belt securely around my waist, I realized things had never been normal at Nightfall. Vivian and I had only thought they were.

When I returned downstairs, Alex had our breakfast on the table.

"How did you happen to come when you did?" I asked.

"My father usually comes in around four and makes

his breakfast before he takes a catnap. I get up and eat with him. I was awake and lying there waiting for him to come. I struck a match to see the clock. It was four-thirty and I wondered if something might be wrong. Of course, I mightn't have wakened, had it not been for the storm. Anyway, I decided to dress and come over here to see if he might be here. On the way I saw Vivian's room flooded with light. I knew then something was amiss and ran the rest of the way."

"I hope your father will be all right," I said.

"I'm sure he will be. But just so there'll be no question of it, I'll send a hired hand to get Dr. Simms."

"He saved my life and nearly got killed doing it."

Alex frowned. "I'm wondering where those ruffians are hiding."

"I wonder too. I figure they'd have to be at Yvonne DesChamps'."

"She has day servants, doesn't she?"

"Yes. They may stay all night, for all I know."

"Would Maggie know?"

"I believe she would."

"Please ask her when you see her."

"I will. Will you have the hired hand stop by and pick up the invitations and mail them?"

"Yes. They won't be able to do much today anyway, unless the rain stops. I'll also have him stop and tell Tim Oliver what happened. He'll come out and talk to my father. Fortunately, you can describe the man."

"Fairly well. But I believe I could identify him."

"Then he won't be back. Yvonne wouldn't risk his getting captured and talking. Fortunately, luck—if you can call it that—has been on the side of Vivian and you. At least, thus far."

"I'd say we were fortunate in having Rolf, you and your father here. Otherwise, Vivian would have been murdered. And I'm sure I would have too, had your father not entered when he did. I'm sorry he was injured."

"I'm just as certain he's relieved it was he instead of you. But it shows Yvonne intends her revenge to be total."

"What do you mean?"

"Has it occurred to you that neither you nor Vivian have any claim to Nightfall with your mother alive?"

"I never thought of that."

"I'm sure your mother did. I'm also certain she wants no part of it."

"I know she doesn't. I feel it's partly because of Vivian and me. She feels we will be disgraced when it's learned how she has earned her living."

"As she said, it's no disgrace in New Orleans, and she's accepted in the best homes. But she's going to have to lay claim to Nightfall now. And a good thing. It will be that much harder for Yvonne to contend with, having three of you instead of two to cope with."

"I wish we could convince Deputy Sheriff Oliver that Yvonne DesChamps is behind all the trouble we've had here."

"So do I. Not only him, but the entire village and those living in the surrounding countryside. But it will be difficult to prove she had a motive—and an evil one—for the good deeds she has performed through the years."

"And now the hospital," I said.

"Everyone is talking about the circus she's bringing here on the day the ground is to be broken," Alex said. "She's a clever strategist."

"We have to outsmart her in some way."

"I've been trying to think of one," Alex said. "Thus far, no luck."

A key was inserted in the lock of the back door and Maggie entered. She was startled at the sight of us seated at the table.

"What's goin' on?" she asked as she took off her raincoat and hung it on a hook by the door.

I explained briefly, mentioning that Jacob was now sleeping in the downstairs library, and adding, "I hope he'll stay there until Dr. Simms comes."

Maggie said, "I'll see to it."

I suddenly remembered Alex asking me about Yvonne's servants and I asked Maggie if any remained overnight.

"None," she replied quickly.

"Do you know if any part of the house is shut off?" I asked.

"I couldn't say as to that," she replied seriously. "Why do you ask, honey?"

"I believe she has thugs living in the house, but with servants there, I'm wondering how she does it. Certainly, strangers are skulking about our grounds, and if they were in the village, word would get around soon enough."

"She'd not allow them to remain in the village," Alex said. "If they got into trouble there, she'd have to come to their assistance. You can be assured she keeps as close an eye on them as she does on you and Vivian and is now probably doing to your mother. Certainly, that poem was written by Yvonne to let your mother know her secret is no longer safe."

"I'm sure mama believes that too."

"I'm also sure her life is just as endangered as yours and Vivian's," Alex said.

"With one difference," I replied. "Mama has Marcel and perhaps a few of his cohorts to protect her. And they will—to the death. There is no doubting their loyalty. Thank God, Vivian has Rolf. I have you and Jacob."

Alex got up. "Daylight's breaking. I'm going to get a hired hand to summon Tim Oliver and Dr. Simms. Will you give me the invitations to the soiree and I'll give them to him?"

A sudden thought occurred to me which I addressed to Maggie. "Do you think you could find out if the servants have had to cook extra food at Mrs. DesChamps' or have been forbidden to enter certain rooms?"

"I could at the church meetin' tomorrow night," she replied.

"If you drove into the village with the hired hand, could you find out immediately?"

"Sure could," she said.

"Then put your raincoat back on and I'll give you the invitations to mail."

Alex said, "I'm going to look in on my father, then I'm going to check the grounds again to see if there's a sign of the assailant."

He picked up the lantern and went out to the hall, followed by Maggie. We paused at the door to the library and Alex raised the lantern so it cast a soft ray of light on his father. Jacob was snoring softly.

Alex said with a smile, "The brandy relaxed him."

I turned to Maggie. "The invitations are on my desk. There are two stacks of them."

She nodded and headed for the stairs, but turned halfway up. "Is Miss Vivian safe?"

"She was awakened, but once things calmed down, I sent her back to bed."

Satisfied, Maggie continued on her way.

Alex donned his raincoat, then held his hat in one hand and the lantern in the other. "Heather, you'd better get some rest. This hasn't done you any good."

I said, "I will if you'll look in on your father. You have a key, haven't you? If not, I'll give you this one." It hung beside the door.

"I have one. I'm going to have the hostler hitch up the buggy. Have Maggie wait on the back porch for him. She won't get so wet. I want to check to see if anyone's still prowling, but I doubt I'll have any luck. Too close to dawn. And no chance of finding footprints with the rain still pounding."

He switched the lantern to his other hand and took the key out of his pocket as I opened the door.

I said, "Be careful, Alex. I need you."

It was an impulsive statement, made on the spur of the moment. It took him completely by surprise. He was halfway out the door, but turned to come back in.

"Not now," I said. "This isn't the proper time. I'm still too shaken by what happened."

He pressed his open palm against the open door, preventing me from closing it. "When will that be, Heather? I'm not made of steel."

"I'm beginning to discover that I'm not either," I said. "I'll let you know."

"Make it soon?" he pleaded. His hand still held the door open.

"I will," I promised. "Please go."

He gave a barely perceptible nod, but his eyes held a ray of hope. I closed the door quickly, lest I weaken. I wasn't ready yet. I couldn't wipe out the brutality I'd witnessed, nor the fear I'd felt when I was pursued down the stairs. I would know when it was time to declare my love.

Twenty-one

OUR ARGUMENTS DID LITTLE TO CONVINCE DEPUTY
Sheriff Tim Oliver that Yvonne DesChamps was behind
all the evil which had occurred at Nightfall. Not even the
sight of Jacob Hale, lying on the couch, his shoulder
bandaged, convinced the deputy. Nor did the knife
which had caused the wound help our story. Tim Oliver
confiscated it and wrote down the description of the assailant which Jacob and I gave him, but I imagined the
villain was on his way back to New Orleans or, more
probably, on his way to parts west, where he'd not be
apt to be identified. However, there were plenty of ruffians in New Orleans who could be sent here to take
his place.

I discussed with Alex the wisdom of showing Deputy
Sheriff Oliver the letter from mama and the poem, but I
felt highly reluctant to do so, stating that it was up to
mama to reveal herself alive, rather than for me to state
she was and that the letter was from her. Proof was what
Tim Oliver insisted on. That, Alex cautioned me, was to
his credit. It was only my word that the letter and newspaper clipping of the poem was from mama. Of course,
the grave could have been dug up and revealed to be
empty, but I was against that. The empty grave was still
no proof mama was alive, and I would not reveal her
whereabouts without her permission. I'd also cautioned
Vivian not to do so. Vivian had made up her mind that
she would go to Rolf's plantation. He'd convinced her
her place was with him and if she'd been there instead
of at Nightfall, she'd not have suffered another fright.

I was relieved to have her go, since I'd not have her to
worry about. Not that she would stray from the house.
She was too terrified. She finally realized that the pro-

tection she'd always felt when papa was alive was no longer there.

Maggie had got some valuable information at the village. She'd learned that the day servants had been shipped to New Orleans to clean up a house recently purchased by Yvonne DesChamps. Joel had accompanied them to supervise the work. That meant he would be her liaison man to keep mama under surveillance. Or, rather, his hired goons would, enabling Yvonne to have someone under her roof to do her evil bidding. And no servants in the house to observe any strangers of an unsavory nature.

What hurt the most was that we'd not heard a word from mama. I'd even insisted on driving to the village with Alex to see if a telegram might have arrived which had not been delivered. He suggested I send mama one, but I refused. Since she'd not answered my appeal, I felt she wanted no part of us. She had apparently felt she'd fulfilled her duty by warning us and suggesting we have the men be on guard at all times.

Vivian didn't seem to mind and I suspected it was because she was secretly relieved that mama's means of support would not be known, thereby eliminating the fear that she would be socially ostracized.

Despite my inner worries, I went ahead with the plans for the soiree. Maggie had help come in from the village. There would be only a light repast. I had hired a small group of musicians to play Strauss waltzes in the summer house. The strains of their music would drift across the lawn to the terrace where we would entertain our guests.

I'd had posts placed at the four corners of the expansive terrace. Wires were strung from post to post and Japanese lanterns were strung on them.

The guests began arriving promptly at seven. They came with gifts, which were placed on a long table. Vivian and Rolf stood there, greeting the guests and accepting their gifts with thanks. Servants opened the packages and made an attractive display of the wide assortment. We'd placed small tables and chairs on the terrace and the guests went to the buffet table and helped themselves, bringing their plates and beverages to the tables. The low hum of conversation mingled with the muted strains of the string ensemble. Fortunately, the day had been beautiful, so the evening was warm with just the suggestion of a breeze to keep everyone comfortable.

I caught sight of a carriage moving up the drive and my hopes rose, believing it would be mama. But I nearly fainted from shock when it stopped and a footman got down, opened the door and helped Yvonne DesChamps out. She was followed by Joel. Both were followed by the footman, who carried an enormous package, which was set on the table with the gifts.

"Do open it," Yvonne said graciously to one of the servants we'd hired for the occasion.

The servant obeyed and in the light of the lanterns a sterling-silver tea service, complete with tray, sent shafts of reflected light from the lanterns.

Vivian and Rolf were as astonished as I, but they recovered and went over to express their thanks to the woman and her son, who had not even been invited.

Yvonne touched Vivian's cheek, as she had that day we visited her, and wished her boundless happiness. She congratulated Rolf for getting such a beautiful wife. There was surprise on the part of many that she had put in an appearance.

There was nothing I could do but be gracious, since I was the hostess. Inwardly, however, I was seething with resentment. Alex, who had been mingling with the guests, was by my side in an instant.

He whispered, "Bring her to the buffet table, as if she were a welcome guest."

I gave him a look of protest, but knew he was right and I went to her.

She accepted readily and Alex moved off, leaving me with Yvonne and her son. He looked very masculine and his comments were as gracious as those of his mother, particularly when he saw the table still heaped with food. Yvonne complimented me on the charm of the grounds and on placing the orchestra where it could be heard, but far enough away so it didn't disturb the conversation of the guests.

"That's not quite the reason, Mrs. DesChamps," I said. "Papa's death is too recent for this to be a gala occasion, but I wanted it to be a happy one without being disrespectful."

She wasn't wearing a veil tonight, but her large hat with soft brim was most flattering. She looked around again and nodded approval.

"It is everything you planned it to be, Heather. Everything. Your mama would be proud of you if she were alive."

"She is alive and she is proud of both her daughters." The low voice was raised so that it carried the length of the terrace.

Yvonne almost dropped her plate in startlement. I was as shocked as she. Joel was looking over my shoulder, his eyes widened in amazement.

I turned to see mama approaching.

She embraced me and then stepped back. "Since I am Vivian's mother, I felt it only right that I make the announcement of my daughter's elopement and marriage."

I managed a shaky smile and said, "I thought you'd never get here, Mama."

"You shouldn't have worried, dear. Please excuse us, Yvonne. I want Heather to be at my side, along with Vivian and Rolf, when I make my little speech."

And so mama had returned to Nightfall after all. Vivian and Rolf had, by now, spotted her, and I saw Vivian whispering to him. His astonishment was as great as Joel's and Yvonne's, but it was quickly followed by a smile of pleasure.

The soft murmur of voices had ceased completely when mama spoke. Yvonne and Joel stood, plates in hand, not even having the presence of mind to seat themselves at one of the few empty tables.

Mama, Vivian, Rolf and I went to the far end of the terrace. There, I'd had a small dais placed so we would be easily visible to everyone. But it was mama who did the talking.

First, she announced the marriage and welcomed Rolf into the family. Following that, she said, "And now, in case some of you in my age group think you are looking at the ghost of Jessica Taylor Gates, you are in error. I am alive. Following the duel, Bryant and I made an agreement that I would leave the plantation out of respect to the girls, whom I had disgraced by causing him to take the life of a gentleman whom I had allowed to persuade me that he cared for me."

She paused and looked beyond the terrace to Yvonne and her son. "You were right, Yvonne. Lemuel fooled me as he had others. That is no excuse for me. I caused grave unhappiness not only to you, but I deprived you of a husband and your son of a father. Afterward, Bryant never knew a moment's happiness, for he had to carry the guilt of his crime with him to his grave. He suffered a cruel death." She paused and looked over the guests. "But he was not a coward, as you've been led to believe. I understand everyone in the village found a copy in their mailbox of a poem which appeared in a New Orleans newspaper. It is headed 'Today's Tattletale.' Since I know you're already familiar with it, I shan't read it. I'm also certain you know now—if you doubted before—I was the wife given a second life. I left Nightfall and began a new life in New Orleans."

Mama went on to describe her way of making a living, and while there were a few gasps in the audience, most people were quiet and, though probably shocked, did not look disapproving.

"I don't know if I will remain at Nightfall," she said. "However, I hope you will not make my daughters suffer if you disapprove of me."

She had an arm around each of us and she turned first to Vivian, who was taller, and stood on tiptoe to kiss her cheek. I was the same height as she and she bestowed a kiss on my cheek next.

I didn't know how the others felt, but I was so happy that I felt like bursting into tears. But I wasn't to wonder for long, for several in the group who had known mama when she was young came up and either welcomed her back or openly embraced her.

Vivian was so stunned that she could only stare. Rolf looked amused, and Alex, standing to one side, gave a nod of his head that indicated all would be well. I hoped so. Jacob stood by his son's side, his arm in a sling to lessen the strain on the wound. He was beaming and I knew he bore mama no ill will.

And so the evening ended, with Yvonne and Joel once again bested. I wondered if Vivian and Rolf would return the silver service, which they must secretly regard with distaste. Mama said later that it would be returned, but not immediately. Perhaps Yvonne would forget her hatred for the family. If so, it could be stored away and forgotten. If not, then it would be returned with a note stating that she had displayed bad taste in coming and presenting the gift, since she bore us only hatred.

After the guests left, I introduced Alex to mama. She approved of him and noticed the warm glances he and I exchanged. She suggested we take a walk while she discussed the plantation with Jacob. Alex regarded me to see if I was in agreement. I nodded and we moved away from the lights. The orchestra had left and their chairs and music stands had been removed by the servants, so we headed for our favorite spot—the summer house.

Not until we ascended the few steps and stood there in the light of the Japanese lanterns did we speak. There seemed to be no need for talk. Alex had held my hand as we moved along the path and our fingers were still intertwined.

But once in the summer house, he said, "I like your mother. I knew she'd come."

"I didn't!" I exclaimed. "I was as startled as Yvonne. I didn't even know those poems had been put in mailboxes."

"It was done during the night," he informed me. "I didn't want you to know. You had enough to attend to without that to add to your worries."

"I wonder if mama will stay," I said.

"I'm inclined to think she will. At least until she knows whether Yvonne will behave herself. She'll never be convicted for the murder of your father. And perhaps she'll be too busy with the coming festivities for the hospital and the circus she's importing to think up further mischief."

"I hope so," I said.

We were silent again, then Alex spoke as he turned me to face him.

"Must we always be so serious?"

"I'm the too-serious one. Vivian said words to that effect and she was right."

Then he said what I wanted to hear. "You're a very genuine young lady and I love you."

"And I love you, Alex. I'm just bursting with love for you. I took you too much for granted. Now that I know,

I'm fearful someone else will come along and take you from me."

"Never." He gathered me close. "Have you anything more to say?"

"No."

"Good. We've wasted enough time."

He gathered me close and my arms went around his neck. Our lips met and it was as glorious as the first time. Only now I knew my reason for being so stirred was not resentment but love. Beautiful, glorious love, and I reveled in the wonderment of his lips on mine, our hearts beating in unison. As I thought before, it was a heady feeling, as if I'd imbibed too much champagne. Only this was much more beautiful.

Twenty-two

THOUGH MAMA CAME WITH TWO TRUNKS AND SEVERAL pieces of baggage, it took some persuading to convince her she should stay. Not until later did the thought occur to me that she had really wanted to return, but intended to make certain we genuinely wanted her with us. Otherwise, she'd never have brought so much baggage.

But what convinced her mostly was when she learned Vivian would now live at Rolf's plantation and I would occupy the house alone. Mama awaited me in the drawing room when I returned from the summer house with Alex, who left me at the door. I was glowing when she called to me, but I felt not a trace of embarrassment that my features revealed my love.

She embraced me when I told her Alex had professed his love and had asked for my hand in marriage. She stated we should have an immediate wedding. After all, she argued, Vivian had eloped, and with Alex in the house, she'd feel that I'd be safe and she could return to New Orleans. She'd had her luxurious carriage transported on the train and Marcel had driven her in it from the station.

I told her Marcel was as welcome to remain as she, though it wasn't for me to say, since Nightfall was her property, not Vivian's and mine. She nodded, well aware of that fact, though she'd never mentioned it in New Orleans. I suggested she take the room Vivian and Rolf had vacated, since it had once been shared by her and papa. But she refused, saying that once Alex and I were wed, it would be ours, since it was the largest. Besides, she added, her sense of guilt regarding papa was still with her and would be till the day she died. Just as papa carried his regarding the duel, I thought.

I gave in to her refusal. As for Marcel, she said he had engaged a room at the inn.

However, I was as stubborn as she when she repeated her suggestion that Alex and I marry immediately. Though the thought was thrilling, I didn't want the shadow of Yvonne DesChamps hovering over Nightfall. I told mama that I hoped her return would persuade Yvonne that her disgusting poem, far from frightening the three of us, would persuade her that we had faced up to the challenge and she had met with defeat.

And so the weeks passed until harvesting time with nothing further happening. Gradually, our apprehension lessened and diminished altogether once the harvesting had been finished and the curing was over for the first crop of leaves. They had been removed from the sticks and more leaves had been added to cure over the smoke from the low-burning fires. All fourteen of our sheds were full. Alex, in the course of two weeks' time, had contacted auctioneers and we would soon begin shipping the tobacco out.

Mama had turned the running of the plantation over completely to Jacob and Alex, but I couldn't resist walking over the grounds. I loved the smell of the fires and the partly cured tobacco leaves as much as Vivian had always hated it, and I had no hesitation about entering the sheds.

To mama's surprise, she had been invited to a few teas, which she had returned. She told me Yvonne had been at two of them and the discussion centered about the hospital she was donating and having built, plus the circus and entertainment she was having brought to Rutford for the ground-breaking ceremonies, which would occur in a week.

One night Vivian invited Jacob, Alex, mama and me to dinner. During the course of it, mama disclosed she had sent Marcel back to New Orleans to negotiate the sale of her establishment. She said her place was here now with her family, since we had accepted her with love. Also, since the villagers bore her no ill will, she wanted to come home. Vivian clapped her hands in delight and the rest of us joined in.

It seemed the next thing to do would be for Alex and me to announce our coming marriage. Certainly, Yvonne had tried nothing more. Perhaps she felt it would be unwise to force her hand further. However, there was one thing that troubled me. I'd asked Maggie to check to see whether the day servants at Yvonne's had returned. She told me they had not, nor had Mrs. DesChamps had anyone else come in to do the cleaning. That gave me pause for thought, for certainly the bediamonded hands of Mrs. DesChamps had never held a dustcloth. But then mama informed me that Yvonne was having meetings at the inn every day and had a sumptuous menu prepared. It was while dining that the ladies discussed the entertainment festivities and who would serve on the various committees. So Yvonne saw to it that she didn't go hungry.

I didn't relay Maggie's information to mama and swore Maggie to secrecy. She obeyed, though reluctantly, feeling a secret such as that should be shared. Perhaps she was right, but mama seemed years younger in the short time she'd been here and her skin glowed with color as she took daily walks in the fresh air. I caught sight of her one day at the cemetery. She stood in front of papa's grave, then moved up to the tombstone, placed her hands on it and rested her head on them. I don't know if she was crying, but I felt it best not to disturb her or even let her know I'd seen her.

Vivian and Rolf were at his plantation, busy with his crop. That is, Rolf was busy. Vivian was planning a formal dinner and had immersed herself totally in the preparations.

We were able to communicate fairly well. It was a carriage ride of about an hour and a half to Rolf's place.

Field hands were entrusted with carrying messages, so we always knew that Vivian and Rolf were safe and how they were occupying themselves.

I saw little of Alex. He was working with his father, supervising the preparation of the tobacco for the market, which required long and arduous hours. I missed him, but fortunately I had mama.

I took to walking in the sunshine, though staying close to the house and keeping a wary eye out for trouble originating from Yvonne. These solitary walks gave me a chance to think about my future with Alex, and about Vivian and Rolf. She loved the house, though she was making plans to do some refurnishing after the crops were sold. It was a lovely place, in need of a mistress. Vivian had proved herself quite competent in the handling of servants and she had hired enough of them. But not without Rolf's approval.

Rolf's farm was about the same size as ours and when, as he suggested, we merged both of them, we would be a formidable power in the raising of tobacco.

By evening I began to experience a strange premonition of disaster. It has been said that twins sometimes can transmit signals of danger or torment over the miles. It had never happened to Vivian and me. Yet tonight, as I prepared for bed, that feeling grew until I found myself trembling with apprehension.

I thought of telling mama about it, but the idea was too silly. Besides, why worry her because of a mere hunch. Yet, shortly before midnight, when the door knocker resounded through the silent mansion, I wasn't surprised. My first thought was of Vivian.

I put on a robe, pushed my feet into my slippers and, carrying a lamp, I hurried down the stairs just before the knocker again resounded. On the veranda stood a man with an envelope in his hand. Not far behind him stood his panting horse, ridden too fast. Just beyond the horse stood Alex, with a rifle ready to fire.

"I'm from Mr. Rolf's plantation, ma'am. There is great trouble. Your sister asked me to ride fast and deliver this letter."

"What happened?" I asked as I began to tear open the flap.

"There was a terrible fire. Every shed burned to the

ground. Mr. Rolf, he tried to put out the fire in one of the sheds and he was burned and hurt bad. You better come fast."

Alex was close enough to hear everything. "I'll harness the carriage and bring it around as fast as I can."

"I'll waken mama, if she's not already awake."

I thanked the man and closed the door. Mama was upstairs in the corridor and I quickly explained.

We were ready in ten minutes. As we hurried along the hallway, mama displayed her anxiety.

"What of Vivian? Did the man say if she was hurt too?"

"No. But he said the sheds were destroyed."

Alex was waiting to help us into the carriage. I noticed that he kept his rifle on the front seat beside him. He had a way with horses and the carriage was soon moving very fast, forcing mama and me to hang on to avoid being tossed about. Mama's silence showed that her worry equaled mine. Alex concentrated on driving.

I said, "If this is Yvonne's doing, I hope there'll be a clue."

"We don't know what caused the fire, so let's not point the finger. Besides, it's Nightfall she's after. Or was."

"Vivian was a part of it," I said remindfully. "Though Rolf's wife, she's still a Gates."

"Be calm," mama advised quietly. "We don't know and we may need our wits about us. What did Vivian say in the letter?"

"All she said was come quickly. Rolf was hurt and she's afraid. I don't doubt she is, because Vivian is most meticulous in her penmanship and I could hardly read her letter."

"Are you sure she sent it?" Alex asked from the front seat.

"Why should we assume she didn't?" mama asked.

"This could be a trick of Yvonne's. To get us into a position where we can be attacked on the road. Or maybe to get us away from the plantation."

"I never gave that a thought," mama said. "We can't turn back. If Vivian and Rolf need help, we have to do what we can for them."

"The man who brought the letter had ridden his horse to a lather," I said. "I noticed that."

"So did I," Alex called back to us. "Though that doesn't prove anything. We'll be there in about forty more minutes. I can't get any more out of the horses."

Well before we reached the farm, we smelled the smoke and the odor of burned wood and tobacco. When we pulled up in front of Rolf's house, every window was showing light. There were two buggies and a carriage already there. From the front of the house, we couldn't see the fields, or the shed area, yet none of us had any doubt but that everything had been destroyed. My heart had never been heavier than when I saw Vivian walk through the lighted doorway to stand on the veranda. She was weeping bitterly.

Mama was the first to reach her. Alex didn't leave the carriage, but drove it around to the back so he might survey the damage and learn what he could. Mama took Vivian in her arms to comfort her. She seemed unable to tell us what happened. She was very close to shock. Mama supported her as they went inside to the drawing room, where they sat down on a sofa.

I heard male voices upstairs and quickly ascended the steps to the second floor. Two men, conversing softly, stood outside a room from which muted light came. One was Dr. Simms, the other, a stranger.

Dr. Simms introduced me to his colleague, Dr. Corman, adding, "Dr. Corman specializes in burn cases and already has a nurse who specializes in that work attending Rolf."

"How seriously is my brother-in-law hurt, Dr. Corman?"

"He has some burns which are very severe, others of a minor nature. We've done everything possible for him. I have one nurse with him now. I'll get a second. I'm sure there are facilities for their living here."

"There are."

"Then that's no problem."

"Will he live?" I asked.

"That depends on whether he can get through the next three days. He has lost a great deal of body fluids."

"May I see him?"

"Of course, but I warn you that you'd better have a strong stomach. He's unconscious. We gave him morphine.

He'll be kept on narcotics for several days. The nurse's name is Miss Bittner."

I walked slowly into the room. Miss Bittner, a competent-looking, middle-aged woman, was seated by the bedside, her attention on her patient. Rolf was covered up to his chin, but his arms were outside the sheet and they were bandaged heavily. Most of his face was covered too, but in one area, free of bandages, I saw how his hair had been burned away.

"I'm Miss Gates, Mrs. Fielding's sister," I said softly.

"I'm glad you're here, Miss Gates." She also kept her tone muted. "Mrs. Fielding is on the verge of hysteria and needs comforting."

"Our mother is with her now."

"That's the best kind of comforting. Mr. Fielding has been burned from head to foot. Luckily for him, most of the burns are superficial, but the bad ones are very serious."

"Have you seen many like him?"

"I've seen burn cases for ten years. They call me every time they get one. Fortunately, Mr. Fielding looks like a strong, healthy man. He'll need care for a long time and I'll have to talk to somebody about another nurse. Unless the doctor decides to send him to the hospital. I don't think he will. The ride is too long, and too rough."

Rolf stirred and she transferred her attention to him.

The two doctors were still in the corridor. "It's shocking," I said. "Does anyone know what happened?"

"Mr. Fielding was trying to check a fire in one of the curing sheds. The roof caved in on him and he was covered with burning timber. He managed to crawl out, but not before being badly burned."

"What of the fire? How did that happen?"

Dr. Simms said, "We've no idea, Heather, but the proper authorities are inspecting the burned area. I think they suspect the fires were set because so many sheds burned."

"Thank you."

Miss Bitner came to the door and both doctors reentered the room.

Instead of going into the drawing room when I came downstairs, I went looking for Alex. If I couldn't find him, I intended to talk to the officials who were investigating the fire. I met Alex coming back, but not before I had a look at what the fire had done. I remembered how well the curing sheds and barns had been laid out, well apart from one another so a fire wouldn't spread. Now, even in the darkness, I could see that there was nothing left.

Alex looked his concern. "How is Rolf?"

"The next few days will tell. He was horribly burned."

He indicated the direction of the sheds. "Every single building is gone. That beautiful crop of fine tobacco burned."

"Have you talked with the authorities?"

"Yes. They found evidence that at least ten fires were set by someone expert at arson."

"We've been living in a fool's paradise," I said soberly.

"You mean Yvonne, of course."

I nodded. "Any proof?"

"None. So without proof we can't make accusations."

"I don't believe she'll cease her nefarious deeds until we're all dead. And I suppose Deputy Sheriff Tim Oliver will still think it's mischievous trespassers."

"In fairness to him," Alex said, "he looked very upset."

"Did he say anything to you?"

"Only that too many things of suspicious origin have happened to the Gates family to make it all seem accidental or the work of a transient who happened on the property."

"But he didn't mention Yvonne."

"No. But I feel I should get back to Nightfall as quickly as possible."

"You don't think. . . ." I couldn't finish the sentence.

"I don't know. The hired hands aren't on the property. There's only my father and Maggie, who's probably sleeping soundly. She doesn't know about this." He gestured toward the charred embers still glowing.

"I'll go back with you," I said. "But first, I must go in and comfort Vivian. She's in shock, which is only natural. I saw Rolf. It's horrible."

"I'd rather you stayed here."

"No."

"Then please don't delay. I'll get the carriage. One of the men is holding the horses in check. I'll give them a drink of water before we start because I'm really going

271

to drive them. I'm thinking of my father alone. Armed but alone."

Vivian and mama were still where I'd left them. Vivian had stopped crying, but she was still shaking with grief and fear.

Vivian looked up at me. "Did you see Rolf?"

I nodded. "The doctors have given him a sedative so he'll sleep. That's nature's best healer. Sleep."

My statement did little to console her. "Did the doctors say he'd die?"

"No. The opinion is he's young and strong. He has a nurse who specializes in burn cases. Dr. Corman is getting another nurse of that type. They will live here. So you'll have to get rooms ready for them."

"I will," mama said, then addressed Vivian. "Do you have a sleeping draught?"

Vivian nodded. "In the small chest in the bathroom off our bedroom."

I said, "Rolf is in a smaller room, isn't he?"

She nodded. "Dr. Simms wanted him in the quietest part of the floor. You know our room is at the head of the stairs."

"I'll prepare it. Bring Vivian upstairs, Mama."

I ran up ahead, found the paper-wrapped powder and mixed it in a glass of water. I insisted Vivian drink it immediately. She did, her movements like those of a human imitating a doll.

Mama started undressing her and I went for her nightgown, talking as I did so. "Be sure to give Rolf all the encouragement you can. He's not going to have an easy time of it."

"I know," she replied, her agony reflected in her face. "I saw him when they brought him in. I couldn't believe it was Rolf. He looked like—like—a burned log." A sob escaped her throat.

"Please try not to sob," I pleaded. "Your voice might carry and waken him."

He was so heavily sedated, I didn't believe it would, but my plea quieted her. I told mama I was returning to Nightfall with Alex. Apparently she sensed my concern, for she eyed me gravely.

"You don't think—"

"Of course not," I said, attempting reassurance. "I'll

send Maggie with some clothes for you. You'd better stay here."

"I will," mama said. She already had Vivian undressed and had helped her put her nightdress on. She pulled down the bedclothes and Vivian got in like an obedient child. I was thankful mama was here so I could return with Alex.

I nodded a farewell to mama, who held up a restraining hand. She stepped out into the hall and asked a question.

"Was it arson?"

I nodded.

She embraced me briefly, then said, "Run along. I fear the worst."

Alex had the carriage in front and was in it, holding the reins. One of the men, unidentifiable with his soot-covered face, addressed me by name and helped me up into the seat beside Alex. I saw the gun on the floor.

Once we were on our way, I asked a question. "Do you know how Rolf's financial situation is?"

"Not good. He mortgaged his plantation to save Nightfall."

"Then we'll sell our crop and give him a fresh start."

"If," Alex said, "there's anything left of your plantation to sell. I'm worried. It would be like those men who work for Yvonne to strike at both places at once to make the loss so tremendous there's no way of coming back."

"And if they have? If everything is lost?"

"I don't know what could be done. It's bad enough now. Our only salvation is to prove Yvonne is a half-crazed woman who should be put behind bars."

"How will you go about that?" I asked.

"All I can suggest," Alex said, "is for us to stay on guard. If your crop brings the price it should, you can easily repay Rolf, with a large added amount, so that you can replant and he can get his plantation back into operation."

"Rolf's requirements will come first," I said resolutely. "He helped us out when we were in dire need and it's no more than right that we do the same for him."

Alex made no reply and when I studied his face in the light from the side lamps, I could see that it was lined with worry. And I knew his worry was caused by one thing. The destruction of our crop.

To reach the plantation we had to drive through the village. It was from there that we saw the crimson glow in the sky and we knew what it was without asking a question. My heart sank and I had trouble refraining from tears.

A friend of Alex's saw us and waved his arms. Alex got out of the carriage to meet him. Mostly, I thought, to shield me from a cruel, firsthand report of what had happened. He came back to the carriage and climbed aboard.

"It's not good," he said. "The fire was first seen from the village about the time Maggie managed to drive a buggy here and ask for help. All of the sheds were burning. The stable and the mansion were not touched, but . . . you're going to view a scene that's a duplicate of what happened at Rolf's."

"With the exception, I hope, that nobody was hurt."

"My father was. Somebody sneaked up behind him and clubbed him down. He isn't going to die, but he's a very sick man and he will be for some time. Can you face up to this, or shall I drop you off at the inn?"

"I have to face it," I said, though I wondered if I could, for I was trembling inside and my stomach was threatening to turn over. I held onto Alex's arm tightly, but I resisted the desire to close my eyes as the red glow grew brighter and the clouds of acrid smoke were beginning to reach us, making breathing difficult. From the area of the glow I was sure every shed was in the process of being destroyed.

When we pulled up at the mansion, I knew it was all too true. The firemen, volunteers from the village, had been unable to control any of the fires.

Alex said, "My father was taken to the house. I'm going to see him for a minute before I go down to the sheds."

"To where the sheds were," I corrected him. "I want to see your father too."

Maggie, tearful and angry at the same time, met us in the reception hall. "I saw one of 'em. I saw him good," she said.

"How do you know it was someone who set fire to the sheds?" Alex asked.

"Because he was holdin' a big torch and it was close to his face. I thought he was going to burn the house down too, but he went on by, ridin' a horse. A big roan. I'd know him and the horse anyplace."

"Good," Alex said.

"Is Mr. Rolf all right?" Maggie asked.

"He's badly burned," I said. "But he's young and strong. That's in his favor."

"Miss Vivian must be takin' it mighty hard."

"Yes, she is, but doing better than I thought. Mama stayed over to take care of her. I'll pack clothes for you to take to her. How bad is Jacob?"

"He's hurt some, that's for sure. I bandaged his head as best I could. I put him in the last room down the hall."

Alex took the stairs two at a time. I turned to Maggie. "It's possible you'll be called upon to identify the man with the torch—and the horse. So remember what they looked like."

"They gotta find him first," she said sensibly.

"True. Will you make a pot of coffee? I'd like some and I'm sure Alex would too."

"It's on the back of the stove. With all that's been goin' on round here, I been keepin' the pot full."

"I'll go up now and see Jacob."

Alex was sitting on a chair beside the bed when I entered. Jacob, his head heavily swathed in bandages, looked wan, but otherwise he seemed to be holding his own. I went over to the bed, bent down and touched his cheek with my hand.

"I'm sorry this had to happen to you, Jacob."

He was as feisty as ever. "I been telling Alex here that before they knocked me out, I saw one of them putting a torch to the first shed. I never saw him before, but I'll know him if I ever lay eyes on that man again."

"Before my father could even raise his rifle," Alex said, "someone rushed up behind him and laid him out with a club."

"I didn't see that one," Jacob confessed. "If I had, I wouldn't be here and he wouldn't be alive. Have you gone down to see the damage yet?"

"Going now," Alex said.

"I'll go too," I said. "Maggie will come in and sit with you."

"You go along with Alex. I'm kinda weak in the knees, but except for that and a headache, I'm fine. Let me know how bad it is. As if I didn't know already," he added morosely.

Maggie was in the hall, but entered the room when we left.

Alex found lanterns, lit them and we used them for light as we made our way along the path which led to the edge of the plantation. We passed the barn and the stables and we stopped long enough to make sure the horses were safe and there was no smoldering spark getting ready to destroy the stable as well. The hostler was nowhere about and I thought it likely he might be down trying to help the firemen.

Alex and I crossed the dusty, cleared area where the tobacco leaves had grown. There were half a dozen small fires still burning, enabling us to see at a glance that not one shed had been spared. I had hoped that the storing shed where the newly baled tobacco was held might have been saved, but it was now a glowing mass of dull fire, as the precious leaves slowly burned.

Alex left me to find some of the volunteers and talk to them. I stood there, gazing at the destruction without emotion because I was no longer capable of it. I couldn't even summon anger against Yvonne. I was numb.

Alex returned, placed an arm around my waist and led me back to the mansion.

"The first warning they got in the village was the beginning of the glow from the fire. About then, Maggie drove in screaming for help. They got out here as fast as they could, but there wasn't enough water, there were too many fires going at the same time and very little could be done."

"Then we're broke again," I said. "All I want to do now is have some coffee and go to bed. Maybe after a rest, I'll be able to think."

He nodded and we increased our pace as we returned to the mansion. There was scarcely enough money to buy groceries. I'd placed what was left of the ten thousand dollars in the bank, to be used for the payroll and supplies which were needed immediately. Since I'd been helping Alex with the books, I knew there was a mere pittance of that remaining.

Twenty-three

IN THE MORNING I AWOKE TO THE BITING SMELL OF burned wood and the incomplete combustion of tobacco leaves, raw and cured. For a moment I couldn't identify that strong odor, but when the truth hit me, I lay back against the pillows in a sort of stupor, brought on by desperation and lack of hope.

What could we do now? Rolf's crop and sheds were gone. Ours were burned out. The two crops we'd depended upon so much were a total loss and we had borrowed large sums on the strength of their sale. There was no insurance. I'd never heard of any company insuring crops, and the sheds were of such flimsy construction they could easily be replaced and were worth little.

True, we still had the barns and the stables, along with the mansion itself. Rolf, too, had the same assets, but combined, they couldn't possibly pay off the indebtedness of one plantation, let alone two of them.

We had been in serious trouble when Yvonne bought up all the notes and threatened us with eviction and foreclosure, but the present situation was even worse. There wasn't the slightest possibility of borrowing any more.

The banks would likely be lenient with their collection of what we owed them because of the fires, but eventually they would have to get their money back and we were in no position to pay off the notes. They could take our land and the mansion and outbuildings. Perhaps it would come to that.

I got out of bed and stood by the window overlooking the front of the estate. It was so beautiful. From here, there was no indication of the blackened ruins at the rear. All I could see were the well-tended lawns, the formal gardens, the boxwood and the great, age-old trees. To lose this now would be almost as bad as losing Alex's love. At least I had that to sustain me. The mere thought of him lifted my spirits.

I dressed hastily and had just finished breakfast when the knocker resounded through the house. I called to Maggie that I would answer. It was Alex and Deputy Sheriff Tim Oliver.

Maggie had already informed me that Jacob was still sleeping, so I relayed that information to Alex. He thanked me, but asked if he might look in on his father anyway. I motioned him toward the stairs and invited Deputy Sheriff Oliver into the drawing room, quite aware of his reason for being here. But he also asked if he could look in on Jacob. I assented, though cautioning him to be quiet, adding that Dr. Simms had come last night and stated that while there had been no fracture of Jacob's skull, he'd been dealt a severe blow and needed rest.

Deputy Sheriff Oliver made a note of that in a book which he held in his hand. He then hastened up the stairs after Alex.

I went into the drawing room to await their return.

When they came down, Alex went to the kitchen first and told Maggie his father was awake and expressed a desire for some food. Deputy Sheriff Oliver entered the drawing room and took a seat opposite me. Alex followed, stating Maggie was delighted to hear the news and said she'd bring a tray up.

I expressed my pleasure at hearing Jacob's request for nourishment, understanding why Alex's features were brighter than when he'd entered the house. The only one whose expression didn't change was Deputy Sheriff Oliver, who opened the conversation.

"I'm afraid I have news of a dusturbing nature, Miss Heather," he said.

"Not Rolf, I hope." I tensed at the thought he'd already lost his battle for survival.

"No," Tim Oliver replied. "I stopped there this morning. Dr. Corman spent the night there and says Rolf is doing as well as can be expected. I asked what that meant and his reply was that he's no worse, but it's too soon to expect improvement."

"Thank you for telling me," I said. "Now, what is the disturbing news?"

"We found a body in the ruins of one of your sheds."

"Have you identified it?"

"It's too badly burned for identification. But he was a big man."

"Apparently, he's the one who set the torch to the plantation."

"I found Jacob's gun just beyond the ruins. I've already sent the hired hands into the village with the body to have the medical examiner perform an autopsy to determine if he was shot before being burned. There is a bullet missing from Jacob's gun."

"Jacob never said he shot anyone!" I exclaimed.

"He didn't," Alex said flatly. "He was struck on the head before he could fire the gun."

"Perhaps he just thought that," Tim Oliver said. "The blow may have caused his finger to press the trigger without his even being aware of it."

Alex said, "My father stated emphatically he did not fire the gun. You even asked him now and he was equally positive he hadn't."

"It could be a slip of memory." Tim Oliver still seemed unconvinced. "Not that I blame him. That's quite a lump on his head."

"My father remembers everything else," Alex argued.

"Maggie saw the arsonist," I said.

"I don't think you'd want her to look at what's left of him," Tim Oliver said. "Our only hope of learning if he was shot is if the bullet can be found lodged in the body."

"Have you thought that the stranger could have been shot by the person who struck Jacob on the head?" I asked.

"No," Tim Oliver admitted. "But it's a possibility."

"Haven't you thought it suspicious that the only two plantations destroyed were Rolf Fielding's, who is married to my sister, and ours?"

To my surprise, he admitted such a thought had occured to him.

"Then wouldn't you say it is possible that someone is out to destroy us?"

"It could well be," he admitted.

"The only enemy we have is Yvonne DesChamps," I said.

"I expected you'd say that," Tim Oliver said. "But we still have no proof."

"Have you looked for any?" I asked.

"I wouldn't even know where to begin," he admitted.

"At least you're honest," I said. "The best place is her house."

"I couldn't do that." He was shocked by my suggestion.

"You could, but you won't," I replied.

"Give me one reason why I should," he said.

"I will," I replied firmly. "Her servants have been in New Orleans for several days, cleaning up a house which she purchased. That means she has the house to herself and to shelter the ruffians she's hired to burn us out."

He pondered that for a few moments. "Miss Heather, I don't want you to think I'm taking sides. I'm an officer sworn to uphold the law. But I can't go to Yvonne Des-Champs and accuse her of hiring goons to burn down your plantation and that of Rolf Fielding."

"Or of burning down our barn, having two of papa's horses shot and then having papa murdered," I said, finding my patience wearing thin. "And please don't remind me of all her good deeds, including the donation of a hospital. I'm well aware of them, just as I'm aware of the poem which was placed in everyone's mailbox to let them know mama was alive. Only one person would do that. Yvonne DesChamps. But mama outsmarted her before the poison poem could be misinterpreted. Mama is now accepted in the community."

"I'm well aware of it," Tim Oliver replied. "Just as I'm aware of the beautiful gift Yvonne DesChamps and her son brought to the soiree at which your mama made her appearance."

"Neither Yvonne nor her son were sent an invitation," I said. "Vivian and Rolf wanted to return the gift, but mama advised caution, stating perhaps Yvonne would cease her deviltry now that mama had foiled her latest effort. The fact that our plantations have been burned to the ground, our crops destroyed, is proof that Yvonne will never stop until she has destroyed us all."

Deputy Sheriff Oliver worried his earlobe, his manner thoughtful. "Tell you what I'll do, Miss Heather. I'm going to pay Yvonne DesChamps a visit. I'll discuss the entire situation with her. I'll state you could think of no one who would have a motive to burn down the plantations except her. I will repeat what Bryant—your father —revealed to you about her swearing revenge after his duel with Lemuel. I'll further comment on the fact that she bought up his outstanding and overdue notes with the idea of further embarrassing him."

"Will you really?" For the first time my hopes rose, believing I'd convinced the deputy sheriff that Yvonne was other than she pretended to be.

But he quickly dashed my enthusiasm. "Now, don't get your hopes up. I'm not going to make any accusation. I'll not even admit I believe a single word you say. I am merely going to repeat what you told me. You know, of course, you may lay yourself open to a civil suit."

Despite the gravity of the situation, I couldn't help but smile. "I doubt Yvonne DesChamps would be so heartless."

He returned the smile and glanced at Alex, who had remained silent through the entire conversation.

Alex said, "I'm inclined to agree with Heather. Yvonne will do nothing to soil the image she's built up of herself as a bountiful lady."

"Well, I'll stop there on my way back to the village. I'm really sorry about all the destruction. I'll let you know the result of the autopsy as soon as I know."

Alex spoke again. "I'd say the man was murdered so he couldn't talk. Both my father and Maggie saw him. If he had been caught, he would have confessed, in the hope of saving his skin."

I said, "You might also ask Yvonne if she would have any objection to your making a search of her premises."

"A good idea," Alex agreed. "There might be others hiding there. I saw a man skulking on these premises one day. I believe he was ready to pounce on Heather, but he spotted me and made his getaway."

Tim Oliver said, "I'll see what I can do about that, but it's asking a lot."

"If she's innocent, she'll have no objection," I said.

Deputy Sheriff Oliver had no sooner driven off than the door knocker sounded. Alex and I were on our way upstairs to see his father, but we paused while Maggie opened it.

To our amazement, it was Banker Bradley. We descended the stairs, greeted him and invited him in to the drawing room. His manner was so cordial and his regrets at what had happened to both Rolf's plantation and ours so genuine that I felt certain he had come to assure us we could borrow to rebuild the sheds and replant.

He opened the conversation by saying, "I've already looked at the destruction on your property. It's total and shocking. It's also puzzling that it happened to both yours and Rolf's and no one else's. It's as if someone has a grudge against you."

Alex spoke before I could reply. "I agree. Can you think of anyone who would wish such misfortune on either Miss Heather or Rolf Fielding?"

"I could not," he replied promptly. "But if you are greatly concerned, you may relax, for I'm the bearer of glad tidings."

Alex and I must have looked so bemused he found it mirth provoking. He chuckled briefly, then removed from a portfolio he was carrying some legal-looking documents.

"Mr. Bradley, did you come here for the purpose of offering a loan?" I asked.

"I did," he replied affirmatively.

"I don't quite know what to say." I felt like laughing and crying at the same time, but managed to get a hold on myself, knowing I was verging on hysteria.

"No need for you to say a word. Just take these documents over to the desk and sign them. I am bringing papers over to Rolf Fielding's also."

"He couldn't possibly sign anything now," I said.

Mr. Bradley gave a sympathetic nod. "I heard how severely he was burned and I'm sorry. But at least he'll get a fresh start. The papers can remain at his home until he is capable of signing them."

"I pray God that will be soon."

I was already on my feet and was reaching for the papers when Alex said, "Heather, your mother will have to sign those papers." He switched his attention to Banker Bradley. "Are you saying that the bank is loaning Heather's mother—since she is the rightful owner—money to begin again?"

"Oh, no," he spoke quickly. "Nothing like that. This is a benevolent gesture on the part of Yvonne DesChamps."

His words hit me with the force of a blow. I said, "You may place the documents back in your portfolio. We will accept nothing from Mrs. DesChamps."

"But why not?" His surprise seemed genuine. "She held notes on Nightfall before."

"She will not a second time," I said. "As Alex stated, I couldn't sign the papers anyway. Only mama can. She is at Rolf Fielding's caring for my sister, who is in shock because of what happened to her husband."

His eyes expressed sympathy, but I could see he was also distressed by my refusal. "You think it useless, then, for me to leave the documents."

"Completely useless," I said.

"My next stop is at Rolf Fielding's," he said. "I hope I will meet with better success there. Since your mama is there, she may not feel as you do."

"You're well aware of the past history regarding my parents and the tragedy of their lives, so I will leave that to you to figure out."

Faint indignation was evident in the look he gave me, but when he switched his glance to Alex and saw his mouth compressed in anger, humility replaced the indignation.

"I won't take up any more of your time." He tied the portfolio and stood up, hat in hand. "I must say this before leaving. Mrs. DesChamps said she is well aware of your pride and would not take your first refusal as final."

"My only refusal is my final one. But since I do not really have any say in the matter, you may discuss it with mama when you go there."

"Which will be at once." He was already heading for the door. "I know my way out. Please don't bother."

We didn't, but our eyes followed him until he opened the door and disappeared from sight.

Maggie stuck her head around the door frame. "If that doesn't beat all."

Before I could berate her for eavesdropping, she had disappeared and her pattering footsteps faded down the hall.

I gave a forlorn sigh. "There's no besting that woman."

Alex's arm went around me and he eased my head against his chest with his hand. "There has to be," he said into my ear. "And we'll find it."

I moved my head back so I could look up at him. "How could I ever have been so blind as not to know I loved you? I never could have kept my wits about me if it hadn't been for you."

He disputed that with, "I told you once you're quite a woman. That still goes. I'm grateful you found out you loved me before I left. I know that Gates pride would never have let you reveal it afterward."

"That's something we'll never need to wonder about," I murmured.

His kiss was tender and I returned it. It made me realize our love would carry us through whatever trials lay ahead.

I suggested we go up and see his father again. I hadn't yet stepped in to wish him well, not wanting to waken him should he be asleep.

Jacob was stirring restlessly, but his tray was empty and from the large platter, I could see Maggie had seen to it that he'd had a man-sized breakfast.

"When am I getting out of here?" he demanded impatiently.

"When Dr. Simms says you can," Alex answered firmly.

"Somebody besides you has to guard the place," Jacob replied.

"There's nothing left to guard," Alex said. "The sheds are burned down, the crops, totally destroyed."

Jacob looked thoughtful. "I didn't kill that thug, though I wouldn't have minded doing so."

"Yvonne DesChamps will make certain there are no witnesses," Alex said. "So she has someone watching to see that the underlings who do her dirty work don't get caught. They did in New Orleans. She'll take no chances here."

I said, "There's nothing for you to do around the plantation, Jacob. Just rest and get well. We're going to discuss our plans now. But first I think we should visit Rolf and Vivian."

"I agree," Alex said.

Twenty-four

MAMA EMBRACED ME, THEN TOLD ME I COULD GO UP and look in on Rolf, and afterward, visit Vivian. Mama wanted to discuss the disastrous events with Alex. She added that when I came downstairs, she had a matter of another nature to talk over with me.

The door of Rolf's room was slightly ajar and I could see the nurse working over him. She sensed someone was about and turned. I stood in the doorway, hesitant about entering. She gave a permissive nod of her head.

I crossed the room quietly, then paused a short distance from the bed. She had just removed a bandage from Rolf's face and the sight of raw flesh was a shock, though I gave no visible evidence of it.

I identified myself and she said, "I'm Miss Jarrell, the day nurse. Mr. Fielding is awake and can see you, but only for a few minutes."

"Sorry about your accident, Rolf," I said.

"Hello, Heather. I want to talk with you."

"Let your sister-in-law do the talking," Miss Jarrell cautioned.

"Go outside for a few minutes, please, Miss Jarrell," Rolf urged. "I'll rest easier after I've talked."

She looked dubious, but I assured her I'd not let him talk more than two minutes. She finished her bandaging, then left, though with reluctance.

Rolf said, "Is there anything left of my face?"

"Yes," I replied. "But one side is badly burned."

There was no need to fool him. Even before the sedatives had been given to him, he had known the pain and had smelled the burned flesh.

"I don't know how Vivian will be able to live with me," he said despairingly.

"She loves you."

"So she said." His voice took on a note of hope. "She even insisted on helping the night nurse change the bandages before she went off duty. So she's seen the ugliness."

"Your heart isn't scarred," I said. "And hers is filled with love of you. She told me that even as a little girl you were the only one she ever loved. But you ignored her."

"Deliberately. She was so beautiful and too aware of it."

"But it's you she loves, Rolf, not herself. I'll tell you something else. For a while, I thought it was you I loved. All the time it was Alex. So you see, I'm the fickle one. Or was. For me, it will always be Alex. For Vivian, it will always be you. That's what you must remember. And now, no more talk."

He looked his surprise. "I didn't know she'd always loved me."

"Don't let her know I told you."

His eyes assured me he wouldn't. Without giving him a chance to say another word, I left the room and nodded to the nurse, standing just outside the door. She returned to her patient and I went on to Vivian's room.

I tapped lightly on her door. She opened it and we embraced, after which we cried, though softly, fearful Rolf might hear. Our tears were caused by what had happened to him and how it might affect his personality. He'd been so handsome and now one complete side of his face would be scarred. She gave me a detailed account of all the doctors had said. I let her talk, knowing it was an outlet for her.

"Were you being honest with Rolf when you said you loved him, despite what happened?"

"It's dreadful, I know," she said. "But the scars won't matter. I just want to be with him, and when he's awake, I am. I only came in now to dress and go back. Of course, he has to have sedatives for a few days until the terrible pain eases, but when he awakens, I'm there. I want him to know I'll always be there when he needs me."

"You've seen his face unbandaged, then." I wanted to make certain Rolf hadn't just imagined she'd been there.

She nodded. "It just serves to enhance my love for him."

"You're quite a woman, Sister." And she was. Her eyes expressed her gratitude, just as I know mine did when Alex made that statement to me.

I embraced her again and we left the room, she, to go to Rolf's, and I, to go downstairs and see what mama wished to discuss with me.

Mama heard my descent and called softly to me from down the hall. I followed her into a small, circular room with a white cast-iron table with glass top and matching chairs which were thickly cushioned. Louver blinds were closed against the midday sun, giving the room a soft light. Mama had sandwiches and iced lemonade on the table and the three of us sat down.

I told Alex about Rolf, but suggested he not go up to see him today. He was still in a great deal of pain. I related the brief talk I'd had with him and his relief when I informed him Vivian had told me there had never been any other man but him. And knowing her, I was certain what had happened would only deepen her love.

"It has," mama said quietly. "I'm proud of her. I'm proud of both my daughters."

"Thank you, mama." I didn't think I'd have much of an appetite, but when I bit into the sandwich and tasted the delicious chicken, I realized the drive had made me hungry. It was apparent Alex relished the sandwiches also.

Mama sipped lemonade.

"No sandwich, Mama?" I asked.

"No, dear. You and I have identical figures. Very womanly and though, despite my curves, I'm almost as slender as you, I've maintained my figure only through very cautious eating. And doing that in New Orleans is far from easy. You remember that as the years pass. You'll have to be either cautious or active. Vivian has a willowy figure and will always be slender."

I was about to reach for another sandwich, but refrained. "Is that what you wanted to tell me?"

She smiled. "No. But it's what I'd have told you had

I been around when you were growing. I have to crowd it all in now with whatever time I have left."

"Don't make it sound morbid, Mama."

"I don't mean to. And we've no more time to waste. First of all, Mr. Bradley, the banker, has come and gone. Once I learned the reason for his mission, I gave him short shrift. Of course, I'm certain he's as innocent of Yvonne's deceit as everyone in the village and surrounding countryside."

"He'd already visited us," I said. "He got the same reception."

"So much for Mr. Bradley," mama said. "Had your mail arrived before you left?"

"No."

She took a lavender envelope from her pocket, removed a card and handed it to me. It was an engraved invitation from Yvonne DesChamps, inviting Vivian and Rolf to a masquerade festival which would be held the evening of the day on which the ground-breaking ceremony for the hospital would occur.

Mama said, "It was addressed to Rolf and Vivian. I'll show it to her later. I'm sorry, my dear, that I had no qualms about opening it, but I had a suspicion as to the sender."

"What do you suppose she's up to?" I asked. "Hasn't she done enough to Vivian and Rolf? Not only destroying the crop, making them penniless, but leaving him with a permanently scarred face."

"I think she feels her method of justice has been served by what happened to Rolf."

"They why the invitation?"

"Because everyone in town will get one."

"Not me," I said. "Or you."

Mama nodded. "I got one also. But I'm sending regrets. Yours will be there when you return."

"I'll not accept," I said firmly.

"Yes, you will. So will Alex, for he'll recieve one also." His smile was quizzical. "*I* will?"

Mama said, "Yvonne knows Heather wouldn't go without you."

"Heather will *not* go!" I exclaimed distastefully.

"Heather *will* go." Mama spoke with quiet emphasis.

"But why, Mama? The very thought sickens me."

"I think she's up to something," mama mused. "Though with so many people about, I can't imagine what she could possibly do."

"Do?"

"To you," mama said. "You're the one I'm worried about now."

"Then why do you want me to go?" I ask indignantly.

"To be around people. I'd worry far more with you back at Nightfall."

"Alex and Maggie would be there."

"And I'd go there to be with you. But you know I'm needed here. I want that woman exposed for what she is. The sooner, the better."

"How can my presence expose her?"

"I wish I could answer that question," mama replied. "But I'd feel much easier with you and Alex around groups of people, rather than alone on the plantation where you'd be completely vulnerable. If you refuse to go to the masquerade, I will go with you. But as I've already said, my place is here."

I couldn't dispute that, and it would have been selfish of me to pursue the argument further. Nonetheless, I found the very thought distasteful.

I said, "I think hate has driven her mad."

"I'm sure of it," mama said.

Alex said, "I told your mother about Tim Oliver's visit this morning and that you told him everything you know about Yvonne. Also, that you suggested he pay her a visit."

"I wonder if he did," I said.

"We'll stop in at his office on our way back and find out," Alex said.

Mama said, "I'll send a telegram to Marcel in New Orleans. I sent him there on an errand for me. I'll have him bring back costumes."

"I don't want to go, Mama."

"You have no choice. I'm ordering you to go."

"Don't you think I'm a little old for you to do that?"

"You won't be too old for me to order you about until you're married to Alex," mama said. "Now, no more arguments. I have some letters to write. You two run along and see what Tim Oliver learned."

"I have a feeling it will be a waste of time, but we'll

stop by anyway." Alex stood up and moved my chair back.

I didn't go back upstairs, knowing Vivian would be at Rolf's bedside and quiet and rest was best for him, for these were crucial days. I doubted she knew just how crucial. It was as well she didn't.

Nor did we have any luck at Tim Oliver's office. He informed us he had stopped by Yvonne DesChamps' home. He had an open and frank discussion about us with her. He said she was deeply hurt by our suspicions, especially since she wished to finance both plantations with her money. He also stated that she had escorted him through her home, from the cellar to the attic. She'd opened the door to every closet and storage room. No one could be concealed in that house. He did state that the furniture downstairs had dust covers, but she said the reason for that was she was planning a voyage to the Orient immediately following the masquerade festival which was to take place in one week.

Alex expressed his thanks and we departed, more frustrated than ever. And mama was right. When we returned home, there were two lavender envelopes. Each contained an invitation. One for Alex and one for me.

"I still say I won't go," I said.

"You must," Alex said, "for your own sake."

"You have no costume."

He smiled. "I will have. Your mother ordered one for me also. I'm going as a pirate. Don't forget, we had a little talk while you were upstairs."

"So you did. I don't know what she is ordering for me and I don't care. I'd rather stay with Vivian."

"Your mother knows that, but I have an idea she has thought of a plan for unmasking Yvonne DesChamps."

"Did she discuss it with you?"

"No. It's just a hunch on my part."

I eyed him warily. "Your hunches usually pay off."

"Heather, I'd like to keep you away from that festival or masquerade or circus or whatever it is, but your mother's adamant. She told me if you refused, she'd insist to the point of going with you. And you know Vivian needs her more than you do."

"Yes," I admitted. "So I suppose I have no choice."

"She used another argument for you to go, stating

Yvonne would believe you fear her if you remained away."

"I do fear her. I'm terrified of her. I don't know where she's going to strike next."

Alex said, "Oh, your mother said if you see strangers on the property, don't fear them. They've been hired by Marcel."

"After what happened here and at Rolf's, how will we know that?" I asked indignantly.

Alex smiled. "They'll be dressed as gentlemen, not as ruffians. They'll speak, should we meet, and continue on their way. But they're armed and as tough as anything Yvonne imported."

"Apparently, she sent her hirelings away after last night."

"After last night, there's not much else to destroy."

"Just mama and me."

He made no answer. There was nothing to say. He knew I spoke the truth.

I went upstairs and changed into a light cotton dress. Then I visited Jacob, who complained he still had the headache. I remained with him, placing cold compresses on his head and answering questions he asked about our plantation and Rolf's. Alex had told him that the destruction there equaled ours.

"Does Rolf know about this one?"

"I don't think so. Nor does Vivian," I said. "I know mama wouldn't tell them just now. Vivian has Rolf on her mind and he was badly burned."

"So Alex said. A miserable shame. When he recovers from the burns, will he be able to work?"

He was asking in a roundabout way if Rolf had other injuries that would make him an invalid.

"Oh, yes. But he mortgaged his plantation for money to get this one going. So while we have the desire, we lack the finances."

I didn't mention Mr. Bradley's visit to Jacob. It would only upset him and the visit had served no purpose other than to inform us that Yvonne was still letting her presence be known. In so doing, we knew she hadn't finished with us. Which was what she wanted us to know. I doubted she ever would be until mama and I were dead. With Vivian, she'd got her revenge. Every time Vivian looked at Rolf's face, she'd know who had been the cause of his disfigurement. But in that respect, Yvonne had failed, though I hoped she never learned about it or she would think up some other form of satanic scheme against my sister. Yvonne thought Vivian was still the social butterfly she'd been before her marriage. But I knew she'd given evidence of having grown up before Rolf's accident. With it, she'd entered womanhood. Either she would have run from him or she would be loving and staunchly loyal the remainder of her life. She'd proved it would be the latter. A wave of pride flowed through me at the thought of her. Though mama and papa's marriage had failed, one thing they both had was courage. Vivian had inherited it.

That reminded me of the medical examiner's report that papa's death had either been accidental or suicide. I was still determined to prove it was murder, instigated by the vengeful instincts of Yvonne DesChamps. I wondered if she had ever been capable of feeling love. Perhaps Lemuel had had reason to look for a gentle woman. I quickly discarded that thought. Mama had learned he had a wandering eye and Yvonne had said he would always have been loyal to her. She knew him and didn't mind his indiscretions so long as he came back to her. Which he always had. But when he had planned to run away with mama, and papa had forced him into a duel which resulted in his death, Yvonne's hatred knew no bounds.

Jacob had stopped talking and his lids were drooping, indicating the cold compresses had eased the ache in his head and sleep wanted to take over. Or perhaps already had, because the lids remained closed and his breathing was even and regular.

I placed the compress back in the basin and carried it out of the room and down to the kitchen.

"How is he?" Maggie relieved me of the basin as she asked the question.

"Sleeping."

"Best healer there is." She poured a glass of milk and handed it to me. "Drink this. Do you good."

"Mama said I have to be careful and watch my figure."

"She's right. Wish I'd had someone to tell me that. Too late now." She patted her ample hips and laughed softly.

"But just now you need nourishment. I made Alex drink a glass."

"Did he tell you about the masquerade Mrs. Des-Champs is giving in a week?"

"Guess I never gave him a chance, honey. I asked questions about Miss Vivian and Mr. Rolf."

So I told her about Yvonne sending invitations to Rolf and Vivian and mama.

"Mama insists that I go."

Maggie looked thoughtful. "If she does, she got a reason."

"Alex said as much. But her reason is she feels I'll be safer around a lot of people than here."

"I agree. Your mama goin'?"

"No. She's sending regrets. She wants to be with Vivian and Rolf."

"That's where her place is."

"Yes. But I hate to go to any affair that woman gives. She's caused us so much grief and trouble. Now we're about to lose the plantations."

"I got a feelin' things aren't as black as you think they are."

I went over and touched my cheek to hers. "I wish I had it. But just saying that lifts my spirits. Any idea where the money is coming from?"

"I got a pretty good idea," she said. "But I ain't sayin'. Reckon you'll hear about it soon enough."

"Oh, come now, Maggie. You know I hate riddles."

"This is no riddle. An' if you used your head, you'd figure it out too."

"I've tried and I can't see any way we can get started."

"Then you ain't tried hard enough. Get out of my kitchen now. I got to get some food ready. You and Alex can eat by candlelight. Go get dressed up."

"It doesn't seem right with Rolf so ill and no telling if he'll make it through the next few days."

"I been prayin' he will and I guess you better start. But get dressed. Walkin' around with a long face ain't gonna change things."

"You're right. I'll dress. Alex will think I'm either heartless or foolish."

"Ever think he needs cheerin' too? His pa got a bad bang on the head."

"I know. I'll do as you say." I started out of the kitchen, then recalled Alex mentioning strangers on the property. I passed the information on to her.

"I know all about it," she said placidly. "I met two of 'em already. Real nice gentlemen."

I felt that "deadly" would be a better word. I was certain Marcel had chosen them to guard the ruins of the plantation. Though I knew it wasn't the plantation they were guarding, but the inhabitants on it. From now on, mama would leave nothing to chance.

I chose an emerald-green tea gown for dinner, and to my surprise, Alex wore dove-gray trousers with matching vest and a dark green coat. His green tie was a perfect match, and for a little while we both felt self-conscious and awkward. Not only because we were so dressed up, but because we missed the chatter of Vivian, mama and Rolf. But Maggie had placed candelabra in the drawing room and she told us to go there first.

We knew better than to argue. We commented on mama's painting, which was lit by two small oil lamps resting on either end of the mantel.

Alex said, "If your mother's hair was jet black, I think you'd look a great deal like her. Certainly, your figures are identical."

"Stop flattering me, darling," I said. "You know as well as I that Vivian's the beauty. She takes after mama."

"I'm not trying to flatter you," he said. "I mean it. I have a feeling that as the years pass, you'll look more like her than Vivian will."

There was no more time for foolish talk, for Maggie entered with a tray on which two glasses stood, half-filled with wine.

"Jus' thought you should make a little ceremony of the evenin' meal by relaxin' with some spirits first," she said in a tone that brooked no argument. "Take your time. When you're finished, you can come in the dinin' room. I put plenty of roses from the garden in there so their perfume will kill the smell of charred wood. I can still smell it, though. Don't think it'll ever go away. Then again, I know it will." She gave me a look of feigned disgust. "First thing, I'll be talkin' as gloomy as you."

I took the glass from the tray and raised it to her. "To your health, Maggie, from all of us, with love."

She stood there while Alex and I took a sip from our glasses. Her tone was soft as she said, "Thank you, honey." She blinked the tears away as she made an abrupt departure.

"What would we do without her?" I asked Alex.

"Let's not even think about it." His arm enclosed my waist and he led me over to the settee.

"I have something to tell you," he said. "Your mother told me I could when I talked with her today. I guess she sensed your despair in regard to Nightfall. I must confess, I shared it, though I knew I could get work as an overseer somewhere and, hopefully, one day own my own plantation. Papa put all his money in an invention that will produce rolled cigarettes. We have faith in it, but while I have my brain, a healthy body and two hands to work with, I know I can make it. I just didn't want you to have to do without, when you've had anything you wanted all your life."

"Alex, you sound nervous." I couldn't help but be amused by the way his thoughts jumped from one subject to another.

"I suppose I am. You know I've already asked for your hand in marriage. Your mother would like us married now."

"So would I," I said. "But not with things as they are."

"With things as they are, there's no need to wait," he said, "Unless—"

"Don't finish that sentence," I said. "I'll marry you. Just let Rolf come through this crisis. I have a feeling he'll mend fast, once the healing starts. I thought it would be nice if he could be our best man."

"And Vivian your matron of honor," he said.

I nodded.

Alex said, "It would be something for him to look forward to."

"And Vivian too. I'll ask her if we could have the wedding in her garden. It escaped the flames. Ours is partially burned."

"Well, now that that's settled," he said, "I'll tell you what your mother revealed to me this morning, while you were upstairs."

I said, "Let's bring our glasses into the dining room. I know you're starved."

"Fine," he agreed. "The aroma of roast chicken really is tantalizing."

"And you know Maggie's sausage stuffing is," I said. "Let's go. I'll carry your glass."

"No, I can." On our way, I called to Maggie that we were too hungry to delay dinner.

She came in from the kitchen as we entered the dining room. "Don't matter. Just let Mr. Alex sit at the head of the table. Way I figure it, he'll be there soon anyway."

"Then you have hope that Nightfall can be saved," I said.

"I never lost hope, child." She spoke with quiet determination.

Maggie outdid herself with the meal, starting with chilled melon balls, moving on to a creamed chicken soup and then the entrée, which was as good as it smelled. I thought of mama's warning about disciplining myself in regard to food, but tonight, I felt, was something special.

Alex felt it too, for before we began the meal, he bowed his head and gave thanks that our lives had been spared in the holocaust which had destroyed the two plantations. He added a prayer for Rolf's recovery.

Maggie stood beside him, head bowed and hands folded while he prayed, and at the end, she joined us in saying, "Amen."

But it seemed that we touched on so many trivial subjects that it wasn't until we were sipping our coffee that he asked if I would remain quiet until he told me the news mama had relayed to him that morning.

I said, "I think it must be the wine that's made me so garrulous. I shan't open my mouth until you say I may."

So it was then he told me that mama had sent Marcel to New Orleans with instructions to her lawyer to sell all her real estate. He said every piece of property was situated in a choice location and she'd already had several offers. He added that the deals would be closed in a matter of days, at which time Marcel would return with the checks and our costumes for the masquerade. In the meantime, he added, both plantations would be guarded by men hired by Marcel.

"A pity it didn't occur to us that Yvonne would burn us out," I said. "If the guards had been placed on the property then. . . ." I didn't finish the sentence. I sounded ungrateful.

"We're alive," Alex said. "Just remember that."

"I know," I said. "I'm sorry I voiced such a thought. Our only concern now is Rolf's recovery."

Alex nodded. "But you see, you don't need to worry about losing Nightfall. Nor does Rolf have any fears regarding his plantation."

"Does he know?"

"No. Nor does Vivian. But Jessica—" Alex paused and smiled. "Your mother gave me permission to call her that."

"Good." I paused, then added, "Sometimes I think she'd like Vivian and me to call her that. She really wasn't with us enough to get used to the term 'mama.' "

"I know what you mean," Alex said. "She's more like a sister than a mother, though there's no doubting her love for either of you."

"I know. Shall we take a walk? I've eaten so much."

"Let's do that. The air won't smell so sweet. But I doubt we'll notice."

Nor did we, for our talk was that of lovers. And when Alex left me at the door, his embrace was so fervent, it left me shaken. I did manage to lock the door, but I leaned against it for minutes afterward until my heartbeat slowed and my steps steadied. I knew he felt as I. I hoped Rolf would make a rapid recovery. I wanted to know the joy and ecstasy of being Mrs. Alexander Hale as soon as possible.

Twenty-five

AND SO THE WEEKS PASSED QUIETLY, WITH ALEX AND I visiting Rolf and Vivian each day. Rolf had passed the crisis and was already seated in a wheelchair, though he was not well enough to leave his room yet and required the care of two nurses. But his spirits were high and made more so by Vivian's constant attention, seeing to his every need.

Rolf joked, cautioning she would spoil him, but she quickly shushed him. She couldn't kiss his face, but she compensated for that by raising his free hand to her lips. There was no doubting her love or devotion to him and the nurses were even now allowing her to change the bandages. Mama and I watched her, our feelings a mixture of amazement and pride.

Maggie had accompanied us a few times and even she shook her head at the change in Vivian. "Just to think," she said on our return journey, "none of us ever gave that girl credit for having an unselfish thought in her head, much less a brain."

Alex said, "Rolf's spirits are high too. It seems as if everything is going to turn out right. Finally."

"You mean," I said, "mama got the money to finance the rebuilding of the sheds and replanting of crops."

"Yes. It's a boost of morale for all of us."

"It is." I only wished I could be as certain that things would now be all right, that Yvonne would attempt no more acts of destruction. Whether of property or life. But somehow I couldn't believe it. I had a feeling she was up to something, but I kept my fears to myself. Especially since Alex made no mention of her name. There again, I wondered if it was because he didn't wish to worry me or he really believed she'd accomplished all she'd set out to do.

Marcel had returned and delivered my costume to the house, along with Alex's. I asked Maggie to bring his to the cottage he and Jacob occupied. Fortunately, Jacob's head injuries responded to rest and he had moved back there, but he still couldn't do anything, other than take brief walks to get his strength back. And then it had to be in the evening, for the sun set his head to throbbing again. I doubted he'd ever be able to do hard labor. Not that he should have done it anyway. But he was like papa, happy in his work and enjoying working alongside the hired help. And Alex was the same.

Mama came one night to see me in my costume.

The full skirt was held out by several crisp petticoats underneath. The skirt was a fiery-red taffeta, which seemed to whisper with each step I took. The blouse was red laced with red-silk lining. It had puffed sleeves which set just below the shoulders and the decolletage was daringly low. I remonstrated with mama about it, feeling it too bold for a village like Rutford and its staid inhabitants.

"It's a duplicate of one I wore once, and if I didn't think it too bold for me, it's not for you."

"I assume you mean you wore it in New Orleans," I said soberly.

"Yes," she replied.

"There it would be accepted," I replied sternly. "Here, I'll be the talk of the countryside. I've been known as the brainy twin, not the beautiful one."

She laughed heartily. "The night of the festival they'll know you have brains as well as beauty. And wear your hair down."

I frowned as I glanced at the low decolletage.

"Oh, goodness!" she exclaimed impatiently. "I knew you'd have reservations about it, so I brought along this large silk rose. Slip the stem into the bodice and that will make you feel more respectable."

"It is an improvement," I admitted.

"It isn't, but so long as you think it is."

"I just don't like to call attention to myself," I said.

"I'm sure Alex will approve of it," she said.

"I hope so," I said doubtfully.

"Wait till you see him in his costume. He'll catch the eye of every female there."

"He'd better not return their admiring glances," I said with mock sternness.

"When are you going to be married?" she asked, sobering.

"As soon as Rolf can be best man."

"Did you tell him that?"

"No. I felt it would be better for him to have a few more days of nothing to think about but getting well."

"He's making a remarkable recovery, thanks to his physical stamina."

"In that case, when you return, tell him we would like him to be our best man and Vivian to be our matron of honor."

"She fully expects to be," Mama said in her matter-of-fact manner. "But she didn't know if Alex would ask Rolf."

I laughed, and when mama looked puzzled, I explained. "It seems only yesterday Vivian scolded Alex for coming too close to the house when she was giving one of her parties."

Mama looked her surprise. "You mean she was a snob?"

"She was. But Alex paid her no mind. After all, we grew up together. But Vivian was spoiled by all the attention she got from the young men she invited."

"And all the time it was Rolf," mama mused.

I nodded. "And for me it was Alex, though I was too stupid to realize it. I even resented her elopement, feeling she'd done a sneaky thing."

"She told me you quarreled constantly during your growing years."

"We did," I admitted. "But if one of us had a problem or a troublesome situation, the other came to the rescue."

"Loyalty," mama said with a nod. "Well, if you weren't close before, what you've been through has accomplished it. I'll have no worries regarding that."

"Never," I said. "We're a closely knit family."

"And a very proud one. I was too proud. My terrible pride brought on the catastrophe that has beset Nightfall and Rolf's plantation."

"Not entirely," I said. "Papa admitted he gambled heavily—or unwisely. He admitted overimbibing. That was after you left him."

"Maggie told me about it," mama said. "I have a terrible sense of guilt. I am completely to blame. I insisted on leaving your papa, even though I loved him. I didn't let him know that. I told him I hated him for what he'd done to Lemuel. I suppose at the time I thought I did. But there never was another man for me but Bryant Gates."

I sensed mama wanted to talk and so I asked a leading question. "Did you ever think of going back to him?"

"I used to walk the floor nights. Lonely nights, wanting him desperately. Knowing the depth of his love and remembering his ardent lovemaking. I even packed my baggage once, knowing he'd welcome me. But I wouldn't give in. And when he wrote, asking for help to save the plantation for the sake of both of you, I turned him down, saying I wanted nothing to do with him or his. How cruel I was."

"He suffered as you did, mama. He drank because of his loneliness, but never when he was here. He would go away."

"And I suppose that she-devil, Yvonne, had him watched and had professional gamblers lure him into card games he couldn't possibly win. That's how she first got him in her clutches. He signed notes, then had to borrow on the plantation, thus signing more notes, which she bought up when they fell due, and he never suspected the identity of his benefactress."

"Not until the barn burned down," I said reflectively. "And then, I think, in some way, she let him know."

"I was selfish," mama said sadly.

"He never blamed you. Only himself. He said he was obsessed with being a successful plantation owner."

She nodded. "The largest one in the state. And I resented it. I wanted to come first, but Nightfall did. Always. It was all he could talk about. The soil, the leaf, the curing sheds, the weather. Every so often he would buy me a bauble or give me money to buy one. My rival was the plantation. Nightfall. I let it destroy me."

"Mama," I said by way of encouragement, "you made a success in New Orleans."

"An empty one." Bitterness tinged her voice. "Love. Everyone responds to love. I was so hungry for it, but I should have been patient. There were times when he came to me, assuring me of the depth of his love. I was always there when he wanted me, but the times seemed too far apart. And for me, that wasn't enough." She paused, then added slowly, "Vivian has succeeded where I failed. Now I must make it up to you both."

"Did you mind selling your holdings?" I asked.

Her head moved negatively, and though she smiled, it was a sad one. "The check will be divided equally between you and Alex, and Vivian and Rolf. There are also investments. You'll never need to worry, even if the plantation crops fail. I had wealthy friends in New Orleans. They advised me wisely in money matters and investments. It will be yours now."

"No, Mama," I disputed. "Alex and I will repay you."

"Not a dime would I accept," she said. This time she

did laugh and it was good to hear, for it was hearty. "I was a neglectful mother, but I am going to make amends."

"Mama, you've been goodness itself since you revealed your love for us. And then, coming here and outsmarting Yvonne the night I was going to announce Vivian and Rolf's marriage."

"She got even."

"She'd have done it anyway," I argued. "I feel certain of it."

"I can't condemn her, since it was my weakness which caused her husband to be killed in a duel with your papa. But I swear to you, my dear, I had not been unfaithful to your papa. I don't even know if I'd have run away with Lemuel. But your papa found the letter Lemuel wrote. We did leave notes for one another in the summer house. I dropped that one. I think it was the fact that I didn't give in to Lemuel that caused him to suggest running away. He knew Yvonne would forgive him another escapade. I didn't know about them until I moved to New Orleans. Everyone there knows about the wrongdoings of others and dotes on telling them."

She stood up. "I've troubled you enough with my past. I just wanted a final talk before the festival. Be sure to wear your mask. It's very beautiful."

And it was. Black silk, lace covered and ruffled, so that most of my face was concealed. Also, it glittered with small, iridescent sequins. She lifted it off the dressing table and held it up to catch the lamplight.

"After you're married," she said, still studying the mask, "enjoy life with Alex while you're young. That's when it's so precious and the sound of lovers' laughter so joyous to hear. Then, when you're older, you'll have all those beautiful memories to share. Or if one goes first, the one remaining will have them to cherish."

Her voice wavered and I felt she was close to tears. For some reason, so was I. Our talk had been warm and sentimental, yet she'd been filled with recrimination too. I suggested a glass of wine before she left, but she refused, saying she must get back to Vivian and Rolf. Vivian had insisted on letting the nurses go, wanting to tend to Rolf herself. But it had proved too much and so mama shared in the changing of bandages.

I went downstairs and saw her to the door. Marcel awaited her outside, and he removed his hat and bowed. He was a handsome gentleman and devoted to mama. He assisted her into the carriage, got in himself, occupied the seat facing her and tapped the roof with his cane for the driver to get started.

I waved a farewell, watched the handsome landau start down the drive, then went inside. Without knowing why, I went into the drawing room and looked up at the painting. I knew the woman who had just left was not the same as the one in the painting. No suffering was visible in the painting. Just a beautiful face and one that was loved.

The lady who left had bared her soul and revealed her years of suffering, just as papa had revealed his. Two people loving each other so much and living out their lives in loneliness. At least, papa had our love. But it wasn't the same. A man needs woman-love to help him grow. And a woman needs man-love for the same reason. Children are the result of that all-consuming love.

I moved about the room, lowering the lamps and then blowing them out. I picked up a small one in the hall to light my way upstairs. On the way, I thought how lucky I was to realize now what it had taken mama years to learn. It would save me from ever making the mistake mama had made. I knew there would be years of hard work ahead for Alex and Rolf. And hours of loneliness for Vivian and me. Hopefully, we would have children to occupy our time and we would have no lonely hours. Or if we did, we'd be content to wait until the man we loved could put his work behind him and come to us, knowing we'd be waiting, arms extended to enclose him.

Twenty-six

WE DIDN'T GO NEAR THE CENTER OF THE VILLAGE THE day of the festival for the ground-breaking ceremonies. The field hands were given the day off, for certainly Mrs. Yvonne DesChamps had spared no expense. She intended to see to it the villagers never forgot this day. A large piece of property at the edge of town had been turned over for the event. Japanese lanterns were strung from one end of it to the other and the acreage was vast.

There was an enormous tent where animals were put through their acts. There were aerialists and acrobats. There was a miniature circus for small children, who were allowed to pet the strange but docile animals. There were ice-cream cones and ice-cream sandwiches for grown-ups as well as children, plus popcorn and cotton candy. Sandwiches containing every kind of meat were available and large glasses of punch, plus iced lemonade and tea and coffee. Deep dishes filled with salads of every description were replaced as soon as empty on a long buffet table. There was a merry-go-round, a Ferris wheel, a tunnel of love, a house of mirrors and other means of merriment.

Yvonne DesChamps had thought of everything. And both she and her son were available all through the day. The ground-breaking ceremony for the hospital had taken place at the beginning of the festivities and dignitaries for miles around were there. Speeches were made and Yvonne's good deeds throughout the years were spoken of. She presented the town with the deed to the ground and a check in full payment for the cost of the hospital.

All this we heard when the hired hands returned. Considerable progress had been made on the ground and Alex and Jacob were impatient to get Nightfall into production again, but today was special for the town. No one worked and everyone spoke of the beautiful Mrs. DesChamps' generosity.

Everyone, that is, except the occupants of Nightfall and those on Rolf's plantation. That wasn't very many. I thought of papa in his grave and couldn't bear to look in the mirror at my reflection, garbed as I was in the costume of Carmen. It was as beautiful as it was daring and I made certain to tuck the long-stemmed rose in the low bodice.

When I came downstairs, Maggie exclaimed aloud at the sight of me. "Honey, except for your hair, you could be your mama. But somehow, with your hair down, you look jus' like her."

Alex said, "I told her the same thing."

"How rakish you look," I chided when he bent to kiss my cheek. And he did. He wore a white-silk shirt with full sleeves. The shirt was open and he'd tied a red kerchief around his neck. The buckled pants were a red silk to match the color of my skirt. He had a patch over one eye, secured with an elastic around his head, and a false line of mustache was pasted across his upper lip. One ear even sported an earring clipped onto the lobe.

"I don't know if I dare let you loose among all those lovely girls," I teased.

"I'm the one to be worried," he said, regarding me with awe. "Jessica couldn't have picked a more beautiful costume for you."

"Nor a more daring one," I added.

"Be daring tonight," he urged softly. "I'm in a reckless mood."

"All right. I'll put on my mask and we'll be on our way."

"The eye patch eliminates my need for one, thank goodness. A pity there isn't time for Vivian and Rolf to see us."

"Seeing who's giving the affair, I think it would be wiser not to remind them of it."

He nodded agreement.

Even before we reached the lighted area, the sounds of revelry reached us. It sounded as if there were several bands parading around the grounds. And when we reached the area and came upon the maze of carriages which were parked haphazardly, I could see men dressed in uniforms, parading around the grounds, their instruments blaring in a tune bound to make you want to move your feet.

There was even a large platform for dancing and an orchestra on a podium, performing for the couples dancing on the floor. At the moment, it was a square dance and the varied costumes seemed strangely out of place for such a dance. But it didn't matter. Everyone was enjoying himself. And herself. Even Alex's face lit up at the sight before him. Neither he nor I had ever seen anything like it. Nor, I thought, would we likely see it again.

He parked the buggy as close to the grounds as possible, so I'd not have to traverse the dirt road. But that didn't matter either. My feet seemed to dance over the ground, which had been well-trampled down during the day.

We took rides on the merry-go-round, the Ferris wheel. We entered the tunnel of love and embraced in the darkness as all lovers did. We walked through the house of mirrors and had hysterics at the grotesque shapes our bodies took on. We enjoyed an ice-cream cone and some punch. Of course, there was pushing and shoving and movement was very slow, but it was all good natured.

I don't know how it happened, but Alex and I became separated. I looked around for him, but he was nowhere in sight.

Then a voice said, "Miss Heather." It was Marcel. "Come this way, please. Miss Jessica wishes to see you."

"But Alex." I tried to turn back and catch sight of him.

"I'll bring you back to him," came the reassuring reply. I couldn't even shake off his grip on my arm. It was too strong and so I could do nothing more than move along with him. But I was annoyed. I didn't want to leave Alex's side, and since mama had insisted I come, I'd decided to make the most of the evening.

Somehow, we had skirted the crowd and were on a dark road that was narrow and seemed little used.

"Where are you taking me?" I asked.

"To the landau," Marcel said.

"Why did mama come?"

"I have never questioned Miss Jessica's orders," came his calm reply.

"Well," I said, "there's the landau. Where's mama?"

"Inside," he replied.

There were two men standing beside the carriage and when Marcel approached, it was as if they'd been rehearsed in what they were to do. One grasped me by the shoulders. The other lifted the lace part of the mask and forced a gag into my mouth. It was pulled tight and secured at the back of my head. I tried to kick out, but my legs were held securely and fastened with a large kerchief by Marcel. The one who had tied the gag now got hold of my clenched fists, which were flailing helplessly, and tied them.

Marcel then lifted me and when one opened the door, he deposited me on the seat. He closed the door and stood beside it. I could look out the window and see the Ferris wheel, its lamps glowing brightly as it moved around in a circle. It would move and stop to let passengers off or to take on others.

I kicked at the doors, but to no effect. I might as well not have been there. I wondered what this was all about. Why had mama had this done to me? Why had she come here? And how had Alex lost sight of me? Had Yvonne's thugs got him and mama had assigned Marcel to watch over me? Perhaps he figured the best way would be to gag and tie me. Was mama coming? And Alex? I tried desperately to loosen my bonds, but I couldn't. It was close inside the landau and the mask made it seem hotter.

I rested my face against the glass pane. At least that was cool. My eyes rested on the Ferris wheel, which would rise, then stop, then rise. It was so brilliantly lit that one could almost make out the faces. I concentrated on that to take my mind off my own predicament.

I heard another band strike up some fast music. The sound of music, mingled with that of the crowds, was cacophonous. I could even hear the steps of dancers beating out rhythms on the wide platform set up for dancing. But it was the Ferris wheel that my eyes strayed back to.

It couldn't have been too far from me, for the brightly colored cages were plainly visible. One person I hadn't seen was Yvonne DesChamps. I hadn't seen Joel either, but I'd not looked for them. I'd not even thought of them. I'd been too carried away by the crowds, bright lights, music and various forms of amusements. To be honest, I'd been enjoying myself. And so had Alex. I suppose because there'd been nothing to enjoy in so long.

My vision focused on two ladies in a cage which was nearing the top. The upper part of the cages weren't enclosed with wire, making it easy to make out their apparel, if not what they looked like. But one lady had on a red blouse. It seemed to be lace and the sleeves were puffed. Her hair was as black as mine and fell loosely on her shoulders, just as I was wearing mine.

The cage was nearing the top when the woman on the opposite side reached over and pulled at the other lady's black hair. It came off and she threw it aside. It fell to the ground. I realized it was a wig! Once the wig was torn off, blonde hair came spilling out. Not Vivian! Dear God, no! The cage started to swing wildly, for the women had closed the distance between them and seemed to be fighting over something.

I saw a bright flash as the woman in black raised her arm and thrust it down in a lightninglike movement. *Woman in black!* Yvonne DesChamps! Then I heard the screams of the crowds, whose attention had been attracted to the cage, which was swinging back and forth though the wheel had stopped. One of the doors swung open and both ladies fell out. At least, that's the way it seemed. Only one screamed and that was Yvonne Des-Champs. The other, whose arm had been around Yvonne, suddenly went limp and her arms dropped. Yvonne couldn't hold her, nor could she save herself.

I closed my eyes, but I couldn't shut out the sounds of the horrified screams, or the music which played, or the stamping of the dancers' feet, who didn't seem to be aware of what had happened up there.

It wasn't Vivian! It was mama! Yvonne had intended to lure me into one of the cages. The gleaming flash I'd observed had been a knife. She had not discovered it was mama until they were almost at the top. Mama knew she was inviting death. She'd done it deliberately. She'd had me kidnapped by Marcel.

Had Alex been in on the trick mama intended to play? I knew differently. He'd never have stood for it. Somehow, mama had fooled him into taking her about. Perhaps she'd even told him it was a game she and I had thought up. *I was even thinking like mama.*

Gradually, the music stopped, the dancers ceased their terpsichorean revels. The crowds were silenced. Tragedy had struck. The landau door opened and the men who had rendered me helpless freed me of the bonds and gag.

"Why?" I asked.

"Marcel's orders, mademoiselle. You are now free to go." They caught me as I took a step and almost fell. "A minute or two, mademoiselle. Let the circulation get back into your legs."

I obeyed, for my legs were almost devoid of feeling. There were a few moments of pain as the blood once again moved freely through my veins, then I headed for the Ferris wheel. A crowd had gathered, blocking my view, but I managed to push my way through it to the area where the two women had fallen. There were three men beside the bodies, both of which lay still in death. Mama lay on her back. The handle of a knife, which had been plunged into her heart, protruded from her body. She had taken the weapon meant for me.

I spoke Alex's name, for he was bent over mama. Joel sat on the ground cradling his mother's body, calling to her over and over to speak to him. He couldn't accept the fact that his mother's latest attempt at vengeance had been her final one.

Alex stood up and gathered me close. I couldn't cry, nor could I speak, but my eyes questioned him.

He said, "Somehow my attention was diverted. The next thing I knew, your mother had caught hold of my arm and was pulling me forward. She whispered you and she were going to play a game on Marcel and you needed my help. She said you'd talked it over a few days before. She spoke as she led me to the Ferris wheel. The next thing I knew, I was grabbed by two men and pulled away from her just as we reached the Ferris wheel. Yvonne appeared out of nowhere and when the man opened the cage door, she said something to your mother and they entered."

I found my voice and was surprised I could speak so calmly. "Mama sacrificed her life for me. She knew

Yvonne was up to something, though I haven't figured that out yet."

"Then you weren't playing a game on Marcel."

"No. Marcel kidnapped me and two of his accomplices —or those he hired for mama—tied and gagged me and kept me in the landau, parked on a back road, but from where I had a good view of the Ferris wheel. I saw the two bodies tumble out."

Deputy Sheriff Tim Oliver, the third man beside the bodies, moved over to my side. "I'm sorry, Miss Heather. You were right, of course. We have witnesses who were in the cages of the Ferris wheel. They heard words exchanged between your mother and Yvonne. They said Yvonne was screaming like a wild woman because she thought it was you she'd lured into the cage. She swore to your mother that after she killed her, she'd get you. She said no one would believe ill of her because of the good deeds she'd performed all through the years. She even confessed to your mother that that's why she did them. She admitted having your father killed, the farms burned, everything. I'm afraid she was mad."

I could only nod.

Alex's arm went around my shoulder and he led me away from the awful sight. I knew now why mama had chosen the Carmen costume. She was wearing one identical to it. I knew why she told me to wear my hair down. She had a wig that matched the shade and length of my hair.

As we moved away from the area, I heard Joel begin to cry. It was horrible. Between his sobs, he kept calling to his mother to come back. But Yvonne DesChamps would never come back. She would wreak no more evil. She had paid for her ill deeds.

And mama! Mama had paid too. I remembered what papa had said the night he confessed to me that he had killed Lemuel DesChamps in a duel: he'd had to live with the knowledge that he'd killed a man every moment of his life. Mama had had to live with the knowledge that she'd been responsible for what papa had done.

She must have found out Yvonne intended to kill me at the festival and so she used the only way she knew to outwit her. Yvonne had met her match in mama, but it was a hollow victory. Hollow for everyone.

Mama lies beside papa, and they are united in death as they never were in life. Nightfall is now a successful plantation and free of debt. So, too, is Rolf's plantation. He made a complete recovery. That is, mentally. Physically, his face bears heavy scars which he will carry through life, but Vivian isn't even aware of them. Nor are we, for his heart is filled with joy and love for his wife and twin sons, born two weeks ago.

Alex and I were married a week after we buried mama. Maggie insisted on it, saying it was what mama would have wanted. Vivian and Rolf agreed. It is over a year since tragedy struck Nightfall.

A year that saw our plantations begin anew and the DesChamps family's go to seed. Joel drank himself into a stupor and became a menace around the village. He is now in an institution for the mentally ill and will probably remain there the rest of his life. His mother helped to make him a weakling by teaching him hate. The sight of her falling body, forced out of the cage by mama, who was even then dying, was too much for him. I know I'll never forget it, though I'm hoping a baby will help. Yes, in a few months Alex and I will become parents. I don't know if we'll be blessed with twins, but I'll gladly settle for one.

The hospital is in the process of being built. It would have been foolish to abandon it, for it will serve a worthy purpose. But it is to be called the Rutford Hospital, rather than bear the name of the woman who donated it for the purpose of hiding her true nature.

As for Marcel, his loyalty to mama was boundless. We invited him to live out his life at Nightfall, but though he was grateful, he refused. He said New Orleans was where he belonged and mama had provided well for him. He revealed how she learned of Yvonne's plan to murder me. Marcel had planted a spy among her hirelings. Though Yvonne had sent them to Richmond after she'd had them put a torch to our plantations, they had returned to hide in her home. It was one of them who had killed the man who fired our plantation. And killed him with Jacob's gun, for he'd been seen by both Jacob and Maggie.

Alex had been pulled from mama at the festival by Yvonne's thugs, so she could lure me into the cage. She had thought it was I and had pretended she wished to talk over all that had happened and make peace. Mama had pretended to fall for the ruse. With the mask and the black hair, Yvonne had been fooled. I doubt mama even spoke until the Ferris wheel was near the top. When Yvonne realized she'd been duped, she lost all control and her madness became evident, as she revealed all she'd done. She even added that she'd told her hirelings she would pretend that mama had had the knife and it was only through luck that she had escaped death. But Yvonne's luck had run out. And so, also, had mama's. But she knew that.

Nightfall, thanks to Alex and his father, has finally become the realization of papa's dream. Yes, there are times when I know the loneliness mama knew, but when Alex comes to me, the waiting is all worthwhile.